ANOTHER DAY ANOTHER JACKAL

CW00820012

ANOTHER DAY ANOTHER JACKAL

LEX LANDER

Kaybec Publishing

First published in 2014 by
Kaybec Publishing
441 Avenue President Kennedy
Montreal
Quebec
H3A 0A4

ISBN: 978-0-9917063-0-3

A CIP catalogue record of this is available from the British Library

Cover and text design: www.mousematdesign.com

Print edition printed and bound by Createspace, www.createspace.com

PART ONE

AUTUMN SCHEMES

Rosarito, near Tijuana, Mexico, 17 October 1995

The job he did before this one was in Mexico, some drug baron. I remember the name of the man who transported the weapon across the border, if you would like it. [affirmative response from interviewer] *It was a man called Regan, a specialist in arms trafficking.*

Ghislaine Fougère to Enrique Dubois, Lieutenant de Police, DCPJ, during interrogation, 11.06.1996.

*   *   *

Professional killer, contract killer, hired assassin, hit man, enforcer. Lux had been called all these and more during his career. All of them described what he did: he committed murder for money.

This latest job was south of the border, in Baja California. The target was a Mexican drug baron who had gone to earth in Canada the year before, but was now being enticed back by one last killer deal. Purported killer deal. In reality, the deal was phoney. The Mexican, a certain Federico Vazquez, had powerful enemies who wished him dead.

As part of his preparations, Lux had crossed into Mexico and checked into an unassuming hotel in the resort town of Rosarito, part of the southern sprawl of Tijuana. His stay would be short. Just long enough for a delivery of goods, a payment, and a transfer of the goods to a secure place. Then back over the border.

The air-con unit in his room had something metallic loose inside. Its incessant rattle was driving him crazy, though he had no complaint over the amount of Arctic air it was pushing out.

His visitor was not impressed by chill factors. Hottest part of the day or no, he insisted on going out on the balcony for security reasons.

'No way is it bugged, Mike,' Lux said for a second time, running a hand through his muddy-blond hair in exasperation. 'I walked in this place off the street, they weren't expecting me.'

'Humour me,' Regan grunted, paranoid about wiretaps and the like, even more so than Lux, who had far more at stake.

Grumbling, Lux clapped a baseball cap on his head and dark glasses on his nose before venturing out. The room being south facing, the balcony was hellishly hot. The sun felt like a blowtorch on the unshaded part of his face.

The balcony overlooked Boulevard Benito Juarez, the town's

main street. It was noisy – another plus for Regan – colourful, and fume laden. Directly opposite the hotel was a stall selling pottery to tourists: row upon row of blues, yellows, and terracottas, a pot for every purpose, even pissing, Lux heard tell. The stallholder had spent most of the morning slumped in the shade, sombrero tilted over his face. Sure to be a pose to attract tourists influenced by local colour.

The briefcase Regan set down on the tiled floor, screened by the balcony wall, was of the rigid variety with a combination lock. He twisted the dial in a 3-9-3 sequence and opened the case. Inside were the components of the M25 sniper rifle Lux had ordered: McMillan polymer stock with customised monopod, detachable barrel, Leupold tactical scope, screw-on bipod, two 20-round magazines, silencer. Chambered for 7.62mm NATO ammunition. Snuggling in nests of polystyrene were two hand grenades.

'All present and correct,' Regan said, like a travelling salesman of the old school displaying his samples. 'It's nearly new.'

'Looks swell,' Lux said non-committally, shutting the case without examining the contents. He trusted Regan. Not only that, the apartments opposite had a fine view of his balcony. 'No problems at the border?'

'Shit, no, Dennis. Short of taking the heap apart with a welding torch, there's no *way* those greasers would find it.'

'It's not the greasers I was thinking about, it's our guys.'

Regan tapped his nose and winked. 'Our guys are taken care of.'

This raised Lux's eyebrows. US border control officers were notoriously resistant to graft. Lux had used Regan on four previous occasions to smuggle weaponry over an international border, but the US-Mexico crossing was a first. An unknown quantity.

When Regan left, ten minutes later, he was heavier by a hundred $100 bills, the balance of his fee.

* * *

In the late afternoon Lux drove to the *Central de Autobuses* in Tijuana and deposited the briefcase in a baggage box he had rented the day before. There it would remain until he received a call that FedericoVazquez was on his way.

Auckland, New Zealand, 18 October 1995

'Almost the first thing he said to me after we'd introduced ourselves was that he was dying. I mean, for God's sake … Here was this guy I was meeting for the first time, crying on my shoulder. Only he wasn't really … crying on my shoulder, I mean.'

Extract from interview with Sheryl Glister recorded by Thierry Garbe, freelance journalist, 23.03.1999

*   *   *

When Eddie Nixon told Sheryl Glister in just so many words that he was a dying man it took several beats to register with her.

His voice carried no timbre of regret, no self-pity, not even resignation. It was as flat and neutral as an electronic message. Seated across from him in the boxlike black leather armchair, one of a dozen strewn about the twentieth-floor lounge of Auckland's exclusive Cavalier Club, Sheryl was nonplussed.

'I … I'm sorry to … er … to hear that, Mr Nixon,' she said, a little hoarsely. It wasn't often she fumbled with words. But then it wasn't every day the third richest man in the country summoned you to announce his imminent demise. She wondered if she should ask what he was dying of, but decided against. If he wanted her to know he would volunteer it.

'Six months the experts give me – at the outside.' Again the matter-of-fact tone.

Sheryl supposed he had learned to live with it, learned to roll with the punch, KO though it was. He didn't look like a man with only six months to live. He was broad and heavily built, but far from obese: bulk, not fat. A cube-shaped head with somehow squashed features, central to which were his blue eyes, brilliant as sapphires. They gave her the uncomfortable feeling they could delve into her mind.

He was sixty-eight, according to a feature on him in an August issue of *The Dominion*; she had taken the trouble to raid the newspaper's archives to brief herself. Three times married, his current spouse less than half his age. Old rich man's folly. Worth, according to the feature, over two hundred million Kiwi dollars.

Sheryl knew him only via the media. He was an international hotelier and casino owner amongst other things, outside the circles in which she, a Greenpeace activist and part time schoolteacher of modest means, circulated. No reason for their twains to converge before today. His summons had come out of the blue, issued by a woman with a voice that had reminded Sheryl of something metallic and shiny.

In the expanse of window behind Nixon, Harbour Bay was alive with boats of all shapes and sizes under a sky of purest blue. The Harbour Bay Bridge, the ugly-eccentric 'coat hanger' that connected Auckland City with the prosperous North Shore, dominated the panorama. It was a holiday brochure sort of scene. But then Auckland was like that. A fair city, traditional and modern, friendly, outgoing, not big enough to be impersonal in the way the aesthetically superior Sydney was.

'I'm real sorry,' Sheryl said again, with a grimace. She wasn't good at dispensing sympathy. 'It must be hard to adjust to. Is there no room for doubt – about the prognosis, I mean?'

'I wish.'

The dialogue lapsed. Nixon studied her: she was tall enough to have been on level terms with him when they shook hands, big boned, small breasted, dead-straight dead-black hair with threads of grey that contradicted her thirty-two years. Not pretty yet certainly not ugly. The face of a woman hell-bent on getting her way with no compromises. A smudge of down hazed her upper lip. He privately bet she scorned depilation as her way of saying stuff 'em. He found himself wondering – without the slightest justification – if she were a lesbian. Whatever her sexual orientation, she seriously impressed him.

Her style of dress was surprisingly sober, not at all Bohemian like many Green supporters. Pinstriped black trousers married to a grey silk blouse; her jacket, which was looped through the strap of her shoulder bag, was a creamy colour with a Greenpeace badge pinned to the lapel. Middling-good quality, none of your Farmer's department store trash.

He had invited her to this meeting, not on the basis of a head-and-shoulders shot in the local press, nor even because of the street interview on Channel 1 television that he had caught last week, but because of her firebrand reputation. Forever at loggerheads with the Greenpeace leadership, on whose fringes she skulked over what she saw as their 'pussyfooting' tactics.

'It's time to show the mailed fist,' she had stormed at the TV cameras, following a demonstration over some whale hunting protest against Japan. 'Our boats are never going to make an impression until we start loading them with torpedoes!'

Hot air rhetoric? Or was she genuinely prepared to back tough talking with kick-ass action? He'd arranged to meet her here to find out.

'Before I go, I want to do something really worthwhile with my money,' he said, reaching for his beer.

To go by Sheryl's expression this was a routine, redemption-seeking line. Do a good deed, make your peace with the Almighty.

'Very commendable,' she said drily as he guzzled from his glass. Her own black coffee was untouched and getting cold.

'Before I go,' he said again, undeterred, 'I want … I *intend* to make an impact. I intend to spend a large part of my wealth doing some good for the world.'

'Wow.'

The flat irony didn't escape him but caused no offence. He was past taking offence over anything. In his case, life really *was* too short.

He paused, an invitation for her to elaborate. She said nothing. Fair enough. It was his party. It was for him to make the running. She was no doubt waiting for the big bang.

He spread his hands, a gesture that reminded Sheryl of an old Jew who used to live next door to her parents.

'I could throw money at a few million starving Africans or make donations to the WWF, UNICEF, Save the Children, or a whole bunch of worthy causes, but I've decided to fry bigger fish … the biggest fish of all in fact.'

Now Sheryl came alert. Suddenly she knew what he was about.

'I got you. You want to save the world.'

His lips twitched, as close as he had yet come to a smile.

'Astute of you. How did you guess?'

'Easy. The fact that it's me you contacted. You know my history and it's not about making collections for Oxfam. As you say, the issue is the state of the world, not its population, which is replaceable. *Very* replaceable. But without a habitable planet it's goodbye human race.'

Nixon settled back into his seat, placed the palms of his hands flat against each other as if about to intone a prayer. 'You've had more practice than me. Why don't you make my speech for me?'

Sheryl was only too glad to oblige. An audience of one was still an audience. This particular individual, with his multi-millions, was worth a whole auditorium-full of Mr and Mrs Averages in terms of what he could help her accomplish.

'It's been said before, by others as often as me.' She shuffled to the edge of her seat. 'First we got to get rid of the weapons of mass-killing – nuclear, biological and chemical. Vaporised, pulped to nothing, buried, whatever it takes. Then we deal with the governments who deploy them, and the scientists, the scum who create these monstrosities …'

'Deal with them?' Nixon interrupted. 'How exactly?'

'Lock them away for fucking-ever.' She almost spat the words at him. 'When we've established the basis for a peaceful world, we take care of the despots, the dictators, and the demagogues. Eliminate them and we eliminate genocide. Afterwards we tackle the problem of pollution – of the air, the seas, and the land. Crippling fines for first offenders, prison sentences if they do it again. And I'm using the term pollution in all its senses. I list the clearing of rain forests and the indiscriminate slaughter of wild life under the same heading. Only then, when the planet's been cleaned up, can we start to improve the lot of the individual and tackle poverty.'

'You paint with a broad brush,' Nixon said, a whiff of awe in his voice. 'How can you hope to accomplish all that, or rather, since you have no powers, influence its accomplishment, in your lifetime?'

Sheryl snorted, causing a lone striped-suit in the nearest chair to glance up from tinkering with his palmtop. She eyeballed him and he looked down at once. Sheryl Glister was not the kind of woman you exchanged loaded winks with.

'This is not a lifetime agenda, Mr Nixon. This is about forever, about infinity. Maybe you know already, maybe you don't, but it's literally gonna take centuries to restore health to the world. The immediate objectives, the ones I feel we have some hope of attaining while I'm still young enough to play an active role, are the removal of all weapons of total war, beginning with nuclear.'

Nixon quaffed what was left of his beer, wiped his mouth on the tissue mat provided. 'Your coffee's getting cold.'

She dismissed her coffee with a discreet snort. 'Okay, so now you know my cause. What are you offering?'

He had noticed that so far had she had not once smiled. Not on account of her teeth, which were white and straight, if on the large side for a woman.

He voiced the thought.

'Smile?' She stared at him, almost with distaste, as if he had just farted noxiously. 'What are you looking for – a cover girl? A candidate for a toothpaste ad? There's nothing about this shit to make anybody *smile!*'

'Accept my apologies.' Nixon was contrite but not about to grovel to her. She needed his money more than he needed her militancy. 'But you should, just occasionally, lighten up a little. It wouldn't diminish your arguments or demean your standing, you know.'

She nodded tersely. Up to a point he was right. She should ease off the gas pedal now and again. So much intensity was hard to maintain. Maybe that was why she had so many migraine headaches, like the one coming on now.

'I'll try,' she said, stern-faced, and when he grinned indulgently at her she found herself grinning back. All at once she liked him. Feeling self-conscious, she brushed her fringe from her eyes and fumbled for cigarettes in her shoulder bag.

'All right then,' Nixon said briskly. 'Down to brass tacks. I've met you and I'm impressed. I reckon you could do the job.'

'What job?' she said, talking around the unlit cigarette. 'Who says I'm in the market for a job? I thought this was about giving money to Greenpeace.' She flicked her lighter.

'This is a no smoking area,' he admonished mildly. 'But you go right ahead. Nobody will say anything as long as I'm with you.'

'Money buys its own house rules, eh?'

'It has its uses. But in this instance it's going to be used to rescue planet Earth. I'm going to place at your disposal the sum of one hundred million Kiwi dollars.'

Clichéd response though it was, the cigarette fell from her fingers. Before she could retrieve it, a passing waiter stooped and did it for her. In unspoken reproof he handed it back.

'Thanks,' she said absently. Then, to Nixon, 'Are you kidding or are you kidding?'

'I'm not kidding or kidding. But there are conditions ...'

Now she actually laughed, again distracting the striped-suit from his calculations.

'I'll *bet* there are. Enough strings for an army of puppets, I reckon.'

'You'll like them. Believe me.' He scrutinised her over his glasses. 'I want you to quit Greenpeace and form a breakaway organisation, dedicated to the aims you outlined a few minutes ago, but using *your* methods, working to *your* formula, and with absolute control over the whole fighting fund.'

Finally he had taken her breath away. Her jaw didn't exactly sag but she lost a little colour and put a hand to her cheek, a feminine act that seemed at odds with her otherwise manly persona.

'Really wow this time. This has got to be a joke of some kind. Father Christmas doesn't come in October.'

'He has this year,' Nixon said, attracted to the human side of her face that she had fleetingly let slip.

'One hundred million you said. For real?'

'That's what I said, that's what I meant.'

'But why me? Why not Steffie Mills, for instance.'

New Zealander Stephanie Mills, leading woman activist in Greenpeace, had been Nixon's preferred candidate. His tentative soundings had been rebuffed. Not only that, but she was banned from France as a consequence of her leading part in the protests at Mururoa Atoll, which he felt might limit her effectiveness one day.

Nixon was too much of a gentleman to tell Sheryl she was only his second choice, so he said, 'I told you. I like your style.'

'Swell, I'm flattered. Where do we go from here?'

'Does that mean you accept my offer?'

'You cannot be serious, as McEnroe would say.' She grinned then, sheepishly, almost girlish. 'Sorry. I didn't mean to be flippant. As for your offer, just to prove how grateful I am, I'm going to give up smoking – here and now.' And she stubbed the last inch of cigarette in her saucer.

'Well done.'

Nixon raised a forefinger and a waiter cruised up, the same one who had picked up Sheryl's cigarette. 'Can I get you something, Mr Nixon?' he enquired. He was part-Maori, impeccably turned out with manners to match.

'The young lady and I have something to celebrate, Mikey. Bring me a bottle of that Dom Perignon I had the other day.'

'Right-o, sir.' Mikey withdrew.

'Before we get down to the detail, there are two things we must settle: first of all, this organisation, unlike Greenpeace, will be undercover. We may publicise its objectives and achievements, but only anonymously. Its personnel – you included – must remain incognito. Do I need to explain why?'

'You do not.'

He gave a satisfied nod, as if she had just passed a little test. 'The other thing is the name of the organisation. It will be yours, lock, stock, and barrel, so to you the honour of baptism. Ah ...' As Mikey approached with the Dom in a silver bucket, Nixon clapped his hands. 'Here's something to baptise it with.'

The ritual of inspection of the label, uncorking, and pouring done, they raised their glasses and clinked.

'I expect you need time to think of a name,' he said, his glass still extended. 'It doesn't matter. There's no hurry.'

'You're wrong, Mr Nixon. I've known for years what I would

14

call it if ever the opportunity and the means to set up my own pressure group arose.'

'Good. Call me Eddie, by the way.' He cocked two quizzical eyebrows, never having mastered the technique of raising one singly. 'So what's it to be?'

'How do you like Greenwar?'

'The President is ready for you, *Monsieur le Ministre.*'

De Charette wiped clammy palms on his trousers, patted his seriously-receding grey hair, and rose from the straight-back chair that was designed to inflict discomfort. Even after six months in office he hadn't learned to quell the rush of nerves that accompanied every presidential summons. He buttoned his jacket. He straightened his red and white spotted tie, ensuring that the knot was correctly aligned between the points of his collar. Now he was ready. He lifted the slim leather attaché case that had been a present from his wife. His initials were gold embossed into the front – H de C – an embellishment he would have preferred to forgo.

The usher, dignified in his frock coat, escorted de Charette to the door of the Salon des Ordonnances. He rapped twice on the door then stood aside to let the Minister pass through.

In the Salon the afternoon autumn sun was streaming through the tall south-facing windows, casting rhomboids of light on the uncarpeted areas of gleaming floorboard. The limes and beeches across the garden, keepers of the presidential privacy, were tall enough to obscure the buildings of the Grand Palais and the Petit Palais. Though the trees were still in full leaf, the green was fading to yellow and their daily increasing alopecia kept the gardeners on their toes maintaining the pristine look of the lawns. At the desk that was positioned in the centre of the room sat today's ADC, Lieutenant-Colonel Marin. He had booked the Foreign Affairs Minister for three o'clock, but JC was running late as always.

'*Bonjour, Monsieur le Ministre,*' Marin said respectfully, rising. Like most soldiers he held all politicians in disdain but woe betide his career if he ever let slip the veil of servility.

'How are you, Marin?' the Foreign Minister said with a stiff smile.

'Very well, thank you.'

The ADC side-stepped to the mirrored double doors on the left of the salon. He tapped discreetly on the right-hand panel, using the knuckle of his forefinger.

'*Entrez,*' came a voice from within, indistinct but recognisably that of President Jacques Chirac.

De Charette swallowed, a vain attempt to lubricate a mouth that was suddenly dry despite the two *cafés grandes* he had consumed during his thirty-five minute wait. Marin stood aside, gave what seemed like a patronising nod. A moment later the Minister was inside the President's private study, the door whispering shut behind him.

'*Assieds-toi, mon cher Hervé,*' the President said without raising his noble nose from the papers scattered before him on his custom-made reproduction Louis XV desk.

The Foreign Minister sat, knees together, nervous as a schoolboy summoned to his principal's study to answer for a breach of school rules. He placed the attaché case precisely across his thighs. Again he checked for hairs out of place. Tugged at the lobe of the left of his rather oversized ears. Tried to relax. Impossible.

The room was dimly lit; though the three tall windows were open notwithstanding the late afternoon chill, the louvered shutters were locked in the half-closed position, letting in only narrow strips of sunlight, the cooing of wood pigeons, and the subdued rumble of traffic in the Avenue de Marigny. On account of the gloom the President was working under a desk lamp, its glow reflected on his balding crown. He was jacketless and his shirt cuffs were folded back, his tie loosened. De Charette spotted a pair of cufflinks in one of a trio of identical octagonal glass ashtrays.

As he waited the Foreign Minister looked around. Access to the President's study, once occupied by Charles de Gaulle and other less exalted leaders, was still something of a novelty. It was an elegant room with furnishings to match: from the genuine Louis XV table on which stood a genuine Louis XIV clock, to the Savonnerie carpet, which had left the loom in 1615. The desk, made to Chirac's own specification, was the only non-antique in the room.

Abruptly, as was his wont, the President looked up, an impatient frown on his naturally stern features, as if de Charette's presence was an intrusion. Unlike Prime Minister Alain Juppé and other members of the Cabinet, the President did not shake hands at every meeting.

'*Alors,*' he said, blue eyes flashing over the half-moon glasses. 'Give me your report.'

'*Monsieur le Président.*'

De Charette flipped the locks of his attaché case and extracted a bound report. It was over two hundred pages long and dealt with the political stance of the Pacific-rim nations in response to the planned resumption of nuclear tests. On the cover was embossed in blood-red TOP SECRET – EXECUTIVE CIRCULATION

ONLY. Ministers used to joke that it was written in real blood. The joke had eventually ceased to amuse and only the most thick-skinned perpetuated it.

De Charette stood the case upright beside his chair, rose and laid the report on the President's blotting pad, where it could be opened without effort.

'You think I have time to read all this,' the President said testily, flicking a dismissive hand at the document.

De Charette remained standing like a junior officer being carpeted by his CO.

'The summary covers ten pages only, *Monsieur le Président.*'

The President made a vexed sound at the back of his throat. 'Give me a brief verbal résumé.' Adding, as an afterthought, 'If you are capable of brevity, that is.'

The implied insult caused the Foreign Minister's eyes to narrow but he was growing used to the President's putdowns. They were not reserved exclusively for him.

'*Bien entendu, Monsieur le Président.*'

'And sit down, *Bon Dieu,* sit down.'

A flustered de Charette resumed his seat.

'The attitude of the United States is well-documented ...' he began, and went on to amplify it, followed by a discourse on the 'attitudes' of Russia, Japan, China, Indonesia, the Philippines, Australia and New Zealand. '*Quant aux Nouvelles-Zéelandais ...*'

'Ah yes,' the President murmured, making a tent of his fingers. ' Our friends the *Kee-wees.* For a little country they make a big noise, *n'est-ce pas?*'

The Foreign Minister nodded energetically. Of all the Pacific Rim countries, New Zealand had the least clout diplomatically so far as France was concerned, yet was the most vociferous in condemning the forthcoming tests. As if the bolshie tactics of Prime Minister Jim Bolger and his cabinet were not enough, the Greenpeace movement there was stirring up a cyclone of protest via the media and threatening all kinds of measures to disrupt the tests. Then there were those disturbing rumours ...

'Rumours?' The President's ears pricked up. 'What rumours? Explain – in plain language not politician's bullshit.'

'*Monsieur le Président.*' De Charette's voice emerged as a squeak.

The President indicated the jug of iced Evian water that reposed on a tray within arm's reach, replenished hourly.

'Help yourself,' he said resignedly.

De Charette needed no second invitation. He slopped water

18

into one of the four tall tumblers on the tray and almost hurled half the contents down his throat.

'*Merci, Monsieur le President*,' he said, gasping. He composed himself swiftly under the President's flinty gaze. 'The rumours … as you might expect, they concern Greenpeace. Our Embassy has reported that two of their key members have defected to form a breakaway movement, about which as yet we have no information. Their objectives are believed to be identical to those of Greenpeace but their methods will be more along the lines of the Basque separatists.'

The President's shrug was expressive. All his shrugs were expressive – this one represented a yawn.

'Another terrorist faction? They will make threats, perhaps kidnap a leading politician or send some letter bombs. The world will go on turning. Who are the two renegades concerned? The Mills bitch and her boyfriend, I suppose … what was his name? You know who I mean – the one we expelled.' The President clicked his fingers in annoyance at the unaccustomed memory lapse.

'Nichols, *Monsieur le Président*.'

'Ah yes. I suppose they are the ones.'

'I am afraid their identities have not yet been released.'

'No matter. What else do I need to know?'

De Charette cleared his throat discreetly behind a clenched fist. 'There is talk ... inside information from a disaffected Greenpeace member who recently fell out with the hierarchy. According to him, big money is behind the breakaway movement.'

The President became marginally more alert. 'How big is big?'

'Very big. A figure of five hundred million francs was mentioned.'

The President whistled, which was out of character. He twiddled with his gold fountain pen for the best part of a minute, his eyes faraway, looking blindly past de Charette.

In the distance a car horn sounded. Beyond that the bustle of a mild autumn afternoon made scant intrusion on the presidential refuge.

'Where is it coming from, this money? It wouldn't surprise me if the New Zealand government was making a contribution.'

'It is rumoured that the source of the funds is a billionaire businessman. Nothing is certain. Our man is still making enquiries, but these things take time. We are not popular in New Zealand. It is not easy, even to buy co-operation.'

'Then spend more!' Petty details did not interest the President, nor petty cash. 'Is that all?'

'Not quite, *Monsieur le Président*. It is said that someone will be … ah, punished, in revenge for the tests.' De Charette polished off the second half of his glass of Evian. 'An important – a very important – public figure perhaps.' He paused to let the President assimilate this.

'The President of the Republic, for example?' The President curled a derisive lip. 'And what form is this … punishment to take?'

De Charette shifted uncomfortably. 'It is said it will be very severe indeed.'

'Very severe indeed? You mean killed?' He threw back his head and released an uninhibited guffaw. 'You have been reading too many thrillers, my dear fellow. Environmental movements, however militant, do not assassinate heads of state.' He arched a sardonic eyebrow at the lugubrious de Charette. 'Not even French ones.'

It was a straightforward enough hit but for the bodyguards. If they were good at their job – and Lux had to proceed on that assumption – they would surround Vazquez, one at the front and back, one on each flank. Lux would have to take out at least one flanker first, before putting his man down.

Lux had done his research. US Army tests conducted in 1959 had demonstrated that average reaction time among a group of trained soldiers when one of their number is downed unexpectedly by an unseen sniper, varied from 1.3 seconds for an unsilenced shot to 2.2 seconds for a silenced shot. A clear case in favour of a silenced gun, provided the degraded muzzle velocity didn't compromise accuracy and killing power.

For the M25 carbine this meant a range no greater than four hundred yards. The only suitable spot at the place of rendezvous was right on the range limit. It offered cover by way of a patch of scrub, about twenty feet of elevation, and a view of the Pacific. Not ideal, but it would do.

Using the US Army tests as a benchmark, the two remaining bodyguards would have about two seconds in which to react. In two seconds, with the semi-automatic M25, a trained sniper could loose off a further three aimed shots, or six unaimed. Enough to be sure of at least disabling the bodyguards and/or taking out Vazquez himself. Worst case scenario he would be still unhurt but without protection. Probably running for cover by then, for the building.

Guessing at where they would park the car, Lux calculated he would have maybe another two to three seconds to take the target out, say five shots. To an expert shooter like Lux this was adequate, even ample. He had originally toyed with the idea of using a sub-machine gun. Until he inspected the killing ground and paced out the range. At four hundred yards, the spread of fire would be so dispersed as to limit his chances of hitting one target, let alone all five. Not only that, but spraying gunfire wasn't his style. He prided himself on precision, on economy. Five targets, two bullets each, no waste.

By eight pm. he was settled in his eyrie, four hundred paces from the cabin driveway. It was a lonely place, desolate even, the nearest habitation being the ranch at Rancho Cepeda, half a mile away. But for the occasional gull's cry, life was non-existent. If you didn't count scorpions and king-size bugs, that was. The scrub made a satisfactory screen. From the driveway he would be invisible. He assembled the rifle and set it up on its bipod and monopod supports. He screwed the scope to the upper receiver and slotted a loaded magazine in place. Finally, he camouflaged the weapon with broken-off twigs of scrub.

In his sleeping bag he passed a restless night, listening to the breakers on their never-ending journey to and from the shore, counting the clusters of stars, going over his escape plan. As ever, it was the getaway that stressed him, not the killing.

Dawn came eventually. The sun peeped over the hinterland, pink light spreading across the hillside and his hide, and tinting the ocean so that momentarily it looked like a limitless pool of blood. The breakers had quietened to a murmur, mostly drowned by the incessant cries of swirling gulls.

His breakfast was orange juice from a flask, and an apple. It left him hungry, but he was used to short rations. Hunger kept him sharp. His biggest problem would be lack of shade, not lack of food.

By ten o'clock the heat was blistering. His precautions against it – light clothes, floppy hat, hand-held, battery-driven fan, plenty of water in a chiller bag – kept the worst effects at bay. He sweated nonetheless, and cast many a longing glance at the ocean, a short sprint and a plunge away.

Vazquez was late. It was 10.38 when a black Buick Roadmaster turned off the dirt track onto the even dirtier track that ran up to the cabin. Lux's Toyota stood in the driveway, posing as the transport of the non-existent men Vazquez had come to meet. Positioned to prevent other cars from getting closer to the cabin than twenty yards.

The Buick had heavy-tinted windows, shiny wheel trims and several layers of dust. It nosed up the track, bouncing on its soft suspension, cautious, suspicious. It would be too remote for Vazquez's liking, too secluded. Anybody would be uneasy, especially Vazquez, ever in fear of his old enemies. Even surrounded by bodyguards. Notwithstanding that one of the men he was coming to meet was an old friend. Trustworthy. Sadly, that same friend was now occupying a grave in the middle of the desert.

The Buick came to a halt more or less where Lux had predicted, immediately behind the Toyota, and some ten yards from the cabin door. The engine continued to run. The front passenger door opened and a thickset bald man in jeans and white T-shirt got out. He was clutching what looked like a pump-action shotgun. Now to test the plan's only obvious weakness. Would they expect Tomas to come out and greet them? Would they be suspicious if he didn't respond to their summons? Whatever their reaction, Lux was ready to take them out, inside or outside the car.

The T-shirted bodyguard scanned the area. He was thorough. Lux's hiding place came in for a long scrutiny, as being the only place where a gunman could be concealed.

Confident of his invisibility, Lux lay still, the M25 butt tucked into his shoulder, his finger hooked around the trigger. The slightest hint from the bodyguard that he was rumbled, and the guy was a dead man. Would be a dead man anyhow, very soon.

The rear door on Lux's side swung open. Another bodyguard, this one in chinos and a dark blue shirt with rolled-up sleeves. Also bald or shaven, taller and thinner than the first, similarly armed.

Lux could have taken them both now, four shots, two corpses. But the third bodyguard was still behind the wheel, waiting for the all clear. In the rear seat a silhouetted head was visible.

T-shirt spoke to Blue Shirt in Spanish. Lux knew a few words but was too far away to interpret their rapid speech pattern. Blue Shirt responded, and he caught the word '*donde*', meaning 'where'.

T-shirt advanced, towards the house. 'Tomas? *Donde estas?*' he called as he walked.

Shit. It wasn't going to go to plan after all. For a clean result Lux needed all four in the open. If Vazquez and the driver stayed put until T-shirt reached the house and found no Tomas, it was going to get messy. A quick decision was called for. Once they discovered the house was empty their suspicions would be aroused; they would all go on red alert, and probably had some sort of procedure to be activated in the eventuality of a double cross. Whereas, for the moment, they were still more or less cool though wary.

Decision made. Lux was already sighted on the blue-shirted bodyguard, so he would go first. He squeezed the trigger – once, twice – the double *phut* of the silenced gun probably inaudible to the victim. He toppled with a cut-off scream.

T-shirt went instantly to ground, his super-fast reactions making a mockery of the US Army's tests, so that Lux's third shot passed over his prone body. The bodyguard responded with a barrage of fire, but the range was too much for a shotgun. Lux's next two shots ended the contest.

By then the car was reversing, wheels spinning, throwing up dust. For good measure, Lux pumped four rounds at the driver, the windshield and door window exploding into fragments. It was enough. The Buick swerved, but being locked in Drive it continued in motion, swerving off the track. Inside, signs of frantic movement. Lux wasn't yet ready to leave his cover. If the intelligence about the numbers was correct, all the bodyguards were dead, and only Vazquez still alive. But he might well be armed.

The Buick ran into a bush and stalled to a standstill, the engine cutting out. Lux replaced his partly-used magazine with the spare, shoved a grenade in each pocket. Bent low, he backed out of the scrub and scuttled along its perimeter, parallel to the driveway. Still nobody exited from the car.

When he reached the limit of his cover, he was beyond the car and at a tangent to it. It was outside grenade-tossing range. Sooner or later he would have to cross open ground, either to blast the car, or rake the inside in the hope of hitting flesh.

He decided to wait it out. With the engine stopped the car would soon heat up. If Vazquez sweated it out, the interior would soon become unbearable. If he tried to restart the engine, he would be visible.

Vazquez opted to sit tight. Half an hour ticked past, then an hour. Even Lux, cooled by a zephyr of wind off the ocean, his head protected from the sun's rays, began to feel uncomfortable.

A faint metallic sound caught his ear. He peered through the telescopic sight. At first, nothing. Then, on the far side of the car, partly screened by it, a man down on all fours came into view. He was wearing a white shirt and black pants, and crawling away from the car. In his hand, a pistol.

This had to be Vazquez. Lux got up, sighted on him. At that moment, the Mexican glanced over his shoulder. Rolling onto his back, he blazed away with his pistol while yelling in Spanish. Lux didn't even flinch. The bullets would have sunk to earth long before they reached him. As if realising the futility of his actions, Vazquez scrambled to his feet. At that point he presented a full size target. Lux fired. Four quick shots, every one striking home, punctuated by yells of pain and fear. The last was a head shot. Blood sprayed. Vazquez crumpled to earth like a demolished building.

Still cautious, uncertain whether anyone remained alive in the car, Lux loped across the rough ground, rifle at the ready. He need not have worried. The dead driver was the sole occupant, already attracting a retinue of flies. Beyond the car, Vazquez was curled up on the ground, groaning. Amazingly still alive.

Lux approached him with caution. There was blood on the front of his shirt, at rib level, and on his shoulder; the head wound was a graze.

'You FedericoVazquez?' Lux asked, though he recognized the wounded man's face from a photograph he had been given.

More groaning. Lux treated wounded men the same as wounded animals. He finished them off.

When he put the muzzle of the M25 to Vazquez's temple the man's mouth opened weakly, as if to protest. Lux wasn't receptive to last requests any more than he was to administering last rites. He knew the man's history and a clean death was more than he merited. He squeezed the trigger.

Vazquez's pulse was still. Laying the rifle across the corpse, Lux extracted a slim Nikon camera from his hip pocket. Ten shots, each from a different angle, of the bloodied body would be proof enough of a contract executed. He was pleased with how it had gone, inasmuch as any pleasure was to be derived from ending a life.

Back at his car he proceeded to dismantle the rifle. As he unscrewed the barrel a faint sound caught his ear. He stood motionless, frowning as he listened. There it was again: sobbing, female for sure. He glanced towards the Buick. No movement there. A three hundred and sixty degree scan of his surroundings yielded no clues either. As a precaution, he screwed the barrel back in place and headed in a crouch for the Buick, his finger on the trigger.

The sobbing grew in volume as he neared the car. One of the rear doors was open; he peeked around it. On the floor, face down, a woman with long black hair in a short black dress. Her shoulders were trembling as she wept.

'Hey,' Lux said softly.

The woman fell silent, stiffening.

'You Vazquez's woman?'

No answer, just a jerk of her head that he took for a 'yes'. A single bullet was all it would take, at this range. A head shot, naturally. He never left witnesses, especially not from the opposing camp. He put the silenced muzzle up close to the back of the sleekly-coiffured skull, not quite touching it. At a technical level, killings didn't come easier. As his finger took in the trigger slack, it struck him that in all his years as a killing machine he had never killed a woman who wasn't the actual target

Don't think of her as a woman, his cold professional self exhorted. She's a hostile witness. She could identify you.

And yet ...

'Don't look up,' he snapped. 'Keep your face in the carpet and listen. You hear me?'

A sniff. Another nod.

'Did you see me?' he demanded, his voice harsh.

'No, *señor.*' It was a whisper, the two words spelling terror.

'You sure?'

'No, *señor.* I no see you. I am here on floor when you shoot.'

Still Lux hesitated, gnawing his lower lip. To let her live would be a professional sin. In his business, sentiment and emotion were *verboten.* He killed for money and self-preservation. Nothing personal about it.

'Okay.' He breathed out heavily. 'Okay, now listen good. You stay exactly as you are for ten minutes. You're going to hear me walk away, and then you'll hear my car drive off. When you can no longer hear the sound of the engine, then you can get up. Understood? *Comprendado?'*

'*Si ... si.* No look. I wait till your car he is gone.'

'If you try to look, I'll be back and you'll be dead. Get it? Bang, bang – dead!'

'*Si, señor, si.*' Panicky now. Lux had got his point across. 'I promise I no look.'

A last moment for reflection, for a change of heart. Something moved him to reach out with his free hand and rest it lightly on her head, appreciating the silky texture of her hair. She trembled anew, perhaps interpreting the gesture as the prelude to the *coup de grace.* With a faint grimace he lowered the gun and backed away. Slamming the door, he retraced his steps to the Toyota. The sun was high, searing his face, his foreshortened shadow beside him, black and hard-etched against the ochre-coloured ground.

Leaving the rifle assembled for now, he stowed it in the trunk. The interior of the car was a crucible of heat, the steering wheel so hot he was barely able to grasp it. He reversed down the driveway in a dust blizzard of his own making. He checked the Buick as he passed. No enquiring head popped up. If he had made a bad decision letting the woman live, he would know soon enough.

On the road between San Vicente and Ensenada, he dismantled the rifle, repacked it in the brief case. Its burial place was already chosen: a cleft in some rocks facing the Pacific, on a wild stretch of coast a few miles north of Ensenada. Too narrow for a body to enter, too deep for the case to be seen. Practically irrecoverable. Lux abhorred the waste, but disposing of guns used on contracts was just part of the whole process.

At the San Ysidro international border crossing, he endured the usual ninety minutes' wait. Come early evening, his fake passport attracting no more than the most cursory examination, he was entering the USA on foot. Safe home.

At 8.10pm precisely, he and a hundred and seventy four other passengers and crew were lifting off the floodlit runway at San Diego airport, bound for Miami. There he would connect with an Air France flight to Paris, due to depart around mid-day. As he settled into his business class seat, sipping a mediocre Bordeaux red, he gave no thought to the four men he had killed, nor to the woman he had spared. He was looking ahead, not behind. Ahead to Paris and Francoise, wondering if she had missed him at all.

When Rafael Simonelli entered the tiled lobby of the Hotel Napoléon, whipping off his sunglasses, the transition from stark sunshine to the shady interior left him momentarily robbed of sight.

'Hi, Napoleon,' came a woman's voice right by him.

He blinked a few times and a face materialised.

'Sheryl!'

'Don't sound so surprised,' Sheryl Glister said, smiling broadly.

'When you said you were down the road, I half-thought it was just your American humour, and this was a wild goose chase,' Simonelli said, his English lightly laced with an American twang. 'I thought you were probably really in San Diego, or wherever it is you used to live.'

They embraced, kissed cheeks then lips, an act that revived in Sheryl troubling memories of a love affair that had ended badly. The passage of five years had not entirely healed the lacerations.

'What brings you to Corsica?' Simonelli asked.

'You, my love, what else?'

His consternation showed on his face and Sheryl laughed, though there was scant humour in it.

'Don't worry, Napoleon, I'm not figuring to take up where we left off. This isn't a social call.'

Only half convinced, he ushered her across the lobby through the bar and out onto the terrace with its exquisite outlook of white sands and azure seas and bobbing palms, marred only by the airport at Campo Dell'Oro where a silver-bodied executive jet was coming in to land.

Simonelli was known to the all the staff at the hotel, and a waiter popped up the moment his bottom touched down. Sheryl ordered lemon tea and Simonelli *un pastis*. The waiter adjusted the parasol over their table and departed.

'It must be three, no, four years,' he said when they were alone again. 'You look marvellous.'

Had she not known him for a glib roué she might have been flattered.

'You always were a fucking good liar, Napoleon. Pity you were such a fucking poor lover.'

Simonelli, who, thanks to his three-year love affair with Sheryl, had as good a grasp of Anglo-American humour and nuance as of the language, was not put out. He chuckled as he positioned a cigarette dead centre between his thin but very red lips.

'You still smoke?' he asked, tendering the packet as an afterthought.

'Given it up. No tobacco, no alcohol.' A tiny pause. 'Or drugs.'

'Remarkable. You are the perfect woman.'

'Only to the tight-fisted,' she riposted drily. 'Tell me something, is this hotel named after you, or are you named after it? Or do you own it even?'

'As you know very well, my little trinket, Napoleon is only your pet name for me.'

'Some pet. And speaking of trinkets, I see you have a new ear ring.'

Simonelli fingered the bauble that dangled from his left earlobe, a teardrop-shaped genuine ruby, taken in payment of a large debt.

'Very becoming,' Sheryl went on, with a grin. 'It matches what used to be the whites of your eyes.'

'And you, I see, continue to scorn such frippery.'

Sheryl made a dismissive gesture. 'Let's quit fencing. Let's come to what was once called the nitty-gritty, way back when you were a young man.'

The red lips squirmed at this reminder of his forty-seven years.

'*Touché,*' he murmured. He had never been able to keep pace with her acrid wit.

'Anyhow, my friend, in spite of your advancing years you may still have your uses. To come to the point – I need your services.'

'My services? I see. Actually, I don't see at all. What, in precise terms, do you need?'

Sheryl edged her chair closer to the table and lowered her voice. 'In precise terms I need your connections.' She checked them off on her fingers. 'I need your leadership skills, your experience in terrorism, and your hatred of France.'

His expression did not alter. 'You need a great deal.'

She checked her little finger. 'Most of all, I need you because you are an outlaw, prepared to commit crimes against the State.'

'Was.'

Sheryl's brow furrowed. 'Was?'

'I *was* an outlaw. Now I am a retired outlaw.'

As if he hadn't spoken, Sheryl said, 'And the pay is very, very good.'

'Pay', especially 'very, very good pay', had enticed Simonelli out of retirement more than once in the past. If the bucks, or francs, or lire, or whatever, were big enough he would even change his plans for the evening, the highlight of which was a cosy supper with a certain Jeanne Mazzetta, wife of his best friend. He mentally cancelled the rendezvous. After all Jeanne was available at the snap of his fingers.

Once a terrorist, specialist in assassination, orchestrator of a string of atrocities on and off the island of his birth, the young Simonelli had committed a series of crimes in pursuit of an independent Corsica. In those days he had been derisive of wealth. Now, having accumulated the means to pursue his idealistic dreams, the dreams themselves had withered away. Now he desired only greater wealth. Corsica, by and large, could look after itself.

For 'very, very good pay', he would even be happy to let Sheryl Glister have the use of his body for an afternoon or two, to help her assuage what he remembered as a sexual appetite even more gargantuan than his own.

He stubbed out his cigarette, assumed a suitably alert attitude.

'You have given me the CV of the person you need. Now tell me, *ma chérie*, why it is you come halfway round the world to recruit such a person.'

When the phone rang Julien Barail was dozing on the couch in his living room. He had nodded off watching the news on TF1 – a news that had been short of the kind of drama that could be expected to keep his eyelids from drooping: a crashed airliner, for instance, or a destructive avalanche, or a gunman run amok. Barail, who held the senior rank of *Commissaire Divisionnaire* in the *Compagnies Républicaines de Sécurité*, more popularly known as the CRS, and commanded the *Corps de Securité Presidentielle*, the Presidential bodyguard, had a penchant for human tragedy.

He came awake just as the ringing ceased. He grunted and half-opened a single eye to regard the flickering screen. The news was over and they were showing what appeared to be an old Delon movie, in which the actor played a lone assassin called Jeff who kept a caged canary in his apartment. Even less diverting than the newsless news, aside from which he must have seen it half-a-dozen times. Then the phone trilled again.

It was just out of reach so, grumbling, he abandoned the couch and walked shoeless around it to the half-moon table that stood at its back. Answering the telephone was just one of the chores he was stuck with since his wife had abandoned him in favour of a twenty-three-year-old fitness instructor. Female, to boot.

'*Oui!*' he snapped into the mouthpiece, making no effort to disguise his irritation.

'Commissaire Barail?'

'Who's calling?'

'My name is unimportant for now. Let us say I am a man with a large sum of money to spread around. The word is that you are in the market for a little palm greasing – in fact, quite a lot of palm greasing.'

Barail stiffened. 'How dare you!'

A silky laugh.

'Do not fear that I am working for those who plot your downfall. On the contrary, I am a friend of the enemies of Chirac.'

The caller's accent carried a sub-stratum of Italian. A Corsican was Barail's guess.

'What is that to me?' he said. As a top government security officer he was far too wily to give himself away to an anonymous caller over an open line.

'What is it to you, you say. Just this: if you are prepared to co-operate, my friend, it is ten million francs to you. And I do not mean *francs anciens*.'

Barail's grip on the receiver tightened. Still clutching it to his ear, he went around the couch to sit down.

'You are obviously a lunatic or a practical joker,' he growled, still maintaining his ingenuous façade. 'Why don't you go and pester someone more gullible?' Yet he stayed on the line.

More soft laughter. The Corsican, or whatever he was, seemed confident of his man.

'And where the devil did you get my name and this number?' Barail demanded, massaging the back of his neck in his agitation.

The Corsican named an acceptable source. Barail relaxed a touch. The man's bona fides were in order.

'Let us meet,' the Corsican proposed, all banter leaving his voice. 'Allow me at least to demonstrate to you my goodwill.'

'By all means let us meet,' Barail rapped. 'Then I can arrest you for causing a public nuisance.'

This was just hot air, as the Corsican would know. A precaution by Barail in case the caller proved to be from Internal Affairs, checking out the CRS *Commissaire's* questionable loyalty and even more questionable honesty. Such subterfuges were not uncommon.

'But of course, *mon cher Commissaire*. For what other reason would you agree to meet a lunatic or practical joker like me? Just be sure to leave your little pistol at home, and I promise to do the same.'

A rendezvous was arranged. Barail tried to hang up first but to his chagrin the Corsican beat him to it.

PART TWO

WINTER CONSPIRACY

Naples, Florida, 5 January 1996

'We met this French police commissioner bloke – Barail – at Eddie's pad in Naples. That's Naples Florida, not Naples Italy. Okay? It was the first time I'd met Eddie's wife, Soon-Ling or something … He was pretty crook by then, I guess, but you couldn't tell from how he looked. He was a tough old bird, all right.'

Gary Rosenbrand to Thierry Garbe, freelance journalist, 19.03.1999

* * *

The view across the Naples harbour was framed between two royal palms whose broad leaves still piddled moisture from the heavy shower of fifteen minutes ago. It was of placid water, rich green vegetation, and other custom-built houses, every last one with its own jetty. Powerboats were tied up at most of them. Though it was mid-winter the temperature was a benign twenty degrees Celsius.

Eddie Nixon was a genial host and Soon-Li, his young Oriental wife, who couldn't do enough for him, an attentive hostess. Sheryl cynically wondered if she had been told that the days remaining to her husband were not many.

Besides Nixon and his wife there were two other people in the room: the Frenchman, CRS Commissaire Barail, recruited by Simonelli as the vital Trojan Horse, and a blond-haired man with a rugged look: his name was Gary Rosenbrand and he was Sheryl's right hand man. Like her, a recent defector from Greenpeace.

Sheryl and Rosenbrand had arrived in Naples the previous day and overnighted at a local motel. Barail had flown in that morning, to be collected from Fort Myers airport by Nixon's housekeeper, a skinny Afro-American with pebble-lensed glasses, who spoke not a word during the entire thirty mile drive to Naples. The three visitors and their host and hostess had lunched on soft-shell crab salad around a circular table on the shaded balcony. When the rain began – unusual at this time of year – the housekeeper operated a remote control that extended a louvered awning. After lunch the party moved inside and now sat in low chairs facing each other, under an idling ceiling fan.

Barail was a burly, bovine character with a look of indestructibility. His clothes were rumpled, but other signs of jet lag after his nine-hours-long flight were absent. He was at ease yet alert, his command of English beyond reproach and all but accentless. Thus far the talk had been mostly of the small variety. Now, amid coffees and assorted liqueurs and tobacco smoke, they were ready to edge towards serious business.

'You fully understand what's required of you, *Commissaire*?' Sheryl said, after treating the Frenchman to a rundown of the job specification. As the project's chief executive to Nixon's honorary president, hers was the responsibility for negotiation and decision making.

'It could not be clearer,' Barail said airily. 'You wish me to recruit a professional assassin. This is not a problem. I have many such men in my files.'

'That's not all we want,' Rosenbrand said in his rather grating voice. 'Not for ten million francs.' And he flicked a sideways glance at Sheryl, who nodded.

Barail's smile fell just short of mocking. 'Indeed, no. And I suppose you will now tell me what other tasks I will be required to perform.'

'Naturally.' Sheryl accepted that, if they were to enlist this man's aid, they would have to come clean about their intentions sooner rather than later. Rafael Simonelli, whom she still trusted despite their emotional incompatibility, had assured her that that if the price was right Barail could be relied on to deliver. 'In addition to recruiting the man,' she said coolly, 'your job will be to co-ordinate his actions, to manage him, if you prefer. You'll be our go-between.'

'This for me is no different from my present job. As head of the President's personal security section, I co-ordinate the actions of many agents.'

'So you'll be able to do it in your sleep. Swell. But that's not all – we're going to need inside information. You'll be our ears and eyes at the Elysées Palace.'

Now Barail's assent was guarded, questioning.

'You must explain further.'

Sheryl swallowed. Unable to delay the exposé longer, she took the big plunge. 'We aim to assassinate someone.'

'Well, that much is evident. May I ask whom?'

'A public figure,' Sheryl stalled, still shrinking from naming Chirac outright. Tough as her outer shell was, plotting to kill a head of state called for a level of ruthlessness that was alien to her public-spirited nature.

'A well-protected public figure,' Rosenbrand expanded.

Barail's 'Ah' of comprehension was barely more than a release of breath. 'You mean you wish to kill President Chirac.'

Sheryl glanced at Rosenbrand, hoping for some subtle signal that he felt the moment was right for disclosure. But, while sharing her worries, he had no guidance to give about how far she should go. She was on her own.

She took a breath so deep it made her dizzy. 'You got it,' she confirmed to Barail at last, her insides churning. 'We're gonna kill the bastard.'

Now their intentions were out in the open, and devil take the consequences. Sheryl lit another cigarette from the glowing tip of the one she was smoking (her renunciation of tobacco had been short-lived). She avoided looking at Barail's face. If she had she would have gleaned nothing. He was devoid of expression, inscrutable as a Ming vase.

'For what purpose?' the Frenchman enquired, so calm, so buttoned-down she instinctively sought to provoke him.

'To set an example.' Now she eyeballed him and her voice hardened as she went on, 'We represent Greenwar, successors to Greenpeace. We make war to save the planet. No one individual, whatever his status, is more important than our objective.'

Nixon's eyes flicked from Sheryl to Barail, fascinated by the interplay. A contest of wills of sorts was taking place. A Frenchman of the old school like Barail would not readily defer to the generalship of a woman .

'I see. And how will killing Chirac save the planet?'

'Figure it out, *Commissaire*. For a start, it'll show other leaders that if they damage it, as Chirac is doing with the Mururoa tests, they can expect to pay the ultimate price. It'll deter them.'

'The tests will be over long before you can get to him.'

'Their impact on the planet won't. The contamination will be with us, in some respects for hundreds of thousands of years.'

'I will take your word for that.' Barail sipped his coffee and looked thoughtful. 'Whether or not it is true, and whether or not Jacques Chirac should be held personally accountable, do you believe me to be the sort of man who would collude in his assassination?'

A frisson of doubt coursed through Sheryl. For the first time since the formation of Greenwar she felt unsure of herself. She wished Eddie would speak up, bolster her authority, but she sensed that turning to him to intervene would diminish her standing. He might even replace her, God forbid.

Dragging down a lungful of smoke soothed her fluttering nerves. She was conscious that every eye was on her, waiting for her to either bluff, back off, or face the Frenchman down.

'Yeah, I do believe that,' she said boldly to Barail, her gaze unflinching under his scrutiny. 'But if I'm wrong, if we've been misinformed about you, it's pointless to continue this discussion.' She stood, her height giving her presence. 'All I can do is thank you for coming ... and wish you *bon voyage*.'

Barail came close to incredulity. 'You would let me walk out of here, now that I know of your plans?'

'Certainly you'll be allowed to walk out of this house, *Commissaire*, though I can't vouch for your safe conduct all the way back to Paris.'

Barail chuckled. His chuckle became a laugh and his laugh a belly-driven guffaw.

'What's so funny?' Rosenbrand growled. He was a man of negligible humour.

'My apologies,' Barail spluttered, dabbing his eyes with a large blue handkerchief. 'I was just thinking how we could use someone like *mademoiselle* in the security service.'

'Thanks for the compliment, if that's what it is,' Sheryl drawled, her tone dry. 'But exactly where does this leave us? Are we in bed together or in the divorce court?'

Barail glanced from Sheryl to Rosenbrand and back to Sheryl, his reluctance to commit almost a tangible thing.

Out in the harbour an outboard puttered past, observing the three-knot speed limit. Inside the room all was quiet but for the whirr of the ceiling fan.

'All right,' Barail said heavily, breaking the silence. He spread his hands. 'You are not mistaken. I will provide an assassin, I will run him, and I will act as your informant.'

'A wise decision,' Sheryl said gravely, keeping her jubilation damped down.

'In return for twenty-five million francs.'

Rosenbrand sat forward, his fists clenched on his knees. 'The price agreed was ten.'

'Not so, my friend,' Barail demurred. 'The price *offered* was ten. I did not accept it, and in any case that was before I knew what the stakes were. For a crime such as this my neck could end up under the knife.'

'What knife?' Sheryl said in puzzlement.

'The guillotine,' Barail explained. 'For certain crimes, including high treason, it is still the official penalty. So you will understand why my price is twenty-five million.'

Once again Sheryl glanced at Nixon for a signal of assent or dissent. He studiously ignored her, inspecting the tip of his cigar as if it were a precious stone he had been asked to value. He had assigned total control over the budget to her. Now she had to prove she could handle it.

Thinking fast, she weighed all the implications, the cost versus the rewards. This project might prove to be the most decisive that Greenwar would ever sanction. It could even bring about an end to nuclear testing worldwide. It was too big to be quibbling over mere dollars and francs.

Rapid mental arithmetic converted twenty-five million French francs to eight million Kiwi dollars, or over a third of the budget she had set for the whole job. The assassin would want at least as much again as Barail, probably a lot more.

She decided that even to haggle as if this were an everyday business transaction would be to demean their historic mission. She sighed.

'Agreed. Twenty-five million francs.'

Paris Latin Quarter, 20 January 1996

Ernest Hemingway's old hangout, the Deux Magots cafe in bustling Boulevard St Germain, was all but empty of clients, but full of bitter-sweet recall of the days when they were lovers, and their every meeting was redolent of Chevalier crooning about springtime in Paris. Even though Hélène was then still married to that Italian bastard.

Now it was winter in Paris, the plane trees were bare of foliage, and the air a too damp and chilly for sitting outside under the canopy as they used to.

He was early; she was on time.

'How are you, Dennis?' she said, after the ritual double air-kiss. In her heels, she was as tall as him. She didn't even try to make the enquiry sound as if she cared. Their six years together were long gone, lamented by neither of them.

'I'm good,' he responded. 'And you? As beautiful as ever, I see.' They spoke in English, though Lux's French was serviceable enough.

'Skin deep, my dear, as you always used to say. You know the real me.'

That was a fact. The real she was almost schizoid, terrific in bed or wherever, a nagging, bad-tempered cow for most of the rest of the time. A serial seductress too. After all, money aside, her looks and sex drive were all she had going for her. Chestnut brown hair worn straight, today with a white band pulling it back off her ears. Rather thin-featured, but with eyes, nose, and lips that no scalpel could ever enhance. Tall, slight of figure, nice curves, legs to drool over. Her mother was an aristocrat, her father a former government minister.

They sat at right angles, just as they used to, back when clasping hands under the table was the natural thing to do. Old habits lingering on.

'You told me it was urgent,' he said, after they had ordered: her choice was some sort of herbal tea, which was a departure. Healthier for sure than his cappuccino.

'I said it *might* be urgent,' she corrected.

'Agreed, you did. Tell me, then.'

She lit a cigarette first, using the solid-gold lighter he bought her on their fifth anniversary. He might have been touched that she still had it and still used it, if he still had those kinds of feelings for her.

'A man called about you. Asking questions.'

Outwardly Lux's features remained bland. 'What man?'

Lux's cappuccino and Hélène's infusion were delivered, causing a momentary break in conversation. As the waiter moved away out of earshot, she said, 'He gave his name as Duval.'

'It's a common name. Could be anybody. What did he want to know, and why?'

She shrugged elegantly, drew on her cigarette. 'He asked if you were in France, how to contact you, that sort of thing.' Her hazel eyes finally locked on his. 'Are you still in business, Dennis?'

'In business? No, I retired last year, after you left me.'

'Really? You've been away, haven't you? I was trying for several weeks to contact you.'

'Vacation, my love. South Africa. It's summertime there, you know.'

She stubbed out her half-smoked cigarette, dribbled her infused tea into the cup from the stainless steel teapot.

Out in the street a car horn blared, was answered with interest. Faintly, somebody shouted an obscenity. All routine behaviour for Paris.

'I don't like your ... associates phoning me,' she said, fixing Lux with what he had always referred to as her *'comtesse* stare'. The put-down look the aristocracy reserved for lesser beings, such as servants and ex-husbands. 'You never told me how you earn a living, and I'm not asking now, but I know it's not legal. Moreover, I suspect it's something very bad.'

'That's you, sweetheart, suspicious of everyone. And this Duval, whoever he is, is not my associate.'

'He told me he's a policeman.'

Now Lux frowned. A policeman, real or bogus, asking about him was not the kind of news he welcomed.

'And you believed him. Some guy phones you out of the blue, says "I'm a cop" and you assume he's telling the truth?'

'I did not assume he was telling the truth,' she flared, her voice raised enough to merit a glance from the only other client, an old man with a black dog, hunched over his *pastis*. 'On the contrary, I assumed he was lying. But in either case, whether he really was a policeman, or he was only posing as a policeman, it was not a call I wished to receive. You and I are over and done with, let us be clear about that. I will not take messages for you, nor will I pass them on.'

'You just have.'

She tossed him an angry look and lit another cigarette. 'That was the last. So tell your friends and your enemies not to call me again. Is that clear?'

Lux toasted her with his cup. 'Message received and understood. Tell me, sweetheart, are you still fucking around?'

No answer was expected and none received. Her cigarette joined the other one in the ash tray after only a couple of puffs. She stood up, smoothing her black pencil skirt over her slender, mannequin thighs. His eyes did an involuntary inspection of her contours. God, she was gorgeous. What a shame that was all she was.

'You can afford to pay for both of us, I suppose,' she snapped, and when he nodded smilingly, she nodded back, smile absent, and walked away, out through the propped-open door. He watched her cross the Boulevard St Germain, swerving around the traffic, or maybe it was the other way around. She was quite a traffic-stopper.

The waiter was behind the bar. Lux flapped a twenty-franc bill at him, before dropping it on the table.

'*Gardez la monnaie*,' he called across, assuming there was some change to keep.

With inflation, you never knew.

Naples, Florida, 29 January 1996

'When they set off the sixth device I predicted it would be the last and Eddie agreed. I don't think it was planned that way though. I think Chirac ran out of nerve.'

Sheryl Glister to Thierry Garbe, freelance journalist, 23.03.1999

*   *   *

The *Washington Post* had devoted only a few lines to the event.
The explosion, the sixth in a series begun in September, was detonated at 10.30am yesterday (NZ time) beneath Fangataufa Atoll and was equivalent to less than 120 kilotonnes, the French Defence Ministry said.

'Oh, *only* a hundred and twenty,' Eddie Nixon muttered. 'Is *that* all?'

Soon-Li, sitting across the breakfast table, peeped at him over her coffee cup. 'I beg your pardon,' she said in that phrasebook English she hadn't progressed beyond, even in bed.

'Nothing, nothing,' He couldn't be bothered to explain it to her in the single syllable words she would require.

'Not bad news, I hoping,' she persisted.

'No, sweetheart.'

He reached across to pat her hand reassuringly and hid behind the newspaper.

French Président Jacques Chirac, he read on, *previously said the test series might be reduced from eight to six and is expected to make an announcement ahead of his visit to Washington on Thursday.*

Then the phone rang and somehow he just knew it was Sheryl, desperate to rage to someone about Chirac's latest atrocity.

He was right.

Gary Rosenbrand slurped a Red Lion beer straight from the can as he settled to watch the start of the news in his favourite armchair. As expected, the headline item was President Jacques Chirac's announcement of an end to France's nuclear weapons tests in the South Pacific.

Translated into an English voice-over, Chirac told the massed ranks of the world's press, 'I announce to you today the final end of French nuclear tests. A new chapter is opening. France will play an active and determined role for disarmament in the world and for a better European defence.'

A scornful 'Hah!' from Sheryl, occupying the couch.

'As do all of you, dear compatriots, I want peace,' Chirac continued unctuously, his smile disarming. 'Solid and durable peace. We all know that peace, like freedom, has to be built each day.'

Sheryl made a pistol of forefinger and thumb and pointed it at the smiling image on the screen.

'Bang,' she said, imitating the hammer action of a revolver. 'You're dead, Mr Fucking Hypocrite Chirac.'

Champs Elysées, Paris, 4 February 1996

'He was real thorough was Rafael, very ... what's the word ... meticulous? I'd planned to dispense with his services once Barail was on board, but I had a change of heart.'

Sheryl Glister to Thierry Garbe, freelance journalist, 23 .03.1999

*   *   *

The shutter of the Pentax camera clicked open and closed, recording the telephotoed image. The motor wound forward, a faint buzz like a bee zipping past the ear, to the thirty-sixth and final exposure of this roll of film, full of images of the route taken by President Jacques Chirac on his way to lunch.

Simonelli laid the camera on the seat beside him and lit a cigarette, his narrow brow crinkled in thought. It was cold, his breath a white plume, his feet like ice from too long sitting still. Paris was not Ajaccio, where winter never came. He raised the car window and twisted the ignition key. The diesel engine of the Mercedes clanked into life. He adjusted the climate control knob and set the fan high. He didn't immediately drive off, but sat for a while, letting the heater warm him.

Barail had chided him for personally visiting all prospective vantage points from which to hit the President. Let the assassin do it, he had grumbled, though the assassin had yet to be recruited. But Simonelli had his reasons and they were not for Barail's ears.

'I don't entirely trust your Commissaire Barail,' Sheryl had admitted, as they lay, limbs still twined together, in the aftermath of their third stint of lovemaking since their reunion. 'He's altogether too smooth.'

'You think *I* trust him?' Simonelli had snapped back at her, resenting the unuttered suggestion that he was gullible. 'Never trust a man who rats on his employers – and especially if his employer is the President of the Republic. I may be a crook but I'm an honourable crook ...'

Sheryl had giggled at that. Right away he saw the funny side too and they finished up clutching at each other, convulsed in laughter which, as it subsided, led to her groping him, which led to his squeezing her tits, which led to a second grand finale. He impressed himself. He had believed the days of two fucks inside an hour were behind him.

It was after the aftermath of their lovemaking when she asked him to work alongside Barail. Whereas he had assumed his job – favour, rather – to be at an end, she'd had second thoughts and offered him the role of overall coordination. His instinctive reaction was refusal. Only when, in the flush of sexual gratification, she offered to match Barail's pay, was he won over. Twenty-five million francs to just keep Barail on track and a watchful eye on the assassin, plus a second watchful eye on his own back. It sounded like a sinecure.

Later, pondering with mixed feelings on the rewards vs. the risk of incarceration or worse, he altered his view somewhat. Nobody on this trip could be just a passenger. As with Barail, he was doing it for financial gain, plus maybe a little of the personal satisfaction that any Corsican of the blood would derive from taking out a French president. But to earn the money was only part of it. He had to be around afterwards to spend it. Ergo, he would do his damnedest to make sure the operation ran as glitch-free as a Rolls-Royce engine and that Barail did likewise. He would baby the assassin by preparing the ground for him. He would wipe his nose and, yes, even his pink little bottom if that was what it took to make a clean kill. All the *mec* would have to do was pull the trigger and get out unscathed. And there, of course, lay the rub.

Over the past month, using schedules provided by Barail, Simonelli had inspected every route used by the President and every venue visited. Some of them formed part of his daily routine, others were patently sporadic or one-offs, such as the ceremony at the new EU headquarters at Strasbourg, the meetings with other heads of state in Brussels, the visit to the Palais-Royal Theatre with that African president of the unpronounceable name and unspeakable reputation. Most of the locations were unsuitable, a few were downright dangerous – to the assassin, that is.

Simonelli, who, unknown to Barail and certainly to Sheryl, was a former contract killer himself, knew better than most what to look for in setting up a hit. He was familiar with angles of fire, allowances for deflection and lay-off, the trajectory curve, moving targets, head shots, body shots. He was also adept at calculating the odds. So far only the itinerary from the Elysées Palace to the restaurant in the Place de l'Opéra showed possibilities and even this lacked a getaway route. Without an assured exit no self-respecting hired killer was going to take this contract, no matter the size of the pay cheque. A lavish funeral would be no compensation.

So here he was, illegally parked across from the Opéra, about to take a last snapshot of the President's favourite eating establishment. According to Barail, Chirac and an entourage frequented the place at least every other month on average. Any of a multitude of top floor apartments along any of the various routes between the Palais and the restaurant might do at a pinch. The security service couldn't check them all. But Simonelli was opposed to hitting the President while he was in a moving vehicle. Such assassination attempts rarely succeeded. A typical failure in this category was the OAS attempt on de Gaulle at Petit-Clamart in the early sixties. No, the moment to do it would be when Chirac crossed the sidewalk from his car to the restaurant entrance.

Opposite the restaurant was a typical apartment building from the 18th century – five floors topped by a mansard roof. About three hundred metres from the nearest fifth floor window to the restaurant door. The range was right on the limit for the kind of lightweight rifle an assassin would most likely elect to use. Not only that, but the *flics* who accompanied the President in two separate cars invariably erected a human wall around him the moment he quit his car, thus ruling out a body shot. So it was the head or nothing, calling for even greater accuracy.

The other difficulty was the random nature of the President's visits to the restaurant. Barail claimed to have little advance notification. To summon up the gunman and get him in position they would need several hours' notice at least, ideally twenty-four. Yet of other prospects there were none so far – or none that Simonelli would be willing to commend to an assassin.

He liberated the handbrake and moved out in the wake of a CD-plated limo with black glass all round and a miniature flag in red and green fluttering from each front wing. At little more than a walking pace he tagged on behind it to head down the Boulevard des Capucines towards the Church of Marie Madeleine.

This job, he reckoned, was going to be an absolute fucking nightmare.

Auckland, New Zealand, 8 February 1996

'The file on Lux made scary reading, especially for Sheryl. It made her think twice about what we were doing.'

Gary Rosenbrand to Thierry Garbe, freelance journalist, 19.03.1999

*   *   *

The padded bag was delivered by Fedex at a few minutes before nine am. Her name was prominent as were the printed words PRIVATE AND PERSONAL. The label denoted French provenance.

Sheryl sat down with her first coffee and cigarette of the day. The package was so securely sealed with packaging tape that she had to cut her way in with a kitchen knife. Inside was a single brown envelope on which her name was again written in upper case. She slit it open with the knife and drew out two pages, to the first of which a post-it note sticker was affixed. She upended the envelope and shook it. A photograph fell face down onto the table; she reversed it. It was a slightly out-of-focus study of a man emerging from a car with his hand extended to shake the hand of another man whose arm, shoulder and half his face were the only parts visible. On the note was scrawled:

This is the dossier of the man I intend to approach. I personally translated it into English. Read it and if you have any questions, comments or objections telephone me on my cellphone before midnight 9/10 February

Cordialement B

There followed a cellphone number.

Sheryl turned the photograph towards the light for a proper look. The man was thirty-plus, good physique, regular features, muddy blond hair worn long on top and at the sides – a lock of it had tumbled over his forehead and he was in the process of sweeping it back with his left hand. He was wearing a sandy-coloured jacket with an open-neck cream shirt and dark blue trousers.

'Not bad,' she murmured, and sipped her coffee. 'You can come into my parlour anytime, Mr Assassin.'

The rest of the photograph was uninformative. Behind the man a line of trees in full leaf gave a clue as to the season but not

47

the whereabouts. Sheryl laid the photograph on the table, peeled the sticker off the first sheet of paper and attached it to the photo. She began to read.

CONFIDENTIAL
PERSONAL PROFILE

Subject's name:	*LUX*
Subject's first name/s:	*Dennis Randolph*
Nationality:	*American*
Place of birth:	*Topeka, Kansas*
Date of birth:	*13th September 1959*
Status:	*Unmarried (divorced)*
Domicile:	*Paris France until January 1994.*
	Marseilles France January 1994–October 1994
	Present abode not known.

Description:		
	Ethnic category	*White Caucasian*
	Height	*184 cm*
	Build	*Medium*
	Hair	*Fair*
	Eyes	*Blue-grey*
	Disabilities	*None recorded*
	Distinguishing Features	*None recorded*

BACKGROUND

The subject is a US ex-infantry corps NCO who also served for a period with the US Special Forces as a sniper. He was honourably discharged from the service in March 1986.

The subject was responsible for several killings during his two years with Special Forces, including the Venezuelan drug baron, Felipe Paulo DIAZ and the Argentinian torturers Lt.-Col Vincente MACTAVISH and Lieutenant Ramon BAIGORRI.

The subject is believed to have committed his first act as a professional assassin in December 1987, when he undertook the killing of Jan VERMUELEN, a senior officer in the South African Police Force, alleged to have been responsible for a number of 'deaths in custody' of black South African detainees. The contract is thought to have been issued by the ANC.

Between late 1988 and July 1990 the subject almost certainly undertook other contracts, including a second South African police officer and a Pakistani nuclear physicist. The latter is noteworthy since it was rumoured at the time that his employer was the Indian Government. Other contracts may or may not have been undertaken.

The subject entered France in July 1990 purportedly on a business visit though at that time he was already active as a professional assassin. According to records the purpose of his visit was the assassination of Antoine FISS, a Swiss banker who was suspected of colluding with Nazi fugitives in the 1950s and 1960s in a bullion-laundering operation. FISS was killed in Basle in August 1990. The murder remains officially unsolved. The contractor is believed to have been one Erasmus KESSLER, a former German Jew, domiciled in Chicago. No formal link was ever established between Kessler and Lux.

Shortly after the Fiss killing, while still in France the subject met the woman whom he subsequently married. Her birth name is Hélène Viollet-le-Duc and she is a member of the aristocracy, though she rarely uses her title. They married in October 1990. The marriage lasted until March 1994 when they separated. A divorce was granted in March 1995.

As a result of this marriage the subject remained in France and applied for a residence permit which was granted in February 1992. Notwithstanding his marriage and despite his wife's comparative wealth he remained active throughout, although it is probable that his activities were curtailed. During this period it is thought that he was implicated in the killing of at least two people.

Between the divorce and the date of this report he has been linked to other further assassinations, the most notorious of which were a British Secret Service officer on behalf of the Provisional IRA, and paradoxically, an IRA brigade commander, on behalf of a Northern Irish Protestant businessman.

Throughout his career as an assassin he appears to have avoided either by accident or design the killing of French nationals and the commission of crimes on French soil.

RESUMÉ

Apolitical, amoral and without loyalty to individuals or factions other than those who employ him. A specialist in assassination by rifle, occasionally explosives. Highly skilled, resourceful, and well-organised, with contacts in a number of countries.

No crime having been committed by him in Metropolitan France or its overseas territories nor against French nationals, and no request for his extradition ever having been received or pending, he is not currently on the wanted list and no charges are currently outstanding against him. The sum total of his criminal record in France is a fine of 400F for exceeding the speed limit (October 1993) and a fine of 800F for failing to stop at a Stop sign (February 1994).

Paris, 05.02.1996

Sheryl's cigarette had burned to nothing in the ashtray, virtually unsmoked, so engrossed had she become in the Lux file. What she read had horrified as well as impressed. Talking about recruiting a killer to remove Chirac was all very fine, the cause was just after all. Yet even if only half of what was contained in the file was fact instead of hearsay, it shook her essentially-Christian beliefs to know that such men really did exist outside of the world of fiction and movies.

Self-doubt and doubts about whether the noble end really did justify ignoble means besieged her. For a minute or so she considered calling off the operation. Then a report at the bottom of the front page of yesterday's *Herald,* opened out on the table from the previous evening, caught her eye. *FRANCE TO SIGN NUKE TREATY BY MID-MARCH* was the headline. One short paragraph in the article stood out; Gary Rosenbrand had coloured it with a yellow highlighter:

French President Jacques Chirac said last month that France had ended nuclear tests forever after the sixth in a series of underground tests in French Polynesia.

Beside it Gary had scrawled in black felt-tip:

Does he think that will let him off the hook?
No fucking way José!

Those few barely-legible sentiments instantly stiffened her resolve. Gary was right. No fucking way José was Chirac going to be let off the hook.

Françoise Yvard was a divorcée of twenty-eight, who lived in a first floor apartment in Avenue des Ternes a short walk from the Palais des Congrès. She was tall and willowy with no chest worth speaking of but a *derrière* that more than compensated. Her brown hair was naturally curly and, although not pretty in the accepted sense, her features were regular, marred only by an over-long, lightly hooked nose.

After being introduced at a mutual friend's home in Chateau La Vallière, near Tours, she and Lux had formed a strictly sexual attachment that was now in its sixth month with no abatement in view. Their trysts were irregular and spontaneous. It was understood that whenever Lux was in town her bed was his for sharing. It was a relationship that suited both their lifestyles.

It was morning but still dark. In the intimate glow of the bedside lamp Françoise lay asleep, belly up, almost but not quite snoring; a bare bony shoulder exposed, a broomstick of an arm protruding rigidly over the side of the bed like the bowsprit of a sailing ship. Only a few hours earlier she and Lux had made love after a fashion, her mechanical body contortions never quite in tune with her panted endearments. It mattered not to Lux. For him, she served a purpose and he did not doubt it was the same for her. He was physically content, that was what counted. He lay beside her, outside the duvet, slurping his first black coffee of the day, marvelling as ever that a woman of such taste and refinement could live amidst such junk. Apart from the oval cheval mirror with the mahogany frame and stand that she had bought in the flea market, and the painting by Manet or Monet, left her by her great-grandfather, there was little to covet. The most expensive item was a portable colour TV fixed to an extending wall bracket. Françoise Yvard was a woman without frills and the decor defined her character.

The mirror was placed to reflect the bed and its occupants. In the glass, Françoise was no more than a bush of brown hair and a pair of nostrils. Lux himself, propped against two square pillows, had a pensive look; the muddy-blond hair was in disorder – he rectified that – the chunky, college-boy features marred by a bewhiskered chin, the old gunshot wound on his left bicep livid in the artificial light. About him an aura of world-weariness beyond his thirty-six years.

He slid a hand beneath the covers to rest on the bony pinnacle of Françoise's flank and she moved sinuously in her sleep. She was sexually undemanding; once a night was her mark which, unless he had undergone a prolonged drought, conformed to his own needs.

He tipped the last droplets of coffee down his throat and got off the bed to patter stark naked to the bathroom. A pee to dispose of the previous evening's wine intake, a fastidious brushing of teeth, an abbreviated shower, and he was ready to confront the day. It was almost seven and Paris was rousing itself.

He switched off the bathroom light and shuffled back into the bedroom, yawning. At that point his sense of wellbeing was rudely demolished. Françoise was awake, sitting bolt upright, clutching the pink duvet to her chest. Well she might, for in Lux's brief absence for ablutions she had received visitors. Specifically, three males, all clad in grey belted topcoats, two of them young, the third in his thirties, sporting wire-rimmed glasses, clearly the leader. The taller of the two subordinates had a pistol trained on Françoise; the shorter one now pointed his at Lux.

'Who are these men, Dennis?' Françoise quavered. She pronounced it Den-eece, as did most natural French speakers of his acquaintance.

Before Lux could reply the taller man told her to 'Shut it, slut!'

She gave him a terrified glance and shut it.

Naked, a man functions less effectively. Nakedness, when all around are clothed, induces inferiority, vulnerability, and a degree of ridicule, all of which lowers one's capacity to think and act positively. Or so Lux was discovering now.

So his first inclination was to cover up – anything, a towel, a sheet ...

'Do not move, please, Mr Lux,' the leader warned and though his tone was mild it demanded, no, presupposed obedience.

'My name is Dubois,' the leader said then, resting one buttock on the corner of the dressing table that had come from Conforama or some other haunt of the shopping proletariat. It sagged but bore up like the solid, veneered chipboard it was.

Dubois. French equivalent of Smith. Narrow shoulders, middle height, average through and through, the way the law likes its employees. For that was what Lux assumed they were, policemen of sorts.

'Apparently,' he said, 'you don't need an introduction from me.'

'No, indeed. And, knowing as much about you as I do, I am confident of your co-operation.'

Lux leaned against the wall, folded his arms. At least now his butt was covered.

'Co-operation?' he echoed. He fought off the temptation to ask them for some form of ID. All would be revealed presently, he was sure of that. Let them make the running for now.

'We are here to discuss your future residency on French soil ...'

'At seven o'clock in the morning?' Lux cut in.

'We do not work by the clock,' Dubois said coldly. 'In any case, you will not contest the authority that brings me here.' He stepped up to Lux and flapped a slim leather wallet at him. Inside was a plastic identity card with an integral black and white photograph of Dubois produced by a computer. It informed Lux that Dubois was an executive officer in the *Direction Central Police Judiciare*, holding the rank of Lieutenant de Police, and that he had been born on 18th November, thirty-six years ago. The rest was mostly gobbledygook.

'The DCPJ, eh,' Lux said, buying time, unsure what to make of it, as he returned the wallet. 'Did I forget to feed a parking meter or what?'

'Nothing so trivial. In any case, I regret this intrusion but I am only following orders, you understand. My apologies also, to *madame*.' A false smile pasted on his face, he executed a stiff little bow towards Françoise, now seemingly upgraded from slut to lady. Unimpressed by the gesture, Françoise bared her teeth in a frozen grimace.

'Now,' Dubois said to Lux, 'you may dress. Unless you prefer to travel in your present condition, of course.'

'Am I travelling?'

'You will be. And please, for your own sake, do not make a scene.'

Lux, outnumbered and outgunned, had no intention of making a scene. Not yet. Scenes should only be made on one's own terms. He dressed perfunctorily in his rather rumpled grey pants, Armani check shirt, also rumpled, and blue jacket, and kissed a pouting Françoise farewell. With the three DCPJ officers in close attendance he descended to the street where a black Citroën XM was waiting. Its engine was running, the exhaust smoke a white bouquet in the near-freezing air. Behind the wheel sat a fourth man – older, thick necked, and with the cropped head of a professional soldier.

They pushed Lux into the rear seat, there to be sandwiched between Dubois and one of his minions. The car was driven fast and slickly through back streets, changing course so often that Lux soon lost all sense of his whereabouts. Eventually they debouched into an ill-lit, *pavé* square with looming tenements on all sides before passing under an archway into a courtyard in miniature where stood another black XM. There was just enough room for the two to park side by side.

'Curious,' the taller of the two subordinates remarked as the driver held open the right hand rear door, 'that you ask no questions.'

'Isn't it?' Lux rejoined with a slight sneer, declining to be provoked and thereby give them an excuse to smack him down.

The taller officer made no further comment and slid out. Leaving the driver with the car, Lux and his three-strong escort mounted three stone steps to the flaking-painted door of the adjacent tenement. No plaques proclaimed its status. Inside it was as cold as a tomb. Lux turned up the collar of his jacket.

Up four flights of stone stairs they went in single file, Dubois leading, followed by Lux. The iron handrail was icy to the touch. At every turn of the stairs a low-wattage wall light burned, just bright enough to see by. Lux was slightly out of breath by the time they reached the top; annoyingly, his three escorts showed no physical discomfort at all.

A number of doors, uniformly stained dark with age and grime, led off the landing. A rap on the nearest gained them instant entry though Lux heard no invitation.

The room beyond was only marginally warmer than outside. The floors were bare board, the window without curtains, each corner had its tapestry of cobwebs. Under the single light bulb that dangled from a gnarled flex, sat a burly man at a table, reading a newspaper – *Le Monde*. Or at any rate he had been reading prior to their arrival. Now, the newspaper lowered, he was staring at Lux, unblinking, incurious. Not someone who would ruffle readily, Lux figured.

The man stood up slowly. 'Good morning, Mr Lux,' he said in English. 'I am Commissaire Barail, of the Compagnies Républicaines de Sécurité.'

No hand was extended to shake.

'The *what*?' Lux said, genuinely mystified.

'Better known perhaps as the CRS. Come ... let us go somewhere more congenial. You would like some coffee?' Barail's English was flawless, which – inexplicably – irked Lux whose French, even after six years of domicile in the country and a French ex-wife, was no more than passable.

'Since I'm here and presumably not free to leave until you say so, I might as well take whatever freebies are on offer.'

'Very sensible of you.'

Barail led Lux through another door into an environment so fundamentally different from the parts of the building he had so far seen, that the American gaped. The room was a long rectangle, furnished ornately with lots of gilt-painted woodwork and scrolled upholstery. The walls were covered in brocade with co-ordinating curtains. The floor was of polished boards but three quarters of it lay beneath an exquisite rug, intricately woven with abstract designs. A silver tray with a coffee pot and two minuscule cups reposed on a round table with a single leg so slender it looked to be incapable of supporting its own weight, let alone that of the tray and its contents. The place blared taste and money. The CRS was no cheapskate outfit, Lux decided.

Commissaire Barail and Lux sat on opposite sides of the fragile-looking table. Barail poured for both of them. They were alone now – Dubois and his sidekicks had not followed them into the *Commissaire's* sanctum. They would not be far away: a shouted command, a hidden buzzer .... whatever the means, Lux didn't doubt that they could be mobilised at a second's notice.

'Well, Mr Lux.' Barail placed a pair of reading glasses on the very tip of his neat and un-Gallic nose and peered over them. 'Let us not beat about the bush. Thank you, first of all, for your co-operation.'

Lux didn't take issue with the term, though he had good reason to.

'You are here so that we can discuss your future residency on French soil,' Barail went on.

'You don't say.'

'No doubt you will recognise the authority that brings you here to my office.' He passed Lux a wallet, slimmer and of softer leather than the Dubois version. Inside was a plastic identity card, also somewhat grander than that of his subordinate. Lux observed that the *Commissaire's* first name was Julien, that he was fifty years old as of last December and an *Officier* of the Legion d'Honneur.

'Presumably,' Lux said, returning the wallet, 'that entitles you to pull people in off the streets at whim.'

'Actually, yes, it does. Not that I often exercise the right. *Noblesse oblige*, and all that.' He tut-tutted then. 'I'm forgetting my manners, do forgive me. Do you take your coffee black?'

'White,' Lux demurred, and accepted the ridiculous little cup that proved to contain barely a mouthful. The coffee was superb though.

Barail settled more comfortably in his chair before lighting a filter-tipped cigarette. He didn't offer Lux one. His file on the

American would contain information on his vices and filter-tips was not among them. Lux glanced through the window at the grey outdoors. The rooftops of the surrounding buildings were the extent of the panorama. He was surprised that such a highly ranked official hadn't rated a more attractive setting. Or maybe it was case of a dreary backcloth for a dreary job.

'Your full name is Dennis Randolph Lux, known to acquaintances as Denny.' He wasn't asking, he was telling, demonstrating the substance of his file.

Don't look impressed, Lux commanded himself. Don't give the supercilious bastard any levers.

'Age thirty-six, domiciled in France for the last five years, profession ...' Barail patted the palms of his hands together softly, as if in mute applause. 'Would you like to hear how we describe your profession?'

'You're going to tell me anyway,' Lux said, with manufactured insouciance. 'Aren't you, *Commissaire*?'

He sighed. 'This is not your first interrogation, is it, Mr Lux? You know how to put on a bold front. Profitless to try and terrorise you.'

'We could play scrabble.'

'Another time perhaps.' He smiled then and some of the fleshiness slid from his face. 'Let us cease all pretence: you are an assassin, certainly responsible for the deaths of at least six foreign nationals and probably twice as many more that no one has managed to connect to you. No French nationals, of that we are fairly sure. You are too astute to foul your own nest. In the USA you are wanted on suspicion of being an accessory to murder.'

In spite of himself Lux was almost impressed. Barail was right about the profession, wrong in his assessment of the numbers.

'You flatter me.'

Barail's lip curled ever so slightly. 'We could invite the governments of your known victims to apply for your extradition at any time. You could spend many, many years in a foreign prison. You could even die there.'

'But I won't, will I, *Commissaire*? Otherwise we wouldn't be having this conversation.'

* * *

The *Compagnies Républicaines de Sécurité* (CRS) were created in 1944, after the liberation of France, and in theory act as a reserve organisation to the national police. In practice they play a variety of parts independently of the police. Their unique functions include protection of the French President and other high ranking officials and dignitaries, including those of foreign nationality, under the umbrella of the SPHP (*le Service de Protection des Hautes Personnalités*). As an offshoot of this activity they also oversee the security of presidential and ministerial residences and foreign embassies. Among their less glamorous duties are highway patrol, lifeguard service, mountain rescue, port security, and, notoriously, riot control.

Over the years, notably during the insurrectional strikes of 1947-48 and student riots of the early 1960s, they have gained an unenviable reputation as an arm of repression and in general are thoroughly disliked by the average French citizen. In Algeria, during the crisis from 1952 to 1962, they enforced law and order – an unenviable task given the mood of the indigenous population during that decade and the methods employed by the *fellagha,* the local terrorists. The CRS emerged with its uncompromising reputation intact.

As at February 1996 the CRS employed some 15,000 active officers of all grades from lowly *Gardien de la Paix* all the way up to Inspector General, plus thousands more in technical and administrative roles. Among their several locations within the *environs* of Paris they counted an eighteenth-century mansion near the south-west extremity of the Bois de Boulogne and within walking distance of Longchamps racetrack. Arguably the most upmarket of the outer suburbs of Paris.

It was early evening when Lux and Dubois' team arrived before the gates of this property in the same black XM, with the same driver. Early evening and dark and cold, with frost already beginning to layer the pavements and verges.

The gates opened outwards, operated by a remote control. Recorded by several CCTV cameras they drove through into a cobbled courtyard hemmed in by a towering wall surmounted by revolving spikes, The building was well-lit outside and most of the ground floor windows were also illuminated. Barail let them in personally, shooed away a sallow-skinned young man in a badly fitting monkey suit who emerged from the woodwork at their entry. Dubois and his two henchmen stayed outside.

It was there, in a sitting room with a bar, a brace of buttoned leather armchairs and a coal fire burning in a black grate, that Barail explained to Lux what was wanted of him and what was offered in return, and this was where the cunning that had gained and secured the *Commissaire*'s place in the top echelons of the security services came into play.

He had reasoned that even a great deal of money would not on its own be enough to tempt the American to undertake such a hazardous contract, but that the prospect of a future without fear might make more of an impression. Accordingly, he had already set the scene with his threats of extradition. Now, as dressing to that threat, he began to unveil the framework of an impending *coup d'état* against the Government.

'I represent an organisation who for the moment shall be nameless,' he said suavely. 'We have infiltrated the Government to a point where we are ready to usurp it.'

Lux kept a straight face; inwardly he was both startled and sceptical.

'The first prerequisite for becoming the new Government of France is the elimination of the President.'

Lux's expression now became one of outright amazement.

Barail nodded a confirmation. 'Your incredulity is understandable, but I mean what I say. The president must die, *will* die. Plans are already under way. They are unstoppable.'

It was too baldly stated, too lacking in passion, to be believable. Lux suspected he was being led up some complicated garden path to an unknown and probably disagreeable terminus.

'Why tell me?' he said, his voice steadier than his emotions.

'Is that your only comment?'

Lux stared. 'You don't mean to say you want constructive criticism?'

'If you have any, I would welcome it.'

Lux wondered if the man was entirely sane. In which case, best to humour him.

'Okay ... if you insist.' He extended his feet towards the fire, gave the subject serious thought. 'In a democracy you can't expect to seize power simply by doing away with the country's elected leader. You have no case, no cause, no justification.'

'Agreed. But seizure doesn't enter into it. Control will devolve upon us; we will succeed to it, just as the first in line to the throne of a monarchy succeeds on the death of the monarch – quite, quite naturally, no fuss at all.'

'That means ...' Lux didn't finish as he realised he was unsure what it meant.

'Work it out. If you will excuse me, I must make a telephone call. I shall not be long. Help yourself to a drink.'

He left by a second door that blended so sympathetically with the panelled wall in which it was set that Lux had been unaware of its existence.

The American's first instinct on being left alone was flight. He dismissed this at once. Even if he slipped past the patrolling stooges, Commissaire Barail was indisputably an official of some substance and could turn him into a fugitive with a single telephone call. His second instinct was to kill the man. Which would probably mean killing the stooges too and maybe the lackey in the monkey suit, plus whoever else might be lurking about the premises. Killing, even in multiples, didn't concern Lux, he was practised at it. But at best his arrest and incarceration would only be deferred. To kill and get away with it requires planning and preparation.

Then Barail, after a ten-minute absence, returned. 'You are not drinking, my dear fellow,' he chided. 'Come, what shall it be to soothe away your rancour?'

'Oh ... er, cognac.'

'I will join you.' Liquor splashed, golden under the concealed lighting above the bar, into balloon glasses.

'You considered escaping?' the Frenchman asked, with a genial curiosity as he rotated his glass. 'While I was out of the room.'

'I considered it.' The cognac was a warming balm to Lux's throat and stomach. He relaxed fractionally under its influence. 'I also considered killing you and your troop of boy scouts and your servants.'

To hear it put so baldly caused Barail to blanch, the first fissure in his veneer of unflappability.

'You could do it? I don't mean physically, but you are capable – morally – of multiple murder?'

'What have morals to do with murder? But to answer your question, yes, if it's justified. In this case, I decided it wasn't.' Lux set his glass down on a table that was the twin of the narrow-stemmed affair in Barail's office. 'But it was a near thing.'

Barail's breath fairly whistled through his teeth. '*Merde*. They said to tread softly around you. But I am pleased ... delighted. It confirms what we have on your file, that you are the man we need.' His eyes were shining now, like the eyes of a rabbit caught in a car's headlights.

'Need? What exactly is this need, *Commissaire*? You've made your threats, explained how my future hangs on your whim, put me in a frame of mind to co-operate. Now tell me what you want from me.'

Barail's answer was mere formality. Merely the nod that punctuates what is already perceived and understood. And, in this case, dreaded.

'From you, *monsieur*? Why, to assassinate our President, what else?'

Lux had made it a rule to steer clear of high profile figures. The heat such assassinations generated was too searing. His niche was private individuals with a justifiable grudge. People without friends in high places. People whose demise rated no more than a single- column five-centimetre write up in the press and no mention at all on TV. People who were not missed.

'Would you care to state your price?' Barail said, once he saw that Lux had absorbed the first shock.

'For killing Chirac?' He shook his head. 'I wouldn't touch the job, not for any amount of dough. It's too big for one man. Especially this man.' He tapped his own chest.

Barail had been primed for rejection. He had two big arguments going for him: even if Lux was able to slip his clutches here and now, the release of his confidential dossier to the DCPJ would lead to almost certain arrest. This was negative reinforcement. It was blackmail, but of the most efficacious kind.

His second argument stood the first on its head.

'Let's look at the other side of the coin,' he said in a tone of great reasonableness. 'Whilst I can offer you imprisonment, by the same authority I can offer you freedom. By that I mean *absolute* freedom. A wiping clean of the slate, an official absolution, the destruction of all records about you, including computer records. And on top of this, a written guarantee of immunity against any and all applications for extradition. You would be free from fear of arrest for as long as you remained in France, for as long as you live.'

Perhaps unknowingly he had touched upon the most exposed of Lux's nerves. Like all transgressors he lived a state of perpetual if generally dormant dread that one day he would be called on to pay the penalty for his sins. It was a dread that never completely let go. It was a dread that kept him looking over his shoulder when walking along a street, that made him suspicious of every glance, nervous of every approach. Now he saw clearly why Barail had him picked up at Françoise's apartment, understood that the incident had been cynically stage-managed to underscore his vulnerability. To make him appreciate how fickle was his freedom, here one day, gone the next.

What Barail was offering was lasting as distinct from provisional freedom. No more uncertainty, no more suspicion. Lux could come as he pleased, go as he pleased, He could even – if he interpreted Barail correctly – kill as he pleased, so long as he did it outside the frontiers of France. No longer need he shun every policeman, plan his moves selectively so as not to draw attention, be constantly on the alert. In France, he would be no different from anyone else. Just another law-abiding citizen.

It was an attractive prospect. It was a lot more than that.

'If I agreed, if I did it ... how could I be sure you would keep your side of the bargain? Afterwards ... you would want to shut me up. You couldn't risk having me tell who hired me.'

Barail took that comfortably in his stride. So comfortably that Lux guessed he had fine-tuned his arguments in advance.

'Let us be honest with each other. A government can – and does – eliminate whomsoever it wishes. Removing you from the face of the earth now or later would require little more than a signature on a piece of paper and a snap of my fingers. No such thing exists as an absolute guarantee. All I can say is that the necessary papers will be drawn up by someone already empowered to do so, and that that someone will have equal if not greater authority ... afterwards. In other words, he will not become one of the ousted. If that is not enough, tell me what will satisfy you. Not that I promise to supply it, you understand.'

If, by appearing so open, he thought to lull Lux's worries he was a mistaken man. Lux raised his brandy glass, let the bouquet satiate his nostrils, drank with slow appreciation.

'You like?' Barail was studying him, a slanted smile dimpling one cheek.

Lux answered with a nod. 'Suppose I told you that I would deposit an exposé with my will, to be opened in the event of my death by any other means than natural causes.'

Barail laughed. 'You read too many *romans policiers*, Mr Lux. And thank you for the advance notice. We will simply have to be sure that you appear to die of natural causes. You must know that there any many ways of accomplishing this.'

'And you, *Commissaire*, must know there are many forms of insurance.'

Barail's hands were spread wide on the desk top. His fingers, Lux noticed, were unusually thin and tapering, like altar candles.

'So we will each be the other's guarantor.' He correctly read Lux's expression at this facile declaration and went on, 'If you would wish to retain the freedom we will give you, not to mention avoid arrest for the assassination then you will obviously remain silent about who hired you.'

The coals in the grate shifted, popping. There was silence between the two men for a minute while Lux pondered. The deed itself was something he had yet to come to terms with. It could wait awhile. Its magnitude was no deterrent. No use deciding whether he could and would go through with it until he was assured that he would survive to savour into old age the fruits it brought him. Unless the aftermath could be made secure, he would take his chances with what he had: eliminate Barail and take off for the nearest frontier.

He didn't trust Barail. Even more certainly he didn't trust the man's political overlords. Any faction that could initiate the murder of a democratically elected head of state was not over-blessed with honour and scruple. Though he didn't know them personally, he was familiar with the type: the power craze that leads ultimately to paranoia – uneasy lies the head, and all that baloney. Whatever deal he negotiated, they would seek to eliminate him in the interests of security *as a matter of course.*

No, he should get out now while he was still able. Overpower Barail, preferably with the minimum of fuss so as not to alert the boy scouts outside. If necessary – and it might well be – he would kill him with his bare hands.

'Relax, my friend.' Barail's voice came as if from another plane, detached and disembodied. Without even being aware of it Lux had tensed to pounce, would have been on Barail while the CRS *Commissaire's* backside was still glued to the chair. 'Relax,' he said again, soothing as a hypnotist to his subject. 'Violence is unnecessary.'

Lux expelled air, felt his pulse rate slacken. He didn't speak, couldn't.

'Let me get you some more of that.' Barail indicated the empty balloon glass. 'Your nerves are in shreds.'

Lux let him go to the bar, wondering whether he would exchange the glass for a gun. He didn't. He poured generously, came back with the recharged glass in one hand and an envelope-type folder of what was probably imitation leather in the other.

'This is the dossier on you,' he told Lux as the balloon glass changed hands and dropped the folder in the American's lap. It was weighty, a good hundred pages. 'It is yours to keep.'

'This isn't the only copy,' Lux said hoarsely.

Barail lit a cigarette, holding it in the root of his index- and middle fingers. 'Hardly. It is merely a gesture. It changes nothing. You can walk out of here and if I wish to have you arrested because of what is in there or on some other pretext, or deported, or simply obliterated without trace, I will do it with or without evidence.' Smoke was ejected from his mouth in little squirts as he talked.

'Otherwise my proposition still stands. An official clean slate, in advance, in return for the death of the President. Think what it means, my friend – total immunity, for the whole of the rest of your life.'

'All right,' Lux said. 'Let's suppose I trust you implicitly to deliver. What happens if your people don't form the next government after all? Where would that leave me – the man who killed the President? Your precious promises won't be worth a *franc ancien*. You won't be able to discharge them.'

Barail's hesitation at this exposure of the weak spot in his hypothesis was so slight as to pass unnoticed by Lux.

'Provided your aim is true,' he said smoothly, 'there is no question of our not forming the new Government. As I already explained to you, there will be no change of government, or of its structure. All that will happen is a minor reshuffle of personnel. A new president, our nominee, will step into Chirac's place. All perfectly legitimate and in strict accordance with the Constitution. Everything is in place.'

Though Barail spoke with conviction Lux was not wholly convinced. Either it was the whole truth, in which case he had no cause to worry, or it was lies, in which case Barail would continue to lie, probably plausibly, and it would be impossible to tell.

'One last question,' Lux said, if only to show he was no pushover.

'Yes?'

'Why me specially? Why not use one of your own assassins?'

Barail smoothed the wings of his thick but lightly greying hair, not hurrying, assembling his reply.

'The truth is, Mr Lux, there isn't one among them I can trust enough to ask.'

Paris, 11 February 1996

One of his rules for survival was to keep looking over his shoulder, metaphorically speaking, that is. He explained this to me when we met up in London. Once he had been approached about a job – even before he accepted it – he would behave as if he were being tailed, whether or not he really was. It must have made life bloody difficult but I suppose it was better than the alternative.'

Sheryl Glister to Thierry Garbe, freelance journalist, 23.03.1999

*   *   *

From here on Lux's every move would be conditioned by the assumption that he was being watched. It mattered not whether the instigator was the Police Judiciare, the CRS, or some other security department. His code of conduct was ever to play it safe.

Accordingly, on taking his leave of Françoise to fly to Nice by Air Inter he did a quadruple switch of trains on the Paris Metro, followed by two changes of taxi and direction. Finally he left Orly on a flight booked under a phoney identity for which he possessed all the right documentation.

His precautions were a huge overkill, for the agent assigned to the task by Dubois lost him after the second switch on the Metro.

They were three: Rafael Simonelli, Commissaire Divisionnaire Barail, and the American, Lux. Three men, plotting to kill the President of the Republic of France.

Unreal, yet real. Fantastic, yet fact. Insanity, yet the project of sane if fanatical beings.

The room in the restored country house was lofty of ceiling and cool, the shutters secured half-open, allowing only a narrow bar of anaemic winter sunlight to enter. The chatter of birds from the garden was just audible. It was a peaceful, restful situation. A place to retire to, to put up one's feet in and reflect with gratitude on a full life or with regret on an empty one. It belonged to a very old, very rich, very right-wing *comte* whose forbears were among the few aristocrats to escape the revolutionary backlash two hundred years previously.

Simonelli and Barail were not natural confederates. On the one hand the slim, black-haired, crook nosed terrorist, former enemy of the State; on the other the big and burly, running slightly to seed professional soldier, sometime aide of the French neo-Nazi, Jean-Marie Le Pen; an ex-paratroop regiment commander and a *pied-noir*. An unlikely partnership. Wedded, nevertheless, for the purpose of ridding France of its present Head of State. Wedded in the highest of high treason.

Simonelli was talking and pacing – short steps, hands clasped in the small of his back in the manner of another, earlier Corsican, who had conquered and lost most of Europe. He paced in circles rather than straight lines. To keep him in sight Lux was required to screw his neck round. Barail declined to make the effort, maintaining a blank stare at some indefinable point on the wall opposite, occasionally taking a deliberate pull at his filter-tipped cigarette.

As for Lux … he was no more than the chosen tool, the hired gun, the man who for payment would bring about the desired end, namely the death of a president. Like most of his breed he was apolitical. He had killed, often and for ever-increasing sums of money, men and occasionally women of varying degrees of deservedness. He had steered clear of kings and presidents and dictators and all whose only crime was that they occupied a throne coveted by others. Until this fine, sunny February afternoon, the day after St Valentine's Day, when the covenant was to be made and his fate, whatever it may be, sealed.

But he was in a quandary. A week's pondering of Barail's proposition had led him to the jaundiced conclusion that, even if Barail and his faceless principals were men of their word, the coveted 'immunity' would have dubious legal gravitas. Would it really bind the next government? If not, he would be no better off than he was right now. Yet his choices were few. If he refused to go through with it, Barail would have him killed, sooner or later. He knew too much now – way, way too much. So if he was to go through with it, he must take out other insurance, he must demand a high enough price to buy him a safe haven and protection for life.

Simonelli wound up his diatribe on the various means by which the President could be assassinated and ended his pacing in front of Lux.

'So what is your professional opinion, Lux?'

Lux altered his position slightly so that he didn't have to crick his neck looking up at Simonelli.

'My opinion? Well, it seems to me you're getting ahead of yourself, pal. I haven't agreed to do the job yet. We haven't even discussed the rate.'

'*Quoi?*' Simonelli glanced towards Barail. 'Is this true? You said – '

'You deduced,' Barail corrected. 'I told you I was confident that he would agree, no more than that.'

Simonelli now remembered Barail's words and suddenly felt foolish. He breathed out hard, angry with no one but himself.

'Very well. So I have wasted ten minutes speaking of practicalities.' He shrugged. 'We will come back to them when ... *if...* we agree terms.'

'Right,' Lux said, straight of face.

'We are offering you guaranteed legal immunity from extradition by any other state for your past crimes committed on their soil, whatever they may be. That is the deal.'

'I've been thinking it over ...' Lux said.

'And?' Simonelli prompted during the pause.

'And I want ten million on top. So that I can really enjoy this wonderful immunity you're going to grant me.'

Again Simonelli glanced at Barail, who made a smoke ring and looked bored. Money was not a problem, at any rate not his problem.

'Ten million francs is a lot of gravy, my friend,' Simonelli said, purposely injecting menace into his tone.

Lux looked amused. 'Did I say francs? Get real, Simonelli.

This is big league. It's not your neck under the knife. I want ten million US dollars and I want an agreement here and now and payment of ten per cent tomorrow or I walk – out of here and out of France. But first ...' He reached down to his left ankle, faster than the eye could follow, and even as Simonelli and Barail understood what was about to happen, a very short, very narrow automatic pistol was in the American's hand and aimed at Simonelli.

'Seen one of these before, gentlemen?' he said, with a tight little smile. 'It's a Beretta Jetfire. It may look tiny but even a .25 bullet in the right place – or the wrong place if you happen to be on the receiving end – can do all sorts of damage, and there are eight in the grip and another up the spout. But I won't need as many as that.'

Simonelli was suitably impressed. 'Weren't your men supposed to have frisked him, *Commissaire*?' he said, in a jeering tone.

'Indeed,' Barail admitted, privately furious with the apparent laxity of his subordinates. 'Heads will roll.'

'Including, quite possibly, ours,' Simonelli observed, eyeing the little pistol.

'No good can come of recrimination,' Barail said. 'Mr Lux wants ten million dollars US, if I understand him correctly?'

Lux nodded, still pointing the gun, still not trusting either man.

'You over-rate yourself and us,' Simonelli said. 'The treasury's not that fat. Two million possibly, just possibly, but ten? It can't be done, *mon pote*.'

'Not so hasty.' Barail was inclined to be more philosophical. Only two days ago he had received a report on Eddie Nixon from the French Embassy in Wellington via the diplomatic bag. It included an assessment of the New Zealander's worth. It reassured Barail that funding was not a constraint. 'Let us at least pass on the message. It can do no harm.'

Simonelli looked sceptical but grunted an assent of sorts. 'So be it.' He plucked a cellphone from the holster on his belt. 'I will transmit your request to the appropriate quarters.'

He composed the number of another cellphone and waited. His call was answered after two rings.

'*Salut, ma petite biche, c'est moi*, Napoleon ...'

Simonelli and I were made to look foolish by Lux. He produced an automatic pistol, a handbag piece but in his hands lethal enough. It made us aware of the dangers of using such a man and after he left we discussed whether he should be allowed to live when the job was done. Naturally Simonelli left that out of his report to Miss Glister whose sensibilities were all against unnecessary disposals.

Translated from written statement of Commissaire Divisionnaire Julien Barail, 03.06.1996.

*   *   *

'He is too good for his own good,' Barail said.

Simonelli was preoccupied in scanning a map. Ash dropped from his cigarette onto it and he wiped it away with a grunt of irritation, leaving a grey smear across the bay of St Tropez.

'Once it is done, you may have to kill him.'

Barail massaged his forehead with his pointed fingertips. 'It would not be as simple as that. He will take certain steps to safeguard himself, he has already said this.'

It was long past midnight, a brilliant full moon bleaching the countryside. The stillness around the house was broken only by the occasional hoo-hoo of an owl; the *comte*, three generations of his family, and sundry retainers slumbered on the floors above. Only the two conspirators were awake.

'Only a fool would trifle with such a man,' Barail went on. 'You do not survive for eight years in his profession by trusting people or by lacking in resource. If ... and I emphasise the "if" ... I decide that he should be silenced permanently once he has done his work, I shall not undertake it lightly, of that you may be sure. It might rebound on me.'

Simonelli's sleek head jerked up. 'Rebound on you? How do you mean?'

'Simply that he might get me before I can get him.'

Simonelli laughed without humour. 'Underrate yourself if you must, *Commissaire*, but don't underrate me. If you want him killed –' that plain-speaking again; Barail winced. '– I will take care of it. At a price.'

That, for Simonelli, rendered further debate irrelevant. He went back to pondering the map, wiping Lux from his thoughts as cleanly and completely as chalk writings from a schoolroom blackboard.

'Nice apartment,' Lux remarked as he wandered into the living room – a room big enough to accommodate a tennis court.

'Thank you,' Sheryl Glister said, 'but it's not mine.'

'Uh-huh.'

Lux wondered if the room or she or both were wired for sound. As always he would stay non-committal, let her do the serious talking.

'My name's Jill Walker,' she said, using her mother's maiden name.

'Hi.'

'It was good of you to come,' she said, watching him, approving of what she saw; physically at least. His dress sense was good too, something she esteemed in a man: a mid-grey suit over a plain pale blue shirt, open at the neck. Casual but classy.

'You mean I had a choice. They said you won't enter France.' Hands in pockets he swivelled round to look her in the eye.

She made a throwaway motion and sank into a very low, tan-coloured lounge chair. She wasn't about to invoke her connection with Greenpeace and the arrests of her former colleagues by the French authorities.

'I have no problem entering France, but I prefer to restrict my visits to the absolutely essential.'

Lux drifted towards the balcony window. 'So this job you're hiring me to do doesn't count as absolutely essential?'

'It's not that. You were able to come here, so why should I go there?'

'Uh-huh,' Lux said again, a form of articulation that offended Sheryl's Masters Degree in English. 'The boss lady beckons and everyone comes running.'

'Just boss will do. Skip the lady.'

'So let's talk … boss. How does an American come to be mixed up in this business?'

Sheryl, fully briefed on Barail's *coup d'état* subterfuge, had her answer to hand.

'It's not so complicated. I represent the purse strings. And the purse is not French.'

'So another country is putting up money to waste a French president.' Lux was bemused. 'Who the hell would that be? More to the point, *why* the hell would that be?'

'An enigma, isn't it?' Sheryl said, with calculated condescension.

'Now do you want to discuss your money or not.'

'Discuss? You know my price. You've had time to do the sums. What's your answer?'

'Ten million US?' Sheryl made a face. 'Those are very big bucks, chum. I wanted to meet you, see for myself if you really amount to so many dollars. What I've seen so far doesn't impress me specially. Perhaps you'd like to run your CV by me, so to speak. Barail seems to think you're the man for the job but I'm not sure I trust his judgement ten million dollars' worth.'

'Uh-huh,' Lux said yet again, irritatingly, declining to take offence at the aspersions she had cast on his talents.

Outside it was dusk. The weather was grey and drizzling, just as Simonelli, a committed Anglophobe, had predicted it would be. Traffic trundled wearily past in the street two floors down, a more or less endless stream as the lemmings headed for home, one body per car, very occasionally two. Cars *per se* offended Sheryl's anti-pollution instincts; under-utilised cars were a criminal waste.

'Who owns this place?' Lux asked.

'A friend and fellow-countryman,' Sheryl said, irked by what she saw as his stalling. She could feel one of her famous headaches coming on and was not in the mood for idle chat.

'In other words, don't ask.' Lux lowered his haunches onto a low chintzy couch and looked at her through an insolent half-grin, letting his gaze travel over her body. She was wearing pants, loose cut after the mode of the day, but her top was scooped low enough at the front to expose a shadow of cleavage. It wasn't that she had dressed with a view to seducing him, merely that at times she liked to be appreciated, admired, faintly lusted after. She was a highly-sexed woman. And since Simonelli wasn't around – the decision to stay home was his, not hers – any halfway attractive male who happened by was a fly to her spider.

'So sell yourself to me, Mr Lux. What makes you so good you can justify such a pay cheque?'

Lux stretched out his legs, crossed them at the ankle, and locked his fingers across his lean belly.

'Well, I could feed you any old garbage, couldn't I? I could tell you how many jobs I'd successfully completed. I could emphasise the risks this one entails – quote risk factors and give you a mathematical assessment of the prospects not only of pulling it off but of avoiding a long stay at the Chateau d'If.'

'And I might even believe you,' Sheryl said. Her head was beginning to throb, not enough to warrant the usual remedy, a fistful of Paracetamol, but it was unlikely to go away on its own.

'And I could tell you to shove it and take off, back home maybe. And by home I don't mean France, I mean Stateside.'

'So why don't you?' Sheryl's curiosity was genuinely aroused.

He sighed long and viscerally. 'If you really got to know, it's because certain people over there want to question me and I'm not anxious to be questioned.'

She nodded slowly. 'You could stay in England.'

'Wouldn't help. Barail has friends at Scotland Yard or whatever they call it. They already checked me in at the airport. They've probably cased this place. Maybe I could give them the slip, but who needs the hassle. Anyhow ...'

'Yes?'

He ran stubby fingers through his lank hair, leaving it in disarray. 'I like France. My wife is ... was ... French. That's why I settled there originally.'

'Is your wife dead?'

'We divorced. She was the daughter of a government minister. She was also impossible to live with.'

'Did she know about you ... what you do, I mean?' Sheryl tried to envisage being married to a hit man. She couldn't. But then she couldn't envisage marriage to anyone.

'No ... and yes. I mean, she had her suspicions. Now and again, usually when she was drunk or high on ... on ...' A shadow passed over his face, like a cloud crossing a meadow. 'Well, whatever, when her guard dropped she used to come out with some remark that told me she was secretly afraid of me. Not that I ever gave her reason to be. I mean, I never smacked her around or anything.' Lux stared out of the window, seeing nothing but memories, like old snapshots in a dog-eared album. 'When she left me, she said it was because I had no humanity.'

Sheryl found herself feeling sorry for this husky, good-looking American, killer or no.

'No humanity? What a strange thing to say.'

'Is it? I thought I knew what it meant, but I looked it up just the same. Just to be sure. I couldn't believe that was how she saw me.' He rubbed his eyes with his fingertips. 'But if I lacked humanity, she sure as hell was short on humility. It was a race as to who quit first, and she won by a nose.'

He got up suddenly, prowled about the room, like a big cat in too-confining a cage.

'And since then?'

'Since then what?'

'No relationships?'

'Not to speak of. Casual stuff, that's all.' He grinned at her, looking almost boyish. 'I haven't gone off women.'

Subconsciously, Sheryl fluffed out her hair. 'Not scarred for life then.'

'No.'

Their eyes met and held.

'So ...' Sheryl said, a hint of tremor in her voice. 'To get back to the matter of money.'

'Tell you what,' Lux said, taking a couple of steps across the green carpet, bringing him to within touching range of her. 'Why don't you forget about money for a while and take your clothes off?'

She stared at him, her mouth parting, her eyes round. 'Are you on the level?'

'Try me.'

Suddenly, as if Lux's words were a cure for all ills, the headache was gone.

Simonelli pressed the disconnect button of his cellphone and turned to Barail.

'She's agreed,' he announced, sounding awed, which he was somewhat. 'Ten million fucking dollars.'

A grunt from Barail, who was pouring his third cognac of the evening.

'Let's hope he's worth it.'

'You would know more about that than I.' Simonelli frowned. 'You know, Sheryl sounded very strange … as if she were … Well, you understand what I am saying?'

'You mean she sounded as if she was being fucked, I presume.'

Simonelli, man of the world though he was, had his prudish side and disapproved of Barail's vulgarity towards his mistress.

'I … er, suppose so.'

'Sounds logical,' Barail said nonchalantly, before taking a swallow at his cognac.

'What do you mean – logical?'

'Well, Mademoiselle Glister is a handsome woman and friend Lux is a handsome man. She's just agreed to pay his price, so he's feeling grateful. Or maybe she's feeling grateful. Do you need graphics?'

Simonelli's eyes slitted. He feared Barail's analysis was accurate and begrudged Lux his apparent easy conquest. He was not in love with Sheryl and was not jealous of her or any of his other current bed mates in the conventional sense. Yet, he did not take kindly to women paying him back in his own two-timing coin.

Simonelli's villa was on a single level and built into a rocky shelf facing out over the Golfe d'Ajaccio, after the town of that name. From the terrace was a precipitous drop onto some rocks that jutted like rotten teeth from the crystal blue waters; behind the house a vast forest on a long shelving slope. A pure blue sky crowned the idyll.

Simonelli was stretched out on a sun bed, face to the sky, using a cordless telephone to speak to Paris. He was dressed only in skimpy swimming trunks and his body was lean and muscular, made imperfect only by a jagged raised cicatrice along his rib cage, wages of an argument with a broken bottle some twenty years earlier.

A girl of about half his age was perched on the edge of the sun bed; she wore a one-piece swimsuit, daringly cut. She was Italian, her name was Angelica and she was Simonelli's mistress of the moment. She also had a penchant for bondage which dovetailed well with Simonelli's penchant for dispensing punishment.

Simonelli was relaxed, having lunched well, and was anticipating an afternoon romp with Angelica before leaving for the mainland.

'Any news from our friend?' he enquired into the mouthpiece, changing subjects and cutting across some political gossip that couldn't have interested him less.

'The briefest imaginable,' was the dry response. 'He telephoned yesterday to say that he was inspecting your recommended locations. So far he is not optimistic. He will be ready to report his preliminary findings the day after tomorrow.'

Involuntarily Simonelli glanced at his watch to check today's date, except that his wrist was bare; he had removed the watch when undressing. A finicky man, he never sunbathed wearing accessories as strips of pallid skin offended his sense of purity. This fastidiousness did not extend to the area of his loins, for, like many Corsicans, he was inclined to be prudish.

Angelica unscrewed the top off a bottle of tanning oil and waved it under Simonelli's nose. Scowling, he rolled over, onto his stomach.

'What else did he have to say?' he asked into the phone as she set to work on his well-browned back.

'Else? That was all. Were you expecting something in particular?'

'No. If you are confident in his ability, I have no quarrel with the slowness of his progress.'

'*Bien,*' from the voice in Paris. 'In any event I have summoned him to a progress meeting at Venoy the day after tomorrow. I suggest you join us, if you wish to keep your playmate from the land of the free fully up-to-date.'

'The *Commissaire* speaks in riddles.' The tone was faintly sardonic. 'Expect me sometime tomorrow afternoon.'

'Have a safe flight.'

'*A demain.*'

Angelica, her red-gold hair swaying in sympathy with the movement of her torso as she massaged oil into the taut skin of her lover, noted the lines of tension that Simonelli's jaw had acquired in the last minute. She left off her oiling to kiss the nape of his neck, just below where his hair ceased to grow. He shrugged off the gesture.

'Who is this man you dislike so much?' she asked, which was unwise of her for Simonelli drew strict lines between business and pleasure and was not in any case loose of tongue.

He rolled over, onto his side and grabbed her wrist; the bottle of sun oil flew from her hand and skittered across the flagstones. She reared back, startled and not a little scared.

'Do not concern yourself with what does not concern you, little dove,' he snarled, and she cringed from him, eyes blinking, mouth working, stammering.

'Silence!' He rose, dragging her up with him. She was tiny of stature and his near-six feet made him seem a giant. Behind him was all sky, and outlined against it he looked like a wrathful god.

'Keep to what you are good for,' he snarled, and his mouth crushed hers, peeling her lips off her teeth. She clung to him, suppressing her fear with simulated desire. Kissing harder and harder.

He pressed her down onto the flagstones. The pebbled surface bruised her back, but she knew better than to complain. Fear and greed made her not merely compliant but passionate. She gave as good as she received, and more. She gave value for money.

And as she gave she wished away the next twenty-four hours so that she could once more be free of him for a while. Free to entertain Jean-Luc, her true love.

Venoy, near Auxerre, France, 1 March 1996

'They met up with Lux a second time, Simonelli and Barail, that is. Same place as before, I'm buggered if I can remember where it was. Some French town, of course. They reviewed Lux's progress which didn't amount to much. It wasn't his fault, mind. But Sheryl was pretty pissed when she heard how little these three supposed experts had achieved between them.'

Gary Rosenbrand to Thierry Garbe, freelance journalist, 19.03.1999

* * *

In the near two weeks since his trip to London Lux had reflected at length and in depth on the feasibility of assassinating the French President. He had perused the reams of highly secret documentation supplied by Barail that detailed the President's official programme and timetable, his daily routine, his habits, his personal friends, and his leisure activities. He focused especially on the strength and nature of the presidential bodyguard and the other routine precautions to prevent attempts on his life.

He travelled about France to visit the more promising of the sites identified by Simonelli. He was not impressed. His conclusions were identical in all key respects to those of Simonelli. He could get in. He could make the hit. But of exits there were none, or at least none he was willing to put to the test. In the assassination business there is no such thing as a dry run. You either get it right on the day or you're finished.

The killing itself was an entirely practical proposition. This was no unconquered peak he was attempting to climb. Round the clock, day-in, day-out celebrity protection is achievable on paper but not in real life. Some chink in the armour plating always comes to light if you chip away for long enough: a subornable bodyguard, servant, or mistress for instance has caused the downfall of more than one tyrant. And no individual, whatever his status, can avoid being separated from his protective shield at times, if only under the shower or in bed. Oh, yes, he could kill Chirac all right, given long enough to prepare. He could do it – but he doubted he would survive to profit from it.

No scruple plagued Lux, no feeling of pity for his victim. From what he had seen and heard of Chirac on French television he was no more or less worthy than any other leading statesman.

Lux had nothing against the man, personally or politically. But he was only mortal, like all the others whose lives Lux had ended. Undeserving of premature death but, as the head of a prominent state, sure to be conscious that it could happen at any moment. It went with the job.

Now here Lux was again, closeted with his employers, to review progress and plan the next step. In the same room of the same chateau with the burble of doves outside complemented by a selection of other gossiping birdlife. It was warm outside and in – warm enough to allow an open window. The log fire crackled cosily in the hearth that was big enough to hold a party in. Simonelli was standing with his back to it, his arms folded, one gleaming foot tapping.

'We must have regular feedback,' he said to Lux who, like Barail, was seated in an overstuffed armchair with a chintzy cover. 'Making contact as and when you feel the need is not acceptable. The timing of the political moves are linked to the ... ah ... fate of the President. Regular progress reports are vital.' He did a half-turn, to confront Barail, as if suddenly remembering his presence. 'Is this not also your opinion, *Commissaire?*'

Barail's nod was acknowledgement not acquiescence. 'You and Mr Lux must work together as you both see fit. For his part, he is a professional. Placing constraints on his technique is not in our best interests. There is no point in employing a man of proven ability, clearly able to function independently, then manacling him to so many rules and conditions that his basic talents are submerged by them.' Barail massaged his bulbous jaw, already shaded with stubble; he would need a second turn with the razor before dinner. 'Having said this, since you ask my opinion, yes – regular feedback is not an option but a necessity. If this creates an impasse, you must find a way around it.'

Working to a schedule was not Lux's style. He was no chessman, operating on a board of black and white squares, to be positioned according to the whim of his employer.

He put this to them bluntly, adding, 'Get this – my dislike of routine reporting isn't an idiosyncrasy, it's a practical precaution. Two reasons: reports can be intercepted, whether they be telephoned or written. An overheard conversation, a letter wrongly delivered ... whichever, the risk of a third party learning of the plot is increased. Secondly, any regular pattern at all is to be avoided. Once it's noticed it becomes a simple matter to monitor it.'

'You're being paranoid,' Simonelli said scathingly. 'Who will notice a weekly telephone call for instance?'

'No, Rafael, he is right.' This support from Barail was unexpected by Lux and Simonelli alike. 'It is like the soldier running across an open stretch of land under enemy fire. He zigzags to avoid the bullets. However, if the pattern of his zigzags are unvarying the enemy will be able to anticipate them and will pick him off.' He turned to Lux. 'You must operate as you see fit. All we ask is that you keep us informed at frequent intervals. If the intervals must also be irregular, we will adapt.'

Simonelli began to stride about, passing and re-passing through the fantail of sunlight from the open window.

'Very well, very well. We will accept sporadic reports but no more than five days between each one.'

Lux sighed. He was against it but willing to compromise.

'If you insist.'

'I will give you a cellphone number,' Barail said. 'It must be used no more than three times, then it will be changed. On each third call I will give you the new number. Now, apropos of other business: did you receive the first draft, the ten per cent of your fee?'

'Sure did.' Lux had checked with the Schweitzer Kreditanstaltbank of Zurich that very morning. 'One million bucks, less transaction charges. While we're on the subject, don't forget another forty per cent is due when I set a date and a place.'

'Ah, yes, the date and place,' Barail murmured, slumping lower in his armchair as if he were about to settle down with a good book. 'Are you in a position to provide us with particulars, or least a ....' he made convex curves in the air with his hands, 'a global impression, an overview?'

'The only overview I can give you is that the restaurant route is a possible, but I figure you already knew that. I just can't see how the hell I would get out of there unless I hire a helicopter to lift me off the rooftops.'

'A helicopter?' Simonelli said, perking up. He hadn't considered that. 'Perhaps that is the answer.'

Barail rejected the concept right away. 'It would not be able to land, which means it would have to hover and lower a ladder for him. A two-minute operation at the least. More than long enough for Chirac's escort to pick him off, not to mention the helicopter pilot and even the helicopter itself.'

'With pistols?' Simonelli was scornful. 'He would be fifty, sixty feet up, maybe more.'

'My men are armed with submachine guns. Spray enough bullets around and you're sure to hit something. Unless of course, our friend here is prepared to risk it.'

'Not this friend,' Lux said with a shake of his head.

'Where does that leave us?' Simonelli queried. 'As we seem to have established that the task is beyond you, do we let you walk away with a million dollars?'

'The task isn't beyond me,' Lux said with grit in his voice. 'But it isn't going to happen tomorrow either. Either you come up with a getaway clause or I do it the hard way and stake out your precious President until I have every mile and every minute of his routine properly sussed.'

'That could take months, a year even,' Simonelli said mournfully.

'It could,' Lux agreed. 'But what's the point in having a man on the inside – ' He directed a nod at Barail, ' – while you and I do it the hard way. You must know the President's programme several weeks ahead or even longer, *Commissaire*.'

'Certainly. In fact I have it here.' Barail dipped into the attaché case that stood open beside his chair, drew forth a green plastic sleeve containing several sheets of paper. This he skimmed across to Lux. 'Not that it will help you much but there you have Chirac's movements until the end of May. Some dates are blank. On such dates he has no official engagements. Ordinarily most of these will be filled up in due course. It is rare for him to have more than the occasional free day, except for Sundays and during his vacations.'

Lux glanced up from the page he was studying. 'Vacations? Is he due any?'

A shrug from Barail.

'Unlikely before June. In August France shuts down, as you will know, and he may then take some time off. Remember, this is only his second year as President. A pattern has yet to be established.' Now he smiled lopsidedly. 'Exalted as I am, he does not confide in me, nor consult with me.'

Simonelli clicked his tongue petulantly. 'Give me the schedule,' he said, snapping his fingers at Lux. 'From the research I have already done I will be able to eliminate most of them. For the rest, it will be quicker and easier for me to check it out and send you to inspect the likeliest places. If there are any.'

'I agree,' Barail said.

Lux remained silent. He was speculating on the prospect of being left in peace to spend the million dollars he had received so far, if it did become necessary to abort the contract. He was not optimistic.

The house high above the rocks was a beacon of white light. It was visible to passengers on the overnight ferry to Marseilles that ten minutes before had slipped from her berth in Ajaccio harbour. Deck promenaders, savouring the unseasonably balmy night air before turning in to their cabins, remarked on it.

From the source of light also came sound: a monotonous throbbing like a distant pulse beat. Music of the most raucous kind.

At Rafael Simonelli's house a party was in progress. Simonelli was not hosting it, being presently in a taxi on the *autoroute* north of Paris Orly Airport. Indeed he was not even aware it was taking place and the only music he was privileged to enjoy was that issuing from the taxi's speakers. Had he an inkling that his Madonna was not only entertaining the smart set of Ajaccio but also cheating on him, his retribution would have been terrible. Also known as Corsican style.

The party had been in full swing for less than an hour before couples (and sometimes three- or foursomes) began to forsake terrace and living room for sleeping quarters. Not that sleep was uppermost in their designs.

Angelica and her latest in a line of secret boyfriends, Jean-Luc, three years her junior at twenty, were the standard bearers of this exodus. Locking the door of the master bedroom behind them they undressed each other, practically ripping off their clothes in their frenzy. In a fusion of tanned flesh they fell across the vast bed, Jean-Luc already hard with the thrill of anticipation; Angelica enclosing his prick between her thighs, squeezing it.

They made love twice in very quick succession, then a third time after only a brief period for recovery. The music continued to pound, unheard by them. Laughter and squeals increasingly overlaid it. Even when a piece of furniture smashed and a squeal became a scream they paid no heed. These were the normal background acoustics to Angelica's parties. The next day any broken items would be repaired or replaced, wounds would be licked, and no more would be said or heard about it.

This night was destined to be different. The scream was renewed, joined by others. Now men were shouting. Feet thudded on the wooden floor. Running feet.

Jean-Luc sat up finally, breaking free of Angelica's possessive clinch. 'What is happening?' he said, as much to himself as to her.

His nostrils twitched as an alien smell was drawn into them. 'Do you smell smoke?'

Angelica, cuddling the pillow where normally rested the sleek, dark head of Simonelli, merely mumbled to herself.

'Smoke,' Jean-Luc repeated, positive now. 'Angie, I smell smoke!'

He bounded athletically from the bed. Now he could see as well as smell smoke – it was creeping under the door, fine, wispy fingers of it. Outside the commotion was at a crescendo. The music stopped suddenly in a distorted wail, as if the stereo had fallen over.

Now Angelica was sitting up, her golden hair in disorder, alarm contorting her pretty features.

'Jean-Luc!' she squeaked, tugging the sheets up to her chin. 'The house is on fire!'

Jean-Luc needed no telling. He also needed no telling that the only bedroom window was on a side of the house that fell away in a sheer drop of a hundred feet or more. Unfortunately, his education did not extend to having the sense to keep the door closed. As far as he was concerned the door was the only escape route.

He opened it. The fire, by then raging madly through most of the living room and hall, leapt towards this untapped source of oxygen. In its leap it consumed Jean-Luc. He died instantly, not even a last scream escaping him. The fire rolled over his charred remains. Angelica froze, transfixed, too terrified to register that her lover was no more. She cringed against the bedhead, still clutching the sheets to her as if they were fireproof, her mouth working.

'Help!' she screeched, finding her voice. '*A seccorro!*'

The furore of the flames and crack of blazing wood smothered her cries. In any case nobody was left within helping range and even if they had been, the screen of fire was impenetrable. Angelica, sobbing with terror, made a desperate rush for the window. Perhaps she could climb up onto the roof somehow. If not, even death on the black rocks below was preferable to death by immolation.

She nearly made it, would have made it if her legs hadn't become entangled in the sheet. As it was, her fingers were scrabbling at the sill when the flames flowed over her lower limbs like liquid gas, turning them from white to black in an instant and such was the shock of the pain that racked her – a pain beyond description – that her screams were cut off. The stench of her own cremated flesh dilated her nostrils. Her death was not so instant as that of her lover; she died slowly and horribly, a literal roasting alive.

The fire consumed the house, destroying all that was in it, even scorching the contents of the wall safe in Simonelli's study, the only room to have been locked that night. Scorching but not making unrecognisable the folder full of photographs of the presidential limousine as it conveyed President Chirac from his place of work to the restaurant at the Opéra.

Commandant Philippe d'Amore left off cleaning his fingernails with the letter opener and scratched the bald spot on his crown with it. While doing this he contemplated the scuffed toe of his right shoe, propped, like his left, on the edge of the scarred, chipped desk.

On the other side of the desk, passively awaiting the outcome of his chief's deliberations, Brigadier-Major Napoléon Bujoli stood as rigidly as the monument to a more celebrated Napoléon in the Place d'Austerlitz. A patient man, d'Amore, (which was just as well since the deliberating was a frequent occurrence and could be prolonged), he had nothing else pressing to attend to and was perfectly content to await the *Commandant's* pleasure.

On this occasion, however, the pronouncement came sooner than usual.

'*Quel merdier*,' d'Amore growled, swinging his feet off the desk to crash on the bare floor; Bujoli winced. 'What a crock of shit!' Now there was real anger in the expletive. 'Now I must decide whether to act on those.' He gestured at the array of partly burned photographs that covered much of the surface of his desk, each individually sealed in a plastic sleeve, 'or whether to destroy them.'

Bujoli, Corsican first and foremost and only French because his passport said so, was in no doubt what should be done with them. He hesitated to express a view until invited to, having made that mistake once in the past. And once had been enough.

So he stayed silent, his eyes screwed up a little, for the morning was bright and the window of Commandant d'Amore's office looked eastward. Two floors below, in the street, traffic honked and shuffled noisily towards the junction with the Cours Napoléon, main artery of Ajaccio. A thin haze filmed the city, blurring the profiles of the stone buildings. In contrast, the edifice of the Préfecture opposite, being closer, was sharply defined.

D'Amore lit a cheroot, his third since breakfast though his wife was nagging him to cut down. 'Why would a man like Monsieur Simonelli have in his possession photographs of the President's car? Could it be that he was photographing the undoubtedly excellent architecture of our beloved capital city and the car simply happened to be there? H'mm?' His head snapped round; Bujoli could have sworn the thick neck cracked. 'Give me your opinion, Bujoli.'

Now at last the Brigadier-Major could air his thoughts, lowly though they may be. He brushed the trailing ends of his black wispy moustache from the corners of his mouth where they tended to get damp.

'To assassinate him?' he ventured, for he was a simple man, and as with most simple men his reasoning was direct and to the point.

D'Amore reared back. 'Assassinate?' His shock was pure theatre for he himself had reached the same conclusion the moment he tipped the photographs on to his desk. Then, seeming to branch off along a different trail, he said, 'Has he been notified of the destruction of his property?'

'Monsieur Simonelli? No, chief. I am waiting your instructions. The press has been told not to publish the story until we release it. Fortunately it broke too late to catch the morning editions.'

The Inspector made a rumbling sound at the back of his throat. 'That won't hold them for long, not without something official from the *Préfet's* office. Meanwhile, what am I to do about these?'

It was on the tip of Bujoli's tongue to offer to chuck them in the basement incinerator. Something made him hold back. Perhaps he felt out of his depth, as if for a mere Brigadier-Major to advise in what was clearly a matter for the highest authority on the island would appear presumptuous.

D'Amore was similarly inclined but the risks were frightful. A number of officers already knew of the existence and nature of the photographs.

'All right, Brigadier-Major,' he said, sighing. 'I'll deal with it from here on. Keep your trap shut and the lid on the press.'

'*Chef.*' Bujoli about-wheeled sloppily and shambled out.

On his own, d'Amore could think more clearly, more objectively. An assassination? Not necessarily, not even probably. Only possibly. He knew Simonelli personally, and was aware of his latent ambitions, his desire to free Corsica from the yoke of the Elysées Palace. Yet the word was that the terrorist in him had been expunged, long since subjugated to love of money. From the look of it, he was wrong, though quite how the elimination of President Chirac would help the island achieve independence was unclear.

Was a *possible* assassination enough to justify alerting his superiors? D'Amore knew it was, acknowledged that his own ambitions for his beloved Corse and his private antipathy towards all and every French Head of State were impairing his judgement. As an upholder of the law and a servant of the State, his duty was clear.

His sigh came from gut level this time. He clawed at the telephone, dragged it across the desk, ploughing through the cracked and discoloured photographs. The person he called was the *Commissaire*, two floors above. A man whose allegiance to Paris was so steadfast that a full-size *drapeau tricolore* permanently adorned his office wall, surmounted by framed head-and-shoulders portraits of that arch-traitor Charles de Gaulle and the President of the moment, before which he was reputed to genuflect first thing every morning.

The *Ministère de l'Intérieure et Décentralisation* is located in Place Beauvau, roughly opposite the Presidential Palace. Cynics say that the site was chosen because French presidents are notoriously nervous of *coups d'état*, and that to have the Headquarters of the police and security forces as neighbours makes them feel less vulnerable. This invulnerability is largely illusory since most of the hundreds of people employed there are clerical and administrative, and perform mundane functions that have no direct bearing on state security and never impinge on the protection of the person of the President in office.

Entry to the circular courtyard is via an ornate wrought-iron gateway over which the tricolour flutters or droops – according to the wind factor – from a short pole. Doric style columns flank the gate, as do two policemen. The building itself, which is constructed of sandstone, dates back to the mid-nineteenth century, and has no outstanding features.

On this overcast Monday morning in March, in a ground floor room at the corner of the ministry that overlooks the Rue des Saussaies, a man was seated behind a red leather-topped desk, speaking into the telephone. His name was Jean-Louis Debre. He was a well-built man with a full head of dark hair, his looks belying by a decade his fifty-two years. His suit was an immaculate midnight blue, his shirt pale blue silk, and his tie a vivid red in keeping with his politics. His tone was subdued, his words carefully chosen, for he was addressing the President, at that moment in his private study at the Palace, not four hundred metres away.

Unlike many of his predecessors the present incumbent to the presidency was not inclined to panic at the hint of a threat to his life. Several such threats had been made during his ten months in power. There had been that business at the Armistice Day anniversary when a man carrying a concealed rifle had been intercepted entering an apartment block across from the monument where the President was to lay a wreath. He denied any harmful intent but was rotting away in prison nevertheless. Naturally, this incident and others less serious had been hushed up. No reports ever featured in the press.

So, when the Minister of the Interior, reckoned to be among the President's closest personal and professional confidants, spoke of photographs found at the house of a Corsican nationalist and activist terrorist, whose present whereabouts were unknown (an unforgivable slip-up on the part of the Police Commissioner for Corsica), the Head of State was unperturbed.

'I am sure you will deal with it, my dear Jean-Louis,' he said in that slightly gravelly tone. He employed the familiar '*tu*', whereas to the Minister, except on social occasions, the President was always a respectful '*vous*'. 'Do not, I beg you, turn it into a crisis. There may after all be some innocent explanation.'

Debre's alarm was not allayed. In the ordinary way he would secretly double the bodyguard strength at the President's home. Such precautions would have to be unobtrusive though: the President, and his wife even more so, were jealous of their privacy. Minders were at best tolerated as a consequence of leadership.

The conversation closed amicably. The Minister would do what he must and the President would bear it like the statesman he was.

Debre replaced the telephone, tilted his velour-upholstered chair backwards and rotated slowly through 360°. The beige distempering on the ceiling needed tarting up, he noticed. And he really must get rid of that old sepia photograph of the Ministry at the turn of the century. He disliked relics; he was a man ahead of his time, a 21st-century man. The past was irretrievable and some of it ignoble. Why perpetuate it?

He debated inwardly whether to call the Prime Minister.

Not yet, was his decision. No sense in stirring up the twittering dears at the Hôtel Matignon (not an hotel in the usual sense, but the Premier's office); Prime Minister Juppé would take it in his stride, no worries about his nerve, but some of those close to him, his purportedly ardent supporters, were less than staunch.

All that was required in the immediate was to put the presidential bodyguard on yellow alert. In practice this meant the suspension of all leave until further notice and putting a few extra men on stand-by.

The Minister flicked his intercom switch.

'*Oui, monsieur,*' his male secretary responded.

'Send for Commissaire Barail, will you please.'

Paris St Germain, 20 March 1996

His carelessness with the photographs was a major factor, the major factor, in alerting the authorities that something was afoot. Of course I confronted Simonelli with it but he simply became irate and in any case the damage was done. Had I known that the photographs would ultimately serve no purpose I might have been more inclined to discipline him, perhaps by recommending that Miss Glister fine him, though such a proposal was not likely to have received a sympathetic hearing. Her motives for using Simonelli were more related to his performance in bed than his qualifications for the job at hand. It was while we were debating how to limit the damage that Mazé entered my office.

Translated from written statement of Commissaire Divisionnaire Julien Barail, 03.06.1996.

* * *

Simonelli mashed a bony fist down on the desk causing most of the bric-a-brac that sat atop it to rise a couple of centimetres into the air.

'You dare accuse me of a lapse of security!' he thundered. 'What was I supposed to do – eat the photographs and convert them into fertiliser?'

Barail moved restlessly in his high-backed leather chair. 'I do not question the security of your safe, merely your laxness in leaving your house in the charge of a ...' His mouth twisted, 'a *poule.*'

Simonelli scowled ferociously. He was all too aware that his over-fondness for women of dubious repute was the indirect cause of the photographs falling into the possession of the authorities.

'Must a man live like a monk?' he grumbled.

Barail, whose own morals were scarcely less lax, opened a brass cigarette case, the only item too heavy to have shifted position under Simonelli's assault. While he rummaged within, Simonelli sat and watched him under lowered brows.

'Until the job is done, yes, perhaps a man should live like a monk. There is too much at stake.'

'Pious bastard,' Simonelli muttered.

'I only said *perhaps.*'

From the window of Barail's first floor study the view was of the treetops of the Bois de Boulogne and the edge of the spectator stand of the Longchamps racecourse. Beyond, the skyscrapers of *La Défense* pierced the sky, one-dimensional against its pale expanse.

'We are fortunate,' Barail said, as Simonelli continued to smoulder, 'that the President regards all reports of a plot to assassinate him as exaggerated. Whether or not any changes are made to the security arrangements at the house is left to the Minister, who in turn has dumped the problem in my lap.'

'Then what is there to worry about?' Simonelli said snappishly. 'Simply do nothing.'

Barail sighed. There were times when he privately questioned the IQ of his fellow conspirator. But then the entire Corsican race was composed of semi-literate peasants, so what was one to expect?

'You must realise it is not so straightforward as that. Knowledge of the incident cannot possibly be restricted to the President, the Minister and me. My superiors in the CRS and others in the Cabinet have to know, have already been informed in fact. If they were not, and it came out through some other channel – the Police Commissioner in Ajaccio who reported the photographs for instance – suspicion would fall on the Minister and I. Our whole project would be endangered. Even to you ...' The insult was studied, deliberate, 'that much should be apparent.'

Simonelli looked sulky, drummed impatient fingers on his knees.

'Action is expected to safeguard the President,' Barail stated flatly. 'I shall have to go through the motions.'

'Then go through them,' Simonelli said with a dismissive shrug. 'So long as they are only motions. On the day, Lux is not obstructed.'

'Do I need you to tell me this? But that may be precisely my difficulty. The *Corps* is now on yellow alert. This is not yet a matter for serious concern, but it may be upgraded at any time if developments suggest that the President's life *is* endangered. Additional defensive precautions may be taken that could make Lux's task impossible.'

Now Simonelli relaxed. Barail's 'difficulty' was purely hypothetical.

'No cause for panic, *cher ami*. I am sure you will oil any troubled waters, as befits your fee of twenty-five million francs.'

Barail glared but reined back his ire. Much as he disliked the Corsican he was stuck with him and no purpose would be served by engaging in a slanging skirmish.

A fine rain began to patter at the window, blotting out the skyscrapers completely. Barail frowned at it. Every Thursday afternoon he went riding with a friend from his schooldays, and every Thursday afternoon for the past four weeks it had rained.

A deferential tap came at the door. Barail made an urgent signal to Simonelli who rose and swiftly crossed to the far side of the room to stand before the window as if admiring the view, his back presented to anyone entering the door.

'Come in,' Barail called.

The man who entered was in his mid-to-late thirties with a complexion that bordered on swarthy, though his forebears were of pure Gallic stock. He was Barail's number two, holding the middling CRS rank of *Commandant de Police*, and vested of ruthless ambition if somewhat crumpled of dress. Under his armpit he bore a slim plastic folder.

'Sorry for the intrusion, *Commissaire*.' His tone was respectful without being servile.

'What is it, Mazé?'

Mazé took a brisk step forward. 'You asked for the dossier on the security dispositions for the President's holidays.'

'So I did. Thank you.' Barail relieved his number two of the folder.

'Will there be anything else, *Commissaire*?'

'No. Thank you.'

In turning from Barail's desk Mazé caught sight of Simonelli. He had been aware that Barail had a visitor whose presence here was hush-hush – so much so that he had been spirited in via a back door to which only Barail had a key. In truth curiosity was partly the reason for his intrusion, for he was as enquiring of mind as Sherlock Holmes and resentful of the extent to which Barail kept him in ignorance of many matters concerning state security and in particular the protection of the head of that state.

The back of Barail's visitor's head was uninformative. But the policeman in Mazé was not readily deterred.

'*Bonjour, monsieur,*' he called to the stranger.

If he expected the stranger to turn and respond in accordance with convention, he was disappointed. A nominal sideways movement and nod was all the reward his temerity earned; that and a near-reprimand from his chief.

'Mazé! That will be all.'

Mazé made a small bow of apology-cum-obeisance and left. Closing the soundproof door behind him he leaned against it, his brow creased in the effort of remembrance. Why did that sleek narrow head seem so familiar? Did he know the man? A member of the Cabinet, a high level Civil Servant, perhaps? No, it was no one in the political or administrative sphere, he was sure of that.

After a minute or so of brain-bashing, he gave up and returned along the bleak corridor to his office. Given time it would come to him. Perhaps his morning coffee would stimulate the memory cells, especially if laced with a little cognac ...

Philippe Mazé's broad Gascon face was much given to frowning, notably when the brain behind it was tackling some inordinately complex question. Today especially he had reason and more to frown, for he had discovered that his chief was consorting with a man once suspected of terrorist activities. A man whose presence on the mainland would be of extreme interest to every security department in Metropolitan France.

Mazé was puzzled. His chief might well have some special motive for entertaining the likes of Rafael Simonelli – to do with some concession on Corsican autonomy, for instance, though Simonelli had no official political standing, indeed stood as a pariah among the official 'separatists'. Maybe he was engaged on some underground mission for the Government. In which case, as Commissaire Barail's deputy, Mazé should have been informed.

What must he do? Must he do anything? Many a trusted lieutenant, confronted by his superior's possible duplicity, had to weigh between conscience, loyalty, and personal advantage – the prospect of stepping into the shoes of the dethroned overlord.

His cramped office in the house at the edge of Bois de Boulogne was somewhat removed from the mainstream bustle and this had been his choice. It was actually at the northwest corner and thus had two walls and two narrow windows with louvered shutters. At the moment these windows were open, letting in the buzz of traffic along the *Périphérique* and the clatter of the motor mower in the grounds on the other side of the building near Barail's office. Mazé was a man of letters, of books and dusty document files: his walls were lined with them, shelves sagged under them, his desk and a stout oaken table by the window were heaped with them. Books on law and on criminal cases and trials, dossiers on men wanted for the commission of a crime, dossiers on men suspected of same, dossiers on undesirables. For Mazé was a criminologist by compulsion as well as by profession. That he now prevented and solved crimes against the State rather than against the Law, was due to his wife's cultivation of Barail's ex-wife, following their meeting at a presentation of police awards, and the instant liking they had taken to each other. Which in turn led to heavy socialising, etc., etc. The result being that Mazé, at the relatively youthful age of thirty-eight, was now poised for elevation to head of one of the divisions of the country's internal and external security network, an elite position since there were less than ten such *bureaux*. Question was, did he attempt to accelerate the natural processes by denouncing his chief, always assuming there was anything to denounce, or did he write off Barail's liaison with Simonelli as having official blessing.

Had he not accidentally learned of the discovery of the incriminating photographs at Simonelli's burned down house, Mazé would have gone for the softer option and trusted in his chief's loyalty to the regime. But this new intelligence, kept from him by Barail, altered everything.

Knowledge of the photographs had come about when a file was delivered to him for signature just a few minutes before midday. He was speaking on the telephone when the clerk deposited the MOST SECRET box in his action tray, otherwise he would have opened it at once to initial the receipt, in accordance with regulations. The presence of the grey plastic wallet marked CD's EYES ONLY would then have been spotted. The clerk, no doubt horrified by this laxness on somebody's part, would have whisked the wallet away and that would have been the end of it. Chance had also further played a part in it. Had twelve noon not come up a bare minute after the delivery of the file, the clerk would have returned for it after completing his round of deliveries. As it was, he went off on the stroke of twelve for his two hour lunch break.

With the soft May sunshine playing on his crinkly coiffure and to the slam of car doors in the courtyard and street as nineteen out of twenty Parisians departed homeward or restaurant-ward, Mazé replaced the receiver and opened the box according to regulations, which stipulated instant receipting of all classified material. It was then that he made his find.

In the ordinary way he would never have contemplated examining its contents. It was from a Minister's office, closed by a padlocked zip; only two keys would open it – the Minister's and Barail's. Two keys, that is, and a thread of wire in skilled hands.

Mazé's hands were sufficiently skilled. His vague unease over his chief's secret assignation with Simonelli provided the motivation. The combination of these two tipped him off the fence of professional rectitude.

Picking the lock was not child's play. It was a matter of sweat and tears and oaths. Of jackets off and shirtsleeves up. When at last the hook of the lock snapped open it was after one o'clock and Mazé's stomach was rumbling, unaccustomed to the lack of midday sustenance. He blew on sore fingertips and dragged the lock away, committed now, his actions confident and unhesitating.

Inside the wallet were a number of photographs, all partially blackened by fire. They had been treated with a special fluid to make them less brittle, but even at that a shower of black celluloid crumbs cascaded from the wallet along with the prints.

Mazé did not immediately draw conclusions from the diverse photographs featuring the presidential car outside a restaurant in the Place Opéra, clearly shot through a telephoto lens. After all, the Press pursued presidents everywhere in droves in the hope of happening on an indiscretion worthy of the front page. He was however intrigued by the hand-written note on plain pale blue paper that accompanied the photographs. It read:

Julien -
Je te rends ci-joint les photos.
Le chef est de l'avis que nous ne devons pas prendre de panique.
C'est sympa, n'est-ce pas? Et bien co-opératif!
    Amicalement

The signature was a single character, either 'R' or 'N' or at a stretch, 'P'. The identity of the department from whence it came was not stated in the little box provided for that purpose, so there were no other clues as to the writer.

So who had taken the photographs? For what purpose? And why were they burnt? A storm of questions assailed him and no answers came forth.

Above all, what of the cryptic note? That '*bien co-opératif,*' for instance, implying that the President's co-operation in taking no panic measures (against what?) suited sender and recipient both.

First things first. Mazé glanced at his digital watch: 13:28. He had half an hour maximum to copy the note and a selection of the photographs and deliver the originals to Barail in the wallet. The *Commissaire*, as always when in residence, was lunching at the exotic Comte de Gascoigne Restaurant, in Boulogne-Billancourt.

The building was all but deserted. Mazé made his copies unobserved on the Canon machine in the office of the secretariat. Having locked them in the safe in his office, he went down to the ground floor. A clerk in the despatch office was drowsing over *Paris Match*. If he noticed Mazé's phantasmal transit he managed not to let it disturb him. In the adjoining larger distribution office, whose desks were unoccupied, Mazé removed the topmost documents box from a stack of seven or eight, barely interrupting his stride. On through the far door and back upstairs to his own office by a different, more circuitous trail. An advantage of old buildings such as this was the diversity of routes they offered for getting from A to B.

As 14:00 tripped onto the rectangular dial of Mazé's watch, he slipped into Barail's office. It took only seconds to place the box, now with the re-locked wallet inside, in Barail's ACTION tray and beat a soundless retreat, back down the corridor to his own paper-strewn cranny.

The appearance of the documents box would create some puzzlement, but not sufficient to merit a witch-hunt. Its recipient would have no reason to suspect the wallet had been tampered with.

Barail did not return until after four, having lunched with his opposite number in the *Service Extérieure* and two high class *poules*. Not, as Mazé supposed, at the Comte de Gascogne restaurant but at a private house set aside for such trysts. Mazé did not see or hear his chief come in. By four o'clock he was in a taxi on the merry-go-round of the Place Charles de Gaulle, the Arc de Triomphe, that tribute to the sacrifice of the flower of French manhood, looming over him, a fat envelope on the seat beside him.

And ahead of him a hard-won rendezvous with the Contrôleur Général of the personal security arm of the CRS.

The real name of the Contrôleur Général was not known to the public and the press. To government ministers and officials he was Monsieur Renard. Within the Service he was referred to as 'Le Renard', the Fox, or, less respectfully, 'Le vieux Renard'. And indeed, he was a man of great cunning, if small imagination.

He was not entirely surprised to hear from Mazé that Commissaire Barail was consorting with a known terrorist and hoodlum. It didn't automatically follow that he was up to no good. In the furtherance of state affairs officers were often called upon to hobnob with the criminal fraternity. The scrawled note on the other hand did make his eyebrows wriggle.

'Who signed this?' he barked.

Mazé shook his head. 'It could be almost anybody whose name or first name begins with r or n or p, *Monsieur le Contrôleur.*'

Le Renard humphed. 'But it must be an insider – a minister or a secretary or a *fonctionnaire.* Somebody within the body of government, no?'

'*Evidemment.*' Obviously.

A tiny vertical crease sprang up from the bridge of the magnificent nose at the implication that the question was superfluous. Above all Le Renard did not take kindly to subordinates, especially one as lowly as Mazé, giving themselves airs at his expense.

'Commissaire Barail doesn't know you have seen this?'

Another '*evidemment*' was on the tip of Mazé's tongue but he decided not to stretch his luck. Le Renard, though close to retirement age, still wielded a hefty club of influence within the Ministry of the Interior, maybe even in the Palais itself.

'And this business with Simonelli.' Le Renard smoothed non-existent hair atop his slightly pointed cranium. It reminded Mazé, a one-time artillery officer, of the business end of a howitzer shell. 'You believe this points to skulduggery on Barail's part?'

'It seems barely credible, I know,' he said, almost apologetically, 'but at worst it could mean that Commissaire Barail is implicated in a plot to assassinate the President.'

'Not so hasty, Mazé. Commissaire Barail has been in the Service for over twenty years. His loyalty and integrity have never been in question. Why would he do such a thing?'

'Money, perhaps?' Mazé was a simple man. He saw life through a monochrome filter: black and white, good and evil, rich and poor. The middle ground between the two poles did not engage him.

'Is there a warrant out for Simonelli?'

'Since we received the photographs from Ajaccio. Only for questioning, at this time. It is not illegal to take pictures of the presidential car.'

'Thank you for enlightening me on that point of law,' Le Renard said drily, tipping back in his worn leather chair. 'As for the *Commissaire*, it seems to me we have two alternatives: we haul him in for interrogation or we put him under surveillance. He may talk under pressure, he may not. If we put a tail on him though, sooner or later he will lead us to the other members of his club, or his employers, as the case may be.'

'I agree,' Mazé announced, though his concurrence had not been sought. 'Better still though,' he went on after a few seconds' pause, 'let us infiltrate his organisation. Get him to condemn himself through his own lips.'

'Really,' Le Renard said coldly. 'Do not forget Barail is not exactly wet behind the ears. He was once an ace in the art of machination and intrigue, before he rose to his present rank. His instincts for sniffing out a phoney are legendary.'

'If they are so legendary, why have I not heard of them?'

The white telephone on the Le Renard's desk rang. He glared at it and it rang no more. A clear case of mute intimidation.

'In any case,' Mazé said, when he was sure the phone really had fallen silent, 'you are perhaps forgetting the *Commissaire*'s weakness.'

'Am I? And which weakness is that?'

Mazé locked his hands behind his neck and tried not to look smug.

'Women.'

'Go on,' Le Renard said, his voice deceptively soft.

'Since his separation from his wife he has developed a taste for slender, dark haired, brown eyed women, with small tits.' Mazé hesitated, as if reluctant to break a confidence. 'Actually, he had these tastes before his divorce.' Further hesitation, more prolonged. 'To tell the truth, *Monsieur le Contrôleur*, that's *why* he is divorced.'

Le Renard did not indulge in rumour-mongering, it smacked of throwing stones inside glasshouses, a reminder of his own occasional trafficking with a *poule* who possessed precisely the physical attributes Mazé described.

'That is his affair.' He reached for his coffee cup, then drew back as he remembered he had emptied it before Mazé arrived. 'A slender, brown-eyed brunette, you say. In other words, a typical Frenchwoman.'

'Precisely. Ten a penny.'

'You have a particular woman in mind for this project, I presume.'

'I do.'

'She works in a government department?'

'She is with the RG.'

'Commissaire Barail may know her,' Le Renard cautioned.

'I doubt it. But I will check with her. In any case, we will make a few cosmetic changes.'

Le Renard smoothed down his non-existent hair again, studied Mazé over his spectacles. He didn't much care for Barail's number two; too self-opinionated, too bumptious. Dangerously ambitious. But he had a good brain and it would be a shame not to exploit it to full advantage.

He gave a nod of assent.

'Proceed, then. With discretion. And report back to me daily in person.'

Out in the corridor Mazé rubbed his hands together, well pleased with the results of the session. With any luck he would be able to prove Barail was deep in skulduggery, oust him, and step into his shoes.

Not that he would let personal ambition influence his judgement in such a matter.

PART THREE

SPRING OFFENSIVE

Madame Q. introduced me to her supposed latest recruit, an exceptionally pretty and unusually intelligent girl. Not only that, but she was bursting with such enthusiasm that it was hard to believe she was performing for money. Contrary to all the dictates of prudence I decided I must see her again.

Translated from written statement of Commissaire Divisionnaire Julien Barail, 03.06.1996.

* * *

Barail always indulged in a cigarette after sex. The more satisfying the sex, the more satisfying the smoke. Now, as he watched the *poule* hook up her red half-cup bra and expelled copious amounts of smoke into the already dense atmosphere of the room at the Hotel Angleterre, he was a very satisfied, not to mention satiated, man.

It had been a fuck to remember, no doubt about that. If points were awarded for enthusiasm she would score *dix sur dix*. As for technique, hers was worthy of an Oscar. His prick although now deflated felt swollen. He was sure it must be patterned with her teeth marks but he was too squeamish about his private parts to examine it.

'Was it good for you?' she asked him as she zipped up her very short leather skirt.

'You need to ask?'

He slid sideways out of the bed and retrieved his crumpled trousers from the floor. His wallet contained a wad of 500 and 100 franc notes. He selected two of the larger denomination and held them out to her.

'What is your name, *ma petite*?' he asked, as she slunk across to relieve him of her wages.

'Lucille. And yours?'

'Raoul,' he said, the pseudonym one of a number he employed so as not to sully his reputation. He proffered his pack of Disque Bleus but she declined with a headshake.

'I don't smoke.'

That was a first. He had never met a professional who didn't use the weed. She went up a couple of notches in his estimation.

She tied her straight brown hair back in a ponytail, shrugged into her black blouse. He was fascinated by her. She wasn't a teenager, his usual preference, far from it. In fact he guessed she was well into her twenties. Yet she had a gamine air about her, and her body, super-slender with perky little tits and the ripest, roundest ass he had ever squeezed, was enough to drive any red-blooded Frenchman crazy. And Barail's blood was of the reddest.

'Will I see you again?' she asked, following the question with the tiniest of pouts, as if in anticipation of a rebuff.

'You have the body, I have the money, so why not? Tomorrow night, same time, suit you?'

St Petersburg, Russia, 1 April 1996

'Our first success was a pretty low profile job. It was more to prove a point to ourselves than to shock the world. To prove we had the ... the power to do it, do you see what I mean? Not that the victim was anything like as hard to get near as bloody Chirac.'

Gary Rosenbrand to Thierry Garbe, freelance journalist, 19.03.1999.

* * *

When the maroon BMW came to a lurching stop at the kerb where he was standing, waiting to cross bustling Nevskij Prospekt, Anatoly Ilyushenko was not immediately alarmed. Perhaps the high-cholesterol lunch in the company of members of his team from the Institute, supplemented by copious amounts of vodka, had lulled him into calm acceptance of the abnormal.

Even when the car disgorged two stocking-masked individuals to seize one of his arms apiece he was more startled than frightened. Not until they bundled him head first into the rear of the BMW and piled in on top of him, did panic hit him.

'Help!' he bawled at the top of his voice, though by then the car doors were closed, muffling his shouts, and the car was on the move. In any case no one was within earshot except for two of his colleagues emerging from the wood-panelled interior of the Nevskij 40 Bar, laughing fit to rupture themselves over a particularly obscene joke.

Anatoly Ilyushenko was not permitted a second call for help. A home-made sandbag descended on the back of his head and his private world turned instant black. He subsided into the footwell behind the driver's seat without even a groan.

The BMW proceeded to Dvorcovaja Place, the golden spire of the Admiralty ahead dramatically outlined against the pale blue of the winter sky. It then doubled back along the Nevskij, ultimately heading south out of town by the Moskovskij Prospekt route. The driver, a squat, incredibly ugly man with a shaven head and multiple rings in both ears, observed all speed limits and drove with scrupulous consideration for other road users. An accident would have been catastrophic. Within fifteen minutes the party was passing the airport at Pulkovo. Beyond lay countryside, lush with forest, and the M20 Gatcina highway.   As it left the last of St Petersburg to the rear the BMW accelerated to over

120kph and was still far from being the fastest on the road. No one paid it heed, which was exactly what the driver wanted. It stuck with the highway until within sight of the steeples and domes of Gatcina, when it turned off on a little-used spur road that ran alongside the forest, signposted to the small town of Kommunar. It had the road to itself apart from an empty lumber truck that roared past them in the opposite direction with a thud of air.

Two miles on the BMW, without noticeably slowing, veered right onto a track that carved a canyon through the forest. It drove deep into the forest, a gradual descent over five miles into the valley of the Jzora River, where silence ruled absolute. At a seemingly random spot it slowed to a standstill. The two men in the rear seat spilled out, hauling the semi-conscious Ilyushenko from the car by his feet. One of his shoes came off in the process.

The driver of the car came around to stand over Ilyushenko, now spread-eagled among the thawing snow and slowly coming round. The driver produced a pistol, a German Heckler & Koch P9 with a concealed hammer. He pulled back the slide, cocking the weapon. Ilyushenko, barely conscious, gazed dopily into the muzzle. Suddenly his head cleared and his eyes opened wide.

'What is going on?' he stuttered. 'Is this some kind of practical joke?'

In his heart he knew that couldn't possibly be the explanation.

'No joke, Anatoly.'

'I don't know you,' Ilyushenko blustered. He tried to rise but the driver's booted foot on his chest dissuaded him.

'My name is Falenki. Feel better now?'

The man's readiness to give his name chilled Ilyushenko for some nameless reason. His bladder voided but in his rising terror he didn't even care.

'Why are you doing this?' he quavered, close to tears.

Falenki stooped to push his face close to Ilyushenko's. 'Why? To stop you creating more weapons of mass destruction, Anatoly.'

This was the explanation he had been given by the people who had hired him. Not that he could have cared less about the nuclear research that went on at the Kerensky Facility, in the little square behind Dom Puskina, but it made a fitting epitaph for Ilyushenko, and it amused him to deliver it.

'But I ...' was as far as Ilyushenko got before a 9mm bullet drilled a hole in the centre of his baby-smooth forehead and terminated forever his dubious contribution to science. Before the echoes of the gunshot had ceased clamouring over the treetops and away down the valley the three men were heading back the way they had come.

* * *

Later in the day a forestry ranger accidentally drove over Ilyushenko's body in his utility vehicle. When he realised what he had done, he sped off to his cottage on the outskirts of Kommunar to raise the alarm.

The following day the killing was reported on page 2 of *Pravda* and most other journals. It was picked up by Reuters but of the English language newspapers of international standing, only the *Tribune* ran the item.

In his bed at Miami's VA Hospital, surrounded by the impedimenta of his treatment for cancer of the liver, Eddie Nixon was a shrunken travesty of the man Sheryl first met seven months ago. His eyes were closed and his breathing regular but his skin was as grey as a winter sky and the massive weight loss had transformed him from a burly rock of a man to a phantom.

Sheryl stood over him, her face crumpled in her shock and distress, feeling like a voyeur. Somehow, the colourful fountain of protea on his bedside table depleted him still further by comparison.

As she pulled up a tubular chair to sit by the bed he stirred, startling her.

'Hello, sweetheart,' he said, his voice faint and scratchy, like a very old recording. 'Good of you to come.'

'Good of me to come, he says.' Sheryl forced a grin and bent to kiss his cheek. His skin felt like dead leaves to her lips, dry and brittle, as if it would crack and flake away at the slightest touch. 'I was summoned to the imperial presence.' The grin faded. 'But I'd have come anyway and a bloody sight sooner if I'd known.'

'Don't fret, girlie. It was inevitable and we've both known it since we started down this road together.'

Sheryl dumped her shoulder bag and the newspaper she was carrying at her feet. She crossed her long legs and the straight knee-length skirt she wore rode up to mid-thigh. Nixon chuckled appreciatively.

'Good to see a bit of flesh for a change. You and your bloody trousers.' He tutted feebly. 'It's not natural. Women should flash what they've got.'

Such remarks from any other man would have got up her nose, brought out the women's libber in her. From Nixon though, especially now as he neared death, they were a huge compliment and raised her spirits a little.

'Has Soon-Li been in today?' she asked.

'She was here this morning. She went shopping – to buy me a farewell gift, I expect. Is Gary with you?'

'Outside, in the car. He sends his best, naturally.'

Not for the first time Sheryl found herself wondering about Soon-Li and her motives. Not that it was her business, or even that it mattered any more. She had brought Nixon pleasure during his last year alive. Now that his remaining lifespan could be measured in days, Sheryl didn't begrudge her a healthy slice of her husband's fortune.

'Any news to send me on my way?' he said, reaching for Sheryl's hand.

'Ooh, yes, I almost forgot.' She reached down for the newspaper, in the process treating Nixon to more upskirt view than was good for him in his present state.

'*Chicago Tribune*.' She held up the front page. 'Do you want to read it yourself or shall I?'

'You read it. I've misplaced my glasses and in any case it's too much effort.'

Biting her lip, Sheryl unfolded the paper and turned several pages. 'Here it is. It's a Reuter's report: "The body of Russian nuclear physicist, Anatoly Ilyushenko was found in the Forest of Gatcina near St Petersburg. He had been shot through the head at close range. An anonymous call to *Pravda* later claimed credit for the killing on behalf of an international green movement whose identity remains anonymous. Police investigations have so far drawn a blank as to the identity of the killers and the caller. Mr Ilyushenko was one of the leading Russian experts on gamma radiation." '

'Is that it?'

'Isn't it enough? Our first blow for the future of the human race. The first of many, I expect, unless governments see sense.'

'Good on you, sweetheart.' His eyes were closed again, as if hearing the news had sapped what little strength remained in the much wasted frame. 'Will you tell the world why?'

'Yes. Without saying who we are, of course. I've drafted a press release stating our cause.'

'Who's next on the list?'

'Another of the same ilk, name of Olga Gratcheva. Her farewell party is set for two weeks from now. Then the press will really start to wake up and take notice, you wait and see.'

Nixon cackled. 'I would if I could.'

At this reminder of his shaky mortality Sheryl fell silent, her head drooping. She craved a cigarette but the red NO SMOKING notice above the headboard crimped even her rebellious nature. Her hand closed more tightly over Nixon's. Sentimental she was not, but this man, who had made it possible for her to realise her ambitions, meant more to her than any number of Simonellis. His dying would leave a black hole in her life.

'The bank account is operating the way it should, I reckon,' he said. 'It's all set up to carry on after I've gone. You've got full power of attorney for as long as you live, you know that. But it's non-transferable, so you'd better keep on living.'

'I plan to. And I'm touched by your faith in me. Eddie … it's none of my business, but have you provided for Soon-Li?'

'Yes, yes,' he said, his tone tinged with impatience. 'She'll be able to go shopping every day as long as *she* lives. But listen …' He came alert again, like a gun dog getting the scent. 'What about the big fish? These Russian scientists are all very well but they're tiddlers compared to that bastard Chirac. Why is it taking so long?'

Sheryl was wondering the same though she wasn't about to let on to Nixon. Instead, she said confidently, 'They're just being thorough and you can't blame them. Don't fret, it won't be much longer … two, three weeks at the outside.'

Badgering Simonelli hadn't worked, he just fed her platitudes. Now she was becoming suspicious of his perpetual reassurances. On her return to Europe she was resolved to pin the Corsican down to something firm, preferably a time and a place, something she could pass back to Eddie. If he was still around to hear it.

A tap at the door; it opened and a nurse's head and arm appeared around it.

'I'll have to ask you to leave now,' she said, softening the injunction with a regretful smile. 'Mr Nixon's due his treatment.'

Sheryl smiled back, a reflex, on-off.

'Okay. I'm on my way.'

She rose slowly, reluctantly, still clutching Nixon's hand.

'You're on your own from here on, sweetheart,' he said.

She wished he hadn't reminded her, wished that somehow he would be proved wrong. Her eyes moistened. She smeared the burgeoning tears away with the back of her free hand. She never blubbered.

'Where to now?' he asked her.

'London, maybe Paris afterwards. A board meeting.'

'Fax me if there's any news. And have a safe journey.'

Sheryl knelt on the edge of the bed and kissed him square on his dry lips.

'You too, Eddie. You too.'

'The President is going to take a holiday in the Var during the first week of June,' Le Renard informed Commissaire Barail, as the latter drew up a chair before his grand desk.

Barail's surprise was unconcealed.

'This is very short notice. His engagements don't allow it.'

'His diary has been rearranged. He badly needs a break, and will spend four days *chez* Crillon, in a house near Cavalière-sur-Mer. Crillon is the friend of a family friend. I gather he is currently in South America and has placed the property at the President's disposal.' Le Renard shoved a file towards his subordinate.

For Barail, providing protection for the President was a daily routine. 'I will make the usual dispositions,' he said, letting the file lie. He would review it later.

Le Renard almost warned him make *un*usual dispositions, in view of the discovery of the photographs. Then he remembered the object of the President's unplanned holiday and kept his mouth shut.

Paris Latin Quarter, 10 April 1996

"As I got to know him a little better, began to recognise his strengths and his foibles, it became obvious that he was a man with much on his mind. Little by little he began to confide in me. Just the occasional hint of what he was up to."

Translated extract from interview with Agent 411, 23 .06.1996. Filed 12.07.1996.

* * *

At Barail's behest all the lights were on in the fifth floor room at the Hotel Albe and a cheval mirror strategically placed at the foot of the bed. He was as much voyeur as participant.

'Let's do it again, my bold lover,' Lucille said, fondling Barail's limp but nevertheless impressive member.

'Not yet, you little rodent.' Barail's voice was hoarse, his breath rasping. 'A short interlude is necessary in which to recharge my ancient batteries.'

Lucille pouted, and though Barail's eyes were closed he sensed it.

'Do not be so impatient,' he said.

'But I must go soon. I am a working woman. I have another appointment ...' She broke off with a squeak as Barail grabbed her arm. Spent or not, there was a frightening strength in his grip.

'You have no more appointments tonight,' he snarled and sat up, glaring at her.

Refusing to be cowed, she glared back until he released her arm. Red fingerprints flared on her creamy skin. She rubbed the spot.

'You are a brute,' she accused, pretending to sulk though privately she was triumphant. His reaction and his actions made her realise that she had more power over him than he over her. 'But I will forgive you. I will also stay. Provided ...'

'Yes?'

'Provided you compensate me for loss of income.'

Barail sighed. Once a *poule* ...

He promised to make good her losses. He was besotted with her and that was a fact. Four trysts and already he was scheming how to get her off the streets. It couldn't work. *Poules* were notoriously incorrigible. But he had determined to try. This one really was special.

As he resumed a supine position Lucille slipped naturally into his arms. She nuzzled his chin where the new day's bristle was already bursting forth.

'Cave man,' she murmured, her tongue flicking at his ear lobe. 'See, I am your adoring slave. You can treat me like a slut …'

'You are a slut,' he cut in. He had no romantic illusions.

'*Quelle gentillesse!* But I will not be discouraged. You can say and do anything to me.'

'For money,' Barail observed, a little sourly.

'Also for other things. I … I do like you, Raoul. Much more than all the others.'

Barail flinched inside at 'all the others', but let it pass.

'You are far too pretty. You are not safe for a man to be around.'

She made a mock growling noise and snapped her teeth just short of his cheek. 'I am a tigress. I will bite and scratch you to death.'

She raked her silver-painted fingernails across his moderately hairy chest leaving four parallel tracks running from nipple to nipple. He sucked hard through his teeth but uttered no protest.

'You are not really in the mood tonight,' she observed. 'You have something on your mind perhaps?'

'Perhaps.' Barail reached for his cigarettes on the bedside table, then, unable to resist bragging, went on, 'If you must know, I am in the middle of a very big deal that will make me a rich man. In the meantime it is turning my hair grey.'

Lucille sat up and began to probe his scalp as if hunting for lice.

'Indeed, you already have strands of silver here and there, my love. But that is perfectly in order for someone of your mature years. You are a distinguished man, so you should look distinguished.'

Barail's jaundiced gaze wandered around the room of the rather seedy, but oh-so discreet establishment. Nothing distinguished about his surroundings or his situation. He clicked his lighter under the cigarette.

'Tell me about it, Raoul,' Lucille cooed, trying without success to smooth the lines from Barail's forehead. 'Take some more wine and unburden yourself to me.' As she spoke she reached across him for the half empty bottle of red Bordeaux.

'*D'accord*, but I assure you, *ma petite,* it is nothing. Why should I expect you to share my tribulations?'

'Because I insist.'

When Commissaire Barail was shown into the President's private study by the ADC he was momentarily put out to find that he was the last to arrive.

'*Mes excuses, Monsieur le Président,*' he said uncertainly as he advanced into the rather under-heated room. 'Am I late?'

It was Le Renard who answered, after a small chuckle.

'No, *Commissaire.* The rest of us were early.'

The other two of the four Beauvais Tapestry chairs ranged before the President's desk were occupied by Jean-Louis Debre, Minister of the Interior and Barail's ultimate boss, and Bernard Provost, Director General of the Gendarmerie National, known to many as 'Charlie' after the gendarmerie's national call sign.

President Jacques Chirac, without looking up from the papers he was poring over, muttered a '*Bonjour,*' and waved Barail to the free seat. Hands were ritually shaken as he passed the other three.

'Now,' the President said, tapping the top sheet of paper, 'let us come to the subject that concerns the good *Commissaire,* then he can be about his business, whatever it may be.' The smile that accompanied this pronouncement struck Barail as distinctly sharklike. It made him feel slightly uncomfortable. That's what came of having a guilty conscience, he said to himself. You started reading your fears into every gesture, every nuance, even every smile.

'The object is to settle the security arrangements for my stay *chez* Crillon in June.' The President tapped the paper again and peered at it through his reading glasses. 'Monsieur Provost's dispositions seem adequate to me, considering the area to be secured. You have seen this, of course, *Commissaire?*'

Barail was in the process of extracting his copy of Le Renard's memo from his attaché case. He nodded.

'*Oui, monsieur.*'

'Have you anything you wish to add, in particular reference to your own obligations?' Debre asked, his deep dark eyes inscrutable.

Barail was well-briefed, as much for Lux's benefit as the President's.

'The President's bodyguard will be quartered in the annex over the garage, with the overspill in a mobile accommodation unit to be installed one week before the start date. They will stand four-hour watches, as usual, so that four men will be on duty at any time. Commandant Petit will have command until my arrival. I propose to attend personally the day immediately prior to the President's arrival and will remain overnight.'

'Any special concerns?' Debre said, directing an elegantly raised eyebrow at Barail.

The President's chief bodyguard was an old, old hand. He had foreseen a general question along these lines. His natural desire for the assassination to succeed made him reluctant to aggravate Lux's task. Yet his own emergence untainted carried a higher priority. His prepared response was thus a fraud, cunningly packaged to appear as a real improvement to the security measures already in place.

'The perimeter wall is over five kilometres in circumference, therefore I would agree that the numbers envisaged are adequate to assure its integrity. What I would like to know is how the men will be distributed along the wall.'

'Over to you, Monsieur Provost,' Chirac said.

The Director General of the Gendarmerie glanced down at the notes in his lap.

'My men will be positioned on the outside of the wall except for the seven hundred metre section on the eastern side of the estate, above the river valley, which is sheer. There is nowhere for a man to stand along that part of the wall, and in any case, in my opinion, it is not necessary. The steepness of the gorge is protection enough. Even so, I intend to station a small number, probably ten or twelve, officers along the *inside* of the wall on that section.'

Barail nodded slowly, his expression pensive.

'*Bien.* I cannot fault your dispositions but if I might make a suggestion ...?'

'Please do,' the Gendarmerie chief said, inwardly berating Barail as an interfering know-all.

'I visited the site yesterday and spent some time on the far bank of the river. From there one has an uninterrupted view of the side of the gorge below the wall. May I suggest an additional ten men be stationed along the river bank. This will prevent a would-be intruder from getting anywhere near the wall, let alone over it.

Barail did not notice the exchange of puzzled glances between Debre and Le Renard. He was silently congratulating himself on having reaffirmed, as he saw it, his bona fides without detriment to Lux's chances.

'That seems to be an excellent suggestion,' Le Renard remarked, stroking the apex of his denuded pate, and Debre murmured his accord.

The head of the Gendarmerie, mildly discomfited at his failure to consider this solution, could only mumble 'I will deal with it right away,' and scribble furiously on his notes.

'I understand from the Director General that a helicopter patrol will also be provided,' Barail said.

The President frowned. 'Not continuously, I trust. My wife hates the noise those things make and I am not keen on it myself.'

It was Le Renard's turn to make notes.

'It will be based outside the estate, *Monsieur le Président*, and will only fly patrols twice daily – at dawn and at dusk – and always beyond the perimeter, not above the estate itself.'

This appeared to mollify the President.

'Any other business in the matter of my vacation?' he demanded, his gaze passing from one face to another. 'If not, I suggest we allow the Monsieur Provost and Commissaire Barail to return to their duties.'

As the door closed behind the two, Chirac, fingers interlocked, hands resting on his snow-white blotter, directed a flinty gaze at the Minister of the Interior.

'Now, if you please, *mon cher* Jean-Louis, is there a plot to assassinate me or is there not?'

Debre motioned to Le Renard to respond.

'*Effectivement, Monsieur le Président*,' Le Renard confirmed. 'Only last night our agent made the first breakthrough with Commissaire Barail.'

'He is definitely implicated?'

'Without doubt.'

The President gave out a long, heartfelt sigh. He was genuinely saddened.

'Have you ascertained the identity of the proposed killer?'

'Not so far, *Monsieur le Président*,' Le Renard said, with a shake of his head. 'We cannot rush this matter. To do so would be to jeopardise the integrity and the safety of our agent and throw away our ace card.'

'So let us arrest Barail,' Debre proposed. 'Even if we can't get him to talk, their plan will probably collapse.'

Le Renard shook his head. 'Perhaps we will. But not yet. If we arrest him our subterfuge will be blown. If he doesn't talk, what then? We will not know whether the killer will still go ahead, whether he will try for it at the Crillon place or some other place and time. Barail is not the mastermind in this affair. Most likely he is only a minor link in the chain. Whoever is in charge is not going to give up just because they lose their fifth columnist.'

'What Monsieur Renard says makes sense,' Chirac said,

nodding. 'I believe his plan should go forward.'

'Very well,' Debre said. 'I understand you have given the killer a code-name, Renard.'

'Indeed.' Renard smirked. 'Henceforth he will be known as ...' He paused for dramatic effect and he was damned if Debre didn't jump in and steal his thunder.

'*Le Chacal*,' the Minister of the Interior trumpeted with a smirk of his own. 'He will be called The Jackal.'

'The Jackal?' Chirac echoed. 'Curious choice. Is there a connection with Ramírez Sánchez, that scumbag terrorist the press call Carlos the Jackal? If it must be an animal I would have thought hyena more appropriate.' He smiled to show it was meant to be a joke.

A dutiful titter from the Minister of the Interior was not duplicated by Renard, who said, 'No, it is not on account of that Jackal, *Monsieur le Président*. There was a book ... you may remember – *Le Jour du Chacal*, *The Day of the Jackal*, about an assassination attempt on de Gaulle. It was written by an Englishman, whose name escapes me.'

'Forsyth, Frederick,' Debre supplied. 'About twenty years ago, was it not? Everybody read it at the time.'

'Indeed,' Renard concurred. 'Actually, I heard Pompidou made it required reading for all ministers and heads of security.'

The President was tapping his fingers on the desk top and looking impatient. He hated conversations in his presence in which he was not a participant.

'This is all very fascinating, but I know nothing of this book. Perhaps you will obtain a copy for me, Jean-Louis.' A nod from Debre, and Chirac went on, 'In the meantime, if it pleases you to christen the killer in honour of a work of fiction, do not let me dissuade you. The Jackal it shall be.'

Paris St Germain, 12 April 1996

209 exposures of the Crillon residence and estate fall into the undernoted categories:

Aerial:	*51*
Internal grounds:	*38*
External grounds:	*33*
Buildings (exterior):	*33*
Buildings (interior):	*57*
Other:	*7*
TOTAL:	*209*

All were processed as positives and slides. 8 sets were distributed as under:

Office of the President:	*1*
Office of the Prime Minister:	*1*
Office of Minister of the Interior:	*1*
Office of CG/CSP	*1*
Office of CD/CSP ★	*1*
Office of DG/DST	*1*
Office of DG/DCPJ	*1*
File (classification MOST SECRET):	*1*

All sets are to be returned to the office of the Controller-General, CSP★ after 10th June 1996 for shredding.

Translated extract of a memorandum from the Private Secretary of the Controller-General of the CSP★to the office of the Minister of the Interior, 11.04.1996. Filed 14.04.1996
★ Commissaire Barail [Author's note]

★   ★   ★

The aerial shots of the Maison Crillon, taken the previous day, depicted a walled estate, roughly egg-shaped, measuring some two kilometres from north to south and a little over half that at its widest point east-west. This added up to a perimeter of about five kilometres. The height of the wall, though not calculable from the shots, was over two and a half metres.

The land was undulating except around the buildings and the asphalt driveway. The ground-level studies showed the house to be an imposing, circa late-nineteenth century structure built in ochre-coloured stone with first floor balconies to each window. A tastefully blended annexe comprising a four-car garage and a guest apartment above had been grafted on. An avenue of trees – silver limes, by the look of them, though the species was not native to southern France – guarded a driveway leading from the southern extremity of the wall. In front of the house the driveway ended in a half circle, with parking space off to one side, discreetly screened by more trees.

Apart from the avenue, an olive grove in the south-west corner, and isolated mimosas, cypresses and pines dotted about the place, there were four distinct wooded areas: a large copse between the back of the house and the east wall and three smaller stands along the west wall. In the northern half of the estate, situated roughly midway from east to west, was a lake, too regular in shape to be natural. A tiny island, accessed by a footbridge, served as home for a single pine tree. Two other small patches of water defined the estate: a guitar-shaped swimming pool (for much of the seventies the owner was an American rock singer) and a rectangular pond at the back of the house. Otherwise, it was all grassland, criss-crossed by footpaths, the only irregularity being a paddock with stables that housed four horses.

Barail reshuffled the stack of photographs and waded through them for the fourth time, noting the service road from the village two kilometres away that petered out into a rutted track. At the end of the track was a ruined cottage, one-time home of some farmworker, no doubt.

His interest in the photographs was twofold. In the first place, as co-ordinator of the presidential bodyguard, he was on the circulation of all material relating to Chirac's outings. To him the ultimate responsibility for assuring the well-being of the President, the last line of protection. If a venue aroused his concern he had the final veto.

In the ordinary way he would merely have stressed the need for thorough searches of the buildings, the outbuildings and the wooded areas. It was not his job to flush out any prospective assassins but clearly his job was made easier if the police and the other security services seconded to the location did their job thoroughly. If his protection squad was called upon to do its duty it meant that one of the other security forces had failed to do theirs.

In the second place, in his role as fifth columnist he had to view the set up as if from the other side of the fence, assess the feasibility of an assassin gaining entry unseen, discharging his obligations without hindrance, and fleeing the scene without being captured. A *triple* tall order. At least a hundred, possibly more, gendarmes and CRS would be drafted to the area to carry out a very thorough search and maintain a round the clock patrol.

The President would arrive by helicopter at mid-day, give or take half an hour, on Sunday 2nd June. The semi-circular asphalt courtyard in front of the house was more than adequate as a landing pad. Barail imagined Lux would want to make the hit as the helicopter hovered above the landing pad preparatory to touchdown. No, wait, that was a non-starter. The helicopter windows were bullet proof. Then it would have to be done at the instant Chirac emerged from the machine, before the twelve-strong Presidential bodyguard could move in to encircle him within a laager of flesh, bone and bullet-proof vests. The tiniest of windows of opportunity; the bodyguards would be swarming all over the President the instant the door opened.

A challenge indeed for the American. Barail was glad that he didn't personally have to make it happen.

It was raining hard in Paris. The pavements reflected the streetlights and the neon signs of the restaurants and clubs. Around midnight the downpour eased and when Lucille stepped out of the revolving door of the Vieux Moulin Hotel, she no longer needed her umbrella.

At the kerb a taxi was waiting, its engine running. She click-clacked over to it on her towering heels and stooped beside the driver.

'Are you booked?' she asked but before he could reply she noticed a dark head outlined against the rear window. 'I am sorry …' she began, then the back door swung open.

'Get in …' It was not a request.

She hesitated.

'*C'est moi*, Mazé,' said the vague form in the back of the taxi. 'Now will you get in?'

'Excuse me, *monsieur*,' she said, feeling foolish, and climbed in, her micro skirt riding up to crotch level and treating Mazé to a flicker of white nylon. He didn't object. Though he was content in his marriage and unlike many of his superiors never made use of other women, paid or unpaid, he was not averse to occasional titillation.

He ordered the taxi driver to move off.

'Where to?' the driver asked, not unreasonably.

Mazé, irritable from his long wait, snarled, '*Je m'en fous, nom de Dieu!* Just drive around.' To Lucille, in a lowered tone, he said, 'I need results – and fast. Most importantly, I need the name of the Jackal and a description and details of his movements. Secondly, I need the identities of his employers.'

'Something has come up?'

'No, nothing special. But I am under pressure, you understand. This is my pet project. Le Vieux Renard expects me to produce results.'

Lucille puffed air through pursed lips. To rush this job would be to court trouble. Barail was no mug. If she started pumping him really hard he would get wary.

'*Ecoutez, monsieur,* that was only my sixth rendezvous with him. You don't cultivate the confidence of a man like Commissaire Barail after a few sessions in the sack – especially if you're a *poule*. You should know that better than anybody.'

He didn't care for the insinuation but let it go. 'Okay, okay. I give you one week. Fuck him sideways and upside down if you have to, but get him to talk. You did well to get him to incriminate himself in the first place. The rest should be a walkover. The door's ajar, all you have to do is kick it in. You're a policewoman, aren't you? You should know how to kick doors in.'

He dropped her at the corner of Avenue Kléber where she had a modest *studio* above a café as part of her 'cover'. She stood at the kerbside and watched the taxi's tail lights dwindle into the distance. It was all very well for Mazé to put pressure on her. If Barail suspected for a minute that she was trying to probe him, she would finish up at the bottom of the Seine with twenty kilos of chain around her ankles. Eight years before, as a police trainee, she had watched as they dragged a real-life *poule* out of the river, minus her head and hands, weighted down by just such a tangle of chain. The impression it made on her was profound and it had stuck.

Venoy, near Auxerre, 16 April 1996

Lux was not forthcoming on the method to be employed or indeed on any aspect of his plans. His discretion both irritated and impressed me. When we met at Venoy in the middle of April to put forward a new suggestion for the place and timing, he refused to be drawn on how he would get in and out. Throughout the weeks of planning and preparation I never ceased to ponder over his method of escape from the scene. I had no doubt that if he fell into the hands of our people he would reveal all our names one way or another, whether willingly or otherwise. In consequence I had a vested interest in his getaway plan.

Translated from written statement of Commissaire Divisionnaire Julien Barail, 03.06.1996.

*   *   *

The curtains were not designed to create blackout conditions and the definition of the slides was therefore not as sharp as it might have been. The room they used was on the second floor, much smaller than the one they recently occupied, and smelled musty. Dust sheets shrouded some bulky pieces of furniture. The chairs were straight backed and made the underside of Lux's thighs ache; Simonelli had hijacked the only armchair. Now wanted by the *police judiciare* for questioning in connection with the photographs, he had been a guest of the *comte* for the past three weeks. He had also grown a beard and sported a pair of heavy-rimmed spectacles whenever he ventured out.

Barail, operating the projector, ran through the slides rapidly and without commentary. There were over two hundred of them, including a number of aerial views. Most featured a large house shaped like an E with the middle stroke missing, set in a walled estate. From some angles a large tract of water was visible in a defile between two ridges of land. Impossible to say from the shots whether it was open sea or a large lake. The countryside was generally rugged, the higher ground rising in steps rather than sloping smoothly. Vegetation tended to be scrub-like with few trees of any size other than those on the estate. The only road in evidence appeared to be that serving the house and two others nearby, and even that was no more than a dirt road, albeit well-maintained as far as one could judge from the slides.

Several shots showed signs of humanity, notably a man and a

woman walking along a terrace that ran the length of the house. The other side of the terrace overlooked an elongated pond, studded with water lilies. Eventually the couple walked out of the frame. There was a swimming pool shaped like a guitar: it was empty so presumably the time of year was winter or autumn, although the foliage of the shrubs was green. Somewhere in the Midi of France, was Lux's guess.

The last slide clunked through the projector and now the screen depicted only a white rectangle. Lux crossed his legs to relieve his cramped muscles and waited for someone to speak.

'What you have just seen is an estate in the Var belonging to a man called Maurice Crillon,' Barail expounded.

Lux silently congratulated himself on correctly identifying the region.

'Chirac will come to this place on Sunday 2nd June for a few days of relaxation. This, in my opinion, is where you should … er …'

'Kill him?' Simonelli suggested, his teeth bared in a vulpine grin.

Barail gave a small but noticeable shudder. Such bald expressions of their intent were distasteful to him. Most would employ euphemism for the word 'kill' – dispose, silence, eliminate. Not Simonelli.

'I prefer to choose my own killing ground,' Lux said mildly, though he privately conceded that the site had much to commend it.

Barail was unperturbed. 'Naturally. But you will not find a better one, and within the time that remains you would be well-advised not to waste it in investigating others.'

A scrap of breeze stirred the curtains, momentarily letting in daylight. In the garden a dog started barking; a harsh command stilled it. Lux was tempted to look, to be reassured that life existed outside this unreal world in which the life of a President was reduced to banalities; to the question of location, and timing, and reporting procedures. The temptation did not translate into movement.

'I will now run through the slides again,' Barail said, reloading the projector. 'More slowly this time … We can examine each one individually. Later I will show you some film, also a plan of the house and a large scale map of the district.'

While Simonelli sighed ostentatiously and lit the latest in a succession of cigarettes, Barail tinkered at length with the focus and managed to eventually produce a sharper image. It became apparent that the photographs had been taken on different days, by the changes in position of items of garden furniture, also the weather alternated between pale sunshine and an all-grey sky that washed so much colour from the scene that many of the slides could have been taken for monochrome.

Lux now perceived that the eastern wall of the estate was built along the top of a sheer drop forming one side of a valley that, according to the lie of the lengthening shadows in one frame, ran from north-east to south west. A slender river wound through the valley, plunging underground beyond the northern end of the garden. The wall seemed in good repair.

The main building, although around two centuries old, was also well-maintained and alterations and extensions carried out over the years had been done sympathetically. Patio doors, obviously not part of the original structure, opened onto the terrace, which was screened from the driveway.

In most of the pictures smoke coiled straight up from the single stubby chimney at the northern end of the building, further supporting Lux's belief that the ground level photographs were taken in winter.

'Who authorised these shots?' Simonelli said, as the screen filled with an aerial study of the rear of the house, partially obscured by some spindly cypress trees.

'The aerial shots were organised by the DCPJ,' Barail replied. 'It was all done quite openly, with the knowledge and co-operation of the owner. Standard practice when the President is to visit a location for the first time. The other photos were supplied by the owner.'

Something clicked inside Lux's head, like a light switching on.

'Why didn't I see it before? You're not just any old security official, are you, Barail? You're responsible for presidential security!'

Barail's face revealed nothing, neither did he deny it.

'You're one of his goddam bodyguards, I'll bet,' Lux said, and followed up with a harsh laugh. 'You might even be the chief bodyguard. My God! Betrayed by the man who's supposed to protect him.' He sat forward on the edge of his seat, stabbed a finger at him. 'Don't bother to confirm it. It's written on your face.'

It would also make Lux's job a sight easier. What bigger, plumper stool pigeon could an assassin hope for than the head bodyguard of the intended victim? Even as he spoke, Lux's mind was sorting through the implications of his discovery. Such an influential ally was an asset not to be wasted.

'Really?' Barail's voice was frosty. 'You must believe what you believe. Perhaps it will induce you to accept my recommendation as to the place and time.'

'Oh, yes,' Lux said. 'I'll accept your advice – provided it checks out.'

'Can we get on now?' Simonelli spoke through a haze of blue smoke. 'We have a lot more material to see and discuss.'

'Why not?' Lux said, and Barail, breathing noisily through his nostrils, nodded.

'So tell us, Julien,' Simonelli said, his dark intense eyes impaling Barail. 'What exactly will be the security dispositions.'

'It has not yet been confirmed officially, it is not my department, you understand. Even so, yesterday I heard through unofficial channels that fifty CRS and two hundred gendarmes, will be deployed. A permanent patrol outside the wall from H-hour minus twenty-four.'

Lux produced a small spiral pad and jotted in it, his face blank. 'H-hour being?'

'Probably mid-day on 2nd June. The President and Mme Chirac will leave Paris around nine-thirty in the morning and fly to Toulon, where they will transfer to a military helicopter.'

'Presumably the grounds will be searched before his arrival.'

Barail lowered himself into a chair that was the twin of Lux's.

'The grounds will be combed immediately prior to the patrol being put in place. In theory no unauthorised person can gain entry from that moment on. Two helicopters will also keep the perimeter under surveillance.'

'The wall looks as if it completely encloses the estate,' Lux observed, still writing.

'It does. The length of the perimeter is estimated at ...' Barail reached across the table and riffled through the papers and photographs there until he found the sketch Mazé had done. 'Five point two kilometres.'

'If we assume that the fifty agents will remain within the grounds,' Simonelli said thoughtfully, 'and if we assume that only half the *flics* will be on duty at any time, that means one *flic* for every fifty metres of perimeter.'

Lux scribbled calculations on his pad. 'That means I can forget about gaining entry after the patrol is in place.'

'Therefore you must enter before,' Simonelli put in. 'You could get over the wall and hide up somewhere.'

Barail cleared his throat theatrically. 'You are forgetting that the grounds will be searched. Take it from me, the search will be very thorough. Normally they will proceed in a line abreast. The estate is roughly oval …' More riffling of papers. 'It is … approximately two kilometres from end to end lengthways, so to speak. So if all two hundred officers are used, this means one per ten metres. The security officers will check the house and the outbuildings.'

Simonelli grimaced.

'Ten metres per man. You couldn't hide a dormouse under those conditions.' Barail skidded an aerial photo, measuring about one foot by eight inches across the table to Lux. 'Pick your hideout,' he said with a mirthless laugh. 'Only you'd better miniaturise yourself first.'

'I'll take a look at the real thing in a day or two,' Lux said, less inclined to be negative than the other two. To them he appeared perfectly at ease. 'Then I'll figure out how to get in.'

'Be careful,' Barail said worriedly. 'The Crillon family are away but a housekeeper goes there every day and two caretakers live there permanently in a mobile home.'

'Perhaps we should take another look at the options we rejected,' Simonelli said dubiously.

'We already looked,' Lux said, his tone abrupt. 'As the *Commissaire* said, this is the best of the bunch. My concern isn't so much how to get in as how to get out.'

'Yes.' Barail nodded earnestly. 'Under no circumstances must you be caught …'

'In case I squeal?' Lux cut in, the words filtered through a sardonic grin. 'But don't worry, *Commissaire,* I have no intention of getting caught. I'm thinking maybe a chopper …'

'To get you *in?*' Simonelli said, staring.

'To get me out, buddy. Like I said, I aim to solve that pretty problem first. If I can't, this place is off the agenda.' Lux raised a hand to still Barail's protest. 'Yeah, I know. We junked the idea of a chopper at the restaurant but here in the country, if it could land rather than hover, that would cut down the time of its exposure to small arms fire.'

'It is your neck, I am thankful to say,' Barail grunted. 'Personally, I would find some other solution.'

It was a matter of indifference to him whether Lux got clean away or was gunned down on the spot. The latter would be preferable. Cheaper, for one thing. But unless his escape was assured the job would not go ahead, therefore he was as keen as the American to come up with an answer.

He stood, silhouetted before the sunlit French windows, and stretched ostentatiously.

Simonelli, shielding his eyes to look at him, said, 'What else can you tell us, *mon ami*?'

Before Barail could answer, Lux, who had been studying the photo, glanced up and said, 'What are these clumps of trees near to the west wall?'

Barail and Simonelli came over together to look.

The Corsican shrugged. 'They are clumps of trees, copses. What of them?'

'They look as if they might be on elevated ground.' Lux turned the photo round so that the light fell on it. 'See how the shadow falls on that patch of ground ...' He rested a fingertip on a spot near the centre of the picture.

Barail checked through the little heap of slides, found the one he was searching for and loaded it in the projector. The scene filled the screen. All three men peered at it.

'The ground is definitely higher along the west wall,' Simonelli declared at last. 'Does it matter?'

'Nope. It's just that I may be able to make the hit from there, from the nearest copse to the house. If these scale markings are accurate it's the best part of a kilometre, maybe a tad more, from the front door. Far enough for me to be invisible, close enough for me to be sure of a killing shot – given a particular kind of hardware.'

Barail rubbed at his chin, his fingers rasping on stubble.

'*D'accord*. But that is still of no account unless you find a way in and out. You said so yourself. Without a guaranteed exit, you won't do it, and I don't blame you.'

Lux eyed him thoughtfully. 'Will you be there when Chirac shows?'

'Yes. It is not unusual for me to inspect the troops, as it were, on such occasions. What do you have in mind?'

'Nothing at the moment. Just establishing what's possible and what isn't.'

Barail frowned at Lux's reticence. He was used to keeping secrets, not having them kept from him.

Auxerre, 20 April 1996

'She trusted that Corsican villain even more than she trusted me. God knows why – unless it was because he was screwing her bow-legged.'

Gary Rosenbrand to Thierry Garbe, freelance journalist, 19.03.1999

*   *   *

The previous September a spat between two of her former colleagues at Greenpeace and the French Government had resulted in the formers' deportation, and Sheryl feared she might have been blacklisted by association. When visiting Corsica in search of Simonelli two months later she had taken the precaution of flying into Rome and proceeding by ferry to the island; passenger transit within the European Union being more or less free of formality she had been able to enter France unmolested.

Now she sought a new meeting with Simonelli and, owing to restrictions on the Corsican's movements, she would have to enter mainland France. The stratagem as before, she flew to Brussels and from there travelled to Paris by TGV then onward to Auxerre by hire car. Again it worked. Not once was she asked to produce her passport.

For Simonelli's part, he was tired of being cooped up in the chateau, benign host though the widower *comte* was, and confident enough in his fully matured disguise to propose dining out. So, within an hour of Sheryl's booking into her hotel, they were sharing a table at the renowned Barnabet Restaurant on the quay in Auxerre, enjoying the views over the River Yonne and the *poitrine de canard à la rôtissoire*, speciality of the house.

Sheryl was not impressed by the Corsican's new guise. 'I must tell you, Napoleon, the beard is crap. It makes you look like the villain in one of those cheap French gangster films from the fifties.'

'It is necessary,' Simonelli muttered, slightly miffed.

'That's another thing. It's only necessary because you left incriminating photographs lying about your house and let a tart have the run of the place.'

Simonelli was not used to being bossed about by women. He lunged across the table with his right hand, his finger and thumb coming together pincer fashion on her left nipple. It was a trick of his, a little punishment he employed to keep his women in line.

Sheryl was familiar with his sadistic peccadilloes. She didn't flinch. Nor, as he pinched and twisted her nipple, did she make an effort to prevent him, merely stared into his eyes.

'Enjoying yourself?'

Something in the tone of her voice made him feel suddenly ashamed. He pulled his hand back on to his own side of the table.

'I am sorry. That was childish of me. Your criticism is justified.'

'As your employer it certainly is.' She gazed round, but no nearby diners spared them a glance. 'As your lover … well, maybe I should have kept my lips zipped.' Sheryl tried to disregard the throb from her maltreated nipple and picked among the bones of her breast of duckling, discovering a scrap of flesh that had escaped her earlier foraging. She popped it into her mouth and chewed slowly and thoroughly. Though her skills in the kitchen were dire, she appreciated well-prepared food. 'Tell me about Lux.'

Simonelli nodded, expunged his rage and guilt, and, in between mouthfuls, brought Sheryl up to date in five minutes. When he explained about the venue her breathing quickened.

'Do you really think this is it?' she said, clutching his arm across the table, her face flushed and animated. She hardly dared to believe that a date had actually been decided, that Chirac's allotted span and with it his capacity for destruction could be calculated in weeks.

'It is not yet certain, *ma biche*, but I am optimistic. Lux will – how do they say it in America? – case the area and make a decision.'

'Tell him he's got to go for it, even if it isn't absolutely perfect. Stop humouring him. He's only the hired hand, for God's sake.'

'Like me, eh?'

Sheryl's glare softened, became impish.

'You're not hired for your hands, Napoleon, darling. Your talents lie in another part of your anatomy.'

He suddenly visualised her naked. She was a big woman; not big as in fat, but big boned, athletic. Firm. Though her breasts didn't amount to much she knew how to employ them to excite him beyond his most erotic dreams.

He took her hand in his, briefly pressed it to his red lips. 'You have finished eating, my love. Shall we go?'

When dawn came and with it an end to the run of warm, sun blessed days, Lux was already awake. He lay, hands locked behind his neck, listening to the rainwater as it gurgled down the drainpipe and the splash of the overspill from the blocked guttering onto the patio. The house was short on maintenance. It belonged to his ex-wife, and she had accorded him squatter's rights whenever it was unoccupied, which was most of the year from October through mid-June.

After a while the rains eased off. The gurgle in the pipe became a trickle and the splashing a stutter. The sun peeked timorously out like a nervous actress making her stage début, plunged back behind a cloud, emerged again more strongly, more certainly, to pierce the gap between the shutters with a lance of white light.

The alarm clock beeped. He wasn't sure why he had set it, since waking up had never been a problem. Maybe it was to remind him that today he would put himself at serious risk for the first time since he accepted this job.

During the weeks following his acceptance at the *comte's* house in Venoy, he had mulled over the promised freedom and though he only half-believed it would happen, the more he mulled the more desirable it became. And the progression from desirability to indispensability was logical. For Lux now, freedom had become a drug: he had been given a whiff of it and he was hooked. Kill a President? Yes, he would do that to get it back, and more. He'd kill the Pope, if it were required.

If God were mortal, he'd even kill him.

That was how badly he wanted it.

*   *   *

His ex-wife's holiday house – a converted barn – was set high in a hillside overlooking the resort of Ste Maxime and the bay towards St Trop. On a clear day, which this wasn't yet, the view was stupendous. The beaches were a couple of kilometres by road, about half that by a precipitous footpath strictly not designed for the unsure of foot.

It had four cavernous bedrooms, a sitting room big enough to play badminton in, and the usual functional appointments. Outside, the obligatory patio with a swimming pool under construction. Excavation equipment occupied a space near the garden entrance; it had an abandoned air and certainly no one had been near it since Lux took up residence, two days previously.

The garden was unkempt, populated by olive trees, fig trees and some haphazardly-planted cypress. Blooms of all shapes and size and hue proliferated. But the scent of it had to be smelled to be appreciated. Even Lux, no flora enthusiast, had been known to rave about it to others back when he'd had a stake of sorts in the place.

Now, as he sauntered onto a patio that still glistened from the recent inundation, the memories of a marriage gone rotten soured the smell of the flowers and dulled the blue of the Mediterranean that twinkled below. It was simply a secluded base for his project, and less than half an hour's drive from the Crillon property. Operating from here also ensured that his own house in Menton remained 'clean' in the event of a security leak.

After a breakfast of black coffee and *brioches* he drove down into Ste Maxime in his hired Renault Safrane, arriving on the sea front just as the skies unleashed another heavy shower, sending flocks of early season tourists scuttling for cover, heads protected by a miscellany of newspapers and shopping bags.

He parked facing the sea and waited out the shower. When it was over but for the accumulated water sliding off the long fronds of the date palms and pinging on the car's roof and hood like so many tiny hammers, he made a dash for the shops, specifically a small supermarket, there to purchase a pack of Evian bottled water, some fruits, cheese, and a *baguette*. His picnic lunch. Even assassins need sustenance to function.

To get to the Crillon house from Ste Maxine the obvious and the only viable route was initially via the N98 as far as the crossroads where it meets the D98, which serves St Tropez, and the D559, the coastal road to Le Lavandou. At the crossroads you have a choice: continue on the N98 for about eight kilometres, then turn off left into the hills of the littoral, or follow the D559 as far as Cavalaire-sur-Mer, turning right just beyond the village.

His choice for today was to stick with the *route nationale*. During this pre-season period when traffic was relatively light, he would invariably opt for the busier route. By mixing with the crowds he would avoid drawing attention, just one of the herd. Anonymity ever lay in numbers.

He drove sedately, was passed frequently and flamboyantly by local vehicles and the occasional Dutch or German visitor. Through the village of Cogolin, a bottleneck of old houses and streets of fluctuating width clogged with illegally parked cars. A large van delivering cartons to a computer shop halted the traffic as effectively as any road block. Lux didn't get agitated, didn't sound his horn. He was in no hurry and to remain unnoticed overrode all other considerations.

Leaving the N98 brought about a transition from wide busy highway to a rough and ready track. It ran fairly straight and level for a few kilometres, then began simultaneously to twist and climb. The rain returned at this point, a solid sheet of it, slowing him to a second gear creep. It quit eventually or else he left it behind and he was back under the Mediterranean sunshine, dazzlingly bright. A red squirrel darted across the road almost under his wheels, tail stiff with fright. When Lux came to a spot where the road ceased to climb he pulled off and braked. He opened up his map of the area. It was one of half a dozen in the same series, covering the whole of the French Mediterranean coastline from Spain to Italy. The other five maps were window dressing, to divert any suggestion of a special interest in the area, in the event of his falling into the clutches of the gendarmerie. In his line of business you learned to cover every angle. Either that or you didn't survive.

The service road to the Crillon property did not appear on the map but purported to be the first turnoff right after the highest point, signposted 'Les Molières'. And there it was, the sign tilted and in need of refurbishment, though the track itself was in a reasonable state of repair.

If this route proved an impasse, the only way in and out, it would be a potential trap. Unusable for the actual hit. To drive along it at all was to attract curiosity. So he would allow himself this one and only reconnoitre on wheels. Future forays would be on foot, posing if challenged as an enthusiastic rambler and bird-watcher. A bit eccentric, like many American tourists.

Rayol, near Le Lavandou, 21 April 1996 (morning)

'The helicopter was not expected. He was caught out when it showed up. So was I for that matter.'

Ghislaine Fougère to Enrique Dubois, Lieutenant de Police, DCPJ,
during interrogation, 11.06.1996.

*   *   *

When Lux set out from the municipal car park in Rayol he carried a knapsack on his back. Inside it, waterproof clothing, binoculars, camera, a book entitled *Mediterranean Birdlife,* a variety of maps by the Institut Géographique National, a bottle of Evian and his lunch. He wore jeans, sweatshirt, heavy shoes with corrugated soles for grip on slippery surfaces, sunglasses, and a battered sun hat. He hoped he looked like a serious walker.

The weather stayed fine for most of his ascent, via a well-defined path to the summit of le Drapeau, a 1000-foot peak two valleys away from that of the Crillon residence. It was warm but not so warm as to make him sweat from it, and his breathing was easy. He made a point of keeping fit without the fanaticism of some, seeing it as a bare professional necessity.

A feather of breeze ruffled the shrubs that grew thickly here and drew the heat from his skin. The sky overhead was still clear but to the west an angry stack of cumulus was on the march. He gave it an hour to arrive. By then he calculated that he should be at or close to his journey's end.

The going was rougher now, for he had left the recognised path and was taking a line of little resistance, skirting impenetrable growths, squeezing through gaps between bushes. Descending brought him into a zone of maritime pines, their carpet of needles springily pleasant underfoot after the hard, rock-strewn terrain higher up. He broke into a lope. The sun was weakening, the air growing chill as the cumulus neared. The first spots landed on him as hail when he crossed the road that ran down into Rayol. He swerved onto the service road leading to the entrance of the estate. The hail was now falling in earnest, he raced for the nearest cover, the estate wall. The distance was less than fifty yards but he was soaked long before he reached it. Nor did it offer much shelter.

The storm was fierce but mercifully short. The sun soon broke through again. Birdsong was restored. Staying within sight of the wall, he resumed his walk, wet through, uncomfortable, his clothes steaming in the heat. It was mid-day. The terrain climbed, yet so gradually that he was hardly aware of it. Only when, after twenty minutes, he took a break and scrambled up the wall to peer over it did he realise how much higher was the west side of the estate than the east. He slithered to the ground and moved away at right angles to the wall and uphill until he could look over it, across the whole estate. He took an apple from his knapsack and munched it while surveying the area. The valley on the west side of the estate was banana-shaped and curved away out of sight. Through the Swarovski binoculars he searched for the service road; short of the valley's edge it split into two, the left fork plunging into the thickly wooded slopes while the right limb veered off towards the two neighbouring villas on this side of the valley, his view of which was obscured by a salient of rock.

He focused more intently on the far slope in an attempt to trace the course of the road. Eventually he lit upon a short stretch where it left the trees to run parallel to the valley. By now he had seen enough to form a fairly clear picture – and it was not propitious.

A single road out meant he couldn't come and go by car – not from this end anyway. Unless there was another road that was passable, not marked on the map. A motorcycle might be the solution, enabling him to travel cross country. After the event, all he had to do was get clear and stay at large for the few days it would take for Barail's political supremo to be installed at the Elysées Palace and for his amnesty to come into force. However, in that interim period it was likely that the full weight of the law would be mobilised against the assassin. It would show no mercy.

Escape from the immediate vicinity and subsequent evasion of capture remained the most elusive of all the answers he sought. Only when he had solved it would there be any point in researching the kill itself.

He swigged Evian, hefted the knapsack, and went on. Still staying close to the wall, topography permitting, taking a short detour when it didn't. In due course he rounded the most northerly point of the estate and continued on down the east side. There he was soon thwarted. The terrain became seriously rugged and boulder strewn and the downward slope perilously steep. Standing on top of a rock the size of a small car, he saw where the slope ended and the canyon began.

It was a no-go zone.

From the wealth of intelligence thrown up by Barail, Lux had gleaned that during extended absences of the Crillon family the staff at the house, normally four strong, was reduced to a single housekeeper who lived in the village. She did not work at weekends, hence Lux's choice of Sunday for his reconnoitre. The only other employees were two permanent security guards who lived on site when the Crillons were away. Not policemen but civilians employed by a security outfit, semi-retired, both in their sixties. These two individuals occupied a mobile home just inside the garden perimeter, screened from the house by shrubbery.

Back at his earlier vantage point on the western side of the wall, where the curve bulged its maximum, Lux again climbed the wall and peeked over the top. Through the binoculars he scanned the house and its immediate surroundings. As he traversed the patch of shrubbery by the gate he spotted what he had failed to spot before: the end section of the roof of a mobile home protruding from the foliage.

As far as he could tell neither of the security guards was out and about. A Citroën Xantia and an old VW Golf stood in the parking area, side by side, the only evidence of human presence. He shoved the binoculars in their case and was up and over the wall in a matter of seconds, dropping flat as he landed on a trampoline of maquis. The nearest of the three copses was less than a hundred metres away, ahead and slightly to his right. If he moved at a crouch the maquis would screen him for most of the way, leaving an exposed patch of maybe twenty or thirty metres of grass to cover. He would do that on his belly.

He sucked air into his lungs and set off, bent double, bushes snagging his clothing. As he came to the open ground he paused to check out the terrain below and the house. No movement at all. He removed his hat, to let the sun dry his hair. It was now pleasantly hot, the hailstorm a faint memory.

Time to go. Down on his belly, hopefully out of sight to anyone down at the base of the slope, he wriggled through the scrawny, still damp grass.

It was his ill-luck that the helicopter chose that moment to pass overhead. He had virtually zero warning: the hammer of its engine was deadened by the hillside that continued upwards beyond the wall, and when it leapt into sight above the copse he was caught in the open between the bushes and the haven of the trees. He mouthed an obscenity and flattened himself to the earth. No use running. Any movement would only attract the chopper's crew.

He turned his head to follow the machine as it flew a diagonal course across the estate. There was no change in direction, no sudden swerve to indicate he had been spotted. It was an olive green painted machine with military markings. It was flying too fast for proper surveillance so maybe its presence was a coincidence. And maybe not.

The helicopter peeled off to head due west and dropped down into the valley beyond the wall. Lux's shoulders slumped with relief. One life used up, how many were left to him?

He recommenced his crawl with more haste than before and was into the copse inside half a minute. It was like a homecoming. A few feet inside the treeline he stood up and brushed soil, grit and other adhesions from his soggy clothing, before taking stock of his haven.

The trees were mostly a species of pine, giving adequate cover from above but less at ground level. Although the copse was about a hundred metres across at this point, sky was visible between the bare lower trunks. It was of no consequence, he decided, as the rising ground and the wall behind would create a dark backdrop when viewed from lower down. By dressing in fatigues and blackening his face, he would be undetectable, especially from where the President's helicopter would land, the best part of a kilometre away.

He struck out through the trees. Underfoot was spongy with fallen pine needles and strewn with dead branches that he knew from experience would crack like a pistol shot if he stood on one. Before each step he paused to sweep aside the branches with his foot and to listen. This retarded progress but was a heap better than running into the resident watchdogs.

Deeper into the copse the trees had thickened somewhat. Now, as he approached the other side they opened up again, letting in bands of sunshine like stage spotlights. A vibrato of wings behind froze him momentarily. It was just a bird, but he twisted round to check behind him anyway. Nothing stirred apart from the occasional quiver of foliage in the desultory breeze.

The end of the treeline was mere paces away. He stopped short of it and once again surveyed the house and the shrubbery through the binoculars. The zoom magnification gave him a close-up image of the semi-circular turning zone at the front of the house. To many, hitting a target as small as the human head at a range of nearly one thousand metres would seem an impossible feat. Even a body-hit would be a challenge. But Lux had supreme confidence in his skills and in his choice of weapon. He had hit smaller objects over greater distances with the same kind of gun. Including moving objects – and he had to assume that the President's head would be a moving object.

None of what he had seen so far helped him in his essential objective of securing a safe exit. If he was to make the kill from here in the copse he would have to make his escape from here. Prior to, during, and immediately after the President's arrival, the grounds would be searched and the walls guarded. So said Barail. Even sticking around until the President was settled in and the guards perhaps grown a little lax, a stratagem he had considered, was not the solution. The longer he stayed here the greater the danger of discovery.

No, short of making himself invisible, he was not going to be able to do this job. So, how was he to make himself invisible?

Sighing, he sank to the ground and unscrewed the cap from his Evian bottle. The renewed stammer of the helicopter stopped him in mid-swallow. Clearing the roof of the house by a few metres, it rushed on up the slope towards the north end of the estate. The feathered inhabitants rose in clusters from trees and undergrowth, wheeling hither and yon like Spitfires and Messerschmitts in a dogfight.

That was when he saw the woman.

She was away to his right, weaving stealthily through the trees towards the open, intent on what lay ahead not to either side. Dressed in a bright yellow anorak and blue jeans, only her slight build and the yellow band around her long straight black hair betrayed her sex.

Wondering what she was doing here, even whether she could conceivably be a security guard, Lux slipped soundlessly behind the nearest tree. From here he took a more leisurely peek, through the binoculars. The first thing he noticed about her was her camera: it was slung from her neck, a far more sophisticated piece of equipment than his. Unlikely to be a bodyguard then. Probably a trespasser. Perhaps a journalist.

He also noted that she was young or youngish, probably slim under the unflattering waterproof, and had a passably attractive profile.

He swung the binoculars back onto the house and the shrubbery. The security men were still lying doggo. The woman's yellow anorak shouted to be noticed. If she left the shelter of the trees and strolled openly down the hill she might just get away with a little-girl-lost plea, especially if she was a looker. But, with the President's visit coming up, the chances were she would find herself in a mess of trouble.

Abruptly, as if she had become aware of how conspicuous she was in her garish outfit, she swung to the left, towards Lux, and advanced in parallel to the edge of the copse. This placed him directly in her line of sight. To change position would be asking to be spotted. He kept perfectly still, hugging the tree trunk, hoping she would pass him by. Her footfall was deadened by the pine needles and other than the drone of an aircraft to the south all was silent, even the birds seeming to hold their breath. As she came into view around his tree he edged to the right, keeping the trunk between them. He heard a startled gasp.

'Who's there?' she challenged, and her voice seemed to be right by his ear. 'Come on out, you piece of shit, I can see you.'

He stepped sideways and confronted her. She was close enough to touch.

'Don't be afraid,' he said, mustering a smile.

She took a pace back, caution not fear, not yet. Something told him she was about to run for it, which he couldn't afford to happen. He darted forward, grabbing for her. Belatedly she turned to flee, her ankles becoming entangled, stumbling …

As he caught up with her he tripped and they hit the ground together hard, his weight pinning her down. She cried out. Instinctively he clamped a hand over her mouth.

'Don't yell!' he commanded in his best French. 'There are two guys in a mobile home down there and you're trespassing.'

She wriggled, tried to heave him off, but at least she kept her mouth shut.

'If I take my hand away will you keep quiet?' he growled in her ear, his lips touching a pearl earring.

She did not immediately react. Finally came a solitary frosty nod.

He still didn't entirely trust her but released her anyway, sat back on his haunches.

'I mean you no harm,' he said, keeping his voice low. 'You're a reporter, aren't you? Me too. If those guys down there see you, you'll be in serious trouble.'

She came up on one knee. 'You hurt me,' she accused, brushing a web of hair from her face while rubbing her hip as if to prove it.

Now that he had an opportunity to study her he was struck by her looks. She had a heart-shaped face with a strong jaw; pale almost pallid skin. Dark brown eyes below thick eyebrows like commas, hair a rich chestnut colour rather than the black he had supposed it to be. The yellow band was fetchingly askew and under his scrutiny she straightened it, tucking in the odd wayward strand. Her camera strap had become wound round her neck and this too she rearranged.

'What are you staring at?' she demanded.

Lux shrugged an apology. 'Let's get away from here.' He extended a hand.

She drew back, eyes flashing.

'Don't be dumb,' he snapped. 'You can been seen miles away in that outfit. *You* may not mind being caught, but *I* do.'

That much at least made sense to her and when he trudged off deeper into the copse she tagged along in his footsteps, grudgingly at first, then caught up and stayed close until they reached the other side of the trees. There, judging them to be out of immediate danger, he turned to her, his concocted story ready should it be needed.

'I suppose I should thank you,' she said, her manner subdued.

'That kind of depends on whether you feel grateful.'

'I do.' She thrust out a hand: a ring with a fat diamond adorned her middle finger.

'Ghislaine Fougère.'

'*Enchanté*,' Lux said as they clasped. Her grip was firm, genuine. He introduced himself as Dennis Hull.

'English or American?'

'American.'

'You speak French quite well.'

He absorbed the compliment. 'Thanks for the flattery. Actually I've lived here for the last few years.'

'That explains it. French speakers are rare among you Anglo-Saxons.' The sound of an approaching helicopter dragged her eyes from Lux to the sky. The machine was not yet in sight but by tacit accord they retreated a few yards into the shadows anyway.

A muffled trilling sound startled Lux. The woman threw him a rueful smile and rummaged under her waterproof.

'*Allo, j'écoute,*' she said into the cellphone, in a tone of long-suffering.

While she listened, her head turned away from Lux, he regarded her profile critically: high forehead, high cheekbones, a short straight nose. You couldn't fault any of it. He now found himself thinking about her as a woman rather than a threat. The option of silencing her permanently receded.

'*Oui, patron,*' she said to her caller. A moment later, '*Oui, monsieur,*' only the '*monsieur*' was tongue-in-cheek.

She said an abrupt goodbye and shut the cellphone off. 'Sorry about that. My editor. My boss.'

'Tool of the trade, I imagine.'

'The cellphone? Indispensable … unfortunately.' She returned the handset to its home under the anorak and rummaged around. Her hand emerged clutching a crushed pack of Stuyvesant cigarettes. 'Well now, *Monsieur 'Ull,* if it's not being too nosy, what exactly are *you* doing here?'

'Thanks,' Lux said when she proffered the pack. He lit up for them both, then went on to feed her a yarn about being a freelance reporter.

'So am I, freelance, I mean.' More rummaging in her pockets, then she flipped a business card at him. 'What a coincidence, our being here at the same time, for the same purpose.'

The words carried more than a trace of sarcasm. He didn't ask what that purpose was. She was regarding him through a haze of cigarette smoke with a faintly jeering air.

'Well, there it is,' he said. 'It's been nice meeting you, Miss Fougère …'

'Ghislaine,' she corrected in a brook-no-nonsense tone.

'Where are you staying?'

'In Rayol.' He tried to remember the name of the big hotel right by the beach.

'At the Bailli de Suffren, I imagine,' she said obligingly. 'I, too, have booked a room there tonight. No doubt we shall bump into each other.'

If it was meant as an invitation he didn't rise to it.

'I suppose I ought to call it a day,' she said then, with a glance southwards. She tapped the camera. 'The light is going. I shall have to come back tomorrow. Can I offer you a lift?'

He stared. 'You came up by car?'

'Not all the way,' she said with a chuckle. 'I am not quite so indiscreet as that. It is parked on the road, out of sight from prying security guards and helicopters. Speaking of which, it seems to have gone now.'

He kept his relief contained. This girl could foul up the works but good. If she really had ideas about a return visit he might have to discourage her. Any prowlers spotted by the two guards were sure to be reported to the police, which in turn might spark off an investigation and a tightening of security measures or even cancellation of Chirac's sabbatical.

'I think I'll stay on here a while,' he said. 'If you will be dining at the hotel tonight, perhaps ...?'

'Yes,' she agreed, coy now. 'Perhaps.'

And she was gone. A girl around medium height, compactly built, with small high breasts, a sleek swathe of hair that descended to her waist; bordering on lovely. Available too, by the sound of it.

* * *

He stayed on only long enough for her to get clear and to make sure the helicopter didn't return. By then the sun was down behind the hills and he could travel with impunity among the long shadows.

In the cool of the evening he set a fast pace and was back in Rayol by seven-thirty just as the street lights came on. His luck was in at the Hotel Bailli de Suffren, they had a couple of rooms available, even for a man as seriously underdressed as Lux. At this hour there was no prospect of finding a clothes shop open, but the male receptionist directed him to a Casino hypermarket on the edge of Le Lavandou, where he bought chinos, a shirt, and a jacket of sorts. Not quite five-star hotel apparel, but it would do to gain admission to the dining room.

At this juncture he had no more in view than to meet up – ostensibly by chance – with Mlle Ghislaine Fougère and somehow deflect her from any more forays into presidential territory. Only if friendly advice failed to produce a result would he consider a more terminal solution.

It was well after nine when he descended to the restaurant, a long narrow room with chandeliers and stucco walls and terracotta tiled flooring. Being early in the season it was by no means crowded and the Maitre d' found him a small corner table next to a window with an uninterrupted view towards the lights on top of Cap Negre. The window was open, letting in the tang of the sea and a breeze that was just the right side of chilly.

No sign of Mlle. Fougère. He was disappointed. Professional needs apart, he could have stood her company for an evening. Sophisticated, agreeable to the eye, obviously intelligent – she was Lux's idea of the perfect dining-out companion.

He ordered a *kir* and browsed the menu. It was predictably heavy on seafood, which ordinarily he couldn't get enough of. Tonight, though, he was in the mood for a fat, crispy, sizzling steak. The waiter tried without success to push the chef's special of the day, *fricassée d'homard aux mousserons*. It sounded mouth-watering but Lux was set on red meat.

The *kir*, chilled to perfection, refreshed him. He was draining the last dregs from the glass when Mlle. Fougère showed up. She spotted him the instant she drifted through the door in a pale pink ankle-length cloud of chiffon with a matching broad headband, like the one she had been wearing when they met.

Their eyes made contact. It was as if a high-voltage electric current leapt across the space between them. In that instant Lux wanted this girl – woman – more than any he had ever known, including his ex-wife. It was far more than just a physical wanting. He wanted, unequivocally, to possess her, to make her his own.

As if she sensed the turmoil inside him she had come to a standstill and was staring at him across the room, her mouth slightly parted, her eyes big and dark and mysterious. He got up, stiff as an arthritic. So unforeseen and unprecedented were the mixed passions that bloomed within him that his usual self-assurance had evaporated.

Reality returned in the form of a man in his early thirties, hair blond like Lux's but cut shorter, a bit above average height. Not bad-looking. A fitting companion for such beauty as Ghislaine Fougère's. He came up behind her, touched her arm. Seeming startled, she turned her head away from Lux, slowly, her eyes staying on him until she was forced to drag them away. Her lips smiled at the man, mechanically so it seemed to Lux. Then he said something that made her smile more broadly and naturally.

Lux was still standing, rigid as a dummy in a shop window, clutching his napkin in his left hand, his empty glass in his right. Ghislaine spoke into the ear of her companion, at which he flicked a glance toward Lux. Lux nodded, forcing a friendly expression on his face. He hoped they would come over. To be in her presence even for a minute, even with her boyfriend in tow, was better than nothing at all.

The Maitre d' bustled over to them. Ghislaine's companion indicated Lux. He stepped deferentially aside. '*Je vous en prie, m'sieu-dame*,' Lux heard him say.

Ghislaine and her escort moved towards Lux, she with her arm slipped through his, he smiling as befits a good looking man with a lovely girl. Lux ground his teeth, envied him, and in his mind consigned him to purgatory.

'Good evening, Miss Fougère,' Lux said, hand extended, a benevolent rictus hoisted in place.

'I told you – Ghislaine.' And in those few words she made it clear there were no secrets between her and her companion. That they had the rare kind of relationship that transcends petty jealousy.

She introduced Lux as 'the English gentleman who saved me from prison,' a calculated exaggeration.

'I am very 'appy to meet you,' her companion said in English. 'Sank you very much for saving my wife.'

His *wife*. The shock was a punch under the heart, robbing him momentarily of the power to think, let alone to speak. Somehow he kept his expression neutral and his hands off the man's throat.

'Anyone would have done it,' he managed to murmur modestly.

Ghislaine begged to differ. 'But you were the one,' and gave him a look under her eyelashes that set him aflame. It told him that his feelings for her were not totally one-sided.

'May we join you?' she said with surprising boldness. Until Lux remembered that sophisticated Frenchwomen often take the initiative. Despite the look she had given him it was yet another demonstration of the rapport between her and her husband, of mutual trust.

His name was Michel Beauregard (Lux learned later in the evening that Ghislaine used her maiden name, again like many of her class), and he was either complaisant or complacent, Lux couldn't decide which. Two more places were speedily set and *aperitifs* summoned. Ghislaine sat opposite Lux and generally kept her gaze averted. It was as well she did so for Beauregard could hardly have failed to get the message had Lux once fixed those marvellous deep-set eyes with his.

The meal progressed as meals do, the discourse with it. Free of incident. Unless her leg brushing Lux's during the dessert, accidentally or otherwise, counted as an incident. The effect was such that he choked on a mouthful of fig, causing concern to his fellow diners. In Ghislaine's case the concern soon succumbed to a roguish grin. Lux began to suspect then that her seduction act was no more than a tease and that he had as much chance of making it with her as he had of discovering the secret of alchemy.

'In the morning, if the light is good, I must go again to the house,' she said a little while later as, cognacs before them, they chatted companionably like old friends. The restaurant was emptying, only a couple of other tables still occupied and the staff were setting places for tomorrow's diners.

It was as Lux had feared, though his expression was unchanged as he said, 'What exactly are you trying to achieve up there? What's the story?'

'I might ask you the same,' she retorted, tossing her head.

'Yes, but I asked first.'

'Oh, all right,' she said and drained the last of her Cointreau. 'It is about Chirac. I suppose you know he is taking a vacation there a few weeks from now. They say.'

'They say? Isn't it true then?'

She moved her head a few inches closer to Lux's. 'There is a rumour from a reliable source that he is there to meet the German Chancellor for talks on a transfer of nuclear know-how to the Germans.'

'Why would France give the Germans that kind of knowledge?' Lux said, mystified. 'I thought you were supposed to be scared stiff of Germany making nuclear weapons.'

'This is what I said,' Beauregard cut in, tapping his dessert spoon on the edge of his dish. 'It is inconceivable.'

Ghislaine was not put out by the scepticism. 'Not at all. It is part of a mutual defence pact. You see they have no confidence in the EU or Nato to defend their countries against new Russian aggression and they do not believe the Russians are now our bosom friends.' She lit a cigarette, sucked in the smoke, let it trickle from her nostrils. 'If ever they do decide to move against the West, Germany will be in the front line. They accept this but they want nuclear weapons and the know-how from the French tests in the Pacific last year would be of enormous value to them.'

Non-political, and an ignoramus on the subject of European politics, Lux was not prepared to argue the point.

'So if the rumour turns out to be fact, you want photographs of Chirac meeting Kohl.'

'Video film … and recordings. I am to place microphones in the house. The evidence of the two combined will be beyond dispute. Chirac will fall. *Phffft.*' She made a gesture with her fingers, to signify an explosion. 'The Left will triumph.' Her eyes moved over Lux's face like a caress. 'I am of the left, not a communist, but very close. I am also a member of Greenpeace, and there are not many of us in France. Since Chirac played with nuclear weapons at Mururoa I have counted the days to his downfall and wished I would be able to play a part in it.'

'If the meeting takes place,' Lux said, 'it looks like you'll get your wish.'

'Will you come with me tomorrow?' The question was aimed at neither Lux nor her husband, rather it was projected into space, as if up for grabs. Lux left the response to Beauregard. Eventually, as though he had likewise been waiting for Lux, he said, covering her hand with his, 'You know I cannot, *ma chêrie*. I have to work all day here.'

Over the meal he had explained to Lux that, like his wife, he was a professional photographer. He was here at the behest of the Tourist Office for the *département* of the Var, doing scenic photography for a promotional leaflet.

'What about you, Dennis?' Ghislaine tilted back her head to exhale, the lights burnishing her hair, enhancing its natural lustre.

Now his professional instincts were creakily reawakened. She was going back, into the valley, exposing herself to the risk of arrest. And if she were to be caught … In his fascination with her as a woman he had lost sight of the professional priorities.

'Do you think it's smart to go there again?' he said ultra-casually, as much to Beauregard as to her. Maybe her husband would overrule her.

'Smart?' She cocked her head sideways as if she didn't understand the word.

Beauregard laughed heartily while lighting his umpteenth cigarette of the evening; he had smoked between courses as do many French.

'If you knew my wife a little better, *monsieur*, you would not bother with such advice. The more hazardous the undertaking, the more likely she is to do it. Compared with some of the risks she has taken, filming the President's retreat is *du gâteau.*'

A piece of cake. Lux thought he was probably right. Maybe she didn't mind paying a fine or spending a week in the jug. None of that was his affair. His only motive was to keep her from making the natives restless, and his job thereby doubly difficult if not impossible.

'Who's commissioned you?' he asked, trying a different approach.

'*Paris Match*,' she replied without hesitation. 'They pay well.'

'A videocassette of the house can't be such a big deal. Suppose I let you have a copy of mine? Save you the trouble ... you can spend all day on the beach.'

She frowned then. Beauregard too looked faintly puzzled.

'Why do you want to keep me away? Why were you there today?'

Sharp and shrewd. Just as Lux had expected.

'Fact is ... I'm not just being chivalrous, but surely you can see that if you get caught it will make it impossible for me. *My* commission calls for shots of the Chiracs at play. But do you imagine they'll still come here if police catch you snooping around?'

'They won't catch me,' she said. Her quiet confidence didn't impress Lux.

'They damn nearly did today.'

Beauregard nodded, lips pursed. 'He has a point, you know, *chérie*.'

Her jaw jutted.

'Don't you start as well. I will not be caught, I tell you. Because I shall have protection.'

'Protection?' Beauregard said, and Lux echoed him.

'Yes.' She gave Lux her most direct look of the evening and he was devastated by it. At the time she was leaning forward, supported on her elbows, right hand clasping her left wrist, while Beauregard was slumped in his chair. From that position he could see only the rear quarter of her face, which meant he saw nothing of what she communicated to Lux by that look. 'Yes. You have to go back, so ... I shall go with you.' Her laugh was gay and infectious. She looked back over her shoulder at her husband. 'From the way Dennis acted today I am confident that he will accomplish his objectives. All I have to do is stay by his side.'

Beauregard applauded, smouldering cigarette protruding from his mouth, eyes squinting against the smoke. '*Tu es drôle!*' You're funny.

Could he really be so naïve about his wife's desirability, Lux wondered. Or was he simply supremely confident of her fidelity. Or maybe he just didn't care.

As for Lux, he was too infatuated to think up a single objection. He suspected she was only using him and that the lowered-eyelids act had been designed throughout to snare him. Okay, he would let her think he was agreeing because he was besotted with her. She would only be half-wrong.

Rayol, near Le Lavandou, 22 April 1996

'Right from the start I could tell he fancied me, though he had this icy exterior, as if nothing ever excited him. He was a man in control of his destiny ... until he met me.'

Ghislaine Fougère to Enrique Dubois, Lieutenant de Police, DCPJ, during interrogation, 11.06.1996.

* * *

This was not like yesterday. The rain was a monotonous drizzle that fell in straight lines from a drab sky and showed no inclination to cease. No dabs of blue, no bright strips along the horizon. '*Gris partout,*' the *méteo* had prophesied and they were not wrong.

However, bad news for tourists was not bad news for the likes of Lux. The murkier the conditions, the better the chances of avoiding detection. The only drawback was the poor visibility that went with the drizzle.

Ghislaine had come prepared. She appeared in Reception wearing a grey oilskin and sou'wester. Lux's oilskin was dark green, so they were both well camouflaged.

Beauregard came to see his wife off. 'Take good care of her,' were his only words to Lux before they departed. He pecked his wife's cheek undemonstratively.

Lux had warned Ghislaine that they would be walking the entire distance, a twelve kilometre minimum round trip. 'So what?' she had rejoined, and he had to concede she looked fit enough for double the distance.

Few people were about when they set off down the promenade. The sea was still and greasy-looking. The palms lining the front drooped despondently.

'I'm looking forward to this,' Ghislaine said as they entered the side turning that was a short cut, albeit a steep one, to the summit of le Drapeau.

Lux glanced at her. Her features were partly obscured by the sou'wester but there was no hiding the animation.

'It's not a Sunday afternoon picnic,' he observed shortly. 'Not for me, that is.'

'Oh, don't worry,' she said, peering at him from under the brim. 'When we get there I'll be deadly serious. This is my job too, you know. I've got a reputation to maintain, just as I suppose you do.'

'It's not our reputations I'm worried about,' Lux muttered. 'It's our heads.'

∗ ∗ ∗

From the top of hill, on the edge of the copse, he could sweep the estate from end to end and beyond with his binoculars. Of the two houses away to the south, believed to be second homes, one was definitely untenanted: all shutters closed, garden generally overgrown awaiting the premier mowing of the season. A car was parked in the drive of the other. Nobody was about though. On a day like this it wasn't surprising.

Rain dripped off the brim of Lux's hat onto the binoculars. Convenient as the bad weather was for concealment, he would have appreciated a break from it. Ghislaine, crouching beside him, seemed oblivious of it. She had her own binoculars and was using them to hop from one object to another at random.

Lux had convinced himself he was only here to keep her out of trouble. To maintain his pretence to be a reporter he took a few listless snapshots while reflecting anew on the practical aspects of his true purpose. If the President's helicopter touched down in the semicircle as was likely, his line of fire would be uninterrupted. The gradual downward slope would also flatten the bullet's trajectory. One shot should be enough. Unless the wind was particularly strong or visibility as bad as today. If a second shot or, God forbid, a third were needed, the prospects of a kill would diminish exponentially. The Barrett, his chosen tool, was a semi-automatic weapon. A top marksman could loose off three shots inside one second, but three *aimed* shots would take three times as long. In three seconds the helicopter could do a fast climb or spin around so that the President was screened from sight. Members of the bodyguard could rush to put their bodies between the bullets and the President. The police could begin shooting back and distract Lux's aim. So many things could go sour on him.

Make the first shot count then. Simple solution. Simple, yet far from easy.

'Time I went and planted a few bugs,' Ghislaine said.

So absorbed in technical detail had Lux become that he had forgotten he was not alone. He turned towards her. She was watching him, her expression enigmatic. They looked at each other for too long; finally she glanced away, colouring up under the sou'wester, to take refuge behind her binoculars.

'You're a beautiful girl, you know that,' he was moved to say.

147

She sighed, as if the compliment had been paid to her so often that it had become tedious. But she immediately went on to demolish this impression by saying, 'It is embarrassing to me to talk about my looks. If I am beautiful, then that is very nice. I do not think of myself in that way, as someone special.' She lowered the binoculars. Solemn brown eyes focused on Lux's grey ones. 'You are also beautiful – in a masculine way, of course. You must have had many women swoon at your feet ...' She made a gesture of appeal. 'Oh, Dennis, what have you done?'

'Done?' Lux was nonplussed. 'I haven't done anything.'

'To me, you fool.' She pushed the sou'wester back from her forehead. 'There I was, happy in my marriage, my career, my young son ...' That was jolt number two; the first jolt had come when he learned she was married. 'Then you come along and upset it all.'

'Not intentionally. And anyway, how have I upset it all? Have I asked you to run away with me?'

A headshake, the lips curving upwards; there was poignancy in the smile.

'No. But you will. And I shall agree. But then you already know that, don't you?'

Lux straightened up, taking her with him. He held her by the shoulders. Her gaze was unwinking, unwavering. Rain dripping from the trees spattered their waterproof clothing.

'No,' he said wonderingly. 'I didn't. But now I do – and you're right.'

Then she clung to him, her cheek pressing his chest, dislodging the sou'wester to release the mass of her hair.

'Then let us love each other here and now. Let us seal the bargain. I don't want to wait, I can't wait.'

They didn't undress fully. Didn't search for a more accommodating, less public site, or dry place; the heat of their desire negated the cold and wet. They simply lay down where they stood, oblivious of the pricking of pine needles. She tugged off her rubber boots, then her jeans and panties down to her ankles and offered him her naked lower body. The depth of her desire was in the moistness he found there. He took what she offered, first gently then desperately and uninhibitedly. He forgot all else, including his reason for being there.

When it was over there was no contrition. They sat just below the top of the ridge, drinking each other in.

'I love you,' she had whispered often during the act, sometimes in French, sometimes in English. Now she said it again, more strongly, holding his gaze as if to convince him of it. Not that he doubted her sincerity.

'I love you,' he shot back at her, the avowal touched with incredulity.

It was a phrase they repeated often over the next hours. Lux somehow felt he would never grow tired of hearing her say it nor of saying it to her.

* * *

To be near her he took a room at the hotel for a second night. It was to be a night of much tossing and turning, of visions mostly of Ghislaine in the same bed as her Beauregard.

She had wanted to leave her husband now, and go with Lux. 'Anywhere, I don't care. Just to be with you ... it's all I need.'

Almost she lured him into this undertow of indiscretion. Only the professionalism that lay ever just below the surface held him back, reminded him of other demands. If he wanted her, if he was prepared to usurp her husband, then the freedom he must buy was more indispensable than ever.

How to keep Ghislaine, while winning his freedom, that was the conundrum.

Not only that – he had had to run the unnecessary risk of a second foray to the Crillon estate solely because of his failure to keep out of Ghislaine's way the previous day. To be ruthless in his self-assessment, he had fallen down on the job.

Well, we're all human, he consoled himself, all allowed one mistake. He resolved there and then, in his hotel room in the stillness of the small hours, that he would make no more. That he would see the job through with ruthless efficiency. No compromises. He would have Ghislaine, yes, but it would be on his terms. When he was ready, and free of encumbrances.

No rain, just wall-to-wall blue sky. Lux and Ghislaine planned to spend the day together, doing nothing in particular, just discovering each other in the manner of new-found lovers. Her husband would be away all day photographing the Var, so no worries from that quarter.

They spent the morning walking on the beach, talking inconsequentially. They lunched in St Tropez, spotting a couple of celebrities and drinking too much red wine.

In the afternoon, Lux, perhaps made maudlin by the wine, experienced the first twang from his conscience. They were strolling along the Mole, admiring the array of floating hardware, blinding white in the early afternoon sun, when some inexplicable impulse made him ask, 'Does it trouble you, deceiving your husband?'

Her pace slowed and his with it since they were holding hands.

'I do not care for this word "deceive."' Twin grooves of displeasure etched above the bridge of her nose.

'You mean the truth hurts?' he said insensitively.

Now she stopped dead, wrenching her hand from his. Her face was puzzled, hurt. 'Why are saying this, Dennis? You are as much a party to this as I am.'

'I feel bad, that's why. I love you, but I feel bad.' He took her by the upper arms and shook her gently. 'Can't you understand that?'

'So you want me to feel bad too. Then you will feel better and everything will be okay. Is that it?'

A couple of teenage girls coming up behind circumnavigated them, gawking openly at what was clearly a lover's tiff. One of them nudged the other and they tittered in harmony.

Lux no longer knew what he wanted or felt, except that he loved this woman.

'I'm not perfect but I'm not an all-out heel either. People's feelings deserve respect. I just want to make sure we handle this in a … an honourable way.' He tugged at his nose self-consciously. 'If that's possible.'

Her eyes were screened behind the oval sunglasses but he had a feeling they were blazing with anger.

'Hah! Honourable, he says. There is nothing honourable about infidelity. All you can do is be honest. I honestly love you. I will honestly tell Bernard. And that will be the end of it. If that is not enough for you maybe it is better we end it now, before it properly begins!'

Lux thrust his hands deep in the pockets of his striped shorts, looked away from her, towards the sea where boats bobbed and jet-skis planed. Looked without seeing.

'Maybe it isn't enough …' he began.

Her fiery Midi temperament would absorb no more of his indecision. She strode away, back towards the town, arms swinging like a skater, the brisk sea breeze flailing her hair and lifting the hem of her short dress to expose the backs of her thighs.

The wine had dulled his reactions. He let her go. Maybe it was for the best. His conscience would be clear if nothing else. His eyes stayed on her until she turned right at the tower and was swallowed by the pastel buildings along the quayside. Then he returned on dragging feet to his car in the Place de l'Hotel de Ville, to find he had been awarded a ticket. A perfect end to a perfect afternoon.

He sat in the car with the engine running and the air conditioning going, half hoping Ghislaine would suddenly turn up in the mood for forgiving, forgetting and sex. If she didn't, well, she would come round soon enough. Love didn't die because of a difference of opinion. He would stay at the villa tonight and pounce on her at the hotel tomorrow, after Bernard had left for the day. Give her an opportunity to work up some contrition. Meanwhile, work first, play afterwards. Better to stay focused on the contract and put the philandering on ice.

The combination of wine, sun, and stress was giving him a headache. He put the car into gear and reversed out of the parking bay.

Invisibility.

The word had stuck in Lux's brain since his first visit to the Crillon estate, like a blackberry seed in a tooth cavity. Worry at it as he might, he couldn't dislodge it. It was the key to killing Chirac and getting away with it. He had to become the invisible man.

Not in the sense of vanishing from sight or dematerialising, impossible as either was. He had to become as unremarkable as a blade of grass in a field, or a sheep in a flock. He had to become another face in the crowd.

The answer came to him as he was driving back from a shopping expedition in Ste Maxime.

'That's it!' he exclaimed, almost driving into the back of a school bus. 'That's fucking *it!*'

At the villa he looked up companies specialising in fancy dress. The nearest was in Fréjus. He phoned them. Yes, sir, they had several such items available but they would need his measurements. He reeled off his statistics and they assured him they could fit him. A deposit of one hundred francs was required to reserve the costume for the specified days. No problem, a cheque would be in that evening's post.

'He did a trial run by night, to simulate the conditions he would actually encounter. If we had been on speaking terms I would have gone with him. If he would have let me.'

Ghislaine Fougère to Enrique Dubois, Lieutenant de Police, DCPJ, during interrogation, 11.06.1996.

*   *   *

From the bed of pine needles where he and Ghislaine had consummated their love Lux surveyed the scene. Not that in the darkness there was much to survey: just the lights along the driveway and in the parking areas below, and a square of yellow cast by the mobile home. Between three o'clock to where he lay the sheen of the artificial lake made a hole in the total blackness in that direction. It was raining again, or rather drizzling, fine dashes of moisture picked out by the lights below, descending vertically in the motionless air.

For almost two hours he sprawled on the sodden hillside, watching – watching for movement, for some indication that the two guards were doing their duty, making periodic tours of inspection. On the hour perhaps, or half-hour.

But no, they were human. The dialogue may be imagined:

'Filthy night, eh, *mon pote.*'

'*Ouais.* You going out?'

'Oh, I think I'll give it a miss until the weather clears up.'

'So what do you say to a game of cards before we turn in?'

'Sure. Why not. Give me a chance to win back a few *sous.*'

There was, after all, no reason to suspect an intrusion. Not even a burglar would venture out on a night like this.

When the light of the mobile home was extinguished it took Lux by surprise. Cupping his hand around his pencil torch he checked the time. It was one-thirty-five a.m. Give them thirty minutes, say, to settle down, then he would move.

*   *   *

His descent to the house was slow and ponderous. Each foot precisely placed to avoid an accident. The slickness of the grass made him even more cautious. He couldn't afford to break an ankle or even twist one. The eight hundred or so metres to the parking area took some thirty-five minutes. On reaching it he paused to take stock. The area was lit up by a low wattage globe on a pole set more or less in the middle of the asphalted area. This was both good and bad. Good in that it would provide light to work by on the night; bad in that he might be spotted by some nosy *flic*. Well, even the best plans contained an element of chance. You couldn't entirely eliminate the unforeseen.

He stood for a while, longing for a cigarette but too professional to risk it. The night was as still as the ocean deep, the only sound the plink-plink of the rain on the leaves of the lime trees that screened the parking area. Satisfied that the security guards weren't walking in their sleep, he followed a short driveway connecting the parking area with the semi-circular turning space in front of the house. Here the illumination was much brighter and he stayed off the asphalt, in the shadows, his black sneakers making no sound as he padded around, imagining the likely run of events and figuring his options. Making provision too for less likely but potentially more disastrous events.

Wiping rain from his face he completed his tour of the semicircle and faced uphill. If he adopted the course that was forming in his mind, he would have to ascend the slope in the darkness. No flashlight, no illumination except the lights around the house, which would be behind him. Well, he had just descended intact, hadn't he? Going up may be more arduous but it was also less hazardous than descending. It ought to be a cinch.

He took a step towards the car park then froze as a faint humming, unmistakably of human origin, came to his ears. He quickly backtracked behind the nearest tree as a man appeared, striding along the driveway from the direction of the gates, a flashlight in hand but switched off, a dog trotting alongside: a big black beast, its ears pricked. Lux remained motionless, even stopped breathing, as the pair crossed the semicircle just metres from where he stood.

The guard was no longer humming but chanting a horribly off-key version of 'Osez, Josephine,' a pop song that hit the charts a few years ago. At mouth level a cigarette glowed. The dog was making intermittent whining noises as if trying to imitate him. Or maybe it was telling him to shut up. There was no wind to carry Lux's scent, though dogs could smell intruder or owner at great distances. Lux tensed, waiting. He dared not risk any movement, not even to reach for his gun, though if the dog went for him he would need it in one hell of a hurry. As the pair passed his tree, he turned his head to keep them in sight without moving his body. The dog stopped abruptly, sniffing the air and whining more sharply, almost a yelp.

The guard slowed and did a lazy U-turn. '*Quelque chose va pas?*' he demanded. Something wrong? He stood by the dog, swaying a little. Lux realised then that he was the worse for drink.

'*Bon, va faire ton pi-pi,*' the guard said, cuffing the dog indulgently.

It let loose a yip of protest and scampered on to the far side of the semicircle. There beside a flowering bush it did its business, while the guard waited, still within spitting distance of Lux. Lux took advantage of the diversion to draw his gun.

The dog was inclined to forage after finishing its ablutions but a whistle from the guard brought it to heel. It received a pat on the head and went off down the driveway, its master steering a wandering course behind it. A smouldering cigarette stub curled away into the night.

Blessed with infinite patience, Lux waited. Silence had been resumed, the guard's footsteps having faded to nothing. Still he made no move. Not until he heard the far off slam of a door did he take off, first checking his watch. Now came the real practice – the ascent.

The lights at his back illuminated the first thirty or so metres, then he was on his own in the dark, relying on his sense of direction and his feet. Though his speed was a little better than on the descent, he did not hurry. He counted every stride and strove to keep them of roughly equal length. The rain intensified, drooling from the front of his hood onto his face. He pounded doggedly on, skidding now and again on the wet grass, tripping once and, as he neared the copse, disturbing a bird that lifted off vertically almost beneath him, chirping in alarm and making him back-pedal several steps, heart bumping.

He stood still, as the bird's trilling receded into the darkness. Listening for other sounds, human or canine. He didn't think anyone was out and about but making sure cost nothing bar a minute or two of his time. As his heart settled back to its normal rhythm he continued his climb. Counting past seven hundred he became aware of a darker patch against the sky, up ahead and to his left. The copse! He ploughed on, swerving left a little. At the eight hundred mark he slowed, sensing more than seeing an obstacle ahead. A couple of paces later he almost walked into a tree. Right on target.

The last short stretch, from the copse to the perimeter, was a breeze. He scrambled over the wall, falling awkwardly. Rolling with the fall saved him from a sprained ankle but bruised his thigh when it came into unsympathetic contact with a large rock. He cursed mildly, at the pain, at the weather, at nothing in particular. Getting to his feet he hurried on, limping slightly, back to where he had left his car.

Ordure !

Excrement. The word occupied most of one side of the plain postcard that Lux had slid unsuspectingly from the envelope, addressed in the same hand to M. Hull. Less complimentary sobriquets had been hurled at him in the past, notably by his wife. Easy to guess who was the author. Lux didn't blame her being pissed at him.

Having handed Lux the missive, the porter had turned away to unhook the key for another guest. When he was free Lux asked him if Monsieur and Madame Beauregard were in.

The man shook his head, jowls flapping like an old bloodhound's. He was a good seventy, probably employed for his cheapness.

'They have checked out, *monsieur*.'

'Checked out?' Lux echoed, slow to register it. 'Did they leave a forwarding address?'

Again the sombre headshake. '*Non, monsieur.* I have an impression they were returning home.'

Home was Paris, that much Lux had gleaned during their all too few stolen hours together.

Lux thanked him, crumpled the card and envelope in his fist and disposed of it in a trash container by the counter. He plodded up the stairs to his room, which he had forgotten to cancel. There, he stretched out on the bed, thoroughly depressed.

Was this all it was destined to be – a one day madness? Love today, gone tomorrow? Surely not. Or not for him, at any rate. Love was not a state he assumed lightly, nor often. Nor so instantaneously. He couldn't let it lie. Then it struck him: she didn't intend that he should. The card carried an unwritten message as well as the expletive. If the affair was meant to be closed she would never have left it. It said *au revoir*, not goodbye. It said come and get me if you really want me. Real goodbyes were unwritten, unspoken. Only no message at all would have meant that.

But she wasn't going to come to him on a platter. He would have to hunt her down. He would have to woo her. That was the test she had set, to determine the strength of his love. Was it potent enough to send him to Paris, to tear him from his commitments?

It was. Though that didn't preclude him from combining business with pleasure. He picked up the phone and dialled the current cellphone number for Commissaire Barail.

The Commissiare answered in person, a rare event. Usually it was switched to his voicemail. He sounded surprised when Lux proposed to meet him in Paris rather than Auxerre until he explained that he had to be there on another matter. He went on to forewarn Barail that he required a special document that was not obtainable through his usual channels. Furthermore, he was owed another document, signed by a Minister of State, exonerating him from the consequences of his crimes. Had it slipped the *Commissaire*'s mind?

Barail assured him that was not the case, that all was in hand.

'It so happens,' he went on in his punctilious English, 'that I was thinking of summoning you to a progress review anyway. So your call is opportune.'

They arranged to convene under the Eiffel Tower at three o'clock in the afternoon, the day after tomorrow, which was Friday.

Air Inter flight Nice-Paris, 25 April 1996

During his one hour flight from Nice to Paris Lux sat with his seat reclined and his eyes shut, refining his escape plan. He made no incriminating notes. He had no need. His memory was excellent and as vast as a Pentium computer's. It was not a perfect plan. It did not guarantee his escape scot-free. It called for nerve and depended on a certain *laissez faire* in the attitude of the CRS and gendarmes who would be patrolling the grounds of the house. If he were given to assessing the odds he would have put his prospects of success at seven-to-three on. Not bad, but not all that good either. Ordinarily he would not have gone ahead with such a modest margin in his favour. But this was no ordinary contract. It was the last, the grand slam, his swansong.

And if he *were* caught, Barail's new regime, whatever its political persuasion, would likely as not set him free. But even without that insurance Lux would have gone ahead just the same and not just for the money. Since yesterday he wanted to do it for the hell of it.

Paris Concorde, 26 April 1996

Lux came to Paris and we met. He was not there for the purpose of seeing me but to trace the woman, as I now know, and decided to profit from his visit. Among other things he was due the not unimportant second instalment on his fee.

Translated from written statement of Commissaire Divisionnaire Julien Barail, 03.06.1996.

* * *

April in Paris, goes the song. The day Lux rose and went out on the balcony of his room at the Meurice Hotel, opposite the Jardin des Tuileries in the Rue Rivoli, it was indeed an April morning worthy of dedication. Traffic? Yes, there was traffic all right, loud and smelly, but that was all part of it. Up here he could look upon it philosophically. Soon he would be in amongst it, placing his life in the hands of a Parisian taxi driver. Well, he was used to living dangerously.

Chilled, he went back inside and took a shower, hot then cold. In the first floor dining room he enjoyed a leisurely cooked breakfast, scanning the *Telegraph*, luxuriating in being thoroughly pampered (and they *do* pamper you at the Meurice, even more so than at its great rival, the Ritz).

Later, ablutions performed, he sauntered through the Jardin, crossed the Place de la Concorde, and continued on up the tree-bordered Avenue Champs Elysées.

Contrary to widespread assumption the Presidential building, officially entitled Palais de l'Elysée, is not on the Avenue Champs Elysées, albeit that the original gardens – the Elysian Fields – do straddle it. No, the main entrance to the Palace is from the Rue du Faubourg St Honoré which runs parallel to the Avenue and is also the address of the British Embassy. Lux had no business to transact either at the Palais or the Embassy; he was merely curious. Although his visits to Paris were frequent and he had driven past the Palace on countless occasions, he had no more than glimpsed it. Viewing it now from a professional perspective, he noted the heavily-armed palace guards, a mixture of gendarmerie and CRS, plus the plainclothes men, three of whom he spotted in the vicinity, their aimless loitering giving them away.

From the Champs Elysées Lux drifted in the warm hazy

sunshine in search of a Post Office, came across one next door to the Chamber of Commerce for Industry. Inside he sat down at a vacant Minitel, the electronic telephone information service unique to France. It consisted of a small VDU with a built-in keyboard. You connected with the enquiry service and simply tapped out the name or business category you sought. No charge.

Lux composed the name Beauregard followed by Paris then 75, the postal code for the city centre. This yielded a multitude of Beauregards, of which two were Michels. He went on to scan the outlying departments of the *région Parisienne*, codes 91 to 95 inclusive, and for good measure threw in 77 (Seine et Marne, a mostly industrial area to the east), and 78 (Yvelines, where many British expats live). He finished up with six leads, including the two in Paris centre.

From the Minitel to a telephone booth was a simple matter of crossing to the counter and requesting '*une cabine, s'il vous plaît*'. The advantage of the booths within the post offices used to be that you didn't need a ton of change; nowadays money was of little use inside Paris since most telephone boxes in the city centre had been converted to accept credit card only.

Lux's two city numbers didn't answer. Of the rest three answered but none was the Beauregard of his acquaintance. He hung up finally, dispirited and frustrated. Okay, so it wasn't going to be a cakewalk, this tracking down of his one-day lover. He still had three numbers to try. If he drew blanks there too it would begin to look as if they were unlisted. In that case, the task would be infinitely tougher.

For the next few hours he killed time with a light lunch at a bistro across from the Opéra. Afterwards, he taxied to his rendezvous under the Eiffel Tower.

He arrived early under that great iron edifice, now past its centenary and its best, yet as popular as ever. In some ways it is more impressive viewed from ground level, dead centre of the four legs, than from the top platform. Looking up through its hollow interior its massiveness is much more apparent, so too is the amount of steel used and the sweated labour that must have gone into its construction.

Barail came upon Lux while the American was in crick-necked contemplation, still visualising the workers swarming about the latticework of girders more than a century ago, high above the ground and probably without safety hats or nets. His tap on Lux's shoulder was tentative. The President's chief bodyguard had a lot of respect for those who lived by the gun, as he himself once had.

'*Bonjour,*' was his simple greeting.

The obligatory handshake, unsmiling, each appraising the other with that ingrained mistrust that hallmarks relationships between fellow-conspirators.

They walked down towards the Military School. Barail wore a sober suit and sported a walking stick, a direct sartorial contrast to Lux's chinos, lightweight sports coat and open-neck Cardin shirt. Lux supposed he was dressed for the 'office'.

'Of what do you wish to speak?' Barail said in English, deceptively offhand, swinging his stick, a crutch he clearly did not need.

'My official immunity, first of all. You have it?'

'Naturally. Since we agreed to provide it and you requested it.' He patted his breast pocket. 'It's here, close to my heart. But before I hand it over I would like to hear about your state of preparedness. Also, you mentioned some, ah, special requirements?' His voice lifted, making it a query.

'Nothing that will tax your resources or your ingenuity,' Lux said, patting the other on the back. 'As to my state of preparedness .... I've solved the bigger of the two main problems.'

'You have decided how you will do it?' he interrupted, clutching Lux's arm above the elbow. His face was flushed.

'That's the easy part,' Lux said, earning an incredulous look. 'No, *Commissaire,* I'm talking about the getaway. You haven't forgotten, have you, that unless my escape can be guaranteed there won't be any assassination? Not by me.'

Barail released his arm, nodding. 'I had forgotten or perhaps taken it for granted.' A low laugh. 'You will forgive my lack of concern for what must be your highest priority. The issues at stake are large ones. The big picture is what concerns me, the tools we use are ... in the main ... expendable.'

Lux's eyes narrowed.

'Don't confuse this tool with others you've used in the past, Barail. As far as I'm concerned it's your big picture that's expendable.'

They overtook a sauntering teenage couple, oblivious of all but each other, the youth's hand exploring the girl's pert bottom. Barail flicked them a glance of what might have been envy.

'Let's speak of your requirements,' he said, now holding his stick upright, resting on his shoulder like a rifle at the slope. 'Nothing too out of the ordinary, I trust.'

'Depends on what you see as ordinary. How does my

recruitment into the police grab you?'

It didn't grab him at all. He looked blank, totally devoid of comprehension.

'I want you to appoint me to a post in one of the security services,' Lux elaborated. 'And provide me with the necessary ID. Just a common officer or whatever the French equivalent.'

Barail cleared his throat, his Adam's apple jerking. 'I see. To what end?'

Lux explained.

Barail protested: it couldn't possibly work. When Lux asked why not all he could do was splutter. Lux elaborated further. Barail listened and finally he nodded assent.

'There will be difficulties,' he said, rubbing his shadowed chin and looking worried, 'but they are not insurmountable.'

'That's not all, I'm afraid, amigo. I will also want a second *passe-partout* for a colleague. Make him a sergeant. Plus a false passport, Canadian for preference.'

They had come to the road that bisects the park. At the kerb, as they waited for an opening in the stream of vehicles, Barail turned towards Lux.

'I shall of course require photographs. Presumably the documents will carry false names. What will the names be?'

'Not yet.' Lux decided it was better to be mysterious rather than admit he didn't have anyone in mind. 'All vital statistics will come with the photo.'

'Just as long as you allow sufficient time – at least a week, preferably ten days.'

Dodging the mêlée of traffic, they gained the far side of the road and the vehicle-free sanctuary of the middle section of the park. They walked on in silence for a minute or two before Barail said, 'If I may speak frankly, I am surprised you see fit to enlist our aid in this matter. Also, why do you require a false passport? Do you plan to leave France afterwards, and if so why not use your own passport? You will be free as a bird.'

'Because, buddy – if you *really* don't know why – we have to plan for possible failure, and if I fail I will want to put a lot of distance between me and a certain location in the Var pronto. I'll only be free as a bird if you gain control, remember? In the other eventuality I'll be a very wanted man.'

'As I have already explained,' Barail said, a weary note in his voice, 'when the President dies the reins of Government will become ours. As for failure on your part ... we selected you because your record carried a one hundred per cent success rate, because you are acknowledged to be the best.'

'Ah,' Lux said softly. 'Then it wasn't just because you have a hold on me.'

'A secondary consideration.' Barail indicated a bench seat. 'Shall we sit. I would like to smoke and prefer to be seated.'

They sat and Barail smoked. It was warm bordering on hot for late April. Lux removed his jacket and folded it on the bench seat beside him. A small boy came up from nowhere and lingered to gaze solemnly at the two men with soulful brown eyes.

Lux grinned at him, and Barail said: '*Salut, jeune homme.* Have you lost your mother?'

'Alain!' Authority calling. '*Laisses-tranquil les messieurs.*' Leave the gentlemen alone.

Young Alain was hauled away by a pretty girl probably too young to be his mother. He went without protest but with his head screwed backwards, his saucer eyes not leaving the two men until the flow of pedestrians absorbed him.

'My grandson is about his age,' Barail remarked.

'You have a grandson? Funny, I don't see you with the trappings of domesticity and normality.'

'There is a lot about me you do not see,' Barail droned, his expression cold. 'I prefer to keep my personal life private.'

'Good idea. So let's get back on track. I'm flattered by your confidence, but I always prepare for the worst eventuality. Here are the details.' Lux proffered an envelope in which were vital statistics of the phoney Canadian personage, together with some mug shots taken in an automatic booth. The shots were of the real Lux, no embellishments other than a pair of glasses.

Barail accepted it with an expression of repugnance as if it were a used condom. 'Very well. If you insist.'

'Your turn now.' Lux stuck out his hand, palm upwards. 'How would you like to cross it with an official declaration of immunity.'

The envelope Barail passed across was cream in colour, had the feel of vellum but was probably imitation. It was not sealed. Lux opened it up: it bore the inscription *Ministère de l'Intérieure et Décentralisation* at its head. The text was larded with flowery expressions such as 'absolute exemption', ' irrevocable', and 'unconditional', and the whole caboodle was rounded off with an official ministry stamp, over which presided the surprisingly legible signature of Jean-Louis Debre, the Minister himself. Expert advice would be required to vouch for its veracity. Lux hoped to have such confirmation within forty-eight hours via a Swiss lawyer friend, whose *bureaux* were less than a mile from where he and

Barail sat.

'Anything else?' Barail asked.

'Just a couple of small items. Do you know what type of helicopter the President will be using, to fly to the house?'

'Most likely an *Armée de l'Air* Ecureuil, but I can check easily enough.'

'Will you do that and let me have either manufacturer's drawings or an exploded diagram of the type.'

Barail was about to ask why, then decided against it. He didn't need to know and sometimes it was best not to.

'Leave it with me,' he said. 'And the other item?'

'Transport. To be specific a gendarmerie car to be parked in the Crillon grounds on the night before I hit him. The key to be sent to me.'

That Barail didn't like the idea overmuch showed in the hardening of his features.

'For getaway purposes, I imagine. Why a gendarmerie car?'

'You'll have to work it out for yourself. My advice is to see no evil and just do it.'

For Barail, whose profession had taught him to see evil everywhere, Lux's suggestion was meaningless. The car, though, he could and would provide.

'You ask a lot,' he complained. 'Perhaps you would like me to do the job for you.'

Lux didn't rise to the taunt, even had sympathy for the man's resentment. After some huffing and puffing Barail promised to have the two IDs 'in a matter of days' from receipt of the CV of Lux's accomplice, and the passport and helicopter drawings the week after next. Time enough. The first week June was still five weeks away.

'You can wait until the passport's ready and deliver the whole package in one,' Lux told him.

'*Bien*,' Barail said with a nod. 'As for the key, it will not be possible to select the car until a day or two before. It will be better if the car is simply left unlocked and the key placed under the driver's seat, for instance.'

This made sense to Lux and he readily agreed.

'Do you not care to confide in me a little?' Barail subconsciously adopted a wheedling tone. 'Tell me how you will solve the matter of getting into the estate and getting out again with the car I will so obligingly supply.'

'Look, pal,' Lux said, 'you want me to murder the President of France.' The word 'murder' in juxtaposition to 'President of

France' made Barail cringe. 'I'm going to do it. Let that be enough. Don't harass me.'

Barail stood, drew himself up. Seen from Lux's seated position he made a commanding figure. The upper half of the Eiffel Tower appeared to be growing from his cranium.

'Let us understand each other, Lux: in this matter I am your master but I am not my own. Others, wielding greater authority than me, seek assurances. You demand a great deal of money. It puts you under obligation to be open about your intentions.'

'Sorry, *Commissaire*.'

'Suppose we were prepared to pay more.'

'Forget it. Ten million bucks and immunity from arrest is enough for me. Now, before you go, there is the small matter of a further forty per cent of my fee, now that the date and place have been set. As a matter of fact, payment is overdue. Settle up and we can part company the best of friends.'

Barail stuck out his redoubtable chin. 'It is in the course of being arranged.'

'According to my instructions?'

'Exactly. I spoke to Simonelli before I left the office. Four million US dollars, by irrevocable Letter of Credit drawn on your Swiss Account, will be wired on Monday next. A further twenty-five per cent on the day itself; the balance within eight days, by the same method, to the same account. You have my absolute assurance.'

'And do you have Simonelli's assurance, and does he have Miss Walker's assurance?'

'Miss …? Ah, Jill, yes, of course.'

Lux allowed himself a wry smile. 'I figured that wasn't her real name. Not that it matters. If that four million hasn't been credited to my account by close of business on 30th, you'll have to find yourself another boy.'

'It will be there,' Barail said stiffly.

* * *

At the hotel that evening, before dining, Lux reviewed his meeting with Barail. Reviewed and wondered if the Frenchman had any inkling at all that, while seeming to place trust in him, Lux's every act was instigated by the fear of a double-cross. He hoped his fears were without foundation. But if they were not, he would be as prepared as anyone could be.

He had come to accept that the death of the President would

result in government devolving upon Barail's principals. No other explanation for the killing made sense. Why the money was coming from abroad and from whom, why the mysterious and sexually aggressive 'Jill Walker' was in charge of the purse strings, were riddles he was unlikely to solve. The prognosis was: one dead president, one new government, and one pardoned assassin back home in Menton, free and richer by ten million dollars. Forget the rest.

So far then, so wonderful. Lux had every reason to look forward to a wealthy and happy-ever-after retirement, hopefully to play house with Ghislaine. The only flaw in this fairy tale reasoning was how the new masters of France would treat him. To them he would represent a potential leak, and leaks, as everyone knew, must be plugged, otherwise they get bigger and bigger and eventually the ship goes down.

A paranoid view, perhaps. But his insurance scheme was already well advanced: a phoney British passport in the name of Paul Hollis, of Dunsford, near Exeter in Devon, was already ordered. In a tiny village in what used to be called Pembrokeshire a man called Freddie would skilfully produce a passport that, being derived from the real thing, would be infallible. This was the passport Lux would carry if he had to flee France. Not a Canadian passport, undoubtedly its equal in pedigree, but whose only purpose was to dupe Barail and/or the authorities into chasing a red herring.

By such devious means had Lux avoided paying the penalty for his crimes for the best part of a decade.

The Beauregards were unlisted. This much Lux had ascertained by Sunday afternoon, when the sixth on his list finally answered his call. Having also failed to track them down under a professional heading in the *Pages Jaunes,* he whiled away what remained of Sunday in a frustrated brain racking about where to go from here in his search for Ghislaine Beauregard/Fougère, whose very untraceability served only to stoke the flames of his longing for her.

Giving up his quest was an option he did not consider. Ghislaine had become his Holy Grail, the cup of desire from which he must drink, if only for one last time – should that be his fate.

On Monday, when everyone was back at work, perhaps he would try calling all the newspapers and magazines. Only when he looked up the classification in the *Pages Jaunes* did he realise how prodigious was the task.

Having drawn a blank with his first twenty or so calls, Lux went to lunch in the Montmartre where, over a *croque monsieur,* an inspiration came to him. Michel Beauregard had been working on a project for the Tourist Office of the Var. Surely that office would have a contact number or address.

The nearest Minitel came up with a number for the office in less than a minute, and a telephone call from a PTT booth yielded a succession of obliging but ultimately unhelpful personnel. The booth grew hot and claustrophobic while Lux repeated his request over and over, his temper wearing thinner and thinner. Only when he had worked his way up to the *Directeur du Bureau* did he strike a seam: yes, certainly he was currently employing a M. Beauregard, was the somewhat guarded response. May one ask why he wished to know?

Lux explained that he had met Beauregard socially, that the photographer had shown him some of his work, and that he, Lux, was a partner in a holiday business and would simply like to hire him. Ah, then in that case, *monsieur,* I shall be only too happy to recommended him. Here is his business address and telephone number ...

More trusting than he had a right to be.

Beauregard operated under the trade name FOTOSCAN, out of a Neuilly address. Lux was too impatient to go there, it was a good half-hour by taxi. Though it was odds against her answering his call – she was not part of the business – he dialled the number. Even to speak to her husband was better than no contact at all. He had even prepared an excuse for contacting him.

It rang just once.

'Fotoscan,' said a woman's voice.

It was her.

'Ghislaine?' he said.

An intake of breath, almost a cry. Then nothing except the sound of her breathing very fast. Lux pressed the receiver hard into his ear.

'Are you still there?' he said, knowing full well she was.

A small 'Yes', instantly reiterated, more firmly, more decisively. 'I have been waiting for your call. What took you so long?'

'You didn't leave many clues.'

Her laugh was happy. Lux joined in, laughing from the sheer delight of talking to her, from the knowledge that she was close to him, that he would certainly see her within the hour.

As if reading his mind, she blurted, 'Come now – at once!'

'To the office?'

'*Merde – non*! What am I thinking of?'

They arranged a rendezvous in the Bois de Boulogne, which reminded Lux of his car ride to Barail's house that crisp February evening, and thence of Barail and the shadowy side of his life. God forbid she should ever learn of it.

*   *   *

'Oh, I love you,' she gasped even as they fell into each other's arms. 'How I love you!'

'It's the same for me ...' Lux began.

'I know, I know! You don't even have to say it. You would never have searched so diligently for me unless you loved me.' She giggled, girlish, flushed with excitement. 'But yes, say it anyway ... say it, say it! You must never stop saying it.' She was shaking him and laughing at the same time. A fat woman pushing a pram glowered at them as she waddled by, in malice born of envy Lux didn't wonder.

He said it. He told her he loved her, even that he would always love her, though he had ever regarded love as a transient, capricious state, the durability of its foundations non-proven.

'I love you,' he said yet again and her perfect lips opened in the joy of hearing it, displaying perfect teeth and a perfect tongue. In his eyes she was perfection.

The Bois de Boulogne is a place where lovers roam and even, by night, make love. But its leafy paths were not for Lux and Ghislaine this day. They found a small but clean hotel on the banks of the Seine, rented a room.

'Where's Michel?' he asked her as he locked the door.

'Oh ... working, in Strasbourg. I don't care. I don't care about anything ...' She hugged him, pressing her face into his neck, breathing him in, savouring him, 'except you.'

The vague sense of guilt was again taking the edge off the pleasure of anticipation. Stealing another man's wife, destroying a marriage, was not a deed to be lightly or cynically done.

'Won't you have to fetch your son soon?'

'He boards at school, comes home every weekend.'

Which took care of matrimonial and maternal obligations. She was making it so easy for him to embark on this affair.

He let himself succumb to the tug of desire. Already she had got rid of her belted jacket and was jerking her high-necked red sweater from her waistband. Her eyes, sparkling with animation, remained on him. She removed her bra – white and lacy – before her skirt, exposing breasts that were his to look at, to inspect, to stroke and squeeze.

'They're yours,' she murmured, offering them like so much fruit to be tested for ripeness. 'Do with them what you will.'

They were pendulous, heavy yet not large, with dark brown nipples as big as thimbles. He covered them with his hands and she quivered, as if an electric current had been passed through her. Her head lolled back, her mouth fell open to release a low groan.

'Darling ... darling ...' The endearment alone was sustenance to his passions.

He drew away, began to undress. Panting, her complexion feverish, she unzipped her slim black skirt and pushed it down over her thighs. Her legs were bare of nylon and from the knees down speckled with fine dark hair. Unbecoming, some would carp. Not Lux. He preferred the human form to be left as nature intended.

Her panties were of the same frothy material as her bra, darkened in the V by the bush of her pubic hair, moulded to her mound of Venus, accentuating it.

'You do it,' she invited. 'Take them off.'

He discarded his shirt, sank before her on one knee. Gently and very slowly he worked the scrap of material down her thighs. The odour of her sex swirled around him like an early morning mist.

'Do it *now*,' she commanded as his tongue flicked at her. 'I can't wait any longer! Fuck me, darling!'

He was still half-dressed, but that no longer mattered. In their frenzy they didn't even use the bed, simply collapsing onto the thin fluffy rug and letting their bodies take charge, lashing up a sexual storm of such force that all they could do was ride it out, let it run its course to extinction, finally to slip into the ensuing calm, exhausted, satiated, fulfilled, to await the inevitable resurgence.

* * *

They dined and danced at the Ritz that night. Krug Champagne and *Canard Apicius*, as befitted a celebration of the beginning of a love affair. No extravagance was too great.

Her evening dress was black and slinky, open to the waist at the front and back, though the front was secured by a silver clasp across her cleavage. Underneath the dress she was stark naked. He had guessed and she had confirmed it. Plenty of men eyed her and Lux smiled smugly to himself because she was his.

As much the haunt of foreign businessmen as of Paris high society the Ritz restaurant hummed with life. Every table was taken, yet no would-be diner was kept waiting.

'Which is why the Ritz is the *haut de la gamme*,' Ghislaine remarked, having confessed that this was only her second visit here and that the first had been financed by a magazine for which she had written an award-winning article.

'What was the article about?' he asked, conscious of how little he knew of her.

'Corruption in Government,' she said, polishing off her third glass of Krug.

'Hot stuff.'

'They threatened me ... threatened to hurt Michel and Marc if I sold the article to the magazine.'

'Who threatened?'

She traced an elegant fingertip around the rim of the glass, making it squeal. 'People. I am not allowed to say. I daren't say.' She shot him a defiant look. 'It's not myself I'm afraid for.'

He leaned across the table, took her hand. 'It's kinda funny, but you don't need to tell me that.' Her aura of dedication and purpose had impressed him from the start. Locating her Achilles' heel would be no mean task. Her son and her husband in that order, and perhaps her parents, were probably the sum total.

'Are you anti-Government? Or just anti-establishment?'

'Both of those and more,' she replied as a waiter came and swept away the dessert dishes. 'Anti-authority would be a more generic way of describing my crusade.'

'Authority in practice or in principle?'

'In practice, my darling,' she said with a smile. 'I'm no anarchist, of that you may be sure.' Her smile dissolved into a kissing motion across the table. 'I love you.'

Before he could respond in kind she had pushed back her chair and extended her arms towards him. 'Let us dance – please.'

It was a waltz. Undemanding enough, which was all to the good for he was rusty. She danced like a dream, light of foot, sinuous of body, titillating with thighs and breasts.

'Tell me more about your politics,' he urged as they glided among other twirling couples. 'I'm intrigued.'

'Not now. Now I want to talk about us and what we are to do.'

It hadn't occurred to him that decisions were required. Not so soon. He was content just to enjoy her company and her closeness. Temporarily all other cares were driven from his mind. The assassination and how it was to be performed, his subsequent getaway, his various subterfuges ... all were consigned to a nether world under the magic of the spell his new love was weaving around him.

'What do *you* think we should do?' he said lightly, sweeping her across the floor to the refrain of the 'Waltz of the Toreadors'.

Surprise widened her brown eyes.

'Must I tell you? Why, we must run away together, of course. To your house in Menton perhaps. I don't really care where we go, so long as we go together.'

'Fine,' he said, though it wasn't as fine as all that, considering his present obligations. Running away with Ghislaine might be interpreted by Barail as a different kind of running away. In which eventuality the togetherness she craved was likely to be of short duration. 'What,' he went on, 'will you do about your son?'

She arched her back to study him. 'Naturally, he will join me ... us. I will make arrangements tomorrow but I must know where we are to live.'

Setting up house together was, notwithstanding the depth of his feelings for her, more a middle-term than short-term project. Yet to establish her in Menton made a sort of sense to him, in that she would be tolerably far from the scene of his forthcoming crime and leave him unencumbered to concentrate on earning his freedom – not to mention ten million dollars. Would she stand for it, waiting out the month-long countdown to the killing?

'Something is wrong.' She stiffened against him. 'You prefer that my son does not stay with us, is that it?'

'Not in the slightest.' He hesitated. To be convincing was no trial, it was the employment of duplicity so early in their relationship that bothered him. 'It's only that I'll have to leave you within a day or two ... a job ... a very big job. It will make me a great deal of money but even more importantly it will create other opportunities that are beyond price.' He felt her relax slightly, soften against him. 'I'm explaining this badly, just trust me for now. I won't let you down.'

'I do trust you,' she said, so immediately and ingenuously that he experienced a renewed surge of love and conscience in equal measure. 'I love you and I know you love me.' She frowned, marring the smooth plain of her forehead. 'You're not married, are you, Dennis? If you are, it doesn't matter, not at all. But I must know. We must be completely honest with each other.'

He suppressed a laugh. 'Not for many years. I'm footloose and fancy free – well, I was. Before I met you.'

The waltz wound down and he brought her to a gradual halt in the centre of the floor. They looked into each other's eyes and beyond and when the music recommenced and the other dancers spun around them they remained rooted, touching only with their souls.

'Just tell me what you want of me, my darling,' she whispered. 'Whatever it is, I will do it.'

'*Do you know he even trusted me with the number of his Swiss bank account, where the money for this job was sent? He explained to me the procedure for making enquiries about the balance and giving instructions by phone. He said it was in case anything happened to him …* [prolonged silence] *Sorry about that. He wanted me to have it. There were two other accounts that I know of – one in the Bahamas the other in some country with a strange name I can't even remember. Not Liechtenstein. In fact, I'm pretty sure it's not in Europe.*'

Ghislaine Fougère to Enrique Dubois, Lieutenant de Police, DCPJ, during interrogation, 12.06.1996.

* * *

His call to the bank was brief and the dialogue consisted mostly of numbers.

'*Compte nombre zéro-zéro-six-six-zéro-un-deux-trois-barre-huit-septante,*' the man chanted back at him.

'*Exacte.*'

'*Et votre code personnel, s'il vous plaît?*'

'*Vingt-cinq, zéro-six, trente-et-un.*' His mother's birth date.

A pause of perhaps a minute. Lux listened to the staccato tap of a keyboard.

A scraping sound as the receiver was picked up. '*Monsieur?*'

'*Toujours là.*' Still here.

'*Votre solde en dollars US est à quatre million neuf cent quatre-vingt dix-neuf mille, huit cent quatre-vingt dix-sept dollars, sans ajouter les intérêts.*'

Five million, less transaction charges. Lux mentally rubbed his hands.

'*Merci bien. Au revoir,*'

'*A votre service. Au revoir, monsieur.*'

If the changes in him these past few weeks had been many and deep, his house on the hill was at any rate the same as ever. Against the grey citadel of the mountains, forbidding in the fading light of evening, it stood like a rock of stability. Lights burned in a downstairs window and over the porch.

He paid off the taxi at the bottom of the drive, for he enjoyed the walk up the winding path, mounting the steps by the pool to the terrace. It was an airless evening, sounds carrying across the valley: a car going up the precipitous Route de Castellar, the note of its engine rising and falling with every hairpin bend; rock music down in the Vieux Ville; even the clatter of dishes drifting through the open kitchen window of a near neighbour. And the air up here at the two hundred metre line squeaky clean, filtered free of impurities by the mountain palisade that walled Menton off from the outside world. Less than two kilometres away was the border with Italy. His bolthole, should he ever need it.

The front door opened as he reached it. She stood before him, the doorway framing her, the soft lights on the hall flowing over her chestnut-dark and slightly tousled hair, turning it molten.

'You're late,' she accused, a catch in her voice. 'I cooked a meal ... salmon ...'

'The air controllers' dispute ... it was late taking off.' He stepped inside, closed the door, lowered his case to the floor.

The banality of the exchange was a cover up for a mutual confusion; hers at being here in his house, waiting for him as if she were his wife of many years and not someone else's; his, at this tangible evidence of his ignobility. For he was not proud of breaking up her marriage. Conscious that, had he not pursued her as though on a vendetta, the fire of their love, with so little to sustain it, must soon have turned to dying embers.

'Oh, Dennis, my love, my love.'

He crushed her to his chest, kissed her with such savagery that she gave a muffled cry. He didn't pull back, nor did she wish that he should.

When they came apart she was gasping. Limp in his arms, almost a dead weight, her jaw slack and her desire laid bare in her eyes.

'Where ...?' he said thickly, wanting her as he hadn't wanted a woman for years if ever. 'Your son ... is he here?'

She shook her beautiful sleek head. Was incapable of speech.

Not that speech was needed. He swept her up into his arms. She snuggled against him, a secretive smile playing over her lips, and he carried her to the living room. On the bearskin rug before the log fire he made love to her as he had never made love to any woman before.

* * *

Naked in the firelight, smoking, sipping a young Bordeaux Red, they talked.

Sending her on a day ahead of him had been a deliberate ploy to avoid making their liaison too public. His motives were largely unselfish: if spotted with him she might easily be regarded as his accomplice. In that eventuality, if – God forbid – the job went sour she would become a fugitive alongside him. But keep her pure and she might yet serve to shelter him. As it was, he did not even have to invent a reason for travelling separately. When he asked her to go to Menton alone and wait for him, she said okay and did not ask why. When he promised to join her as soon as his business in Paris was finalised, she said okay and did not seek reassurance. Her trust in him was absolute and left him bemused and humbled.

If he had his way this was to be their last night together until the job was over and done with, though he shrank from breaking this news to her. He hoped she would agree to stay here in Menton, while he would be based at his wife's villa.

'Where's your son?' he asked as she knelt before the fire to rearrange the logs, her skin turned the colour of old gold by the licking flames.

'At school.' She stared into the fire, her expression remote. 'At the weekend, when normally he would come home, he will go to his *mami's* – my mother. This will give me time to make other arrangements.'

'And Michel? Did you tell him.'

She prodded moodily with the poker; sparks whooshed, a log collapsed. 'I left a note.'

A note didn't seem much for a marriage ended. They had been living together, initially out of wedlock, since she was seventeen. If she was to be believed, Lux was her first extra-marital lover. 'And my last,' she had said fiercely, as he plunged into her that afternoon in the hotel on the banks of the Seine, pumping a breathless scream from her lungs. 'I will always love you – I swear it, oh God, I *swear* it!'

'Tomorrow I must go away,' he said, here and now, his tone

matter-of-fact. 'Out of the country.' A necessary white lie.

Still on her haunches she rotated towards him. 'Ah yes. Your big special job.'

'That's the one.'

'I cannot come with you then?'

'It wouldn't be a smart idea.'

Apart from an insignificant flaring of the nostrils her face did not alter.

'It's not that I don't want you with me,' he insisted, and to his ears it had a lame ring. 'And I can't tell you more ... it's confidential. When it's over, I'll explain, and you'll understand.'

She sank onto her bottom, ran a hand lightly up his thigh. Such was her effect on him that his prick instantly stiffened, though they had already savoured intercourse twice within the last hour.

She gave a soft laugh. 'You do not need to explain, my love. I have already told you – I trust you. I know you want to be with me and that if we must be apart it is because it is unavoidable. You see – ' Another laugh, liberated, happy. ' – I am a very uncomplicated, undemanding woman. Aren't you lucky to have me?'

She was sitting now, legs apart, leaning back supported by her spread hands. Her breasts drooped sensuously, the nipples casting sideways shadows over them like sundial pointers. She stirred restlessly under his scrutiny, not out of modesty (that much he had already learned about her), but out of the fires inside that her nakedness and his appraisal of it kindled. She had not been embarrassed to admit that she loved to display her body.

'You'll stay here, of course,' he said, and made it a statement.

'A few days only. I must also go to Paris to see Marc, no later than the weekend after next. Also, I must see Michel. I was not totally ... forthcoming in my note. It is only fair and right that I tell him about ... about us.'

Secretly Lux approved, though the jealous side of his nature, usually slow to inflame, resented the continued contact between her and her husband.

'I also have to work,' she said, after a pause.

'Work? Look ... I'll give you all you need. From now on you're my responsibility.'

Little sparks that owed nothing to the reflection of the fire flickered in her eyes.

'Never!' she snapped with such emphasis that he was taken aback. 'Never. I am my own responsibility.' She perceived his hurt and held his hands, twining her fingers with his. 'I love you, my darling, more than you can imagine. Whatever you wish I will do, I am your ... your ...' She searched for words, found them: '... adoring slave. But my adoration does not extend to giving up my independence. Not yet, not for a long while ... maybe never, even if one day we should marry. I am a career woman. I enjoy my work.'

The pride with which she made this declaration was stark. With the firelight suffusing her features, creating deep dark planes where normally there was none, she resembled a warlike goddess, a Joan of Arc, ready to do battle for her rights.

He grinned his admiration, counted himself a lucky man. 'You're terrific.'

She made that languorous kissing motion with her lips. 'As you know, I still have to finish my article on the President's vacation home.' Which Lux had forgotten. 'It must be delivered by the 15th May, and I always meet my deadlines.'

'So you should,' he agreed, while thinking furiously about the implications. For her to go trespassing again on the Crillon estate, stirring up the natives, was to be avoided at all costs. 'Do you absolutely need to go there again, to the house?'

'You don't want me to?'

'I don't want you to get into trouble.'

He gathered her to him and she sighed into his chest.

'You smell like a man,' she murmured.

'Glad to hear it. I do my best.'

She chuckled then and snuggled closer.

'So?' he prompted. 'Will you stay away?'

'I must go, my darling.' Her tongue flicked his nipple. 'It is my duty.'

Already he knew her well enough to accept the futility of further entreaty. Hadn't her husband warned him? 'I wish I could come with you.' And he honestly did. 'If you get caught, you could be arrested. Must you really go through with it?'

She had already given him the answer to that. Quite rightly she didn't repeat it.

'I will be careful.'

And with that meaningless assurance he had to be content.

'Dennis?' came the disembodied voice from the recorder. '*Ici* Jules.'

Lux's lawyer, Swiss-born, French mother, now Paris domiciled.

'I have made enquiries into the veracity of the document.' Pause. 'If the photocopy you sent me is a true facsimile then it is indeed genuine.' A more extended hiatus. 'I will qualify that: conditional on the signature being genuine, then the document is good.'

As a fount of legal advice, Jules was infallible. Lux accepted his findings implicitly.

He took that to be the whole of the message, but as he reached for the STOP button Jules went on, 'I have a question.' If he had any faults it was that he was too inquisitive for Lux's liking.

'Who is the subject of the pardon?'

Lux had obliterated his name from the photocopy. Not that he didn't expect Jules to guess correctly, more as a precaution against having such an incriminating piece of paper in circulation.

'You know better than to ask that,' Lux said softly to the machine and switched off.

The day after tomorrow at the latest Jules's bill would turn up on Lux's doormat. Minimum 10,000 Swiss Francs plus expenses. A reminder, as ever, that of the two of them the lawyer had the more lucrative profession.

Le Renard was in poor humour. He had overslept, thanks to a dinner party that had lasted too long the previous evening, and was suffering from a splitting headache. It was one of those days when he would have preferred if not to stay in bed, at least to be faced with nothing more demanding than a stack of reports and minutes to yawn through.

It was unfortunate then that at this, his introduction to Agent 411, aka 'Lucille,' he was irascible and impatient. And, worse, she was flanked by Mazé, Debre, de Charette and his minion, Victor Le Bihan. His office had the potential for a veritable Babel.

'In résumé,' he said, 'we know about Barail, possibly Dubois, Simonelli, and the killer, our Jackal – an American whose name we think we know but who is not on file under that name …' He checked them off on his fingers as he spoke. 'Also an unidentified woman from New Zealand whom we believe is masterminding the whole business.'

Lucille nodded.

'Let's move in now, *chef,*' Mazé urged. 'We can't lay our hands on the woman but there's nothing to stop us picking up the rest of the bunch.'

'No!' It was Debre who responded. 'We must have them all. Cut off the tail and another will grow in its place. We must have the head, though I cannot believe myself that it is this woman, whoever she is. This is not a woman's project. She is merely a messenger, an intermediary of some sort.'

'I believe there is another man, who may be the man behind it,' Lucille said warily. 'Listen again.'

She stabbed the rewind button of the recorder on the conference table and backtracked until the digital display showed 21:00, 21 minutes into the session.

Barail's voice entered the room. It was slurred, rambling.

'…. if you were not so anti-Chirac I would never, never, not never tell you, my little orchid (Lucille and Mazé grimaced together) … but … but ….' A lengthy pause. 'What was I saying? Ah, yes, but big changes are coming … coming. Mr Chirac is … is going to retreat … no, no, I mean retire … yes, retire from public life. In a manner of speaking, you understand, my love. Also, from private life.' Another space. Glass clinked on glass. 'Ah, *zut!* Excuse me …' Sound of drinking. 'It will happen soon, very soon. It is strange, is it not …? Is it not strange …?' Barail's voice degenerated into a mumble.

'What are you saying?' This was Lucille. 'Speak up, my brave warrior.'

'Brave *warrior*?' Mazé said, through an incredulous grin

'… I am saying -' Barail again, more forcibly, ' – that it is strange that it will happen because of a woman coming from a country twenty-thousand kilometres from here.'

'You mean Australia?' Lucille again.

'No … no, but close, very close. They are the same. Australians speak English as if their tongues were tied in a knot.' Barail seemed to be getting his second wind, becoming more coherent. 'And so does the man, her associate. She is American by birth, possibly Canadian.'

Lucille prodded the stop switch.

' "And so does the man, her associate," ' she quoted. 'Fairly conclusive, *non*?'

'They could be referring to the woman and the moneybags,' Mazé demurred. 'The one who is funding the whole show.'

Lucille bit her lip. 'Ah. I did not know about him. Is he actively involved in the operation?'

'We are pretty certain he is not,' Le Renard said. 'According to our sources he funds the breakaway group not the operations. He has not broken any laws, so we cannot touch him.'

'Have we identified him, the moneybags?' Lucille asked.

No one answered.

'Hervé?' Debre prompted.

De Charette's head jerked up at the mention of his name. He had been about to nod off, penalty of a heavy lunch.

'We have some leads. Greenpeace won't even talk to us, for reasons you can guess. But a possible lead came up a few weeks ago.'

Debre blew up. 'A few weeks ago! *Mon Dieu*, what are you saying, man? You have had this information for a matter of *weeks* …?' He found himself lost for words, a unique event.

Le Renard, who was so far slumped in his chair that he was in danger of sliding beneath the table, suddenly sat up.

'Who is he, this moneybags?'

De Charette snapped his fingers at his *chef de cabinet*, Victor Le Bihan, who hastily flicked through his notes.

'His name is Edward Noble Nixon,' Le Bihan said shortly. 'Sixty-nine years old. Owner of a hotel chain and several nightclubs.'

'Doesn't sound a very likely activist,' Debre remarked.

'Married to a Chinese,' Le Bihan droned on. 'Soon-Li Ying, twenty-seven, former prostitute …'

'How sure are you that this Nixon is the moneybags behind it?' Le Renard said. As holder of a CRS rank equivalent to that of a three-star general and bearer of ultimate responsibility for presidential security, he too was peeved at the failure of the Ministry of Foreign Affairs to pass on this new intelligence but he didn't make an issue of it. It was not his place to remonstrate with his *soi-disant* betters.

'We are not sure at all,' de Charette snapped, still smarting over the implied rebuke from his fellow-Minister.

'Question him then.'

'Not so easy. Apart from the need to observe certain legal niceties, especially in New Zealand, there is a major practical impediment.' De Charette's expression became doleful. 'Nixon died last month.'

'*Merde!*' Le Renard flung himself back in his chair so violently that it rolled backwards a good metre.

'And his wife?' Mazé said.

De Charette frowned and looked enquiringly at Le Bihan who in turn stared blankly at Mazé.

'His wife,' Mazé repeated. 'Did she also die?'

'Er … *non*,' Le Bihan said. 'Why?'

Mazé did not answer, but a slow grin evolved on his face. 'You may return to your duties, Agent 411,' he said to Lucille, who promptly stood up to attention. 'Continue your excellent work. We have a name, we know the place. We now need to know the date and the precise method. We also need the name or names of the people behind the plot. To guarantee to foil it we must have this intelligence. *Compris?*'

'*Monsieur*. But could we not …' Lucille faltered. She would not dare to speak too much out of turn in such exalted company. 'Perhaps we should cancel the President's vacation or at least change the venue.'

'Absolutely not,' Debre said. 'If we do that we will be completely in the dark as to their intentions. This way we can at least give the President the best possible protection throughout his stay at the Crillon residence.' He glanced over at de Charette who was tapping his wristwatch as if this would somehow slow it down. He had an appointment over at the Defence Ministry and he was already late.

De Charette nodded. 'I agree.' Anything to bring this meeting to a close.

'So be on your way, my dear,' the Interior Minister said, in that patronising tone he always used on women.

Lucille kept her umbrage off her face, saluted, and wheeled about.

'Attractive girl,' the Foreign Minister remarked, when she was gone. 'I can see why the *Commissaire* is prepared to roll over on his back and let her tickle his tummy.'

Wellington, New Zealand, 8 May 1996

The Ambassador has made a formal complaint about the local representative of your International Terrorism Directorate. His Excellency does not approve of the officer's presence, his methods, or his morals.

Extract from memo from the Minister for Foreign Affairs to CG/CRS, 13.05.96

*   *   *

It was set to be another grey, windy day in Wellington. From the second floor office at the embassy, Jacques Le Blanc, French Ambassador to New Zealand, watched the incoming ferry from South Island battle through white horses just outside the harbour. He didn't envy those who plied the strait between the North and South Islands, one of the roughest stretches of water in the world.

A rap at his door turned his head towards it.

'*Entrez,*' he called.

A man by the name of Maurice Incardona entered. Short of stature, receding black hair, with bright beady eyes that always made Le Blanc think of a rat, he was not officially a member of the Embassy staff. That he was a nifty dresser merely intensified the Ambassador's dislike. He had no time for fops.

'You wanted to see me, sir.'

The Ambassador gestured to the easy chair before his low modern desk, on which reposed the contents of last night's diplomatic bag.

'Make yourself comfortable, Incardona,' he said and resumed his own seat behind the desk.

Incardona purported to be a clerk in the tourism section. In reality he was an attaché to the Embassy from the Ministry of Defence, whose brief consisted chiefly of spying on Greenpeace and other pressure groups likely to interfere with French policy, nuclear or otherwise.

'Have you had any success tracing this new green faction?' the Ambassador asked, not that he cared overmuch. In fact he wished the whole issue of the Greens and France's nuclear tests would go away and leave him to run the embassy without interference.

'Not much. You have seen my latest report?' A nod from the Ambassador. 'It is a case of see, hear, and speak no evil. If anyone knows, they aren't talking.'

'What about this report you sent to Paris a few weeks ago, about the source of the finance for these people?' The Ambassador waved five stapled sheets at Incardona. 'This Edward Nixon. Third richest man in New Zealand, it says here.'

'Gossip,' Incardona said with a shrug of his slight shoulders. 'It couldn't be verified. And anyway, he died just after I wrote that report, so that's a dead end.' He tittered. 'Excuse the pun, *M. l'Ambassadeur.*'

'Not quite a dead end. Or at any rate, Paris doesn't think so. The Minister wants you to contact his wife, Soon-Li Nixon.'

'A Chink. I've seen a picture of her. She looks about eighteen. Juicy.' Incardona pretended not to notice the Ambassador's moue of censure. 'So they want me to chat her up, do they? Well, it won't be a hardship.'

The Ambassador handed a sealed envelope to the intelligence agent. The covering note, addressed to him and signed by de Charette, had merely provided an outline. Though out of curiosity he would have loved to see the contents of the envelope, it was best to stay ignorant of the machinations of Ministers and their minions.

The cassette arrived in a padded bag within a bag as always, the inner one marked EYES ONLY – COMMANDANT DE POLICE MAZE / CRS.

The plastic container bore the label No 14 and a date, 05.05.96. Mazé fed it into the mouth of the recording machine on the shelf behind his desk and sat back to listen while running a battery-driven shaver over his stubble. He had developed the habit of shaving at the office ever since the traffic got so bad as to require him to leave home ever-earlier in the morning.

'Agent 411,' Lucille's voice announced. 'Recording of conversation on 5th May 1996 …'

Mazé's face remained immobile if not his emotions. Lucille's endearments carried a new intensity that caused him mild surprise. She was quite the actress. Hidden talents to go with the more obvious ones.

The actual lovemaking did nothing to arouse him beyond a fleeting envy. It was the psychology of interaction between people that fascinated him professionally, not the physiology. Vicarious sexual gratification was not for him.

The cassette ran for two hours. Occasionally he made a note. Much of it was unusable mush. Great material for a cheap erotic novel. Maybe that was the source of her inspiration.

The tape came to a conclusion in mid-sentence – '*Je t'aime, mon amour … oh, je …*' God, what corn. That line was lifted verbatim from the hit record by Gainsbourg and Birkin, punctuated by her heavy breathing, that caused such an uproar in the 70s.

From a strict intelligence viewpoint it was a dud. She was doing her damnedest to earn Barail's trust, that much he did concede. But the man was above all a pro. Under the influence of sex and alcohol he had dropped his guard enough to confirm that, in cahoots with Rafael Simonelli, he was probably implicated in a plot to assassinate the President. He had also let slip that the attempt would be carried out at the Crillon place, and that an American female and a New Zealand male were co-ordinating the show, if they were not actually the principals. The Jackal had been identified, though the name – Dennis Hull – was probably a phoney. No criminal record existed of him in Western Europe or North America.

The date, the time, the method, and the names of the coordinators were blanks waiting to be filled in. One thing was certain; the assassin wouldn't be firing blanks.

'While I was back in Enzed I visited Eddie's grave. Gary wanted to come with me, but I wanted … needed to go alone. You know it's funny but I barely met Eddie a dozen times since that first time, at his club, yet I felt closer to him than to any other man, apart from my dad, who's been dead for years. Don't you think that's weird?'

Sheryl Glister to Thierry Garbe, freelance journalist, 24.03.1999

*   *   *

The monument was not ostentatious. About four feet in height; grey and black marble, gilt lettering, the simplest of epitaphs.

HERE LIES EDWARD NOBLE NIXON.
1927-1996.
Noble not only by name.

A fresh spray of flowers already occupied the solitary pot. Sheryl bent and laid her bright bouquet on the tombstone. She remained there for a minute or so on one knee, not praying exactly, for she was not devout, just remembering, just trying to convey to his spirit that the cause he championed lived on and would continue to live on. That she would remain true to it, however rocky the road ahead. She was the trustee-in-chief of his cause. The custodian of a good half of his fortune, no matter how much Soon-Li, not content with her hundred and twenty million legacy, might remonstrate with her lawyers.

'Rest easy, Eddie,' Sheryl said aloud. Her knee cracked as she straightened up, a reminder of the arthritic tendency in her family genes.

The sun went in and a typical Auckland shower abruptly started, as from a hose in the sky. She had come prepared and put up her umbrella. The transition from a Northern Hemisphere spring to an Antipodean autumn had been barely noticeable, and she was wearing the same summer-weight suit with short sleeves she wore in London only a few days before.

She stood looking down at the grave for quite a while.

Even when, around mid-day, she eventually walked away, her steps slow and deliberate, her head bent, she remained unaware of the dapper little man on the wooden bench by the entrance to the

Purewa cemetery, taking snaps through the zoom lens of a dinky camera. Even if she had noticed him she would have had no way of telling from his appearance that he was a member of the staff of the French Embassy whose sole purpose was to monitor and report on the doings of Greenpeace and its contemporaries.

Paris, 17e Arrondissement, 13 May 1996

'Agent 411. Time – seventeen forty-four hours, Monday 13th May, 1996. I am on my way to a meeting with Commissaire Divisionnaire Barail, Julien, at his apartment, number 1, rue Barye.'

Opening extract from transcript of recording by Agent 411, dated 13.05.96., Filed 19.05.96

*   *   *

Her ears still on fire from Mazé's latest harangue, Lucille snapped the flap of her cellphone shut and slid it in her shoulder bag. Cassettes nos. 15 and 16 had been as uninformative as no. 14, the one that had sparked his previous remonstration, and now the *conard* was threatening to pull her off the case with all its negative implications for her future advancement within the service.

Fuming, she took out her compact and opened it, peering critically at the circle of her face by the meagre interior light of the taxi. Her make-up was overdone in keeping with the norms of her supposed trade – black eyeliner, lurid turquoise eye shadow, lips drawn beyond those endowed by nature. A generous dab of foundation on each cheek and she was ready for him.

This was to be their first rendezvous outside the hotel. Barail, sensitive to gossip, had always deemed it 'inappropriate' until now. The unexpected and unexplained change of heart troubled her somewhat, though she had kept her reservations to herself. Already familiar with Barail's penchant for perversion, she suspected that he meant to introduce more elaborate and less portable sex aids into their intercourse. She could only hope that they did not involve pain. Pain was not a source of pleasure for her.

The taxi deposited her at the corner of Rue Médéric and Rue Barye, just across from the Lycée Technique. It was a fine mild night, not quite dark. This part of the city lay under a respectful hush, is if in deference to its high class residentia. Apart from the occasional car the streets were bereft of activity. The steel tips of her heels clacked on the paving slabs as she proceeded past the apartment block towards its high portal. Dress discreetly, had been his injunction, 'like a secretary'.

So she was attired in a chic business suit with a knee-length skirt, her hair drawn back in a schoolmarmish pleat. Underneath these trapping it was of course another story: the skimpiest of G-strings in black silk, matching half-cup bra that barely covered her nipples, and black self-support stockings. His tastes in women's underwear were wholly consistent and wholly typical.

The male concierge at number 1 watched from his cubicle as she passed under the archway but issued no challenge. The two-hundred franc note reposing in his wallet, courtesy of *'le Commissaire,'* had purchased his blind eye for the evening. Though as the *Commissaire's* visitor entered the side door into the vestibule, he couldn't resist an envious smirk.

Barail answered Lucille's buzz at the door even before she removed her thumb from the button. He had no wish to keep her lingering in the corridor where his mealy-mouthed neighbours might catch sight of her and draw the obvious conclusions.

'Come in, come in,' he urged and expedited the process by dragging her through the doorway. She cannoned into him.

'What a caveman!' she gasped and attached her lips to his. He kicked the door shut with his foot, leaving his hands free to grope and grasp.

Inside five minutes they were under the duvet of the vast four poster bed. Five minutes more and already they had had sex. Unlike many men Barail had not promptly turned over to go to sleep. A cigarette as usual and he would be ready for more. His libido was voracious and, herself naturally highly-sexed, she encouraged him to exercise it to the limit while she pumped him for new scraps of intelligence. It was even quite fun.

An hour later, with her wrists and ankles chained to each post, the tatters of her underwear scattered about the room, the fun was beginning to pall and she felt the first tremor of unease.

Barail was straddling her thighs, smoking; now and again touching the lighted end of his cigarette to her pubic hairs. They burned with a little fizzing noise and an acrid stink. It could have been no more than a harmless fetish. It didn't hurt in the slightest. Not yet. But unless she came up with satisfactory answers it was going to. He had told her so and she had no reason to doubt him.

In trying to do her job she had gone a question too far, a probe too deep. When he turned on her, half-angry, half-suspicious, she was unprepared. She became flustered. Her stammerings made matters worse. That she was already chained to the bed had weakened her ability to answer back, to fake indignation. Now she was faced with the prospect of pain, perhaps even serious pain, if she failed to allay his suspicions.

'You are so interested in my plans for the President, my angel,' he said, his eyes caressing her nakedness. 'It begins to trouble me, to make me wonder if your questions are motivated by something more than your natural nosiness.'

'But I love you, *chérie*,' she protested, willing her heartbeat to slow down. 'I want to share everything with you. You know this is true. How often have I already asked you to leave your wife?' Lucille managed to form her lips into a prize-winning pout.

For once, it made no impression on Barail.

*   *   *

Lucille's skirt lay crumpled on the floor. The tiny microphone sewn inside the waistband transmitted every spoken word, every movement, to the recording device in a cramped third floor office in the *15e Arrondissement*, where two plainclothes DCPJ men huddled, their heads shrouded in cigarette smoke. Their expressions were without emotion, their eyes cold as those of dead fish. Even when sounds of distress travelled along the wire they did not visibly react. Nor even when the groans graduated to screams. It was left to them to judge whether intervention was necessary. According to their instruction from Mazé it should only be in the case of a matter of life and death.

Mazé had granted her a few days' 'rest and recuperation' for the hurts she had suffered at Barail's hands. Not that they amounted to much: a couple of bruises the size of ten franc coins on the inside of her thighs, nipples that bore indentations from his fingernails, and a really sore anus where he had buggered her with a lighted cigarette. *That,* admittedly, had been nasty. Sitting was no longer a pleasure.

Her subterfuge as the Barail's paramour had run its course, so there was no prospect of her extracting more secrets, always supposing he still trusted her enough to confide any. She had got off lightly, the torture session having been more of a game to him than a serious attempt to make her confess. Afterwards, she had readily consented to a new assignation, making light of his sadistic treatment, even pretending to have derived a sexual buzz from it. It was a tryst she would simply fail to keep. She would disappear from the streets, and the powers-that-be would make sure the traitorous *Commissaire* never came anywhere near her place of work.

Later, she would pack a bag and board the TGV to journey south to Nice in search of a little healing in the sun.

St Tropez, 16 May 1996

'Lux was suspicious of everything we did to the point of paranoia. When he met Rafael in St Trop for handover of the second instalment and the fake documents, he questioned the precautions Rafael took to ensure he wasn't photographed handing over the package. We were in a state of mutual mistrust.'

Sheryl Glister to Thierry Garbe, freelance journalist, 24.03.1999.

* * *

Lux's appointment with Simonelli was for five o'clock in the afternoon. The Corsican was to come equipped with the phoney Canadian passport, the phoney Renseignements Généraux ID, a technical drawing of the Aérospatiale Ecureuil helicopter, and a certified copy of a Letter of Credit for forty per cent of his fee – though the last mentioned was mere formality, as the money had been accumulating interest in his Swiss account for the past fortnight.

The designated meeting place was the Remparts Café in St Tropez, the only drinking establishment from which both the Citadel and the sea are visible. Lux was there ahead of Simonelli and perched on the crumbling stone wall of the terrace bar in the hot sun, watching the underdressed girls go by.

Most of the sitters at table looked like holidaymakers, with their beach paraphernalia and sun hats. The Remparts was not the sort of haunt locals would frequent. Brigitte Bardot in particular, as the most celebrated local, didn't come and take coffee and garner the inevitable adulation, or even pass by with one or more of her family of dogs in tow, though it was less than a kilometre from her St Trop residence.

Simonelli arrived by chauffeured Citroën XM. It deposited him by the entrance, a flowered archway, and went off in a fusillade of gravel.

His smile when he saw Lux was wide and white and radiated pleasure for all the world to see. His suit was white too and his buckskin shoes, and as if in empathy his pallor was more deathly that ever.

'An unusual place to rendezvous,' he observed

'Not to me. Lonely spots on lonely roads are not only more obvious, they are also less secure.'

Simonelli made a face. 'I'm not devious enough for this business,' he lied blithely. 'All I want is ...' On the brink of committing an indiscretion, he checked, smiled abruptly.

'We all want something,' Lux said, gazing out towards a sea that was as flat as a pane of glass. 'Money, sex, power.'

'Freedom,' Simonelli put in.

'Yeah ... freedom. One man's freedom, another man's life.' The taste in Lux's mouth was sour.

'Everything has a price. Console your conscience with the ten million good American dollars that will make your freedom that little bit more free.'

Lux twitched his lip in a sneer. 'I don't need your money. I'll take it, since it's being stuffed inside my wallet, but I can get by without it. No trouble at all.' He slid off his perch. 'Enough chewing the fat. You can buy me a drink and cross my palm with documentation.'

The key on the table between Lux's glass of Vermouth and Simonelli's Ricard had a plastic tag numbered 333. The other side bore the letters SNCF moulded-in.

'You know where the station is?' Simonelli asked.

'There is no station in St Tropez,' Lux said, suspicious. 'Is this a joke?'

'No joke – the station is at Fréjus. You will find everything you requested there.'

Lux lifted the key by its tag, dangled it. 'Why so far away? More sensible surely to let me examine the merchandise before you leave.'

'*Comme ça.*' Because. An evasion not an answer.

'Try again, pal. Try harder.'

Simonelli looked as if he might get ugly, the lips peeling back, the spade-shaped chin coming up. 'If we didn't need you ...'

'But you do. So tell me what game you're playing.'

A further internal struggle with his fragile temper, then Simonelli said, 'Let me put it this way, Lux: we realise you do not trust us, that you are taking precautions in case we break our promises. This is understandable. We do not blame you for it. So you must not blame us if we do not trust you either. If you chose, you could cause us much embarrassment, could even expose our plan to install our nominee as President. At the very least you could retard our schedule. We are conscious of this. So, it is natural that we should take precautions of our own. To be photographed handing over a package to you – for instance – whether or not the contents of the package were revealed, might compromise me and my associates.'

'If that were my intention – ' and it wasn't such a lousy idea at that, Lux reflected, ' – I would surely have picked a less public place to meet and arranged for my photographer to record what was in the package whilst in your presence.'

The Corsican acknowledged this with a tilt of his gleaming head. 'But before I came we could not know that this place was not secluded. And even if we had it would have made no difference. Like you, we leave nothing to chance.'

He clicked his fingers and a waiter swooped.

'Not for me,' Lux said.

'As you wish.' Simonelli requested another Ricard. '*Encore un Ricard*,' just like the billboard stickers.

'I need a man,' Lux said

Simonelli quit dabbing his red lips with his polka dot handkerchief. 'A man? You disappoint me. According to your dossier you are something of a Casanova.'

'Don't be funny. I need a driver who can be trusted to keep his mouth zipped tight when the going gets nasty.'

Simonelli considered this until his Ricard showed up. Then he drank to help the considering.

'This man will be involved in the ... operation?' With so many ears around even Simonelli resorted to euphemism.

'He will be an accessory. He will be in ignorance of my real intent.'

'You cannot use one of Barail's people – he will not allow it.'

'If that was what I wanted I would ask Barail. I'm asking you because I expected you would have the right kind of connections. If I'm wrong ...' Lux gave a dismissive shrug, implying contempt. 'Forget it. I'll go elsewhere.'

'No! If you need outside help you must not go elsewhere.' Simonelli looked earnest, which was rare in Lux's experience of him. 'I will provide someone ... a countryman of mine and loyal to me. But he will want paying. What will be expected of him?'

Lux dabbed with a fingertip at a runnel of perspiration that was threatening his eye. 'As I said – drive a car and keep his mouth shut. If he could provide the car too, this would be worth a bonus. A dark saloon, new or nearly new – Citroën or Renault, French anyway. As for payment ... ten thousand *francs nouveaux*? Does that sound like the going rate?'

'It is a starting point for negotiation, no more than that. Where should he meet you?'

'Tell me where and I'll go to him.'

Simonelli nodded. 'Telephone me tomorrow morning. I will

stay in this area for twenty-four hours anyway, in case there should be any problems, *c'est à dire,* any questions concerning the merchandise I have delivered.' He opened his wallet and slid out a blank piece of white card, wrote on it with a svelte gold fountain pen, four groups of two digits.

Lux tucked the card away without so much as a glance at it. A crowd of new arrivals, young, garrulous, and Italian, came onto the terrace and whipped the spare seats from Lux's table to make up a shortfall. Under the umbrella of their staccato chatter Simonelli asked Lux what progress he had made.

'All's well for the 2nd,' Lux assured him. 'Let's hope the President doesn't change his plans.'

'How will you do it?' Simonelli asked. 'How will you gain entry to the estate?'

'Who said anything about gaining entry?'

A sneer. 'Because of the wall you must, unless you plan to use a missile launcher.' He smirked, pleased with the logic of his reasoning, elementary though it was.

'Maybe I'll do it from a chopper.'

Simonelli looked incredulous. 'You would never be allowed to enter the airspace over the chateau. It will be patrolled, you know this …'

'It's not your concern.'

'That's where you are wrong,' he retorted, shoving his face close to Lux's. 'To fail is not an option. We are all in jeopardy here, not just you. I am already a wanted man. I will console myself with the money I will be paid, though I do not need it. But to make the attempt and fail means I remain on the run – for nothing.'

'Aw, quit shooting off, Simonelli. Let me do the job my way. At least you're not risking a bullet.'

Simonelli lit a cigarette with an unsteady hand. 'In some ways that would be preferable.'

* * *

'Darling … oh, darling, is it really you?'

Lux grinned into the mouthpiece. 'Hi, there, gorgeous. Missing me?'

'Missing you? I'm dying for want of you. Why am I here in Menton all on my own. Where are you? You sound as if you were in the next room.'

'Still in the land of pasta. How are your problems? Did you talk to Michel?'

'Yes.' More subdued now. 'It isn't good but at least we are still speaking.'

'How did he take it?'

'How do you think?' Her tone was harsh. He had exposed a raw nerve.

'Sorry, my love. I'll leave that side to you. But yell if you need me.'

'I need you all the time – every minute, every second.' The tone reverted to soft, alluring. 'But I wouldn't know where to yell to. Why don't you have a cellphone. Everyone has them now. Can't you at least give me a number where I can reach you? If I can't have your body on tap, I'll have your voice. I do so long for you.'

He put her question on hold. 'How did your third visit to the Crillon place go? You weren't arrested, I hope.'

'*Pas du tout.* I was in and out inside half an hour and saw no one and was seen by no one. Satisfied? It was not a new experience for me, you know.'

'I know. You're brave as well as beautiful and talented.'

'You say such nice things to me. You should be here saying them not ... not ... wherever you are.'

Lux stared out through fly-speckled glass at a sea bathed red by the setting sun. Two men were loading fishing tackle into a small sailing boat down on the pebble beach, attended by two small children and a black-and-white dog. Somewhere close by but out of sight from the telephone kiosk, a woman laughed.

He wished Ghislaine were here with him, wished it so intensely it was a physical hurt.

'Darling ... are you still there?'

'I'm here,' he said, 'and I love you, and no, I can't give you a number ... we're continually on the move. It won't be long now, though, before I'm back home.'

Home. With Ghislaine there the word, the idea, had real meaning. Wasn't just a convenient caption to describe his base.

'Hurry. I'll be waiting. I'll always be waiting.'

Ste Maxime, 17 May 1996

'He told me how he had always loved guns, from being very young. He told me a little story about it.'

Ghislaine Fougère to Enrique Dubois, Lieutenant de Police, DCPJ, during interrogation, 12.06.1996.

* * *

At the Ste Maxime house the swimming pool construction team had turned up in force with a mechanical digger and were hard at it transforming the once immaculate garden into a First World War landscape. Back from his drive to Fréjus Station Lux made coffee *espresso* from freshly ground beans and tried to ignore the roar of the digger's motor as he unwrapped the surprisingly bulky package and spread its contents across the bare wood of the kitchen table: the Canadian Passport, dark green with a soft cover was superficially okay; he would compare it with a genuine article at a later date. The RG *passe-partout* was in the name of Richard Lefranc. It was of plastic and the photograph – taken from the kiosk facial he had provided for the passport – was reproduced by computer and formed an integral part of the card. Nowhere in the text was the RG mentioned; intelligence and security outfits never provide their operatives with papers proclaiming their real function. He was classed as an *Attaché Personnel*, and there was an assortment of codes together with a telephone number, otherwise it was an austere piece of work.

Authenticating the card was outside Lux's competence. Certainly it was not within a lawyer's remit. Much as it went against the grain, he would have to take it on trust. It was a reasonable assumption that Barail would not employ him to perform so critical a task as killing the President only to issue him with a useless Identity Card. The more he thought about it, tapping the edge of the card on his knuckle, the more he came to accept that above all his RG credentials were flawless, that if anything was dubious it would be the passport.

The third document was a confirmation copy of the Letter of Credit, drawn as specified, on the Schweitzer Kreditanstaltbank of Zürich. Four million United States dollars made a lot of noughts. Somehow, seeing it in writing made it more real than having it read out over the phone.

'Four fucking million,' he breathed. It had a sweet ring to it, though ten million would ring sweeter still.

Thus far then, Barail was playing ball. Had given him all he had demanded with the minimum of fuss.

The fourth and final item was a colour brochure and a maintenance manual for the Ecureuil helicopter. After leafing through the latter to verify that it contained the diagrams he sought, he set it aside.

Next on his shopping list was the gun, that essential tool of his bloody trade. From being small he had always loved guns. Oddly, a minor incident from his boyhood was lodged in his memory with total clarity of recall, possibly because it was the first occasion when he had confessed openly to this fascination with weaponry. Not really an incident even: he was in his tenth summer, and the little girl from next door, a year younger, had come round to play. Ordinarily he would never have entertained a *girl* (yuk!) in his domain. According to the perception of the day they were such boring creatures, only interested in dolls and things. He should have been goofing off with Buzz, Des, and Spex at Buzz's place with its spacious yard and tree house, or maybe over at River Bay. But all three of his regular buddies were away on vacation or at summer camp and, lacking other lures, he had condescended to devote an hour or so to Joanna. Admittedly she was above average in the looks department – long blue-black hair and beseeching brown eyes. Five, six years later there would have been no holding him.

'What do you want to do, Denny?' she had asked him, as they lay on their tummies on the rug on the sweeping lawn. 'When you grow up, I mean.'

'I am grown up.' Had he not overhead his mom say so the other day: 'My Denny's very grown up for his age.'

Joanna tickled his nose with a long blade of grass. He brushed it away irritably.

'I mean ... when you're *really* grown up, when you're a man, like our daddies.'

'Oh.' He was flummoxed. Fact was, he hadn't given it a deal of thought. Life was too full of just being a boy, school a chore that had to be endured because your parents made you go, not because it prepared you for the future, a dimension too remote and imprecise to figure in the scale of priorities.

'Well then?' she prodded when he didn't answer, persistent as a wasp at a picnic.

'Oh,' he said again, then, abashed, plumped for 'a cowboy.' It was the first thing that entered his head and he recognised the absurdity of it.

So did she.

'Don't be stupid! They don't have cowboys nowadays. That was hundreds of years ago.'

'Course they do,' he countered. 'They still have cows, don't they? Who's supposed to look after them?'

'Yes, but they don't call them cowboys and I expect they drive around in cars and things. Anyway, Mommy says it's all nonsense and that it only happens in movies and the funnies.'

That, he was sure, was not true, but he didn't have the proof at his disposal. So he resorted to a dismissive grunt and rolled over onto his stomach, pressing his face into the grass, savouring its coolness and freshness. An ant was marching across a bare patch of earth near his splayed hand. He flicked it away, chanting, 'Ant, ant, fly away, come back another day.' Then, still irked by his inability to get the better of Joanna, he said, 'I know! If I can't be a cowboy, I'll be a soldier, a general.'

He expected her to be impressed but all she said was, 'Why?'

He remembered his answer because it was so patently honest.

'Because ... because ... I like guns and shooting.'

And here he was, a quarter of a century on, still liking guns, still liking shooting.

Tomas Leandri was the man recommended by Simonelli and he might have passed for the Corsican's younger brother: scraggy features, lean jawed, with slick black hair and eyes like two blobs of tar. He wore lightweight caramel-coloured slacks with matching shoes, a pale green shirt with some subtle interweaving that flashed in the sun like polished armour. He was the type who would carry a shiv and wouldn't need much encouragement to stick it between your ribs. Simonelli rated him 'the most trustworthy man I know, and an implacable enemy of Chirac and France. If he agrees to work for you, I guarantee his secrecy.'

For maximum privacy Lux had arranged to meet at Leandri's house, a single-storey log cabin affair not far from Toulon and with a spectacular view of that city. Several warships, lean and grey, were berthed side by side in the naval dockyard.

The man was married – or at any rate he presented a curvy but otherwise rather plain blonde girl who wore a wedding ring as '*ma femme*'. She smiled coyly, addressed Lux respectfully as '*monsieur,*' making him feel like a grandfather, and left them to their negotiations. They parked their bottoms in comfy outdoor chairs under a eucalyptus tree too sparsely foliated to give much protection from the mid-afternoon sun, which shone with its usual relentless brilliance, churning out heat like a flame thrower.

Leandri hailed from Bonificia at the extreme southern tip of Corsica. Profession dubious, earnings – to judge from the size and style of his property and the nearly-new Mercedes and Alfa Sports that squatted under the car port – substantial. He came swiftly to the point.

'Simonelli says you want a driver.'

'A little more than that.' Lux enlarged on the job specification as the blonde girl brought cold beers in chilled glasses.

Leandri sucked in his top lip contemplatively. 'The car will be obtained by someone else; I am not in that line of business. It will cost *about un million de francs. Anciens,*' he appended, chuckling at Lux's expression of dismay. The American still hadn't gotten used to the tendency of many French, especially in the Midi, to calculate in old francs.

'That includes a respray and the special plates,' he said while Lux was still doing the mental arithmetic.

Twelve thousand dollars American, maybe a bit less, for a 'clean' stolen car. It was a fair price.

'Agreed,' Lux said. 'And for yourself and the second man?'

'What second man?'

'Another man will be required to assist you. He will be your choice and must be guaranteed by you.'

Leandri adjusted fast. 'Shall we say … fifteen times the amount for the car for the two of us.' His voice was like silk, almost a caress. He had unusually long eyelashes and he fluttered them like a tart giving the come-on.

Lux unstuck the front of his shirt from his chest and tutted, shaking his head.

'If not,' Leandri said, grinning broadly, 'I can recommend someone cheaper.'

Lux was pretty sure he was bluffing but it was quality bluffing. Pretending to consider it, he quaffed his beer, already losing its chill.

'If I agree there must be no questions asked. I want absolute obedience, absolute discretion, from you and your helper.' He was talking for the sake of it. Had he held doubts on either count he should not have been here. Surprisingly for him, who bestowed trust but rarely, he trusted Simonelli and therefore his judgement.

A point Leandri uncannily proceeded to make. 'Simonelli is an old friend, also we are related by blood. We trust each other implicitly. Do not forget, *mon ami*, I also will be taking risks. And, please …' A raised hand, like a policeman stopping traffic, 'Do not insult my intelligence by continuing to pose as a journalist. Whatever you are, you are not of the paparazzi.'

'Did Simonelli …?' Lux left the question unfinished; such an indiscretion was unthinkable.

'It is my own deduction.' Leandri smiled and wiped an errant black forelock from his eyes. 'You and I are perhaps, in the loosest sense, of the same breed. Or do I flatter myself?'

Lux let that go. Agreed his three hundred thousand franc fee.

'Half now,' Leandri said and the hand was already outstretched.

Lux scuffed at the turf with his shoes. It was as fine as baize and cropped short. It would not have been out of place in an English Country Garden.

'Well now,' he said slowly, 'I thought a quarter now another quarter when you show up with the car, the rest after the job's done.'

These were the terms Barail had imposed on Lux. He didn't see why he should be more magnanimous when sub-contracting work out.

Leandri got to his feet, very fast like a switchblade springing open. And the simile was apt for, even as Lux tensed defensively, just such a knife was inches from his solar plexus. He made to move; Leandri discouraged him by pushing him back with the flat of his free hand and shoving the blade of the knife under his ear lobe.

'Stay perfectly still if you don't want to lose an ear, *mon ami*.'

For now Lux opted for caution. He couldn't tell how much of this performance was front and how much was the McCoy. The man was an unknown quantity. The knife point stayed below Lux's ear lobe as his free hand wormed inside Lux's jacket, lighted on the fat envelope there. Tugging it loose he stepped away, again very smooth, very fast ... so fast that by comparison Lux's own reflexes were those of a snail, and an old tired snail at that.

'Now what do we have here?' Leandri crooned, slitting the envelope with the knife and thereby demonstrating its sharpness. At this point his wife came out of the cabin. Leandri prancing around with a foot-long sticker was clearly a regular event for she came and cleared away the glasses, detouring around him without so much as a flickered eyelid.

'Another beer, *chérie*?' she enquired.

He looked up from groping inside the slashed envelope. 'Why not? For my friend too.'

As his wife went off, hips in full gyration, he extracted the wad of 500F notes with a triumphant '*Voila!*'

Lux eyed him sourly. If Leandri's behaviour amounted to no more than theatricals he would go along with it, humour him; the stakes were too high for outrage. But if this was a shakedown he'd be one sorry *mec* when Lux got through with him.

'It looks to me like about two hundred notes,' Leandri said, measuring the depth of the wad with an apparently expert eye. 'Maybe a little more. A hundred thousand francs?' He snorted. 'You think I come that cheap?'

'One hundred and twenty five thousand,' Lux corrected. 'I figured a half a million was about the rate for the job. That represents twenty-five per cent.'

Only slightly mollified, Leandri said, 'We have agreed six hundred thousand.'

'So I'll send you the difference tomorrow morning by special messenger. Okay?'

Leandri nodded slowly as if unsure. His wife brought the beers, twitched a timid smile at Lux. She reminded him of a little mouse. She came, she went, disturbing only the blades of grass she trod.

Lux added, 'But the deal is twenty-five per cent up front – not a *sou* more.'

Leandri laughed suddenly and it was like seeing someone undergo a personality change. 'You win, Yank. Send me the rest of the deposit tomorrow.'

Lux eased himself out of the chair, stretched, making a big show of it, flinging his arms out. Leandri was no longer interested in him. He was stuffing the money back in the envelope when Lux brought his fist round in a loop that caught him high on the cheekbone, tearing the skin, lifting him clean off his feet.

Just beyond where they had been sitting the lawn sloped away and Leandri went down this like a rolling barrel, losing the wad of money and the knife. Only when his shoulders thudded into weeping willow at the base of the slope was his descent arrested. The impact squeezed a yell of hurt from his lips and brought his wife out at a run. She didn't spot him right away, obscured as he was by the willow's drooping foliage, and stood there, rigid with fright, staring at Lux.

'*Qu'est-ce qui s'est passé?*' she demanded. What happened?

'Your husband slipped and lost his balance,' Lux said blandly, indicating the groaning form below.

'Oh, *Bon Dieu!*' She rushed off down the slope like a hundred-metres sprinter leaving the blocks.

Leandri's groans intensified when she arrived at his side. As Lux suspected, the man was a great one for theatricals. Lux retrieved the dropped money and knife and resumed his seat. He crossed his right leg over his left knee and ripped the Jetfire automatic free of the two strips of masking tape that secured it to his right ankle.

Leandri's recovery, like everything else about him, was fast. He stormed up the incline, dabbing his bloody cheek with a handkerchief, his wife scampering behind him, hands fluttering.

'Give me the knife,' were his first words to Lux.

'Here.' Lux tossed it to him, waggled the gun gently to make sure he had noticed it. 'See this, Leandri? Any more tricks like that and I'll put a bullet through one of your kneecaps, or both if you really beg for it. Take it from me, the pain is excruciating. Plus, it'll be a year before you walk without crutches.'

'You don't scare me,' Leandri sneered. 'All I have to do is make a phone call and you'll be riding home in a hearse.'

'Bigger men than you have made threats like that and I'm still around.' Lux lowered the gun, let it dangle at his side, a flag of truce. 'Now, do we still have a deal, or don't we?'

Still pressing the red-stained handkerchief to his face, Leandri glowered briefly. Then came that abrupt joyful laugh that sounded as if it belonged to another person. He snapped the switchblade shut.

'You're all right, Yank,' he said, which Lux translated as praise. His wife, stopping a couple of paces short of him, broke into a smile of pure relief. Lux guessed Leandri wasn't above taking out his annoyance on her by way of good old-fashioned chastisement.

'Now we've gotten the crap out of the way,' Lux said, 'let's talk practical matters. First of all I need a passport size photograph of you.'

Leandri's eyes reduced to slits. 'For what purpose?'

'For the purpose of providing you with phoney documentation. If you want to alter your appearance, by wearing a false moustache say, or colouring your hair, that's up to you. But no glasses and no beard. You can choose your own name.'

'What about my assistant? Will he not also need identification?'

'Yes, but his face will not be his own.'

'Really?' Leandri nibbled at his lip. He waited for Lux to elaborate, his features composed in an enquiry.

'When the time comes, I'll explain. The less you know now, the less you can tell to others.'

As a fellow outlaw Leandri could not dispute the logic of Lux's preoccupation with security. With the best grace he could muster he gestured his acceptance.

It was early evening and cool up here in the foothills of the Massif when Lux left. He had achieved an understanding with Leandri. Under the flash exterior there beat the heart of a true pro, a man who would not cave in under pressure. A man who could act out a part and not forget his lines. A man who would choose his assistant with infinite care. A man, in short, who could do the job.

'Not that I know much about guns, but I understand the one Lux used was a monster, with a range of a mile or more. That may be an exaggeration, I wouldn't know. He bought it in Belgium, from some shady back-street gunrunner, I gather. Don't they call them armourers?'

Sheryl Glister to Thierry Garbe, freelance journalist, 24.03.1999.

* * *

Belgium is the legitimate supplier of an estimated eighty per cent of all illicit arms purchased in Europe. It is the only country in the EU whose citizens could buy a firearm literally 'over the counter' with minimal fuss. Of course, proof of identity must be produced. To the purchaser with no ulterior intent, this requirement causes no inconvenience. To the wrongdoer it causes no inconvenience in practice either: he or, occasionally, she, produces his or her forged or stolen documents and the transaction proceeds as smoothly as would the purchase of a box of Belgian chocolates. The purchase is logged in a register which can be, and is, inspected periodically by the police. But an entry is hardly ever checked and the false names and addresses that account for a significant proportion of the total do not call attention to themselves. Even 'Donald Duck, Disneyland, USA,' transcribed from the apparently bona-fide passport of a recent purchaser at the Boghe establishment in Leuven, raised no inspectorial eyebrows when the local *flic* dropped in for a casual thumb-through the register a few days after the entry was made.

Jean-Louis Boghe, known to his Anglo-Saxon clientele as the Bogey man, ran a legitimate retail gun store, trading as JLB Aarmz SA/NV. It was a business of respectable pedigree, established by his uncle in 1958. Following his uncle's death in 1982, ironically in a shooting accident, and in the absence of any direct heirs, Jean-Louis had taken over the business at the request of his aunt, to whom he paid a share of the profits until her death in 1994. He handled mainly hunting rifles, shotguns, and handguns for personal protection, in that order of sales volume. His wares were displayed in the window and on racks along two walls inside the spacious shop, and, in the case of handguns, under glass topped counters. The glass was bulletproof and all weapons were locked or chained in one manner or another. Ammunition was stored in a strong room in the back, the door operated by a combination lock. In short, Jean-Louis

Boghe complied with the regulations – such as they were – and was perceived by the local police as a 'responsible' arms trader.

That was the public JLB Aarmz. A profitable, secure retail outlet, with no debts and no worries. Behind the scenes or, more accurately, at his mini-chateau twenty kilometres from St Pieterskerk in the centre of Leuven, Jean-Louis Boghe ran and still runs another kind of arms operation. Here would-be purchasers need show no papers or ID. The only paper required to complete a transaction is the cash variety, any hard currency will do, but there are discounts for US dollars and Swiss francs, and gold qualifies for special terms. The hardware too has little in common with that on display in the store. Here, in the cellar with the concealed entrance below Boghe's chateau, are to be found the whole gamut of personal weaponry – from submachine guns through grenade launchers to handheld missile launchers. Boghe can also obtain killing machines with even more grunt, all the way up to surplus Russian Sukhoi strike aircraft that even come with a 12-month international warranty, courtesy of the Russian Air Force.

It was to this place that Dennis Lux was driven, from the Martelarenplein Station, on a sunny May afternoon, one of Boghe's perks to his regular clients being a chauffeured collection service. It was perhaps Lux's twelfth visit in seven years. He knew the route by heart and was particularly attracted to the rolling, wooded countryside through which it wove. The driver was Flemish, his French was non-existent, and what was more he never spoke. Or not to Lux, at any rate.

Jean-Louis Boghe was his employee's exact converse – effusive and voluble, always delighted to welcome a client back for more of his deadly wares.

'It's a pleasure to see you again, Dennis,' he burbled, wringing the American's hand as if it were a wet cloth from which he was trying to remove all moisture. 'It must be at least six months ...'

'Seven,' Lux said, blowing on his mangled digits. He was not one for flamboyance, preferring to deal at arm's length in every sense. 'And how are you, Bogey?'

'Very well, as always,' Boghe said as he hustled his visitor through to the sitting room.

Lux was pressed into the ornate Louis Quinze armchair with its tapestried upholstery. While Boghe went off to make coffee Lux looked around for recent acquisitions, the arms trader being an avid hoarder of antiques. He saw only one that he did not recognise from his last visit: a painting of a ruined mill by a placid stream, with two boys rod fishing and a dog burrowing in a patch of bare earth nearby. Far off a stand of trees in full foliage, the whole scene under the evening sun and pink tinted sky.

'Do you have the merchandise?' Lux said to Boghe, as the latter deposited a silver tray containing a coffee pot, a milk jug and two diminutive cups on a side table between Lux's chair and another identical chair. From previous meetings he knew the importance of steering Boghe straight onto the matter in hand, otherwise he would ramble for ever about old times, politics, art, the never-ending stream of regulations spewed out by the EU Commission, anything at all but business.

'It is here,' Boghe said, pouring coffee for both of them. 'It is not easy to get hold of, you know, this particular rifle.'

'Oh, quit hyping up the price, Bogey. You know me better than that.'

Boghe's grin was sheepish. Now in his fifty-first year he looked and behaved like a much younger man; only his thinning blond hair devalued the impression. He was very sensitive about his depleted locks and forever resolving to consult a trichology practitioner. Too vain, too self-conscious, he would probably put it off until it was too late for anything but a full-blown wig.

Lux drained his cup in a single swallow. Boghe made superb coffee and he gladly accepted the offer of a refill. Boghe, sipping his, eyed the American speculatively, wondering who was going to be on the receiving end of the prodigious half-inch calibre bullets that his chosen weapon fired.

'A big job, eh?' he hazarded.

'One day your curiosity will get you killed,' Lux said, his tone light, his meaning serious. 'Like the cat.'

'You are right. Me and my big nose.' Boghe polished off his coffee. 'Shall we go?'

'Lead on, pal.'

To access the underground store-room involved entering a study whose walls were lined with bookshelves. A two-foot wide section was designed to swing out on command from a remote control; beyond lay a steel door with a digital combination lock. Boghe would key in a five-digit code and lo! the door would swing inwards. Stone steps, much worn, led down to the vast, air-conditioned cellar where in days gone by only wine had been stored.

Here, on a very long oak table, stood the gun Lux had ordered and already half paid for. It was propped on a bipod, facing towards three conventional round targets, standing side by side, as yet unblemished. Beside the gun a square carton of ammunition, bearing the red Winchester cowboy logo and prominent 'X' for excellence, and beside the carton a set of ear muffs.

Lux descended the steps behind Boghe and together they walked over to the table. Without touching the rifle, Lux circumnavigated the table, viewing the gun from all angles. The Barrett Model M82A1 "Special Application Scoped Rifle" (to cite its US armed forces designation) is manufactured in the USA by Barrett Firearms Manufacturing Inc. of Murfreesboro, Tennessee, and is in service with the US Marine Corps, the Navy SEALS, and Special Forces in a number of countries. It is nearly six feet long, fires a 0.5in calibre round, and is accurate at over a mile – a distance that the bullet takes about two seconds to travel. It has an exceptionally flat velocity up to half a mile, one reason why Lux had chosen it. This particular version was fitted with the detachable arrowhead muzzle brake which, for the job in hand, would be replaced by a sound suppressor. The fold-down carrying handle that was normally attached to the upper housing had been removed at Lux's behest.

'A magnificent weapon,' Boghe remarked, dwelling on it as if it were his personal creation. 'None better for range and hitting power.'

Lux grunted his agreement then reached across the table and hefted the gun. It weighed a muscle-aching thirty pounds fully-loaded with ten rounds. 'A monster' Boghe had called it and the description was apt. But it was the gun for the job. Because of the size of the bullet a hit on what is euphemistically known as a soft target almost anywhere above the waist was almost guaranteed to result in death – if not from destruction of a vital organ, then from the trauma to the system or massive loss of blood.

Lux walked to the far end of the table and set the gun down there. He looked pointedly at Boghe.

'It is loaded,' Boghe confirmed.

'And the silencers?'

'The sound suppressors are ready. I made three and tested one to destruction. Do you wish to test another one here?'

Lux shook his head. 'I trust you.'

'*J'espère bien.* Now I will leave you to test to your satisfaction.'

'Give me thirty minutes.'

Lux waited until he was alone. He peeled off his jacket and hung it on the nearest of a row of coat hooks screwed to the wall. He rolled up his sleeves. He positioned the ear muffs headband very precisely on his head. He climbed on to the table and spread-eagled himself behind the Barrett. He tucked the rubber-padded stock into his shoulder and cocked the gun, appreciating the healthy clack of the first round entering the breech.

Even with the Swarovski scope set at a modest 3X magnification, the middle of the target's three roundels filled it. He positioned the crosshairs plumb centre of the bull. He wrapped his fingers around the pistol-type grip. He caressed the trigger lightly, assessing the amount of slack in the two-stage pull.

He fired and took out the whole bull in one.

* * *

Lux counted the last five-hundred-franc note onto the table.

'Delivery included – right?'

'But of course. And the address?'

The address was always different, always used only once. Accommodation addresses prepared to accept illicit merchandise were scarce and commanded a high premium but were a necessary precaution. Lux dictated the details and Boghe scrawled them in a hand that to Lux was indecipherable. Nonetheless, the goods always seemed to get there, so he had long since ceased to ask the arms trader to read it back.

'On the 23rd,' Boghe said. 'Probably late afternoon.'

Lux didn't even bother to emphasise the need for delivery not to be delayed. It was never necessary to repeat any instruction or double check with Boghe. The rapport and mutual understanding between client and supplier was absolute, as it must be between all lawbreakers.

'Two more things,' Lux said, as he shoved his wallet back in his jacket pocket. 'I prefer the Ubertl Mil-dot scope to the Swarovski. See to it, will you?'

'Perfectionist. You realise they are only made for the US Marines and the FBI. They are as hard to come by as square eggs.'

'Just get me one, Bogey. Bribe and corrupt in high places.'

'And the other thing?'

'Raufoss ammunition.'

Boghe looked mildly startled. 'That is even more difficult than the scope. I don't traffic in that stuff.'

'I know.' Lux put his arm around Boghe's shoulder and they walked towards the door like that. 'But I'm sure you know someone who does.'

Boghe went through a pantomime of lip-pursing and eyebrow-writhing before finally nodding. 'But it will be very expensive. Maybe thirty dollars apiece. The risks are considerable.'

'Twenty rounds, okay, Bogey?'

'Okay, Dennis. You're the boss.'

They had reached the door.

'You got it,' Lux said, and with a farewell pat on the arms trader's shoulder he went out to the waiting car.

We questioned the Senator unofficially but he refused to name the Minister concerned. He claims that it is privileged information. He intends to resign shortly so we have no levers to use on him. Otherwise he was co-operative and provided a detailed account of the only meeting he attended when both Commissaire BARAIL and Rafael SIMONELLI were present.

In my opinion it would not be appropriate to employ sterner interrogation methods on such a public figure unless we are prepared to send him on a holiday afterward, which decision I leave to the highest authority. (AUTHOR'S NOTE: the precise phrase used in this top secret memo was 'faire le passer ses vacances', understood to be French Security Services doublespeak for 'kill.')

Extract from memo from CG/CSP to Minister of the Interior, 20.05.1996. Filed 21.05.1996.

*   *   *

With the walking stick he affected when posing as a member of the landed gentry Commissaire Barail slashed at the clump of dandelions that lay in his path, and succeeded in causing an explosion of spores. It was a childish act and he derived a childish pleasure from it. He began to hum under his breath.

As he and his three fellow walkers breasted a gentle incline, the chateau ahead rose in magnificent contrast to the backdrop of hills, chequered yellow with rape and green with young corn. The sun shone from a velvet blue sky that was blotched only lightly with benign cumuli. It was spring, and the land was aglow with it.

The man on Barail's left, a Minister of State in the Socialist Government of Alain Juppé, glanced at him, his brow corrugated with anxiety. Shorter than Barail he had difficulty keeping up, and the uneven, uncultivated terrain did not suit his city-trained feet. The other two members of this exclusive group found the pace no hardship: a bearded, bespectacled Simonelli positively loping along on his long legs, and the youngest of the group, a Gaullist member of the Senate and hard-line nationalist, bursting fit from a rigid regime of exercising.

'Jean-Marie is not as sanguine as you appear to be about using this ... this mercenary,' the Minister puffed, arms swinging wildly as if to generate momentum. The uncut grass whipped at his legs.

'How do we know he will not attempt to extort additional payment from us afterwards?'

'*I* know,' Barail replied confidently, 'and that is enough. You must trust me, Patrick, and so must our revered leader. You have put me in the driving seat, you must leave the choice of tools to me. Do not interfere, *je t'en prie*.'

'At least tell me his name, anything ... Is he a Frenchman?'

'He is not. And this I have decided on reflection is preferable. The man must be seen to be a renegade, an outsider ...'

'An outlaw,' Simonelli put in.

The Senator gave a grunt of accord. 'All who will be in and with the new cabinet must be ... be untainted.' The choice of word pleased him to the point of absurdity, and he nodded to himself, smiling. 'You must insist on it,' he emphasised, with a sharp look at the Minister.

'Self-delusion,' Simonelli sneered and was surprised when the Senator did not rise to the barb.

'Tell me then,' the Minister said, almost in desperation, 'what can I convey to Jean-Marie? I cannot go back empty-handed. Can you give me a date? The political moves must be planned too, you know. For you this may be just a military operation, but unless we of the Government act in concert with you and with each other, the blow will have been struck for nothing.'

Barail stopped suddenly. Waited for the others to gather round him, anticipating.

'Tell him that we are meeting our man here, tomorrow, to settle the practical aspects. Tell him ... in June at the latest we will strike. The exact date cannot be revealed yet, not until our man has made his preparations. But it shall be no later than June.' He treated the Minister to the smile that could disarm as readily as that of an attractive child. 'Will that do?'

The Minister squinted at Barail, for the sun was behind him, white and brilliant; the heat of it brought pimples of sweat to his forehead. 'It is not much. But if that is all you can give me ...' He shrugged. 'I will leave you now. Come, Georges.'

Hands were shaken. The two politicians walked on, leaving Barail gazing at their backs.

'It will take more than the likes of such men to make France great again,' he lamented. He looked sidelong at the inscrutable Corsican. 'Only such as you and I could do that.'

Simonelli, hot in his dark wool suit, snapped a twig from the overhanging branch of a pear tree.

'And we care only about the money,' he said simply.

'*Allo, allo!*' he blared into the mouthpiece.

'Napoleon?'

'Ah, Sheryl, *ma chérie*. Are you in France?'

'Soon will be. Listen, Napoleon, I want to call a final meeting of the full committee – you, me, Barail and Lux. I'll be bringing Gary with me.'

Simonelli smoothed a slim eyebrow with a moistened finger. 'To what end? Everything is in place. We don't need to talk about it. The talking is over.'

'For once just do as you're told,' Sheryl said in a voice that resembled the crunch of a bad gear change. 'I'm running this show, not you. Set it up for Thursday next week, or Friday at the latest.'

'Very well,' Simonelli conceded sulkily. 'Telephone me this time tomorrow. I can't guarantee Lux will have called in. If not, it will be the day after. Where is this meeting to take place?'

'Wherever is easiest for everyone to converge. Auxerre, I suppose, if we're to keep you out of jail.'

'And afterwards, shall I see you?'

'Before *and* after if you like, darling. It's been a long famine.'

'Then I forgive you.'

'Napoleon?'

'Yes?'

'You're an asshole.'

The line went dead.

The French term for display dummies is *mannequins pour étalages*, and it was under this heading that Lux tracked down an outfit called 'Window', in an industrial zone in the town of Carron, not far from Nice.

They were manufacturers not distributors and reluctant to supply a one-off to a private individual.

'It is not that we ourselves have any objection, *monsieur*,' the large lady from the sales department explained, 'simply that, if the word got around we would lose the confidence of our wholesale customers. You understand, I am sure.'

Oh, yes, Lux quite understood. Now, he wheedled, how about selling him two standard models from stock for 2,000 francs cash each. Just parcel them up, put the money in your pocket and none would be the wiser.

'*Monsieur*!' came the affronted response.

Lux sighed. 'Okay, okay, three thousand each.'

Five minutes later he was arranging the dummies in the trunk of his car, cocooned to the point of unrecognizability in brown paper, mute and unresisting, their joints malleable and conforming to his every wish and whim. The large *dame*, flapping about him like a torn sail, was anxious for him to be up and away, the banknotes scorching the bodice of her voluminous flowered dress, where she had stuffed them.

He drove back along the dusty, unfinished road, off the industrial estate, and took the N202 down into Nice.

* * *

'A two-piece suit, *monsieur*? Our selection is infinite. Do step this way, if you please.'

Staff in the retail drapery world are the most well-mannered of all shop assistants, Lux found, irrespective of nationality and the quality of the establishment. Maybe the rag trade exercises a peculiar attraction to those of servile disposition. If so, he couldn't understand why.

The fawning assistant at this draper's store in Fréjus, male, homosexual naturally, fifty or so with bifocal-lensed glasses, led Lux into an inner sanctum, where suits were suspended in ranks as if on parade.

'I want a middle quality,' Lux said, and reeled off a few

measurements. 'And I want two identical.'

'*Ah, bon!*' the salesman exclaimed, overtly gratified. 'But *monsieur* is quite broad of shoulder, our stock of suits in your size is limited ... Is it absolutely essential that they are identical?'

'Absolutely.'

From then on the salesman went to it with a will. In the end he dug up five suits that would fit and which he could supply in duplicate. Lux settled for a charcoal grey with a subtle beige check costing over 3,000 francs apiece. Steep for what would be a single wearing, but what the hell? It wasn't every day he knocked off a Head of State. The least he could do was dress for the occasion. With a little arm twisting the salesman threw in two identical ties for free. He paid in cash.

*   *   *

Just a few streets away but as spiritually remote from the bustling shopping precinct on rue Jean Jaures as is New York's Bowery from Fifth Avenue, was the fancy dress hire business where, almost one month ago, Lux had booked his gendarme uniform. He went on foot. It had a shop front but only just, barely a door's width of window.

The gendarme's uniform was bagged up and waiting for him. He paid the balance of a week's hire charge in cash. The male assistant showed surprise at the length of the hire term. Lux offered no explanation, put his anonymous cash receipt in the bag and ten seconds later he was gone.

To Philippe Mazé, that most scrupulous and conscientious of police officers, it was a nightmare scenario: seven days from now the President of the Republic could be off on his holidays in the Var, knowing that an assassin was waiting for him and that, notwithstanding the elaborate precautions now pending and shortly to be in place, he could be gunned down or blown up or whatever. Bodyguards galore would surround him. The house and grounds would be swept for interlopers and explosive devices. All the extensive security machinery would be brought into play to preserve and protect France's ruler. Yet no measures on Earth could wholly eliminate the jeopardy in which the President would be placing himself. Only when the assassin and his employers were caught and put behind bars would he be able to resume his normal routine, with only a squad of bodyguards instead of an army.

From his north-facing window Mazé could just make out part of the anti-clockwise carriageway of the *Périphérique*. Traffic was almost stationary, as ever at nine-fifteen on a mid-week morning. It was a windless day and over the city as a whole lay a dirty brown pall of pollution. He didn't like to dwell on what it did to people's lungs, breathing in that muck, so he stepped away from the window and hunted for a cigarette.

He decided to set down on paper an evaluation of the present status, a gathering of his thoughts, and present it as a memo to Le Renard. If nothing else it would clear his fuddled head and shovel some of the shit upwards instead of letting it all heap up on his desk. A smouldering cigarette in the corner of his mouth, he contemplated the mass of files on the groaning shelves, stuffed with records and reports that went back to the late seventies. All that information, all that sweat, and none of it was of the least value in this unique case.

He considered the protagonists one by one, starting with Barail, *Commissaire Divisionnaire* in the CRS, number two in the presidential security corps to Le Renard. Professionally speaking, he was finished of course, would end up in a cell on a diet of bread and potatoes. Meanwhile, he surely had more secrets to impart than Lucille had extracted from him. But to haul him in was to blow the plot and maybe they would, maybe they wouldn't get him to name the top dog. Or bitch. The last thought brought a wry smile to Mazé's face. He personally still doubted a woman could or would initiate an assassination attempt. There was something un-womanly about it. The moneybag's wife, the Chink, had been more or less ruled out following Maurice Incardona's enquiries.

Stubbing out his cigarette and igniting another, he returned to his appraisal of Barail's role. Le Renard had been adamant about leaving the *Commissaire* to go about his business for now. He didn't want the conspiracy aborted, end of story. Since Barail was no longer a menace, Mazé was not disposed to argue the point. Recommended course of action then? None, as far as Barail was concerned.

So what about Simonelli. Officially a fugitive but no one had a clue where he was. Lucille had confirmation from Barail that a man he referred to as 'the Corsican' was in cahoots with him. On the recordings he didn't speak of this man as a straight partner, or his confederate, or his equal, rather as someone who had been foisted on him. Her hunch was that this person acted as the intermediary between the principal and Barail, and Mazé tended to agree with her reading. So find Simonelli and just maybe he would lead them directly to the boss. Right then. Recommended course of action: set in train an all-out manhunt for the Corsican.

The other lead player was the Jackal Mk 2 himself – Hull, or whatever name he was masquerading under. His Menton home was under permanent surveillance but whenever he was away, which was most of the time, he was left to travel freely. Mazé's reasoning, shared by Le Renard, was that putting a tail on Jackal 2 (or should it be 3?) would be the same as telling him he was rumbled. An even greater danger was that the American would ambush the tail and make him sing. So his comings and goings were allowed to remain a mystery. Would it really make any difference knowing where he was, what he was doing, Mazé had continued to ask himself over the past weeks. His reluctant conclusion was invariably that it would not. It simply offended his professional mores to leave a contract killer loose on the streets of French cities. No, what really mattered was his timetable and his method. The two key questions, still unanswered.

Mazé thrust spread fingers into his unruly hair and created hirsute havoc. The responsibility of it all didn't worry him – not much, it didn't. The fact was, though he kept it well hidden, he was fucking *frantic*. If anything went wrong it wouldn't be Le Renard's head up for the chop; the old bastard wasn't called Le Renard because he lacked cunning and the survival instinct. Even if the President was blown away, the CG would still be there at the end of it all, sitting in his flash office, immune to the crisis that a successful assassination would unleash upon France.

So Mazé's preference would be to pull the Jackal in when next he showed up in Menton. Grill him for every last syllable of information and get rid of the husk. The man was already on record as a killer so why go easy on him? Yet with the Jackal as with Barail, no direct connection with the mastermind of the operation had been established. The Jackal generally reported to Barail. If he couldn't name names from higher up the tree it would be a pointless, indeed destructive, exercise.

For all that, Mazé felt on balance that the Jackal should be rendered inactive, prevented from making his attempt on the President's life. It was the more sure option. Recommended course of action: arrest Hull and question him. Rigorously.

So be it. His notes completed, Mazé threw down his much-gnawed pen. He would dictate a memo to Le Renard this instant and insist on discussing it with him tomorrow at the latest.

He picked up his dictaphone, frowned as he composed his thoughts, then clicked the record button.

'After long deliberation,' he intoned, as always slightly uncomfortable speaking into a machine, 'on the options open to us I have arrived at certain conclusions …'

A telephone call to Barail confirmed that Leandri's phoney RG pass was ready. It would be available for collection in the place where Lux collected his documentation, two days hence. The key would be left in an envelope at the Razzmatazz Bar in St Raphael. Ask for Frédéric, who would expect a generous tip in return.

'Our leader wants a final meeting of the Board,' Barail said, cutting into Lux's '*Au revoir.*'

'What for?'

'To satisfy herself that all is in place according to plan. Simonelli will be present too.'

Lux wasn't wild about the idea. 'Why add to the risks? All of us together, that's asking for trouble.'

'She insists, and Simonelli is right behind her, naturally. In front of her too.'

Lux had wondered about the relationship between Rafael Simonelli and the woman he knew as Jill Walker. Barail's off-the-cuff remark didn't come completely out of the blue therefore.

'Okay, so we meet. Where and when?'

'Probably Auxerre, next Thursday. Call me tomorrow at the same time.'

In France gunshots are commonplace and one does not prick up one's ears at the sound. Hunting guns are sold over the counter with few constraints and the killing of game is widespread. If you choose to pump lead at anything that moves or at a caricature of President Chirac, none will say you nay so long as you do so within your territorial boundaries, i.e. in your own backyard. If you wish to extend your bloodletting farther afield you need a *Permis de Chasse* – a hunter's licence – for which a kind of examination must be sat, to prove you know when to shoot which species of game. It's a straightforward enough process and the exam itself, provided you've swotted up on the subject, does not require a high IQ. Lux had obtained his permit after moving to Menton, nearly two years previously.

Because he did not want his neighbours to hear him blasting off with an abbreviated field gun, he drove up into the Massif to put the Barrett through its paces. Unlike many he did not regard forests as suitable screening for clandestine deeds. The concealment it provides works two ways, it allows you to be spied on. His preference was for a bare chunk of land, ideally with some high ground or other eminence between it and any nearby highway. Such a piece of real estate is to be found beyond the village of Plan-de-la-Tour, out on the D74, heading west. An overgrown track serves an uninhabited house, burned down by its owner in the summer of 1994 in an insurance scam, so local mythology went. It is about half a kilometre from the road, which is little used, especially early in the season, and anyone on the far side of the house cannot be seen. The landscape thereabouts is of rolling hillside, descending to the coast, and relatively treeless for most of the distance. Ideal for his purpose.

Just after dawn he parked the hired Safrane behind the burnt-out house. He was wearing shorts, a drill shirt with big button-down pockets and epaulettes, and Nike sneakers that were showing their age but were as comfortable as carpet slippers. On his head a forage cap, also of a certain antiquity, and Polaroid sunglasses.

Getting out of the car, he perched on one fender and smoked a cigarette, slowly and with relish. When it was finished he stubbed it in the car ashtray. He unloaded the two naked window dummies from the trunk and set them up against the house's blackened end wall about a metre apart. He fetched a length of yellow chalk from the shallow tray on the car's dashboard and proceeded to draw a crude round target of about fifteen centimetres diameter on the wall space between the dummies' heads, adding a single bulls-eye the size of his fist. At eight hundred metres anything smaller, even magnified to the limit of the telescopic sight, would be too small to hit. He tucked a roll of clear plastic sheet down the back of his waistband, shoved one of the two silencers Boghe had supplied in his hip pocket, hooked a headband of ear muffs around his neck, and slung a bag of loose .50 calibre shells over his shoulder. Finally he hoisted the Barrett rifle across his other shoulder and began to walk, away from the house and across the scrubby ground in roughly an easterly direction.

The sun peeping over the skyline had as yet no warmth and the dew sparkled on the rare patches of grass like scattered gemstones. It was the sort of morning that takes a couple of years off your age and puts bounce in your step. It was his favourite time of the day.

His paces were even and measured. He counted them as he had counted up the slope from the Crillon house to the copse. At eight hundred exactly he stopped and turned towards the house. He could afford to be fifty paces out plus or minus and it would make no difference to the accuracy of his shooting. Anything more and he would lose maybe a millimetre of precision for every metre of distance. He would have to be out in his calculations by a hundred metres or more to miss altogether.

Apart from his indoor trials at Boghe's chateau, he had zero first-hand experience of the Barrett. But he had worked with a variety of rifles in the past and so long as the sights were correctly set, the model, calibre, size and style of gun – unless it was of substandard manufacture – was a matter of indifference to him. The Barrett had several advantages over more conventional riflery. For a start its long barrel gave it greater range and a flatter trajectory. Its large calibre also meant that a clean kill was more likely. And its bipod provided stability. It was the ultimate assassin's weapon.

Keeping hold of the gun, he one-handedly shook out the plastic sheet and spread it on the dry earth. He swung out the bipod legs and splayed them. He placed the gun carefully on the sheet, muzzle pointing towards the house. The bill of the forage cap shielded his eyes as he studied his targets. His vision was near twenty-twenty but at this distance the dummies were no more than pink smudges against the wall.

The sun was behind him and he could feel its growing heat on the back of his neck. The forecast was for twenty-five degrees Celsius, with a mistral predicted to arrive in the evening. He got down on his knees then on his belly. He removed the magazine and flipped the ten Winchester rounds it contained onto the plastic. Taking his time, he examined each one for flaws. It takes a lot of imperfection to make a cartridge jam and an absolute guarantee against a misfire doesn't exist. But it was his custom and he stuck to it religiously. Satisfied that they were as good as factory-made ammunition would ever be (which, it has to be said, is pretty good), he reloaded and refitted the magazine. His last act of preparation was to transfer the ear muffs from his neck to his ears.

The two sound suppressors Boghe had supplied were identical and not designed for longevity – a truly efficient silencer never is. Presently he would test the one he had brought with him, then discard it. To begin with he would fire the gun unmuffled.

At a range of eight hundred metres, which is long bordering on extreme, he expected to achieve a 6-inch grouping with all shots. But the object of this expedition was not to check out his shooting skills – though it would serve to reaffirm them; it was to put the weapon through its paces in 'field' conditions and above all to set up the sights for optimum results.

He tucked the stock with its soft recoil pad into his armpit. He wrapped his fingers almost lovingly around the pistol grip. His body was completely relaxed, his breathing regular and light. He flipped open the hinged covers of the Ubertl mil-dot recticle scope and set it to full magnification. A squint down it brought the dummies up close, the equivalent of less than a hundred metres. He sighted on the left hand one. He operated the cocking lever and a round slid without effort into the firing chamber. The wall of the house faced almost true east and was therefore brightly lit by the rising sun and the pink plastic of the dummies stood out well against the blackened crepi. He altered the position of the gun slightly, bringing the crosshairs to bear on the bull of his chalked target, roughly midway in the space between the two heads. His hold on the pistol grip tightened. His finger hooked around the rather wide trigger and commenced a gentle caress. The application of pressure to the trigger creates a reflex contraction in the tendons in the space between thumb and forefinger, so that the space between grip and trigger is caught in a clamp that grows tighter and tighter until the trigger mechanism trips and the process set in train by which the firing pin travels forwards and discharges the cartridge. It is this equalisation of pressure which ensures a true aim; conversely, the tendency among the unskilled to drag or jerk at the trigger guarantees a miss.

He breathed in, once-twice-three times, and held the air in his lungs. The crosshairs were so steady on the bull they might have been drawn there. A final squeeze of the trigger and the massive round sped on its way with a boom that sent every bird within five hundred metres erupting into the air and doubtless every mammal scurrying for cover. The recoil shoved him back several inches on the plastic sheet, the pad absorbing most of the kick. The report racketed off across the open ground with no echo and hardly any lingering resonance.

His opening shot struck the wall pretty much where he intended, raising a puff of crepi and brick dust. He examined it through the scope. The hole was not round but more or less trapezoid in shape. He hoped the bullet had been stopped within the ruined building and not travelled on through all the walls to emerge from the other side. Although properties in the vicinity were few and far between, there was always the danger of a stray bullet causing collateral damage. Barrett-propelled bullets travelled a heck of a distance.

For his second shot he placed the crosshairs on the hole. In theory, if his aim was perfect, the bullet would pass through without touching the brickwork. In practice, because no two rounds are exactly the same, this was an unlikely outcome. Again the pincer action of finger and thumb, the pressure on the trigger, the sensation of metal moving against metal. *Boom*! A much smaller puff this time. He checked it through the scope. A minuscule alteration to the shape of the hole was just detectable. It was a near-exact bull, the payoff of years of practice, a regime never neglected, never compromised. That, coupled with a first class weapon.

The third shot was a whisker to the right, chipping a notch in the blackened crepi. Numbers four to six passed through the same hole without visibly touching its sides. Seven was a repeat of three, but a smidgen lower. Eight to ten were spot on. Overall, it was an even better performance than he had hoped.

The outside of the muzzle was threaded to a depth of about 1cm to accommodate the arrowhead muzzle brake, which he now unscrewed and replaced with a silencer. The thread was coarse and required only three turns to lock it fast. The silencer was a top notch job made of fibre glass, and was maybe two inches in diameter and ten inches long. A pure silencer would have knocked about twenty per cent off the gun's power and lowered the velocity of the bullet to below that of sound, which in turn would make for a less flat trajectory – at eight-hundred metres to target, an unacceptable penalty. Hence Lux had specified a sound suppressor, which has negligible retarding effect on the bullet's velocity. It would deaden the crash of the discharge, though the supersonic crack of the bullet would still be audible. Crucially, the suppression of the blast would make it difficult for anyone in the target area to trace its source, thus alleviating the hazards he would face in the immediate sequel to the kill. It would buy him valuable seconds that could make the difference between escape and capture. Or death.

A major drawback of the most effective silencing products is their limited life. After six shots it would be finished, or at least unreliable, the internal baffles burned out. In this instance it was not a factor. Lux reckoned on taking out the President with one or at most two bullets. If he needed more the attempt would be a bust, no matter what.

When fitted the ten-inch tube added to the already considerable length, of course, though he would carry it separately and only screw it in place just before the kill. Because of its lightness the silencer barely influenced the balance of the gun and any tendency to muzzle heaviness was negated by use of the bipod.

Removing the ear muffs, he refilled the magazine, not rushing, inspecting every round. The brass cartridge case of one bullet had a shallow dimple; he returned it to his pocket. The gun reloaded and cocked, he sighted on the hole. Holding his breath, he fired. A cough, no, a grunt, the gun's kick no less vicious than normal; the smack of the round into the wall a good inch below the hole was as loud as the whip crack of the bullet travelling at the speed of Concorde. Surprised by the extent of the miss, he loosed off the next four rounds with great care and precision, noting that the last shot made more noise than its predecessors as the silencer began to degrade. He had produced about a three-inch grouping, thrown a shade low and to the right. Still within his personal tolerances. With the jeweller's screwdriver he made a tiny adjustment to the horizontal hair to compensate for the trajectory curve. None at all for the throw to the right. It was insignificant, a couple of millimetres, and the other silencer might throw to the left and he wouldn't know until the day.

To make sure he wasn't imagining the deterioration in performance of the silencer he tested it to destruction: after five more rounds – a two-inch grouping – it was displaying a marked loss of efficiency as the sound suppression material was burned away by the muzzle blast.

His eardrums were ringing from the noise of the last few

rounds, so he replaced the ear protection. Leaving the silencer in situ, he reloaded yet again and slammed the first round into the firing chamber. With the stock snuggling into his now-aching shoulder and his finger hovering over the trigger he positioned the crosshairs dead centre of the left hand dummy's moon face. One, two, three breaths, hold it, squeeze the trigger. The now unsuppressed crash of the gun galvanised wildlife anew but Lux heard little of the commotion, cocooned as he was within his ear muffs. Through the telescope he watched dispassionately as the head was literally blown to fragments, leaving a neatly decapitated body.

'Right on,' he whispered to himself. 'Say your prayers, Mister Chirac.'

He swung the barrel on to the other dummy and went through the now familiar procedure. The result was identical, the head bursting asunder as if a grenade had gone off inside it. It was a testimony to the awesome destructive force of the high calibre bullet.

By now the sun was well clear of the hills to the east and already signalling hot times to come. It was almost seven. Early risers would be up and about and maybe getting curious about the gunshots. He dragged the ear muffs off and left them around his neck. The birds were beginning to settle down once more. Now there was only the odd chirp, the drawl of an aircraft too high to be seen. Few realise how remote are some parts of the South of France. Even at the height of summer it is still possible to escape the milling multitudes by avoiding the coastline and the more obvious tourist attractions.

He hunted round for the fallen cartridge cases. It took a while to find them but he persevered until all twenty-two were accounted for. He dropped them in the shoulder bag with the remaining live rounds and carried bag, plastic sheet, gun and the other bits and pieces back to the car. Under the dash was a vacuum flask. He swigged the lime juice, kept chilled by fast shrinking ice cubes. He loaded the headless dummies in the trunk of the car, plus the larger fragments of plastic scattered about the immediate area, and stamped the smaller pieces into the earth. The only other evidence of his handicraft was the holes in the wall of the house. He yanked a tuft of grass from the soil and scrubbed at the holes with the root, artificially ageing them. The bullets themselves were long gone, scattered about the countryside.

A last look around and he was all through there, never to return.

All his efforts to secure an interview by consent having failed, Maurice Incardona had spent most of the preceding week tailing Soon-Li Nixon all over the city. She only ever ventured out in her chauffeur-driven Mercedes, with a minder riding shotgun. And the minder, a Schwarzeneggar clone in build, was not someone Incardona, for all his skills in unarmed combat, cared to tackle.

Today he was in luck. Soon-Li, accompanied by a relative or friend of the same ethnic origins, went shopabout in Auckland's snooty Newmarket district. After a protracted dawdle through the shopping mall they finished up in the trendy Modes of Broadway fashion store, leaving the minder on sentry duty in the doorway. Incardona avoided him by entering via a side door and tagged along behind the two women as they meandered from skirts to trousers to lingerie to dresses, chattering endlessly and incomprehensibly to each other. His chance came when the companion went off to the rest room and Soon-Li plunged into a changing cubicle, staggering under armfuls of cocktail dresses. A quick glance left and right assured Incardona that the only sales assistant in this section was otherwise occupied and he darted into the cubicle to confront a startled Soon-Li, already stripped down to fetching apricot-hued bra and pants.

As she opened her mouth to yell Incardona clapped his hand over it, forcing her back against the wall, and for good measure rammed an automatic pistol into her cheek.

'One sound and you're dead,' he said in his passable English, putting on the tough gangster voice he used when intimidating people. 'Understand?'

She stared back at him with fearful eyes.

'Do you understand?' he snarled, and thrust his knee between her thighs, promptly giving himself the first stirrings of an erection.

Soon-Li was no shrinking violet. She had had a tough upbringing in Hong Kong and her education had included the best part of a decade as prostitute and stripper, starting while she was still a schoolgirl. Incardona's pistol wasn't the first she had seen from the business end.

So she recovered fast. Nodded three or four times and was rewarded by a fractional lessening of the pressure on her cheekbone.

'All I want is a little information,' he said, which produced another series of nods.

With her nearly naked body pressed against his he was finding it hard to keep his mind on priorities. His erection was now full-blown and he guessed she could feel it.

'You want rape me?' she said in a childlike voice, on the surface not in the least perturbed at the prospect. 'You want make jig-a-jig?'

He wouldn't have said no but the murmur of voices was all around, only feet away. Apart from which she would probably yell 'rape', the minute it was over. The resultant uproar, if they were discovered, would finish him forever as a Government employee.

'Shut up, bitch. All I want from you is the name of the person who runs the Greenwar organisation.'

Soon-Li gaped. 'You not want rape?'

'Greenwar,' he repeated, in his gangster snarl. 'Who's in charge?'

'You not want jig-a-jig?'

Incardona raised his eyes to the ceiling and wondered if her vocabulary was limited to words with a sexual connotation.

'Green-war,' he enunciated, slowly and precisely. 'Who is boss?'

Her expression cleared and she smiled, further feeding Incardona's lust.

'Ah, Greenwar. Boss is Sheryl.' She had difficulty getting her tongue around the name; it came out as 'Sheller.'

'Sheryl Glister?'

'Yes, that her name. Eddie give her lot of money. I try to get back, it my money. I Eddie's wife.'

'Are you all right in there, madam?' called someone on the other side of the cubicle curtain.

'Answer,' a nervous Incardona hissed in her ear, jabbing anew with the gun.

A second telling was not required.

'I okay,' she called back. 'Trying dresses, okay?'

'That's fine,' said the assistant and was heard moving away.

'You help me get money back from Sheller?' Soon-Li said, tugging at the lapels of Incardona's jacket.

'What?' he said. He backed away, holstered the gun. Then, thinking quickly and reminding himself to speak as to a five-year old, 'Yes, yes ... I detective. We find Sheryl Glister. We get your money.'

She swayed towards him, eyes sparkling mischief, her nipples salaciously defined through the thin silky material of her bra.

'It true, you get my money?' Now her hand was at his fly, unzipping. 'Okay, mister, I let you make jig-a-jig.'

*   *   *

That evening he sent a short note to Le Renard via the overnight diplomatic bag. The note read:

Sheryl Glister confirmed head of Greenwar. No other known executive. Present whereabouts uncertain, presume Europe. Await your further instructions.

The last item on Lux's list of material needs was a face mask in his own likeness. Enquiries via an acquaintance who worked for Canal Plus, the pay-tv channel, led to a special effects outfit in Fontainebleau.

To avoid leaving traces of his movements as D-Day drew nearer, he went by car, a journey of some nine hours, excluding breaks. After an overnight stay at the rustic Legris et Parc Hotel he presented himself at the reception desk of SPEFEX at nine. A woman – brisk, business-like, early forties and very Irish – took charge of him.

'You're going to make a lovely mask, Mr Vincent,' she said after introducing herself – her name was Moira; well, that's what it sounded like. The spelling was probably something like Maireagh.

'You wouldn't make a bad one yourself,' he riposted in kind.

She cackled, nudged him, and said something like 'G'wan with you. I expect you use that kind of blarney on all the girls.'

That was as far as the flirting went. She whisked him off to a room that reminded him of a hairdresser's salon, with its padded reclining seats, wall-width mirrors, wash basins and impedimenta of the trade. There he was handed over to yet another obvious queer. This one had a Canadian accent and was called Timothy.

The next two hours were among the most uncomfortable he could recall ever spending. His hair was tucked under a hair net, which made him feel foolish – especially when Moira poked her head around the door and sniggered, 'Hello there, Granny.' His eyes were covered in small circular pads, two slender plastic tubes like drinking straws were stuck up his nostrils, and he was ready for the plaster to be applied.

Timothy used his hands for this part of the process, smearing the stuff that smelled like splatch over every exposed piece of skin from hairline to Adam's apple.

'Whatever you do now, you must not so much as *twitch* a facial muscle, dear. Don't talk, don't lick your lips – it tastes positively *awful,* I can tell you. Grunt if you understand.'

Lux grunted.

Timothy puckered his lips into a blown kiss and minced out, leaving Lux to his own devices. He sighed through his nose and resigned himself to 'ninety-minutes minimum' immobility. Only a CD player, from which a soothing sonata trickled forth, remained to keep him in touch with reality.

When Timothy returned, one hour and forty minutes later, Lux was ready to start smashing things. The eye pads and tubes were discarded. Then began the unpeeling process. This was slow and tedious. 'It tears easily,' Timothy explained. In the event it came off in one-piece, like the shed skin of a lizard.

'*Voila!*' Timothy rejoiced, dangling the mask before him for inspection. 'Aren't I a clever boy, then?'

'And aren't I an ugly one?' Lux said. The only likeness he saw in the facsimile was to a chamois leather, and a well-used one at that.

He mopped his face with the damp towel Timothy handed him.

'Now what?'

Timothy simpered. 'Now, you lovely man, we put your spare face on a dummy's head to preserve its shape and put it in a padded box to keep it intact.'

'Sounds very organised.'

Timothy made humming birds wings of his eyelashes. 'Are you staying overnight in Fontainebleau?'

Lux shook his head without regret. 'I have business down south.'

'Oh, well,' Timothy pouted, and flounced off, dangling the mask from finger and thumb.

Lux was done here. The finished article was delivered to him at the front desk by Moira in person. The carton that contained it was a solid affair. 'Uncrushable,' Moira assured him. 'You can sit on it if you like.'

The wad of banknotes Lux passed over raised her eyebrows but she made no demur.

'I'll get your invoice made up,' she said.

'No invoice necessary. Put the dough in your Thanksgiving Party fund and have a real good time.'

It was a little after 2.00pm when he walked out into the stark sunshine and collected his car from the visitor's bay in the parking lot. He hadn't lied to Timothy about heading south. By midnight he was in Menton. He had meant to stay in Ste Maxime but his desire to see Ghislaine got the better of him.

To his chagrin the house was in darkness and not because she was asleep in bed. He found a note pinned to the bedroom door.

Darling.
Missed you like mad. It's Thursday and I'm going to Paris for a few days. Sorry but it's business and cannot wait. Call me on 47 71 11 91

which is the number at my new apartment. I will phone you here
anyway every day. I'm going to buy you a present, a cellphone!
My love forever
Ghislaine

Pity. But maybe it was all for the better. She was a distraction
he didn't need.

For his second meeting with Tomas Leandri, Lux again went to the man's rural retreat. It was hot and Leandri was dressed like a tourist, in a multi-striped shirt outside a pair of khaki shorts.

After a perfunctory handshake the Corsican beckoned Lux over to a two-car garage some twenty metres from the log cabin house. In the left hand section stood a black Citroën XM with special registration plates. The car was not new but it was immaculate.

'Open the trunk,' Lux said.

Leandri obliged. Lux bent forward and tapped on the panel behind the rear seat.

'It is empty,' Leandri pointed out.

'It needs modifying. Nothing major … just a false panel inserting about here …' Lux stabbed a finger at a point slightly over a foot short of the rear bulkhead. 'It must blend perfectly with the existing trim and be undetectable. It must also be easy to remove.'

Leandri stroked his chin. 'It is not a problem. I will of course do it myself, therefore it will not be cheap. And I must know the purpose. What do you wish to conceal behind it?'

'A body.'

'Are you joking?' Leandri said, then saw that he was not.

Lux allowed a small smile to creep onto his face. 'Let me explain …'

After they had finished discussing the car they went to sit in the same comfy chairs under the eucalyptus tree in the garden, to be served cold beers by Leandri's '*femme*'. She was wearing denim shorts a size too small for her plump backside but Lux had no objection. Leandri certainly didn't; he patted her rump without fail whenever she came within range. Her squeak of protest was for Lux's benefit only.

The view over Toulon was still superb, superficially altered by the presence in the naval dockyard of an aircraft carrier and some shuffling about of the smaller warships; one was in dry dock.

Leandri examined the ID card bearing his photograph and the name Laurent Castel, making a clicking sound with the tip of his tongue against the roof of his mouth as he did so.

'*Bien*,' he said at length, sliding the card into his breast pocket.

The two men, by coincidence, produced packs of cigarettes

from their pockets at the same time. Same brand too, Gitanes. Leandri laughed. 'I insist you have one of mine.'

Lux accepted, grinning back, and lit both cigarettes.

Leandri said, 'And now, my friend with no name, I presume you are going to explain to me why I need this card, how I will earn the considerable sum you are paying for my services, and what part my assistant will play in this venture.'

'That's why I'm here,' Lux said and hoped the man's nerves were all Simonelli had claimed them to be. 'Let's deal with your assistant, first of all. The rest will become clear as I explain.'

'*Bien.* I am listening intently.'

'Your assistant will ride in the hidden compartment,' Lux said, watching the man's reaction.

Outwardly, there was none.

'Go on,' Leandri said, tapping invisible ash from his cigarette.

Here was the point of no return. The point when Leandri would have to know all, and therefore put Lux at risk of exposure. The point when he must place his trust in a blackguard whose only credentials came from another, probably greater blackguard.

He drew in a deep breath.

'Afterwards he will impersonate me.'

Charles de Gaulle Airport, Roissy, Paris, 29 May 1996

All points of entry and airports have been instructed to report the arrival of Miss Sheryl Glister in France.

Translated extract of a memorandum from Philippe Mazé, Commandant de Police, CRS to CG/CRS, 26.05.1996. Filed 27.05.96

* * *

'Hey!' cried the young male clerk in the passport control centre at Charles de Gaulle Terminal 2, to whoever happened to be within earshot.

'What?' a fellow-clerk said sleepily. He'd had a busy night with his girlfriend and was suffering for it.

'One of the foreign arrivals this morning is on the DST notification list,' said the first clerk. He pointed to the display on his monitor with its flashing notice 'to report the entry into France of the above-named to the DST immediately'.

The second clerk's drowsiness was dissipated somewhat.

'You lucky bastard! I've been here twice as long as you and I've *never* had one of those. Who is it?'

'A woman. Name of Sheryl Glister.' He pronounced it Glee-stair. '*Américaine*.'

The second clerk propelled his castored chair across to his colleague's desk.

'What else does it say?'

'See for yourself. Passport number, date of birth, place of birth, description, distinguishing marks, the usual garbage. There's a telephone number to ring. Should I ring it?'

'Should I ring it, he says. Of course you fucking ring it, *crétin*. Do you want to find yourself in an interrogation cell with your testicles wired to a generator? Not a nice way to end the day!'

The first clerk took his point. He reached for his telephone and composed the central Paris number on the *ordonnance*.

It was eleven o'clock at night and warm for the end of May. Lux lay on his back covered only by a white satin sheet, smoking, satiated and exhausted after a reunion that had been worth the wait. Beside him, Ghislaine was sprawled untidily on her front, her face turned towards him. The sheet clung salaciously to the double bulge of her bottom, leaving Lux in a state of constant desire the likes of which he had never known before.

'So?' she said, breaking the silence of the aftermath. 'What do you think of my son, my parents, my new apartment?'

Lux, who had never been into kids, had been genuinely touched by her son, Marc. A ringer for his mother and well-behaved without relinquishing the essential impishness of small boys, he had unfailingly addressed Lux as '*monsieur*', resisting blandishments to use his first name. The three of them lunched *al fresco* in the Champs Elysees, rode to the top of the Eiffel Tower and strolled through the Pompidou Centre. Marc had advanced a case for a jaunt to Disneyland but time was too short. In the end he had settled for a visit to the cinema where "Back to the Future II" was showing.

Now he was in his bed in the next room, hopefully asleep and undisturbed by the boisterous activity in his mother's room.

'I think they're all great, especially your son. He's a terrific kid.' It sounded flat, but on the spur of the moment he couldn't think up any better way of expressing his feelings.

'You could be his father, do you think? Could you love my son?'

Lux hesitated, not wishing to merely placate her. Honesty was her credo. He owed it to her to be honest when he had no need to deceive.

'I could try,' he said eventually, amending this, when he realised the tense was wrong, to, 'I *will* try. For you.'

She turned on her side, propped her head on her clenched fist.

'No, not for me, darling. You must try for him. Do you understand the difference?'

'Oh, sure,' he said confidently, though he wasn't as sure as all that. 'Say, how have you explained it to him, what I'm doing here in place of his pa? Or haven't you explained it.'

'I have told him as much as he will understand. He's too young for the unvarnished truth, and too innocent. So I told him papa has gone away for a few weeks and that you're a special friend who is staying here to take care of us.'

Lux's inhalation of smoke turned into a splutter. 'You mean he thinks I'm standing in for his pa? Keeping the bed warm till he gets back?'

She glared at him. 'Not in exactly those terms, no. It's too complicated and if I had to relay it to you in French you wouldn't understand.'

Touché crossed Lux's mind but he didn't say it aloud. What he did say was, 'Does Michel have your new address?'

'No. Maybe I will tell him when I am sure he has accepted our separation. It depends.'

'Uh-huh.' Lux wasn't worried about the prospect of an enraged spouse on the doorstep, he just preferred to be ready to receive him. 'Look, sweetheart, things are moving. On Sunday we have to go away.'

'We? You mean *us*?'

Lux nodded. Her hand crept under the sheet like a burrowing animal to make contact with his aroused member.

'Where? Why?'

'Business. Urgent and necessary, and we'll be away a long time. Months, anyhow.'

Now she released him and sat up. He was watching her, his eyes lightly slitted. Her own gaze was quizzing, as if seeking a clue as to his real motives, his intentions. During this lull in their conversation the sound of cheering from the TV in the sitting room intervened and a commentator could be heard yammering about a truly magnificent goal.

'All right,' she said finally. 'But where will we go?'

'Switzerland. To begin with.'

'Must I come?'

'If you want to go on. With me, that is.'

She reached for his face, explored it with her fingertips. 'You doubt it?'

His shrug was slight. 'I guess not.'

'You do, a little, I think. But you shouldn't. I may have to return from time to time for my work … I will not abandon my career. But Switzerland is not so far. So dispel your doubts, my darling. Let me demonstrate to you again how much you mean to me.'

Lux wasn't sure he could respond to yet another such demonstration, which would be the third in as many hours. Still, he stubbed out his cigarette and prepared to give it his best shot. In the event she made it easy for him simply by being irresistible.

St Lazare, Paris, 30 May 1996

The digital alarm clock read 3:50 and still they weren't tired. They lay in the dark, hands clasped, talking.

'I must leave for the south after breakfast,' he told her.

She tightened her grip on his hand to show she had heard, understood, and hated the idea of another separation.

'You must go to Menton,' he pressed on. A pause then, 'You and Marc.'

'No, not Marc. Not right away. He will stay with his grandparents. You must not expect me to turn his life upside down so readily.' She sensed he was hurt by her defensive tone and gave his hand another squeeze, of appeasement now. 'Which airport will we fly from, for Switzerland? Nice, I suppose.'

'We won't be flying. We go by boat, a private yacht.'

'Is that a joke? Switzerland is landlocked. How will you achieve this impossible feat?'

'We sail to a place where there is an airport,' he said patiently.

'Oh.' She was puzzled but didn't pursue the point. 'From where do we sail?'

'Does it matter?' His tone was curt and she recoiled a little. 'All I want from you is to be at the house from tomorrow evening and to stay within earshot of the phone. I will call you there sometime on Sunday, probably early afternoon, with instructions where to meet me.'

'Why can't you tell me now? This is all very mysterious. You are beginning to frighten me, Dennis. Have you done something – something bad, I mean?'

'No, my love, but there is a lot at stake. Some people might try to prevent me leaving.' That much was the truth at any rate. 'Make sure your cellphone is on and charged up. I'll call you on it sometime after one in the afternoon and say where you must go. I'll be at the rendezvous about an hour after my call.'

'But why can't you tell me right now where I am to go?' she persisted.

No reason, was his private answer. Only that he had always kept his plans to himself and on the subject of security he was a creature of unshakeable habit. The need to know was a personal commandment.

He refused to be drawn further and the subject atrophied. After a while he lapsed into a fitful sleep; Ghislaine stayed awake, listening to the hum of the city and watching the curtains gradually lighten with the coming of a new dawn.

Paris, 1e Arondissement, 30 May 1996

This meeting was not instigated by me. The MoI in person summoned me to what he termed an informal exchange of ideas. I understood it to be off the record until the MoI informed the CG of it the following day. Consequently this aide-memoire *serves to place on record my recollection of the dialogue while it is still fresh in my mind in case any questions should arise in future.*

Translated extract of note dictated by Philippe Mazé, Commandant de Police, CRS, 31.05.1996. Filed 03.06.96.

'It reads like Mazé covering his ass.'

Sheryl Glister to Thierry Garbe, freelance journalist, 24.03.1999. (on hearing Garbe's translation of the above note)

*   *   *

It was a grand day for a saunter in the Jardin des Tuileries. Sunny, pleasantly warm, the sort of day that Paris was made for but did not experience as often as Parisians like to broadcast.

Not that Philippe Mazé's itinerary for this day had included the Tuileries, any more than his timetable included a saunter. But when the Minister of the Interior summoned Mazé in person to pass an hour of gentle exercise with him, how could he refuse? *A vrai dire,* he dare not.

It was a surprising slap in the face for protocol and especially for Le Renard. To such an extent that Mazé even contemplated alerting his boss. After five minutes of mind wrestling he decided that the smaller of the two evils was to upset Le Renard rather than the Minister.

Debre was in good form. Cheery, full of aimless chitchat that Mazé suspected was designed only to put him off guard. This breezy monologue lasted for so long that Mazé began to wonder if the Minister merely sought a willing ear into which to feed his tendency to liberal notions about law and order and human rights.

Then, in mid-sentence, so it seemed to the bemused CRS officer, the Minister of the Interior stopped by a bench seat overlooking the Seine and, propping his posterior on the back of it, said to Mazé, 'Tell me your proposals for assuring the President's safety on Sunday. Not the official line, not Le Renard's line, but Mazé's line. *Your* line. Understand?'

Mazé, more than a shade bemused, indicated that he understood. 'But you realise that the President's security is not my speciality, *Monsieur le Ministre*. My brief gravitates more towards surveillance …'

'No matter. They tell me you have an excellent brain. You must have given the question some thought.' The Minister spoke abstractedly, his gaze tracking a pleasure boat packed with goggling tourists as it passed beneath the Pont Royal.

'It's true, I have, and I have some ideas that may or may not appeal to you and the President. But Monsieur Renard gave me to understand that he is handling this aspect. I am fully committed to tracing and ultimately apprehending the protagonists.'

'Nevertheless,' the Minister said with some asperity, and that one word left no more room for debate. 'Air your ideas. Even if I discard them, what have you to lose?'

Initially hesitant, Mazé complied, even throwing in a suggestion by his wife that she introduced into the conversation over a meal at their local *brasserie* the previous evening.

He rounded off his verbal treatise with the comment, 'I have concluded that the attempt will be made between the moment the President's helicopter lands and his entry into the house – ' He broke off to concede *force majeure* to the ululating siren of a police car as it ripped along the Quai des Tuileries, painting a pained expression on the Ministerial visage. 'Or possibly,' he resumed, as the whooping subsided, 'the killer will try to hit him while he is still in the air.'

'You have a basis for this conclusion?'

'Yes.'

The Minister did not ask him to postulate. 'If it happens while he is in the air this would require a missile launcher of some kind, I should think.'

'In theory the helicopter patrol will forestall any such attempt. They will be using infra-red search equipment, so I am told.'

At the Minister's instigation they moved on, approaching the Orangerie. Out of the blue he said in a low, almost reverential voice, 'Do you attach any credence to the report that a senior government minister is implicated in this affair?'

Mazé didn't point out that he was the source of this particular report.

'Yes,' he said. 'I have seen the evidence for myself.'

'Ah, yes, of course. The famous note with the photographs. That was you, was it?' He sighed, side-stepping a small boy who was coming at him on a collision course, a matronly woman in wheezing pursuit. 'This is a very complicated affair, *Commandant*. The assassination attempt itself does not appear to be politically motivated but there are those of the right who see an opportunity to foment instability and perhaps even insurrection.'

Startled, Mazé glanced sharply at Debre. Surely he was exaggerating?

'So you see,' the Minister continued, as they turned right at the Orangerie and approached the octagonal lake, 'there is more at stake here than the life of the President of the Fifth Republic.' He patted Mazé's broad back. 'The Fifth Republic itself may be imperilled. In any case we will consider your suggestions. I shall speak to the President this very afternoon. Well done, well done.'

Mazé grinned uncertainly, happy to bask in the Minister's praise but mildly alarmed at the prospect of brickbats from his immediate superior should it get back to him. 'Thank you, *Monsieur le Ministre*. If I could ask a small service ...'

'Name it, my dear Mazé. A modest pecuniary advantage, perhaps?'

'No, no!' Mazé protested (later reflecting that perhaps he was a shade too hasty with his protest). 'It's not at all that. But I would be most grateful if you could you speak to Monsieur Renard and explain that I was not trying to go over his head.'

A light shower began as Barail walked from the door to where his government-issued Renault Safrane was parked, beside Lux's identical but-for-the-paintwork model. Simonelli accompanied him and stood by as Barail slid behind the wheel.

'Have a pleasant drive south,' Simonelli said, leaning on the top of the open door.

'I am already late,' Barail grumbled, 'thanks to this unnecessary meeting.'

The shower was developing into a serious precipitation. The shoulders of Simonelli's cream suit were acquiring a dark rash.

'Do not be so disgruntled, my friend. From now on you can relax. Your job is done and, unlike me, your official record has not been besmirched. You will still have your government pension to fall back on in case your new-found wealth slips through your grasp like a piece of wet soap.'

The simile did not improve Barail's humour. As Simonelli stood back from the car he pulled the door shut brusquely then lowered the window.

'We may not meet again,' he said, twisting the ignition key. 'Let me remind you though, that *your* job is not yet done. You have received the down payment, and all the financial arrangements are in place for the balance. Now earn it.'

'*Bien entendu, Monsieur le Commissaire,*' Simonelli said waggishly. 'In any case it has been a privilege to work with you.' He thrust a hand through the open window. Barail took it with a hint of reluctance.

A thoroughly wetted Simonelli retreated to the house, turning to watch the black Safrane accelerate down the driveway on the final leg of its journey that would terminate at the Crillon estate.

'When I told Lux that in many ways I admired him he seemed taken aback. Almost as if the possibility had never occurred to him that a contract killer could possess admirable qualities. His self-esteem was shaky. It was the last time we met before D-Day. He was still cagey about his preparations but after a glass or two of Burgundy he opened up a little. Oh, and he also confessed to being in love. Mister Ice-in-his-veins himself. Not in so many words, he was too coy for that, but he admitted there was a new woman in his life and I deduced the rest. Call it woman's intuition.'

Sheryl Glister to Thierry Garbe, freelance journalist, 25.03.1999.

*   *   *

The restaurant of the old auberge was half empty and they were able to find a corner table, far enough from the nearest diners to be able to talk freely.

'Won't Rafael be jealous?' Lux asked playfully, as they worked through the main course of *venison en croute*.

Sheryl was amused. 'Of what? Us having dinner together? You flatter yourself, my friend. Just because I succumbed to your seduction routine in a moment of weakness and sexual deprivation, doesn't mean I fancy you.'

'That's okay by me,' Lux said as he forked the last morsel of venison into his mouth. 'Anyhow, since we last met I'm spoken for.'

If Sheryl was disappointed by this piece of news she kept it off her face.

'Well, congratulations or something. Is it serious?'

'Kind of.'

Sheryl eyed him thoughtfully. Certainly she could detect a subtle change in his attitude, a new maturity. All of a sudden she wondered if he was still capable of going through with the contract. If his new love had perhaps softened him, even made him decide to go respectable.

'So, Jill, or whatever your name is,' Lux said, 'if this dinner isn't about a repeat performance of London or to get Rafael fired up, what *is* it for?'

'Good question.' Sheryl tore a piece from the bread roll and mopped the last of the sauce estragon from her plate. 'First of all let me ask you how you think the meeting went this afternoon.'

Lux laid his knife and fork on his plate as he assembled a reply.

'A lot of hot air, but essentially we covered all the ground.'

'You didn't say a lot.'

'In case you didn't notice, Simonelli had elected himself my mouthpiece. You and he are close so I figured you were happy to let him make the speeches.'

Sheryl somehow combined a grimace with a grin. 'His heart's in the right place where it concerns me, but I'm not sure he's a hundred per cent reliable. Let me put it this way: I want assurance from the horse's mouth, not from the jockey's. Or should it be the other way round – and do I mean *re*assurance?'

'That it's going to happen just the way Simonelli told it, you mean? I can buy that. The only feedback you've had so far is from him and Barail so I'm not surprised you're looking for comfort. No offence meant towards Simonelli, I guess you have confidence in him, but neither of those guys are exactly stand-up, are they?'

At that moment the waitress approached to enquire '*Terminé?*' and whisk the cleared plates and accessories off the table, darting a winsome smile at Lux that Sheryl didn't miss.

'You're right that I have confidence in Rafael but that doesn't mean I treat everything he tells me as if it were lifted from the pages of the Holy Bible. Barail's the one I'm wary of and Rafael is very dependent on him. So when Rafael says we're steaming ahead very nicely and no worries, I'm pretty sure most of what he's feeding me is parroted from what Barail's fed him.'

'And Barail's parroting what *I've* fed him in many cases,' Lux reminded her. 'So maybe I'm the one you should mistrust.'

Sheryl folded her arms and rested her elbows on the white tablecloth. She looked right into the American's eyes.

'I don't think so, Dennis. I'm a good judge of character. You're an outlaw … ' Darting a glance towards the nearest occupied table, she dropped her voice to an octave above a whisper, 'An assassin … a murderer some would call you. The worst kind of criminal – a taker of human lives. I hold no brief for that, yet I can't condemn it because I'm using your skills and your willingness to kill for my own ends, and it wouldn't matter to the rest of the world that those ends were unselfish and for their own good. So whatever you're guilty of, so am I. To get back to the point … my gut tells me you're straight-talking and straight-dealing. A man of your word. A man of honour.'

'Phew! Me?' Lux tilted back on his chair, running both hands through his hair. 'All those things? Maybe I should get you to write my CV … Jill.'

'My name's Sheryl,' she said on an impulse, letting out a hollow laugh. 'You see, I'm even trusting you with my name. 'Sheryl Glister. Now you can turn me in any time you like.'

Lux shook his head slowly, in bemusement as well as denial, that she should reveal her identity when there was no need, merely to underline a point.

'I really appreciate your faith in me. And your instincts are good, take my word. So how do we play this – like a quiz game? Ask me what you want to know and I promise to either answer honestly or, if I can't, I'll explain why to the best of my ability.'

'That sounds fair. But we don't need to set out a precise format. We'll start off that way and see how it develops.' Sheryl glanced across the restaurant. 'Here comes the waitress ... are you having a dessert?'

Venoy, near Auxerre, 31 May 1996

Early in May I instructed Dubois and his team to mount a twenty-four hour tail on Lux. This proved to be a frustrating business as he was skilled in the art of giving tails the slip. It was almost a month before we learned about his love affair. The woman was not known to us at the time, apart from a name, that she was divorced and had a small son. My concern was not over the affair itself but over the security implications. Lovers tend to be loose-tongued, as happened in my own case. I had to satisfy myself that he had not betrayed us.

Translated from written statement of Commissaire Divisionnaire Julien Barail, 03.06.1996.

* * *

As Lux was checking out of the hotel an unexpected visitor turned up.

'Good morning, Lux,' Barail said. From his stern expression this was not a social call.

Lux pocketed his credit card wallet and acknowledged the *Commissaire* urbanely enough. He didn't like surprises. He couldn't recall mentioning the name of his hotel to Barail.

'May we talk?' Barail said, taking Lux's elbow peremptorily. 'Here will do, in reception.'

'All right,' Lux said curtly and lugged his suitcase after him to a table across the lobby screened by a lush cheese plant.

'Did you pass an agreeable night?' Barail enquired, settling in a basket weave chair and crossing his legs.

'Get to the point.' Lux sat down opposite, more to blend with the décor than to be sociable.

'I would like to know the purpose of your liaison with Madame Fougère.'

Lux goggled. '*What?*'

'According to information passed to me last night, Madame Fougère is a divorced woman, currently unattached, with a small child by her marriage to a certain...' Barail pulled a notebook from his pocket and flipped it open, 'Albin Fougère, at present living in Belgium. You have installed her in your house. This raises certain, ah, security issues and I would like to have your assurance that you have not been indiscreet.'

'Are you following me?' Lux's voice was controlled, unlike his emotions which were running amok. Ghislaine *divorced*? So who the hell was Michel Beauregard, who had posed as her husband?

Barail shrugged. '*Désolé*. A precautionary measure, you understand.'

The urge on Lux to sock Barail was powerful. He restrained himself. A public disturbance only two days from the killing would not have been smart.

'What else do you know about Madame Fougère?'

Barail checked his notes. 'Not a lot. She is a *fonctionnaire*, that's all we can say. Please understand we have not been following *her*. We have no interest in her background.'

Lux snorted. 'Just enough interest to check into her marital status and her job.'

'It was volunteered to us by an informant. We were not seeking to know. But it matters not who she is or what she does, simply that you clearly have serious intentions towards her and I must be assured that you have not discussed our ... business transactions with her.' His gaze was direct, unapologetic. 'The way lovers do.'

Lux got to his feet, buttoned his sports coat.

'I insist on knowing,' Barail said, rising with him, 'or we will consider you to be in breach of contract.'

Lux's anger deflated before the reality. 'All right, so I'm having an affair with her,' he said between clamped teeth. 'The timing's unfortunate but it has nothing to do with the job.'

'I see it differently. You know too much to be allowed complete freedom. You will cease all contact with this woman until you have completed your task.'

'You can go and fuck yourself, Barail. Do you think I don't know when to keep my mouth shut?'

Lux hefted his suitcase and left a visibly fuming Barail with the cheese plant for company.

* * *

At 150 kph on a near-empty *autoroute* a driver can almost switch off. All you have to do is stay in lane and avoid contact with the central barrier or another vehicle. Once past the toll booths south of Lyon Lux had ample opportunity to reflect on Ghislaine's apparent deception, she who claimed to rate honesty above all other personal attributes.

Why say she was married if she was divorced? The other way round would have made more sense. Yet she had almost flaunted her so-called husband, made much ado about leaving him, with her great shows of contrition and conscience. Now, if Barail's intelligence was reliable – and why would he invent it? – she had been merely playacting. Even her job as a journalist was a sham. The lies didn't trouble him as such; he had told more than a few of his own. But he had to know the reason.

Given that their meeting on the Crillon estate was chance, a possible explanation was that she had created a bogus identity to cover up her real activity. That she was perhaps part of an anti-Chirac faction, a terrorist even, and that instead of spying out the Crillon place for a magazine feature, her goals and Lux's were not so far apart.

It was a far-fetched hypothesis yet not without credibility. He found himself laughing aloud at the irony. Not that he really did believe it. Coincidences happened, but not on so momentous a scale.

As the miles flew by his speculations became ever more arid. In a conscious effort to break the trend he pulled off the *autoroute* at the service area near Montpellier. There he freshened up and ate an indifferent salad with *tarte aux pommes* for dessert, washed down with a glass of Perrier. When, around three p.m., he resumed his journey southward, he forcibly shunted Ghislaine's subterfuge into a siding in his mind, there to remain until the job was done.

By design Barail was excluded from what was expected to be the final meeting with President Chirac. Le Renard had despatched his second-in-command a day early – overruling protests that it was quite unnecessary – ostensibly to review the arrangements for security at the Crillon residence. Barail had planned to go in any case, though not until Saturday.

When Debre and Le Renard were summoned into the presidential study at a little after eleven, Chirac was standing at one of the open windows looking out into the gardens. He was jacketless, his hands in his pockets.

He greeted them without turning. '*Bonjour, messieurs. Asseyez-vous.*'

They responded in chorus like a stage duo and took their seats before the desk.

The meeting proved to be of short duration.

'We still do not know *how* it will be done,' Le Renard could not resist reminding the other two. He was still smarting over Mazé's hobnobbing with his chief, of which he had only been informed ten minutes previously, as he and Debre kicked their heels in the Salon des Ordonnances.

'Quite so,' the President said, increasingly irritated by the whole business. 'Let me see if I understand the security procedures correctly, gentlemen: the grounds will be thoroughly searched before nightfall on Saturday by a team of one hundred gendarmes. The outer wall will be simultaneously guarded by a further one hundred gendarmes and continuously guarded thereafter by shifts of one hundred gendarmes.' He glanced enquiringly from Debre to Le Renard.

The former nodded; the latter said, '*Oui, Monsieur le Président, c'est exacte.*'

'This means,' the President said, 'that no unauthorised person can be in the grounds at the intended time of my arrival, nor can enter the grounds before, during, or after my arrival. Is my understanding correct?'

'Entirely,' Le Renard said. 'In addition, we have decided to illuminate the whole exterior of the wall, to ensure that no one slips through under cover of darkness. The work is under way at this very moment.'

'Forgive me for saying this, *mon cher* Renard, but it rather sounds as if you will make the place so secure that no assassin could possibly penetrate it. Doesn't that rather defeat the object of the exercise?'

Neither Debre nor Le Renard had thought of that.

Le Renard said, 'Barail knew of most of these precautions, indeed he was involved in the discussions when they were agreed. Yet as at 13th May, before his affair with Agent 411 came to an end, the project was going ahead. Nothing has changed.'

'Except the lighting,' the President reminded him. 'May I suggest you reconsider the question of lighting. If our Jackal friend comes by night and sees the place illuminated like the Arc de Triomphe he may well turn around and go home and our elaborate preparations will all have been for nothing.'

'As you wish, *Monsieur le Président*,' Le Renard muttered, secretly fuming at the implied rebuke as well as the prospect of looking foolish when he rescinded the order.

A pigeon, newly alighted on the window sill, cooed softly and the distant voice of someone calling from below, probably a gardener, filtered into the room after it.

'Continuing my appraisal of the precautions,' the President said, 'I understand that the house, annexes and outbuildings have been swept for explosive devices and will be swept again on Saturday and on Sunday morning, and that a full complement of bodyguards will be in place.'

'All correct, *Monsieur le Président*,' Debre confirmed.

'Good.' Chirac glanced at his watch. 'Then as I am required elsewhere twenty minutes from now I shall call this meeting to a close. We will not meet again, gentlemen, until next week, when I trust it will all be over.'

As Debre and Le Renard stood up to leave, the President pulled out the top right hand drawer of his desk and depressed the stop button of the recording machine.

PART FOUR

SUMMER EXECUTION

The Crillon estate had taken on the look of a military encampment. Blue and khaki uniforms by the dozen and great comings and goings of vehicles. Watching this bubbling cauldron of activity Mazé found himself questioning the point of it all. No assassin with a halfway functioning brain was going to try and penetrate such defences.

Was he?

Even as he convinced himself new doubts assailed him. He strolled across to where a beige-suited Commissaire Barail stood, smoking and contemplating the hillside.

'Everything seems to be proceeding very smoothly, *Monsieur le Commissaire*,' he remarked, extracting a cigarette of his own from a crumpled pack.

'Quite. I feel almost superfluous.'

'My wife is not happy about me working the weekend,' Mazé said conversationally, though he did not grudge the loss of leisure time in the slightest. This was big league and he was excited to be a part of it, this bringing to fruition his toils of the past ten weeks, to have serendipity turn into a major success for the security forces. Not to mention playing a key part in saving the life of the President of the Republic.

Barail, who had spent the past twenty-four hours at the Crillon house supposedly overseeing the security operation but largely kicking his heels, grunted neutrally. He couldn't have cared less about Mazé's domestic vicissitudes. To observe the results of his labours first-hand and thereafter verify the transfer of the balance of his Greenwar pay check to his account in Liechtenstein, were his only missions.

Unlike Mazé, he was not at all uneasy about the extent of the security screen. Lux had been made aware of the numbers and the dispositions, and still had expressed no reservations about his ability to go through with it. Barail was absolutely confident that, by this time tomorrow, Jacques Chirac would be dead.

Sheryl came awake in the early dawn half-light, her mind instantly alert. This is D-Day minus one, was her opening thought.

Rafael Simonelli lay beside her on his back, lightly snoring. She smiled at him with real affection if not real love. Once she had loved him but those feelings had not after all been rekindled. Now it was partly companionship, partly the sex, which was bloody great, that made her relish his company. Once this Chirac business was over she would be off back to Enzed, probably never to see him again and with no regrets.

'Napoleon,' she said, digging a finger in his flank.

The snoring stopped, punctuated with a snort, and he came lazily awake.

'Napoleon,' she said, more sharply now.

'*Qu'est qu'il y a?*' he complained.

'Fuck me, will you?'

Silence. Then he rolled onto his side to bring his groin into contact with hers.

'You want me to fuck you – *now*?' He was having difficulty unsticking his eyelids but lower down all parts seemed to be working fine.

'Would you mind?'

'*Tu es folle, ma biche,*' he said, coming wide awake and grinning. 'You're crazy.'

'Oh, shut up and just get on with it. This might be your last chance. I'll be too tense tonight.'

As he climbed on top of her he frowned. 'Too tense? Why is that?'

'You mean you won't be? Like it's every day you organise the assassination of a head of state.'

He stopped what he had started to do and swore obscenely. 'Can you believe it? I completely forgot tomorrow is the day.'

'Yes, I had heard that excessive snoring dulls the brain.'

'Cheeky bitch. For that I will make you sorry you didn't let me sleep on.'

Sheryl stretched her arms above her head and let her tongue circumnavigate her lips, giving them an ephemeral gloss. She couldn't recall when last she was so aroused.

'Go right ahead, lover boy. Make me sorry.'

That was when they discovered that the bed creaked.

* * *

In the next room Gary Rosenbrand listened to the rhythm of the creaking bed and the girlish squeals that beat time with it. He wished he were the one doing the rogering. It wasn't so much that Sheryl turned him on sexually. He just missed his home comforts, presently twelve thousand miles away.

To think of Sheryl shagging that greasy Frog brought out the racist in him. He pulled the duvet over his head like a tortoise withdrawing into its shell and tried to go back to sleep.

Lux ran through his mental checklist while perched at the breakfast bar scoffing a muesli, the aroma of percolating coffee titillating his nostrils. It was a longish list: rifle (loaded), spare magazine (loaded) handgun (loaded), spare ammunition, silencer, hunting knife, a short spade, a hammer and some six-inch nails, sunglasses, clear protective glasses (to prevent low-level branches from poking his eyes out), oilskins, fatigues, forage cap, towel, black boots, gendarme's uniform complete with kepi, belt, holster (empty for now); knapsack to carry all these things, excluding the rifle and the spade. Also an ID card, though that would go in his pocket. Provisions would include a bar of chocolate, a couple of apples and a 1.5 litre bottle of Evian. He would stoke up before he left to keep the worst of the pangs at bay.

The morning news on the radio was fairly bland and included an item about the President's impending short break '*dans le Midi*'. Just a flat statement to the effect, no commentary or nameless quotes.

Lux munched away, his appetite as voracious as if tomorrow were just a day like any other. He thought he might try calling Ghislaine, though she would most likely be on the *autoroute* by now, heading south. He didn't want to distract her from duelling with the traffic. Everybody knew all French motorists were homicidally mad and that you messed with them at your peril.

Later, donning shorts, he went for a stroll along the foreshore towards the Cap des Sardineaux. The sun kept going in and the sea was choppy, foaming white around the base of the lighthouse of the Tourelle de la Seche-à-Huile. When he reached the Cap he sat there for quite a while, the dry, brittle grass prickling the backs of his bare legs, savouring the miracle that was planet Earth and revelling in the power of life and death such as he possessed – a power that soon, very soon now, he would exercise for the good of that planet.

*   *   *

It was early evening. The clouds had dispersed, the sky in the east was a deepening blue, the first subliminal hint of the night to come. Lux was demolishing a sandwich consisting of a baguette with a cheese and tomato filling when the scrunch of gravel in the driveway announced a wheeled visitor.

A glance through the kitchen window reassured him that this visitor was expected – Tomas Leandri in the bogus RG Citroën. Plus accomplice. Dusting crumbs from his hands, Lux strolled out through the front entrance to greet them.

Leandri was first out of the car. A salutation and handshake later he presented his companion, who was coming around the car to meet his employer. Although he was expecting it, Lux found the experience of confronting his mirror image, even down to the identical grey suit and tie, disturbing beyond belief.

The man thrust out a hand. 'Robert Bernanos.'

'Hi, Robert. Tomas calls me Yank and it's all you need to know.'

In build Robert Bernanos was as specified, a near-clone of Lux. His hair was muddy blond, styled like Lux's, his eyes were grey-blue. Appearance-wise, to anyone other than an intimate, he would pass for the real thing.

'Satisfied with your other self?' Leandri said with a smirk.

'He's me all right,' Lux said, still a little unnerved. He subjected Bernanos's neck to scrutiny, in the area where the mask blended with real skin. Only the faintest hairline join was visible. 'Is the hair colour natural?'

'It's a wig,' Bernanos confessed, a mite sheepishly. 'I'm bald really.'

Lux decided it was irrelevant. Nobody was going to inspect his hair.

'*Bien.*' Leandri went to the rear of the car and opened the trunk lid. 'Now, come and see the trunk.'

Lux went and saw the trunk. At first sight it looked no different from when he first viewed it: empty, lined with grey moquette.

'What about the modification?' he asked Leandri.

The Corsican's smirk widened. 'It's there.'

And so it was. On closer examination Lux saw that the space between the lip of the trunk and the panel that separated it from the passenger section was smaller. He whistled his appreciation of the craftsmanship. No means of moving the panel were evident. It looked like an original fixture.

When he rapped a knuckle on it, it sounded hollow.

'How does it open?' he said.

Leandri produced a stubby screwdriver from his hip pocket and thrust it beneath the rear parcel shelf, about a foot in from the left. He levered with the screwdriver tip. There was a popping noise. He repeated the procedure a foot from the right and the panel suddenly fell open, revealing a space which, if Leandri had used the measurements given to him, should have been forty cm deep. Lux noticed that the top edge of the panel had a hinged strip along its entire width, into which two large press-studs had been set. The lower edge of the panel was also hinged, but screwed to the floor. Being attached to the inner side of the panel, the hinge was invisible in the closed position.

'Simple, eh, Yank?' Leandri said, looking smug. 'You don't need a degree in engineering for something like this.'

'It looks good,' Lux agreed, as he examined the top edge of the panel. The hinge there was no more than a separate length of wood, of identical thickness to the panel itself and about two centimetres wide, joined to the panel by the carpet. A gap of a few millimetres between the two pieces of wood allowed the hinged strip to flex back and forth and air to enter.

'Take a look at this,' Leandri said, a boastful note entering his voice as he led Lux around the side of the car and opened a rear door.

Lux looked. He saw nothing out of the ordinary. Just seats and a carpeted floor.

Leandri broke into a guffaw. 'The seat back is about five centimetres forward from its usual position and most of the padding has been removed.' He tapped the narrow panel of leather that had been inserted at the end of the seat cushion to fill the gap created by the repositioning. It blended seamlessly with the rest of the upholstery.

'By moving the rear seat forward I didn't have to encroach too much on the trunk space, which is why you don't notice the loss of depth. Effectively, I shared the space taken up by the compartment between the trunk and the inside of the car. Clever, no?'

'You're a genius, my friend.' Lux slapped him on the back, genuinely impressed, before turning towards Bernanos. 'And you? Are you clear on what's required of you?'

'*Certainement*, Monsieur Yank.'

Assurances on their own meant nothing to Lux.

'So tell me.'

With a shrug of insouciance, Lux's double ran through the expected sequence of events and his role in them without a stumble. He concluded with, 'And do not forget, *monsieur*, when we change places you must give me your ID.'

'Thanks for reminding me,' Lux said but the irony was lost on Bernanos. 'Now, let's get ready to roll. Just give me a minute to make sure there hasn't been a last-minute change of plan.'

From inside the house he called Barail's current cellphone.

'Everything okay at your end?' he asked the *Commissaire* in English, without identifying himself.

'No problems here. JC is due to arrive at 11.30 plus or minus thirty minutes. The grounds have been checked and the men are now stationed around the wall. All you have to do is get inside.'

'Plain sailing,' Lux agreed nonchalantly. 'And my wheels?'

'A Clio. It is in the car park, about halfway along.' He reeled off the plate number. 'Keys under the carpet to the left of the clutch pedal.'

'If anybody else takes it I'll hold you personally responsible. Now listen – in the next hour or so you ll be visited by two RG men, making a special delivery.'

A beat, then, 'A delivery? What of?'

'Nothing. You're simply playing a part in my method of getting in undetected.'

'What!'

Lux imagined he could feel the spray from Barail's splutter.

'Only a bit part, don't worry. All you have to do is be there and receive an envelope.'

'What's in it?' The suspicion in Barail's voice was an almost tangible thing.

'I told you – nothing. Chill out, Barail. Just play along.'

Lux hung up, slicing through Barail's next question or protest, whatever it was. On the couch was a bulging garbage bag, a short-handled spade, and a long bubble-wrapped package sealed with masking tape that contained the Barrett. He gathered them all up and went outside to where Leandri was adjusting the knot of his tie in his reflection in the window. He dumped everything in the trunk, closed the lid. Bernanos was already occupying the rear seat, gnawing his nails.

'Let's go, Tomas.'

'Before we do,' Leandri said, restraining Lux with the flat of his hand on the American's chest. 'I wish you to explain something to me.'

Lux tensed but said nothing.

'It seems strange to me that you do not ride in the hidden compartment yourself? If you did, Robert would not be necessary. When we arrive *chez* Crillon you would simply emerge from your hiding place and do what you must do. I drive in alone, I drive out alone. *Voila!* One less mouth to blab, one less wage to pay.'

'You really want to know, Tomas?' Lux bared his teeth. 'It is because I never place myself in a situation where I am at someone

260

else's mercy. With all that you know about what I intend to do, I am trusting you with the success or failure of this job. That is one hell of a lot of trust, and it's already more than enough. But to make myself helpless as well, to place my life in your hands? Uh-uh.' Lux's headshake was emphatic. 'No, my friend, I wouldn't trust any human being that far, even a Corsican one.' To soften the slight he made a fist and threw a mock punch at Leandri's jaw. 'A dog, now, I *would* trust a dog.'

'But not a dog like me, hey?'

'You're saying it, pal.' Lux heard a hoot of laughter from inside the car. 'Now, if you're happy, can we get moving...?'

The dashboard clock read 21:50. It was dark and it was dry. Up here, as the road climbed past the two hundred metre level the faintest suspicion of a chill in the air. Down at sea level, in Ste Maxine, it had been balmy.

The props were as authentic as bribery could buy: the car with the government plates, the guns, the IDs. All from an impeccable source – the CRS, courtesy of Commissaire Divisionnaire Julien Barail. In a suit, off-the-peg and ill-fitting, Leandri had the authentic air of an underpaid security thug.

'After all,' Barail had said sardonically to Lux, 'that is precisely what the security forces of this country are made up of – thugs.'

'You should know,' Lux had retorted.

All the more reason not to fall into their hands, he thought, as the Citroën passed the sign that informed one and all that the Col du Canadel alt. 267m was one kilometre ahead. The night sky was a panoply of sparkling stars that decorated the windshield. Then the road twisted to the left and dipped, and the heavens were replaced by the looming mass of Le Drapeau.

Leandri was inclined to be taciturn. He drove the car, that was his job. He wasn't being paid to natter. Once, when the undipped headlights of an oncoming vehicle dazzled him, he shouted '*Merde!*' and shook his fist. Lux let him be. Himself focused on the task ahead, he was content to let the wiry Corsican keep his counsel and his attention on the road. Bernanos too was tight-lipped, perhaps increasingly queasy about his pending confinement. In the mirror his head was a silhouette without features.

When Lux did break the silence, twenty minutes into their journey, it was to direct Leandri to take the next right. Even as he spoke the sagging 'Molières' sign came up and Leandri swung the wheel. The ascent grew steeper.

'Here's the dirt road,' Lux said suddenly, indicating a gap in the hedge, beyond it a track, overgrown, leading to nowhere apparent. A pair of animal eyes sparkled in the headlights then were gone.

Leandri drove along for about a minute, only stopping when the track faded to nothing. The three men piled out. Leandri popped the trunk; Bernanos scrambled in, over Lux's baggage, and wriggled into position in the compartment, which had been left open. It was a snug fit. His body was angled at forty-five degrees, his trunk twisted, his legs bent and intertwined at the ankles. A couple of cushions helped smooth the hard surfaces. Even so, the next few minutes, the last lap to the Crillon place, was not going to be a comfortable ride.

Lux upended the garbage bag: a bulging knapsack tumbled out, followed by oilskins, fatigues, gendarme's uniform complete with kepi, provisions, and the rest. The boots he was already wearing; the sunglasses and protective glasses would go in the breast pockets of his fatigues.

The butt of the gun fitted between the Bernanos's legs. The barrel, being the lightest part, simply by-passed his chest and was propped on the curve of the wheel arch, a bare inch from his nose. The spade and the loose items were packed wherever they would fit. When the panel was closed it would hold everything, animate and inanimate, securely in position.

'*Ca va, mon vieux*?' Leandri enquired of Bernanos.

A grimace and a nod from Bernanos, and Leandri swung the panel upwards and clicked it into position.

'Sooner him than me,' Lux muttered, almost wishing he had come up with a different solution. The lifelikeness of the mask still bothered him. It was like shutting himself in a coffin. Creepy.

'Relax, Yank,' Leandri said as he secured the hinged strip. 'He's been in tighter spots than this for a lot less money.'

'Yeah. It's too late for a Plan B anyhow, even if I had one. Now, let's roll. The Crillon house is only a few minutes from here.'

Leandri got back behind the wheel, Lux beside him, fondling the MAB PA-15 automatic under his armpit. A bullet was already up the spout. If he needed to use it, if his plan went askew, he would be fast on the trigger. Leandri was similarly armed and prepared. He was under no illusions either. Lux had made sure of that.

They reversed back to the road and rejoined it. Less than half a kilometre later the headlights picked out the fallen pine that denoted the fork. Last opportunity to take a different route, Lux reflected. To get the hell out of here and forget about the contract. To go home, to a waiting Ghislaine. To his woman.

God, he was missing her like he wouldn't have believed possible.

Ahead, the entrance to the estate. Less than a hundred metres to go. Lights everywhere. The place was illuminated like a football stadium.

'*Nous sommes arrivés*, Robert,' Leandri called over his shoulder. 'We're here.'

From behind the rear seat a muffled expletive.

The wrought iron gates stood open, white in the glare as if freshly painted. Uniformed figures in little clusters, almost to a man turned their faces towards the approaching car. Mostly CRS, toting sub-machine guns, with a dash of *gendarmes*. Lux quailed before this display of manpower. If it came to a shoot-out he was a dead man. The fifteen rounds in the magazine of the MAB would not save him even if he managed to get off every shot and make them all count.

Leandri brought the car to a sighing stop, its nose well short of the gates so as to leave room for manoeuvre in case a speedy retreat was called for. He lowered his window and displayed his plasticised ID between finger and thumb. Two CRS men came up; one shone a flashlight into the interior of the car.

'*Ca va, ca va*,' Leandri protested, shielding his eyes and passing first his, then Lux's IDs across to the CRS man with the flashlight. It had been agreed that Leandri would do the lion's share of the talking.

Only the lower half of the features of the CRS man examining the IDs were visible to Lux; he had a moustache, trimmed very short and thin.

'RG, eh?' he said, the initials shaded with grudging respect. 'And the reason for your visit?'

There was no hint of suspicion in the man's voice or his manner. It was casual, even bored. No doubt there had been many such comings and goings during the day.

'We've been summoned by Commissaire Barail,' Leandri responded, making it sound resentful.

'Ah, *bon*. What for, exactly?' It was an idle question. The other officer, the one wielding the flashlight, was yawning.

'How the fuck would I know?' Leandri said, projecting just the right amount of irritation. 'He's one of your lot so why don't you buzz him and ask him. We're underlings, like you. We obey orders, we don't ask questions of *commissaires* and the like.' He swivelled his head towards Lux. 'Do we?'

Lux grunted. The CRS man thrust the IDs back through the open window.

'Will you be staying the night?'

'Shit, no. We'll be out of here in fifteen minutes, I hope. I have a little friend waiting for me in town.'

'*Moi aussi*,' Lux ventured, trying to look pissed off. '*Ma femme*.'

The CRS man nodded. A smile seemed to be beyond him,

which was perhaps why he had chosen employment in the most hated organisation in France.

The flashlight clicked off. Both CRS men took a step back.

'*Allez-y*,' the churlish one said, with a sloppy salute. 'Just follow this road to the house. Don't leave it or you might get shot.'

Sloppy in other ways too, was Lux's professional view. The elaborate modifications to the trunk to accommodate Bernanos had been wasted on these two.

The avenue of silver limes was illuminated. The effect was striking, making the trees appear to be covered in snow.

'Nice place,' Leandri observed, as they cruised along the well-maintained asphalt.

'With money you can make a trashcan look like a work of art,' Lux said.

Leandri surprised him with his comeback. 'You're nothing but a cynic.'

Ahead, the house and more floodlights and uniforms. Quite a few plain-clothes too, a mixture of *Police Judiciare* and CRS from the *Corps de Securité Présidentielle*, Barail's crowd, gathered in front of a barrier. One of their number waved the Citroën to a standstill.

The ritual was identical. The flashlight, the lowered window, the scrutinised IDs, the casual banter. The plain-clothes officer was more affable than the CRS man, though he did at least check the trunk.

'*Où est le Commissaire?*' Leandri enquired.

The officer pointed at the house; lights burned in several downstairs windows.

'In there. Not far from the drinks cabinet.'

Cue for roars of laughter.

'But don't leave the car here,' the officer went on. 'Put it in the visitors' car park, over there behind the trees.' He indicated the oblong parking area off to the right that Lux had already noted on the aerial photographs and during his recce.

The barrier rose. They drove through and turned in the semi-circle. Lux lifted a hand to the officer in acknowledgement as they proceeded sedately down a short connecting driveway to the car park.

'Well, we're in,' Leandri said under his breath.

'Park well away from the light,' Lux enjoined. 'We don't want to be seen unloading.'

'Right.'

As they passed down the line of parked vehicles, many of them bearing *gendarmerie* livery, a van pulled out just ahead; the uniformed driver bipped his horn at them, lawman to lawman. They responded with raised hands. The parking area was lit by a single light on a pole more or less in the centre. It left the cars on the periphery in deep shadow.

Leandri continued on until the asphalt ended, parking on grass. He killed the engine and he and Lux got out. Lux had allowed two minutes for unloading the car, after which an alert security man might start wondering why they were taking so long to park. Now their movements were swift, urgent. Leandri lifted the trunk lid. With a small penknife he prised down the top hinge of the false panel; it flopped into the well of the trunk. Bernanos tumbled out, cursing, in a heap with the gun and the rest of the cargo.

'Shut up!' Leandri snarled at him.

A minute already gone and the odds on some nosey cop checking on them were growing. Working fast, Lux and Leandri transferred Lux's kit to the grass beside the car while Bernanos flexed his cramped joints.

'That's the lot.' Leandri slammed the trunk lid.

Lux's self-imposed time frame was almost up. He proffered his fake ID card to Bernanos, who took a break from knee-bending exercises to grasp Lux's hand.

'Good luck, Monsieur Yank,' he said. 'Is my face okay?'

'As far as I can tell in this light.' Lux felt along the edges of the mask, where it merged into Bernanos's neck. The join felt smooth and unbroken, the thin silicone of the mask almost like real skin.

'You'll pass. Just don't forget yourself and try to shave.'

Bernanos chuckled, then Leandri was elbowing him aside to bid Lux farewell, his handclasp knuckle-cracking.

'Be sure to shoot straight, my friend.'

'You can count on it. I'll see you tomorrow.'

'I'll be there.' He reached inside the car and lifted a brown envelope off the rear seat, then locked the car with the remote key.

'If it gets stolen with so many *flics* around, nowhere in France is safe,' he cracked, and Bernanos, despite his tautened nerves, gave a snort of laughter.

A last bob of his head for Lux and he set off towards the house, with Bernanos hurrying to keep up. A good man to have around in a tight corner, Lux reckoned. So far he had merited his high wages.

* * *

Lux got moving. He pulled the fatigues on over his suit; they would make him hot but it beat carrying them. The smaller items of gear he shovelled into the knapsack which he then slung over one shoulder. The gun in its bubble wrapping he would carry in one hand, the spade in the other. He stepped behind one of the trees that encircled the parking area and stood listening. Waiting for the challenge to Leandri and Bernanos; the shouts of alarm, the gunshots ... So much could still go wrong. For the first time this evening he found himself sweating. Instinctively his fingers tightened around the Barrett. They wouldn't take him cheaply. Barail had already convinced him that if he was arrested he was unlikely ever to face a judge, so why surrender?

Another minute dragged past. All was quiet. Lux loosened his hold on the Barrett. Sagged against the tree trunk, weak in his relief. What price Mister Cool now?

But he was inside the grounds and nobody knew.

He was invisible.

⋆   ⋆   ⋆

Leandri and Bernanos walked side by side past the parked vehicles, back towards the house. None of the *gendarmes* and security officers milling about accosted them as they crossed the semi-circular area. At the door, a bored-looking plain-clothes officer demanded their passes. A quick scrutiny and they were cleared through.

'The *Commissaire* is in the room on the right.'

Barail was indeed in close proximity to the lavishly-stocked drinks cabinet and even closer to a chunky glass of amber liquid. He toasted Leandri and Bernanos with it as the pair entered, then froze.

'Lux? What the fuck are you doing here?' He spoke in English, and Leandri and Bernanos exchanged uncomprehending glances.

'Commissaire Barail?' Leandri said warily. 'I'm Brigadier-Major Castel.' The name on his phoney ID.

Barail, staring in mixed horror and disbelief at the man he took to be Lux, said, addressing Leandri, 'I don't care a fuck who *you* are. What is *he* doing here, in my office?' He pointed with his glass at Bernanos/Lux.

'This is Gardien Villeneuve, my assistant, *Commissaire*. We are here to make a special delivery.'

Leandri passed across the envelope marked SECRET in red. It contained several blank sheets of A4 paper – a precaution in case the CRS guards had demanded material evidence of a 'message'.

Barail shook his head as if trying to clear it.

'Are you telling me you're not Lux?' he said at last to Bernanos.

Bernanos snapped to attention. 'Gardien Villeneuve *à votre service, Commissaire.*'

'Well, you look like Lux to me,' Barail growled, tossing the envelope on a table. 'Why didn't you tell me you had a twin? I mean, why didn't Lux tell me he had a twin.'

'Who is this Lux you speak of, *Commissaire?*' Leandri queried, fashioning a frown of puzzlement.

'Never mind, never mind. Do you want something to drink?'

'*Non, merci,*' Leandri replied for both of them. 'We must leave.'

Barail swirled the amber liquid around his glass. 'You had better be on your way then, whoever you are. Good luck.'

Leandri offered a sloppy salute, Bernanos likewise, and they took their leave. The same plain-clothes man flagged them out of the building without re-checking their passes. In silence they retraced their steps to the car park, just two security men amidst a multitude of security men. Invisible.

* * *

Lux started up the slope, using the lights of the driveway and the house to maintain a sense of direction, just as he had on his trial run. So long as the ground was rising and the house square on to his back he was confident of not straying off course. Sooner or later he would come to the copse or, if he overshot, to the wall, which would suffice to orientate him. Barail had assured him that, apart from a short section along the western side of the estate, the wall was only patrolled from the outside. The grounds had been swept and in theory were free of unauthorised persons.

The moon was in its first quarter, providing only a meagre glow, just enough to enable Lux to avoid most obstacles, though at six hundred and twelve paces up the slope, he put his foot in a rabbit hole and went sprawling. He landed painfully on his shoulder, losing the rifle but making no disturbance. Even his curse was mouthed not spoken.

For a minute or two he lay there, face to the sky, looking – really looking – at the rest of the universe for perhaps the first time since he was a child. It left him unmoved. It always had. He was an earthbound creature who could relate only to that which he could touch and taste, and harboured no ambition to learn about other worlds.

Retrieving the gun, he went on, the ground steeper and becoming more rugged as he left the cultivated area closer to the house. From his previous outing he was sure that the copse was close. Even as the certainty entered his mind he saw it on his left quarter, the ragged outline of the treetops, near black against the night-blue backwash. If it was the copse, the wall was not far away, and where there was wall there were police. He stood still, listening. For voices, a footfall, a cough, a striking match ... a challenge. He heard none of these, only a distant pulsation around the house, now far below, an illuminated oasis in the arid darkness of the countryside.

A few more steps and he entered the resin-perfumed embrace of the trees. He transferred safety glasses from pocket to nose, a precaution against branches and twigs at eye level. Now he could risk using the penlight. He propped the rifle and spade against a tree trunk. Making a tube of his left hand he inserted the penlight in it and thumbed the switch. Counted two seconds as he got his bearings and noted obstacles in his path and switched off. Then a three-minute wait for his night vision to return before shuffling forward, gun and spade held out in front of him to ward off protruding branches. The spade connected with wood almost at once and he swerved to the right. Then his sleeve caught on a jagged branch and held him there until he picked it free, careful not to snap the branch.

In this way he proceeded some twenty metres into the copse, far enough he judged to make him undetectable come the dawn. Another two-second flash of the penlight. He placed gun and shovel on the ground and sank down beside them, feeling for a tree trunk to rest his back against. He positioned himself to face down the hill, towards the house, though the massed trees largely obscured the buildings and only a yellow penumbra marked its position.

He unbuckled the knapsack, extracted the bottle of water and took a couple of swigs. Up here the air carried a slight nip and as the warming effect of his exertions diminished he began to notice it. In his suit and fatigues though, he was snug enough. He closed his eyes and listened without fear to the nameless rustlings and scurryings above and in the undergrowth. This was the music of the night and it didn't trouble him. His analytical mind rejected phantoms and bogeymen. Now and again the buzz of an engine overlaid nature's diapason, and once the clearing of a throat – the phlegmy crackle of a heavy smoker – startled him with its seeming nearness. He realised that it was a trick of the acoustics of the amphitheatrical shape of the terrain, but it was also a reminder of the presence of the gendarmes on the other side of the wall, not a hundred metres away. Soon afterwards he drifted into semi-slumber, a disciplined state that allowed him to stay alert while trickle-charging his energy for the coming day, D-Day.

Les Molières, Var, 2 June 1996 (morning)

'On the day, he did what he was paid to do. He earned his pay.'

Ghislaine Fougère to Enrique Dubois, Lieutenant de Police, DCPJ, during interrogation, 13.06.1996.

*   *   *

A single shaft of sunlight reached out across the valley like a laser beam. The ray broadened and was joined by others, spread fingers of brilliance. They gradually merged into a single broad fan, creating instant colour where before was only grey. A bird cheeped, was joined by a second of the same species; a pause then an exultant trilling, like a bugler sounding reveille.

Lux came fully awake with the birds, chilled and stiff, bladder close to bursting. In the copse it was still near-dark, with just enough light to see by. He stood up, stamped his feet to rouse the circulation, brushed fallen pine needles from the shoulders of his fatigues, before relieving himself at some length.

Directly overhead a bird took off with a shrill of alarm. Lux hunted out the binoculars and slung the strap around his neck. He made for the edge of the trees. Keeping to the shadows, he focused the glasses on the house. Two plain-clothes men stood by the front entrance, yawning and smoking. No other humanity. All was calm. Lux grinned to himself. The proverbial lull before the storm.

Retreating to his overnight bivouac, he stripped off the fatigues and the redundant suit, letting the suit lie where it fell. He donned the gendarme's uniform, pulling the fatigues over the top. He drank some water. His stomach gurgled. Maybe later he would munch an apple. Right now his appetite was zero. A cigarette, *that* he could use. Mindful of the gendarmes a hundred metres away, if that, beyond the wall, he rejected the temptation. In all probability the smoke would disperse as it filtered upwards through the foliage but even so there remained a small element of risk. So he refrained, self-discipline overruling the craving for nicotine. This small sacrifice even gave him a perverse pleasure, was proof that he was the master of his vices.

*   *   *

Before the day began to heat up he dug a trench in the earth, some five feet long by two wide and eighteen inches deep. It took about forty minutes. The earth was bone dry but loose packed. Into it he dumped suit, shoulder holster, oilskins, since it clearly was not going to rain, and the emptied knapsack. All he kept was the kepi, the belt and holster, and the MAB automatic. It wasn't the standard gendarmerie sidearm – which is a Beretta M92 – but no one was likely to check unless he was caught, in which case it wouldn't matter what make of gun he was toting.

He had just finished digging when a helicopter flew over, first patrol of the day. After circling each of the other two copses in turn it came bowling along towards where Lux was resting from his toils. It was a routine check but no less unsettling for all that, watching the machine pass back and forth only a few feet above the treetops. Inspection over, it chattered off to the south.

Lux checked the time: it was a few minutes from 7.30. H-Hour was 11.30 give or take thirty minutes. So any time from eleven o'clock onwards. If he were to allow, say, an additional thirty minutes either way as a comfort zone, he would have to be at readiness from 10.30.

The morning dragged by. As the sun rose he became overheated in his two sets of clothes. It was a penance he would have to bear. The need to transform himself quickly into a gendarme as soon as Chirac went down took precedence over comfort. As for the fatigues, their function was twofold: to keep the uniform clean, and as camouflage. Well, shit, he couldn't expect to make ten million bucks without some suffering.

Helicopters came and went every thirty minutes. As the beat of the rotors of the ten-thirty patrol faded, Lux began his final preparations. He peeled the bubble wrap from the rifle, folded it flat and dumped it in the trench. He tipped the Ubertl scope sight and the sound suppressor from their bubble wrap tubes. The scope he clipped on its mount and the suppressor he screwed into the muzzle, extending the gun's overall length to well over five feet. He detached the magazine and individually re-checked the ammunition for the slightest blemish. All ten rounds passed. He patted his left breast pocket where reposed a spare magazine containing ten more rounds, also previously inspected.

With the gun cradled in his arms, and the hammer with its padded head and a couple of six-inch nails in his pocket he advanced cautiously to within three metres of the edge of the trees. From here he had a clear field of fire yet would still be deep enough in the copse to stay undetected. He hammered a nail about four centimetres deep into a tree trunk, at shoulder height. Using the nail as a rest for the gun barrel, he adopted a firing stance. The scope came naturally to his eye. He swept the sky, like an anti-aircraft gunner searching for bombers. Imitated *sotto voce* the tacka-tacka-tacka of a machinegun. Suddenly felt self-conscious, and shook his head sheepishly.

He was ready. He stood the Barrett against the tree.

Eleven o'clock. A helicopter showed up, swooping over and, for the first time, alongside the copses, skimming the ground. Lux retreated a good twenty metres into the trees and was spread-eagled on the ground when the machine flew past at walking pace. No reason for its crew of two to suspect the copse concealed a prospective assassin. After all, it had been combed before dark the previous evening, since when the estate had been sealed tighter than a pharaoh's tomb. Nobody had entered who hadn't been accounted for.

Satisfied, the helicopter went away, the crew complacent in the certainty that the estate was impenetrable. Perhaps they forgot that the tombs of the pharaohs had not proved quite as impenetrable as their architects intended.

Lux fetched his provisions and resumed his firing position. Squatting, his back supported by a tree, he drank water, nibbled at an apple. It was coming up to 11.30 and the heat was beginning to seriously bother him when a flurry of movement down at the house drew his attention. A stream of men, mostly plain-clothes but interspersed with a few uniformed CRS, spilled from the front entrance to join the dozen or so already outside. Through the binoculars Lux sought out Barail, but in vain. The *Commissaire* was no doubt continuing to direct operations from behind the drinks cabinet.

A shortish, stocky man seemed to be in charge, his mouth going like a fish's as he barked orders, finger stabbing here and there. The bulk of the force formed a border to the asphalted semi-circle; a tight cluster, six or maybe seven. Lux guessed that these were part of the President's personal bodyguard. Others were sure to be accompanying him in the helicopter.

No sooner were the dispositions completed, the stocky man looking about him, fists on hips, when the far-off stutter of a helicopter entered the valley. The engine note was vaguely different from that of the gendarmerie machine; deeper, more obtrusive.

While the new arrival was still no more than a speck on the sky's flawless blue Lux trained the binoculars on it. It was approaching from the southwest. This then could be the President.

A good half-hour late. He estimated it would touch down no more than five minutes from now. He brought the machine up close with the binoculars' zoom facility. The pilot was alone at the controls; shaven-headed with a droopy moustache, speaking into the transmitter mouthpiece that curled around his jaw. The Chiracs, assuming they were on board, would be in the four-seat passenger section behind. From hours spent studying the manual Lux was well acquainted with the internal layout of the Ecureuil. The passengers would only come in sight if the machine turned sideways on to him. Whether they did or didn't, would have no impact on his plans.

The patrol helicopter batted overhead and Lux prepared to hit the ground if it repeated its previous tactic of coming alongside. But no, it circled the copse once and headed off towards the approaching machine. Just going through the motions.

Lux hurried back to his bivouac and flung everything expendable into the trench: binoculars, protective glasses, bottle of water, provisions. When he returned to his firing position the approaching helicopter was much closer and on its descent. He hoisted the Barrett onto the branch and folded his fingers almost tenderly around the pistol grip.

Les Molières, Var, 2 June 1996 (afternoon)

The presidential helicopter almost filled the scope lens. Lux placed the crosshairs in the centre of the pilot's forehead. He could take him out now and the chances were the machine would plummet to earth and explode on impact, killing its occupants.

Lux never relied on chance. The helicopter was now nearly over the house and maybe two hundred feet up; the gendarmerie machine took up position to its right, maintaining a stationary hover. Lux dragged back the cocking lever of the Barrett. Again he put his eye to the scope. The helicopter was still head on to him. Even as he silently willed it to turn, it commenced a leisurely anti-clockwise pirouette on its axis. The glass panel of the passenger compartment was presented to Lux: there were only two passengers, a man and a woman. No bodyguards, surprisingly. The man was on the right, Lux's side. It was Chirac all right, his head turned towards his wife and tilted a little as if he were having difficulty hearing her; her face, partially obscured, was close to his ear.

The American's finger instinctively tightened around the trigger but the helicopter was still rotating and such a small target as a person's head required virtual total absence of movement, if only for a second.

Which was why he had decided not to shoot the President.

As the helicopter came fully broadside on he squeezed the trigger. A sound no louder than a cough as the bullet left the muzzle. The crack it emitted as it passed through the sound barrier was lost in the din of the two engines. One second later the projectile struck the helicopter near the base of the fuselage, behind the cabin. It pierced the unarmoured metal and, being a bullet that was designed to explode on impact, it burst into a million fragments. The contents of the aft bay fuel tank that had been pierced by the bullet exploded in their turn, ripping the helicopter apart and dealing instant death to all living souls in it.

Even as torn metal and plastic rained to earth with the remains of the mortally wounded machine, supported by its still-twisting rotor, descending more slowly in its wake, Lux was going hell for leather back into the depths of the copse. He stopped by the trench, dropped the rifle in it, followed by the fatigues. He jammed the gendarme's kepi on his head and strapped the gun belt, complete with automatic, around his waist. Working fast and frantically with the spade he filled in the trench with the loose earth.

A third explosion made the ground shudder under his feet. From close at hand came shouting. The gendarmes guarding the wall, he supposed; no one from below could have gotten up here in the time. He finished levelling the trench and stamped the earth flat.

More shouts. Through a slender gap in the trees he saw the back of a gendarme running down the hill, towards the devastation at its foot. Then another, then a third, stumbling but recovering. From somewhere below a siren brayed.

Now Lux was entering into the truly unknown and unpredictable. His next move would be governed by the behaviour of the security forces, especially the gendarmerie with whom he proposed to mingle. If the gendarmes were assuming that the explosion was accidental or had been caused by a bomb, they would have no reason to continue to guard the wall. So if the general trend was to rush to help, Lux was happy to conform. What he could not do was simply march brazenly out of cover in full view of the police.

Still clutching the spade, he set off for the other side of the copse, a distance of perhaps a hundred metres. Nearing the end of trees, he ducked back behind one as a gendarme dropped from the wall and ran straight towards him, apparently bent on taking the shortest route. Here it was – the unforeseen. The thing he had dreaded.

He slipped behind a tree and waited, listening to the thud of the man's feet as he blundered through the copse. As he passed Lux, he stumbled over an exposed root, and measured his length in the pine needles, his kepi spinning away. Lux froze and prepared to take action. The man cursed, went after his kepi on hands and knees. On recovering it he got up and, to Lux's relief, went on at a stagger, oblivious of his brush with certain death.

Lux shoved the spade under a clump of bushes. It would be found easily enough but not, he hoped, until he was long departed and might not even be connected with the destruction of the Presidential helicopter. He covered the few remaining metres to the edge of the trees and cautiously checked right and left. Farther along on his left, yet another a gendarme was scrambling over the wall. He fell awkwardly but was back on his feet at once and blundering down the hill. Lux chose right, running along the edge of the copse. At its southern end he followed it round. Now the results of his handiwork were revealed to him: the blazing wreckage of the helicopter, the milling security forces, their numbers swelling by the second as gendarmes arrived literally from all corners of the estate.

The patrol helicopter whirled by overhead as Lux took off after the other gendarmes. He forced himself to disregard it. He had nothing to fear from that quarter as the crew could have no way of knowing the explosion had been caused by a bullet. This was the beauty of his chosen method of killing Chirac.

As he reached the foot of the hill he became just another cop among many in the midst of chaos. He drew as close to the burning wreck as the heat would allow, noting that a number of bodies lay about, each with a small group in attendance. The Chiracs were not recognisably among them, so these were most likely victims of falling debris. A number of CRS men were tackling the blaze with fire extinguishers and making no impression at all; two gendarmes were in the process of connecting a garden hose. Unpreparedness was absolute.

'It must have been a bomb,' he heard a plain-clothes man say to a gendarme with sergeant's stripes on his sleeve.

Good, Lux thought. That was what he meant them to assume.

The best time to slip away was now, while confusion was at its peak. Putting on an air of a man going about his business, he jogged off to the car park in search of his car. It was where Barail had said it would be and so were the keys. He started up and drove out. No one paid him any heed. A left turn onto the driveway. Accelerating hard, like a man on an urgent errand, but not too hard like a man on the run. The next and last obstacle was the barrier at the gate. The driveway was deserted apart from a CRS man hurrying towards the house. The barrier was down, manned by two more CRS. Security hadn't entirely relaxed then. Lux prayed that neither of the men was the one who checked him in last night.

He braked. The shorter of the two CRS, whose epaulettes denoted the rank of brigadier-major, ambled up.

'*Salut, mon vieux,*' he hailed Lux. '*On a entendu une explosion. Qu'est-ce qui se passe?*' What's happening?

'A bomb. The helico has been blown to pieces.'

The CRS brigadier-major blanched. 'You don't say! What about JC?'

Lux shrugged. 'Injured, at least.' Straining to speak accentless French.

'*Où vas-tu?*' Where are you going?

The man's life hinged on his acceptance of Lux's answer. 'We've called the fire brigade. I've been ordered to wait at the end of the road and guide them here.'

The barrier was on its way up even as he spoke.

'*Allez-y.* Don't drive too fast, hey?'

Lux felt he had already pushed his French too far so he settled for a nod. He slipped the clutch and passed through the barrier.

After the first bend he let the engine rip. Down the track at teeth-rattling speed to where Leandri was supposed to be waiting in the Jeep. Almost home free and another five million dollars in the bag.

Leandri was at the old barn, sitting astride the front wheel of a dilapidated tractor, exploring his teeth with a match. Inside, the black Citroën, its nose in a band of sunlight, the rest in shadow. Bernanos was not in evidence. Lux drove straight into the barn and climbed out.

'*Va bien?*' Leandri asked in greeting.

'So far,' Lux replied. 'Bernanos gone?'

'Last night. The suit is in the car and I have the ID.'

Lux stripped off the gendarme uniform, exchanging it for the charcoal grey suit that lay neatly folded on the back seat of the Citroen, the same suit that recently adorned Robert Bernanos. It smelled faintly of cigarette smoke.

'I heard an explosion,' Leandri said, unconsciously parroting the CRS brigadier-major. 'Was that you?'

'Don't ask, pal. Give me the ID.'

Leandri handed over Lux's CRS card.

'Right,' Lux said, in his haste making a hash of knotting his necktie. 'Let's hit the road, Tomas.'

Blasting along the D27 they passed two fire appliances going the other way, beacons flashing and sirens at full scream, and a kilometre or so farther a whole convoy of ambulances led by a police car.

'They'll be setting up road blocks,' Leandri mused.

'Not for us.' Lux patted his pocket containing the ID card. 'We're with the good guys.'

* * *

But road blocks cannot be organised at a snap of the fingers. The security forces were initially convinced that a bomb had been planted on the helicopter and that no fleeing assassin existed to be stopped. Barail, the senior security officer present, issued no instructions. It was left to Mazé to take the initiative and, as a precaution, arrange to have the whole area cordoned off within a five-mile radius, despite the pooh-poohing of Capitaine Petit, the senior gendarmerie officer present.

'It was a bomb, *mon vieux*,' he protested as they stood together and watched the futile efforts of their men to douse the blaze with a garden hose and fire extinguishers from their cars' emergency kits. 'Do you think the assassin came here to observe the results of his handicraft?'

'We cannot be sure,' Mazé returned, 'therefore we must not squander the opportunity.'

Even so it was after one pm. when the first road block was set up on the D27, north of Les Molières, this being the likeliest escape route. An hour more elapsed before every route out of Les Molières was covered within a radius of ten kilometres. By then the black Citroën with the government plates was in a private garage beneath an apartment block in Cannes, awaiting new plates and a respray by a local firm that specialised in providing new identities for stolen cars. Lux was stepping out of a taxi in the Place Wilson, in Nice, and Leandri was enjoying a *café cappuccino* at Cannes central station as he waited for the 2.45 train to Toulon.

*   *   *

Unable to bear looking upon the outcome of his machinations, Julien Barail remained in his makeshift operations centre. In his hand a glass of whisky, his fourth of the day.

When the explosion occurred at 12.07pm it blew out most of the windows in the upper floor of the Crillon house but left the lower more or less unscathed. His senses blunted by alcohol, Barail's flinch was no more than a reflex. He did not at once connect it with the President. Even the crash to earth of the wrecked helicopter and the further explosions, one of which did shatter both windows of the study, failed to stir him. While all outside was in uproar he continued to stare down at his hands; splayed flat on the desktop they resembled a pair of anaemic starfish.

He knew he should join his deputy outside, take charge, issue orders. It was his job. To remain in the house was to invite attention and comment. Yet he could not bring himself to mingle with his colleagues. His perfidy had come home to roost.

It was after one o'clock before anyone entered his temporary office (though he was not aware of it, two CRS men had been stationed outside his door since ten minutes after the helicopter plummeted to earth). At about the time Lux and Leandri were turning onto the D25 at Ste Maxime, Mazé barged in without knocking, the two CRS men in tow.

'Commissaire Divisionnaire Barail,' Mazé barked, coming to

279

attention before the man who, conspirator or not, remained his superior. 'In the name of the Republic, I am placing you under arrest for complicity in murder.'

Mazé's proclamation with its death knell ring took a while to sink in. Barail's face remained empty of emotion and he did not stir.

'Did you hear me, *Commissaire*?' Mazé said, fidgeting, still at attention.

With a long sigh Barail rose. 'What are you raving about?' he said, bluffing to the last. 'Are you insane?'

'We have known of your complicity for several months, *Commissaire*, so it is useless to expostulate. If you co-operate I will leave the cuffs off.'

A further blast outside accompanied by more crashing of glass triggered renewed shouting: '*Attention! Gardez-vous tous!*' Something metallic clattered on the asphalt.

'Is the President injured?' Barail's voice had a dead quality, like a machine-made recording.

'Need you ask? Every living person in that helicopter was killed instantly when it blew up.'

Barail abandoned the refuge of his desk, his movements those of an octogenarian, his shoulders no longer square. A broken man.

'Are you armed?' Mazé asked.

Barail shook his head, but Mazé had him frisked anyway.

'One more matter before we leave,' Mazé said. 'We must know if it was a bomb, and if the assassin is here or has been here.'

'You speak in riddles, Mazé. If sabotage has occurred it is none of my doing.'

Mazé's smile was without humour or warmth. 'When you have listened to the tapes of your conversations with Agent 411 you will cease to protest your innocence, *monsieur*. Now … is he here or not?'

Since Barail presumed Lux was long gone he could have honestly replied 'No.' Instead he chose to maintain his virtuous stance.

'As I am not involved in this unspeakable crime, I cannot help you. Who in God's name is Agent 411? If you feel a compulsion to arrest me, go ahead. I will not make difficulties for you.'

At heart a compassionate man, Mazé felt almost sorry for his chief. He touched his shoulder, conveying a little of that sympathy while asserting his authority.

'Come, *Commissaire*,' he said in a soothing tone, such as a doctor might use on a hypochondriac patient. 'Le Renard is expecting us and he is not in the best of humour.'

Menton, 2 June 1996 (afternoon)

'The transition was sudden – like a coup de foudre. *Afterwards I was no longer in charge of my destiny. You understand what I am saying?* [prolonged silence] *No, you don't understand, do you, Enrique?'*

Ghislaine Fougère to Enrique Dubois, Lieutenant de Police, DCPJ, during interrogation, 13.06.1996.

*   *   *

When her cellphone tinkled, Ghislaine was on the couch, her legs tucked under her, skimming the fashion page of *Nice-Matin.* She unclipped the phone from the waistband of her cords.

'Dennis?' she said, before her caller could announce himself.

'Yes. Listen, I want you to take a taxi to Monaco. Meet me at the Café de ...' A squiggle of static briefly erased his voice. Reception in Menton was always patchy owing to the high ground surrounding the town. ' ... in about forty-five minutes, but if I'm late, don't worry.'

'Repeat the name of the café, please, *mon amour.* Your voice faded.'

'Café de Paris,' he said, enunciating precisely. 'Give me an hour.'

'I know it. By the Casino.'

'Take a table. If you want to eat, eat. Don't wait for me.'

'I am not hungry. Where are you?'

'Cannes.' A silence; she could hear him breathing. 'I love you,' he said.

'And I, you.'

And then he was gone. She listened to the dialling tone for a long moment, nibbling her lower lip, the questions she had meant to ask left unasked.

Decision hour. To run away with the man she loved or to stay with the security of the status quo. It wasn't such a dilemma. The elements of her life she would lose if she chose love over pragmatism, she could bear to lose. The same couldn't be said for the converse: a future without Lux was too barren to contemplate. For good or ill, he was now essential to her wellbeing.

The cellphone trilled again. She checked the number on the screen and grimaced. She had no wish to speak to her boss. After ten rings the voicemail cut in. She left the phone trilling on the couch and went over to the telephone table to hunt for a taxi service in the *Pages Jaunes*.

* * *

As the taxi driver slid her valise into the trunk of his long-in-the-tooth Mercedes, Ghislaine's cellphone summoned her again. Not unexpectedly, it was her boss again, the persistent bastard. The temptation to hurl the phone from her was strong. She resisted it. Apart from its general indispensability, she had to keep the line of communication open for Lux.

In the back seat of the taxi she reflected on the consequences of her decision to throw in her lot with Lux, to effectively reject her lifestyle and entrust mind, body and spirit, and her so-precious son to uncertainty, no matter what the ultimate cost.

And found she didn't care a bit.

Such was her distraction that when the cellphone claimed her once more as the taxi filtered onto the *autoroute*, she absently put it to her ear and thumbed the *oui* key.

Even as her mouth opened to speak her caller pre-empted her. '*Agent quatre-cent onze? Ici Mazé.*'

* * *

As Ghislaine was paying off the taxi by the *acenseur* station on Avenue d'Ostende she noticed the green Peugeot that had stuck too close to her the entire drive from Menton to Monaco cruising past in search of a space. The two occupants of the car were plain-clothes CRS, part of a team designated to keep Lux's house under continuous surveillance these past months. Fifty metres on the Peugeot gave up its quest for a legal slot and came to a stop, double parked. The man in the passenger seat got out.

'Call me as soon as you get parked,' he ordered his junior colleague.

The Peugeot sped off with no consideration for approaching vehicles, nearly causing a minor pile-up. The CRS officer turned towards the kerb and promptly blundered into an elderly overweight woman with a poodle under each arm who was emerging from a gap between two parked cars. He sent her reeling and fell on top of her amid canine yaps and flying curses, the woman outdoing the policeman in the latter respect. His elbow cracked painfully against the bumper of one of the cars.

'You stupid fucking cow!' he rasped, as he strove to disengage himself.

'How dare you!' she shrilled back at him. 'I'll report you to the police, you hooligan!'

'I *am* the fucking police.'

Leaving her to round up her pets, who had chosen to abscond in opposite directions, he staggered onto the pavement, nursing a throbbing elbow. The Fougère piece was of course long away and no amount of '*Merdes*' would bring her back.

Acting on my instructions, Simonelli went to Menton to track down Lux. Naturally there was a fee involved.

Translated from written statement of Commissaire Divisionnaire Julien Barail, 03.06.1996.

* * *

While the hapless CRS man floundered in the Avenue d'Ostende, another interested party was doing somewhat better.

Rafael Simonelli had travelled by hired Honda Civic from Auxerre to Menton, entering the town in the late morning, leaving time enough for a leisurely *plat du jour* at l'Oursin Restaurant, watching the boats come in and the girls go by. His lingering worry about venturing out soon dissipated, secure behind his dark glasses, beard and floppy coiffure, and not least his Belgian passport, for which he was indebted to Barail. Not that the *Commissaire* had supplied it free of charge, damn his grasping ways.

Simonelli punctuated his excellent repast of "fruits of the sea" with a second herbal tea. While he sipped he pored over Barail's sketch of the location of Lux's house.

* * *

It was approaching two o'clock when he came to the cul-de-sac in the heights above Menton, where Lux's villa snuggled amid a half dozen similarly exclusive properties. To park in the cul-de-sac itself would be a little too blatant. Not only was there Lux's girl to consider, but also, Barail had warned, the CRS surveillance team lodged in an empty villa opposite. So Simonelli parked on the Route de Castellar, a few metres short of the turn. From there he enjoyed an outlook of spectacular beauty: the red rooftops of Menton, the jutting nose of Cap Martin with its toytown dwellings, and above all the dazzling blue of the Côte d'Azur. Almost the equal of the view from the terrace of his house in Corsica, alas no more.

Among the other goodies provided by Barail was a transcript of a conversation between Lux and his floozie, presumably obtained by tapping the telephone, which made reference to the couple's exit plan

– but only up to the point where she was to leave the house and rendezvous with him. The location of their assignation was still unknown. Follow the girl, Barail had suggested, and she will lead you to Lux.

'And then what?' Simonelli queried. 'They will probably be inseparable.'

'Then do what you must do,' Barail said, no change in his expression.

Simonelli was patient by nature and did not mind the heat. What they called hot here on the mainland was merely balmy to a Corsican. Whenever he felt like dozing he did a couple of circuits of the car, smoked a cigarette. Thirty-five minutes into this wait an old Mercedes taxi rolled up and turned into the cul-de-sac. Simonelli went on full mental alert. He got out and walked briskly – not too briskly – to the corner. From there, ostensibly lingering to light a cigarette, he perceived that the taxi's destination was indeed Lux's villa.

Back in the Honda he started the engine, waited for a dusty Deux Chevaux to pass, and executed a three-point turn that left him facing down the hill towards the town.

The taxi with its solitary female passenger edged out onto the Route de Castellar and turned right. Simonelli was about to set off after it when a second car, a green Peugeot containing two men, shot out of the cul-de-sac and away down the hill in the taxi's wake.

This was not unexpected. If the girl was the CRS team's only lead to Lux, the Corsican reasoned, they would have to keep track of her. He allowed them a two hundred metre lead before moving off.

Keeping the Peugeot and the Mercedes in sight was no hardship at first. The Sunday afternoon, pre-season traffic was light and the drivers less combative than their weekday contemporaries. It was only when the taxi and the Peugeot descended into the tangle of Monaco's streets that he came close to losing them. Fortunately for him, the gendarmerie tend to be less numerous and less alert on Sundays, and his occasional minor infractions (jumping red lights, overtaking on prohibited sections of road, and so on), went unnoticed.

The taxi came to a halt opposite the Acenseur on Avenue d'Ostende to disgorge a brunette in a short blue and yellow print dress. Ever the Romeo, Simonelli almost ran off the road ogling her. Lucky Lux, he reflected, to have a piece like that to warm his bed. He stopped just short of the taxi, unlike the Peugeot, which continued some fifty metres or more beyond. As good fortune would have it a Jaguar with a GB sticker on its backside vacated a space two cars behind the taxi. He backed into it, parking untidily, and leapt out. The woman, a large suitcase and a grip by her feet, was paying off the taxi. Farther along the street a man in a dark jacket was climbing from the double-parked Peugeot. A passer-by jostled Simonelli as he bent to manually lock the Honda.

'*Excusez-moi.*' Foreign-accented, like half the inhabitants of the Principality.

Simonelli hardly registered the apology. His eyes were only for the woman, now descending the stairway to the Quai des Etats-Unis, luggage and all. He watched her for a moment, out of basic male appreciation rather than professional interest. She had nicely-shaped legs that the short dress did proud and tits that bounced a little with each step. Remembering why he was there, he privately upbraided himself and set off towards the steps.

The Monaco-registered fifty-foot motor cruiser *Ocean Deep*, ploughed through the rolling swell at a relaxed fifteen knots. Her course was east-north-east, her position some twenty nautical miles off the Italian coast. At the wheel was a man called Edwin Keating, a husky American with a head of thick grey hair; beside him his stepson, Nick. Keating owed Dennis Lux a huge favour and was in the act of working it off.

In the stern of the boat, under a blue awning, Lux and Ghislaine sat thigh to thigh, each seeking comfort of a different kind from the other. As the euphoria engendered by his successful hit faded, Lux was beset by unease, increasingly convinced that he had made some fatal slip-up that would lead to his downfall. Ghislaine on the other hand was beset by a whole gamut of emotions, from misgivings to exhilaration. The sudden discovery, less than twenty-four hours earlier, that she truly loved this man after weeks of pretence had thrilled and devastated her. So intense was that love that it had driven her to stay by his side and in doing so cross over from lawmaker to lawbreaker.

Lost in introspection, they had barely spoken since leaving Monaco harbour under benign skies and the still-hot late afternoon sun. Now, after an hour at sea, Ghislaine was the one to end the silence.

'Are you ready to tell me what is happening, Dennis?' she said. Although she well knew that today was the day he was supposed to shoot the President and it was reasonable to suppose he had gone through with it, she could only guess at the outcome. Had he succeeded in the crime of the decade or not? She was determined that he would be open with her, that he would speak of it first.

Lux's arm was about her shoulders. He squeezed her, and she interpreted this as a substitute for the truth that he was not ready to tell.

'Not yet, sweetheart.'

Not that he could delay long, he well knew. She would hear soon enough on the radio or TV and put two and two together.

'I do so love you,' she said earnestly, stroking his forearm so that the blond hairs stood up like stalks of corn in miniature.

'Me too, you,' he said with a quick grin.

'No, I mean I really *do* love you,' she persisted.

Now he looked surprised. 'Well, sure, sweetheart. I never doubted it.'

Such an accolade to her acting ability. From the start, when she contrived for him to 'stumble on' her in the copse at the Crillon Estate, she had flitted from one lie to the next. From simulated fright to fake flirtatiousness, from demonstrations of lust to avowals of love. Hardly an utterance passed her lips nor act was performed that was not counterfeit. Yet falseness was not in her nature. Her professed honesty was real. Only her job – *this* job – required deception.

Since two hours ago she was free of all that. From now on she would speak only the truth.

'I love you, darling,' she said again, snuggling into his embrace.

He didn't speak. He was suddenly remembering those lies that, thanks to Barail, he *had* found out about. Soon he would confront her with them. But not yet, not here. Better wait until they were safe in Lausanne.

* * *

Ocean Deep hove to off the Italian seaport of Genova at around ten-thirty that night, just in sight of the city's lights. A motor cruiser of about half her length came up on the windward side. The two hulls nudged, sausage-shaped fenders keeping the paintwork from rubbing, and Nick secured them to each other with a length of line.

A man wearing a black T-shirt and baseball cap vaulted aboard from the small cruiser, leaving its outdrive engine ticking over.

'Good evening,' he said to Nick, strongly Italian accented.

'*Caio*,' Nick responded. Just then, Keating joined them and hands were clasped. Some rapid Italian ensued.

'Denny – you can come out,' Keating called, and Lux and Ghislaine appeared from behind the superstructure. More greetings. Nick bustled about transferring luggage to the small boat.

Ghislaine bit back a question about the reason for the transfer. Her mind was trained to think like a criminal, so she guessed that to go ashore in an Italian registered craft – the square stern showed the smaller boat's port of registration to be Genova – was to make it less likely they would be noticed, though these enlightened days nationals of EU member countries traversed borders more or less without constraint.

Lux exchanged fraternal hugs with the bearlike Keating and mock-punched a grinning Nick. Ghislaine kissed cheeks with them both, thanked them, and was wished all the luck in the world. She spurned a helping hand in the transfer to the Italian boat. Lux went after her and they descended into the tiny cabin under the foredeck.

The boats separated. As the note of *Ocean Deep's* engine rose and she curved away into the night, the Italian, an unprincipled rogue called Zeppi – from Guiseppi – dropped into the cabin hatchway. *Lire* changed hands. It looked a lot but with the *lira* at about 1300 to the dollar it was less than a thousand.

'Will we stay in Genova tonight?' Ghislaine asked Lux.

'No. We're sleeping on board.'

Ghislaine patted the cushion of the bench seat. 'Not exactly four-star. Why can't we go ashore?'

Zeppi stopped counting *lire* to look at her. His brown eyes in their whiter than whites were appraising, perhaps appreciative of her loveliness.

'In daytime you go on shore. It is safer in daytime. More peoples, more busy. In night *polizia* always watch. Bad guys always come at night.'

It made sense to her. She didn't contest it.

Zeppi finished counting, saluted Lux with the wad of notes and returned to the helm. The deck angled upwards as he piled on the knots.

As the little boat bucked its way to Genova with unnecessary haste – or so it seemed to Ghislaine, a poor sailor – the thud-thud of the keel on the water was a constant refrain. Surprisingly quickly she grew inured to it. She curled up on the seat, her head on the lap of her lover and was soon asleep.

Monaco, 2 June 1996 (evening)

The sky over the Palace was red and the city cowered in the shadow of the Tête de Chien *massif.* The lights around the port came on as the sleek motor cruiser entered the passage between the breakwaters, its engine beat amplified in the hush of the evening.

From the quayside bench Rafael Simonelli watched impassively as the boat manoeuvred to reverse into its berth. The lettering of the name on the stern, *Ocean Deep,* was gilt and glistened under the lights. A two-man crew, one about sixty, the other in his twenties. Father and son possibly. Simonelli smiled to himself thinly. A blood tie was good for what he had in mind.

With the older man at the helm the boat crept into its space under minimal power, fenders nudging those of the craft on either side, making little whimpering sounds. The young man leapt onto the quay, line at the ready and hooked the end loop over a bollard on the starboard quarter, then repeated the exercise on the other side. The engine died. Words were exchanged, American-accented English that Simonelli didn't quite catch. The young man plugged a power line into the quayside power supply and followed the older man below. Lights sprang on. Simonelli heard them talking, the crackle of laughter. 'Hell, no!' someone exclaimed.

Darkness was fast spreading its cape. The quay was deserted but for a couple walking a dog and, three boats up, a man working under an arc lamp on the bow of a tired-looking ketch.

Simonelli left the bench and made for the nearest payphone.

Once he had extracted Lux's whereabouts from the grey-haired American, Simonelli would be faced with a greater Rubicon – how to discourage the man from alerting Lux. He had toyed with the idea of silencing him and his companion permanently. But even Simonelli, a man of few scruples and fewer nerves, shrank from a double murder without proper preparation. So he phoned a couple of fellow-islanders who lived in Nice.

Tracking them down to an inevitable bar took until well after midnight but, tempted by a twenty thousand franc payday between them, they finally rolled up in a wreck of an open-topped Renault Floride. One of them was the worse for drink. It took a succession of black coffees at the all-night café where Rue Grimaldi intersects Albert *1er* to restore him to a tolerable level of sobriety.

In lowered tones Simonelli explained his requirements: overpower the two Yanks, take the boat out to sea and stay there and baby-sit them for three days. The older of the pair, a hook-nose, muscular individual with an ear-ring like Simonelli's, except that the stone that dangled from it was less precious than a ruby, was a former fisherman who had the skills it took to handle a boat the size of *Ocean Deep*. He was known as Le Boeuf – the Bull.

Both men accepted the contract as if it were no more routine than walking a dog. Simonelli had already drawn half the agreed fee from a nearby cash dispenser. He doled it out, sixty-forty in Le Boeuf's favour.

The operation went as smooth as glass. Dawn was still an hour away and the Americans sleeping soundly when Simonelli and his helpers boarded *Ocean Deep*. A gun under the grey-hair's chin secured their full co-operation. He parted with an address in exchange for his stepson's life. The pair were then bound and gagged and locked in a cabin with a single porthole too small for even a child to wriggle through.

When Simonelli took his leave, the engines were ticking over and Le Boeuf was down among them, poking around knowledgeably.

'Three days, *mon pote*,' Simonelli reminded him. 'Come back early and you can whistle for your other ten.'

Le Boeuf's grin displayed more gap than tooth.

'Don't worry about us, chief. I always fancied a cruise. We might even take a week.'

From the quayside Simonelli hung about to watch his hirelings cast off and nose out of the berth to chug towards the port entrance, the first shafts of sunlight silvering the bridge windows.

'Bon voyage,' he chuckled and walked away, hands in pockets, well-pleased with his night's work.

'The helicopter was not destroyed by a bomb,' Le Renard announced to the room.

'Not destroyed by a bomb?' the Minister of the Interior echoed, his brow crinkling. His puzzlement was reflected in the scrubbed, rubicund features of Roger Billaud-Varennes, his Chef de Cabinet, seated to Debre's right.

'Are you serious?' Billaud-Varennes said, feeling he ought to say something.

'Why was I not told this sooner?' the Minister cut in. Anger simmering.

'Because I received the report only minutes ago, on my way here, *Monsieur le Ministre*,' Le Renard said smoothly.

'So did I,' Bernard Provost, Director General of the Gendarmerie, murmured, in a show of solidarity, to lessen the heat on his colleague.

Debre's scowl retreated. 'If it was not a bomb, what was it? How do you create an explosion without a bomb, pray?'

'It would appear that our Jackal used an explosive bullet. Fired into the rear fuel tank which on the Ecureuil is essentially unprotected. Very effective and very very clever on his part.'

'Clever?' Debre snapped. 'How so?'

Le Renard yielded the floor to Mazé.

'Precisely because he intended us to think it was a bomb,' the newly-elevated *Commissaire de Police* explained. 'It was a perfectly natural assumption.'

'Yes, yes,' the Minister said irritably. 'But why is that so clever?'

'Because, *Monsieur le Ministre,* we were lulled into the supposition that the assassin had not after all entered the grounds. That the bomb had been planted in the helicopter, in which case there would be no need for him to be at the scene.'

Provost elaborated. 'Which meant that instead of immediately sealing off the estate most of my men rushed to the scene of the crash.'

'Does this mean that the assassin was there all along?' Billaud-Varennes framed the question that Debre had been about to ask.

'Regrettably, yes,' Le Renard said. 'He was dressed as a gendarme. He left by car within minutes of the shooting, under the pretext of guiding the fire appliances. We also discovered the weapon he used and some of his belongings in a copse, presumably where he was hiding.'

The Minister rolled his eyes. 'Now we have a killer on the loose and you don't know where. Your agent – 441 or whatever she is called … '

'411, *monsieur.*'

'Whatever, she does not appear to have been very effective in extracting information from her lover.' His lip curled as he spoke the last word.

'She is missing,' Mazé announced, looking uncomfortable. 'She cannot be contacted by her cellphone.'

'A litany of incompetence and ineptitude!' the Minister fumed. 'Whoever was in charge should be disciplined.'

'Commissaire Barail was in charge, *Monsieur le Ministre,*' Le Renard pointed out, 'and as you know he is already under arrest.'

'Ah, yes. Stupid of me.'

At least, Mazé thought, the man had the grace to admit when he was behaving like a typical politician. A moment later he had cause to revise his opinion when the Minister glared at him.

'But you were there, were you not, *Commandant*? Excuse me … I mean *Commissaire.*'

'*Oui, Monsieur le Ministre.*'

'*Bon.* Consider yourself reprimanded. Off the record, naturally, as it is only down to you that we were alerted to Barail's treason in the first place.'

'Has the press got wind of it yet?' Mazé asked. A strict clampdown on reporting had been promulgated within an hour of the incident. To keep all two hundred policemen not to mention twenty-plus *pompiers* and the ambulance crews from loose talk would be an on-going challenge, but all had been individually and collectively warned that their livelihoods were at stake.

'Amazingly, no,' the Chef de Cabinet said. 'Not so much as a single request for confirmation.'

'There was an enquiry from *Nice-Matin,*' Provost volunteered as he slopped water from the communal jug into a glass. 'An eyewitness reported a helicopter crash to the *Nice Matin* office and they checked it out with the local Gendarmerie. Our people professed ignorance but took it seriously enough to pass it down the line. Since nobody knew anything, it seems to have died a death. I only learned of it myself in passing.'

'Woe betide anyone who goes sniffing around the Crillon place,' Le Renard said. 'My men will stay in place at least until the wreckage has been moved and all traces cleaned up.'

'Very good.' The Minister stood, buttoned his jacket; Billaud-

Varennes did likewise. 'Everything seems to be in hand, apart from allowing the assassin to slip away. I have every confidence that that slip will be rectified inside twenty-four hours, *messieurs*. Keep Billaud-Varennes fully informed.'

Le Renard, also standing and stuffing papers into his attaché case, asked, 'Has the President communicated with you since the incident?'

The Interior Minister, also shuffling papers, permitted himself a shadow of a smile. 'Naturally. He is keenly interested in the case. He said – absolutely straight-faced, I promise you – he did not think that the dummy we used as his stand-in was very flattering. Now, gentlemen … I bid you good day.'

Paris 15e Arondissement, 3 June 1996 (morning)

'I will co-operate.'

Commissaire Divisionnaire Julien Barail to Commissaire Divisionnaire Frédéric Le Page, DCPJ, during interrogation, 03.06.1996.

★   ★   ★

The interrogation of Commissaire Divisionnaire Julien Barail took place in a first floor DCPJ office near the Porte de Versailles. It did not involve electricity or water or extreme heat, or even injections of thiopental sodium. By police standards it was a remarkably civilised session.

The team of interviewers was four strong: Commissaire Divisionnaire de la DCPJ Frédéric Le Page led the interrogation; his helpers ironically included Enrique Dubois who was also a witness against Barail. They played him extracts from some eighty hours of cassettes, mostly consisting of conversation between him and Lucille alias Ghislaine Fougère alias Agent 411. These pieces of dialogue demonstrated more effectively than any rough stuff the futility of denial. When Barail learned that his *poule* and Lux's lover were the same girl he even laughed at this further irony.

One of the few secrets he had withheld from the bogus courtesan was Lux's real name. He assumed Lucille/Ghislaine must by now have exposed it and passed it on to her superiors, so he referred to him as Lux from the start. He even confessed to fixing Lux up with a Canadian passport. The particulars were immediately transmitted to the DST for circulation to all international airports and frontiers. Barail also confirmed Simonelli's complicity, but since the man was already on the wanted list this did not affect his status. He even implicated the old Comte, who had done no more than provide a meeting place and haven for the conspirators. The only area where uncertainty still remained was the identity of his employers. In this respect his inquisitors used the oldest ploy known to police all over the world: they pretended they had already arrested their chief suspect, Sheryl Glister.

'Your lady boss is singing like a lark, Julien,' Le Page said with a smirk.

Barail was well acquainted with police chicanery and not so readily duped.

'Which lady boss would that be?'

'*L'Américaine*,' Le Page said, poker-faced. 'Mademoiselle Glister. We picked her up in London this morning.'

'*Ah, bon?* My congratulations, *Commissaire*.'

'We had to get heavy with her. She is not so pretty as she was.'

Barail could imagine how heavy they would have had to get to make the Glister woman 'sing like a lark'. He was a little surprised that his opposite number in the DCPJ was prepared to put a foreign national through the mill. If their methods became public the hierarchy could be hauled before the Court of Human Rights, a humiliating experience for a democracy and member of the EU.

'If she is being so obliging you will need nothing from me,' he said, still wary.

'Just a few lines on your statement, Julien,' Le Page crooned. 'To tidy the loose ends. For example, she told us it was you who contacted her with an offer to kill the President, not the other way around. What is your version?

Was there any point in stalling? Barail thought not. He was going down for ever, come what may, but life inside might be a little sweeter if he worked with them instead of against.

So, with a certain amount of resignation, he talked. Over the space of eight hours they milked him as dry as an Egyptian mummy.

At least a dozen taxis were lined up in the rank off Genova's hectic, indescribably noisy Corso Quadrio. The driver of the first in line was sitting at the wheel of his car, head lolling out of the window.

'Do you still think you are being followed?' Ghislaine asked Lux as they approached it, hand in hand.

'Maybe.'

'By whom?'

'Not now, sweetheart, please.'

To the best of his knowledge the police had no one to look for. No name, no photograph, not even a description unless someone tied the assassin in with the CRS officer who had called to see Barail, or the gendarme who was allowed through the barrier to 'meet the fire appliance'. By the time a photofit was circulated, even if it resembled him, he would be safe in Switzerland under the protection of his British passport. And even Switzerland was but a seven-day stopover, an interlude.

Lux opened the door of the leading taxi and almost deposited the catnapping driver on the pavement.

'Airport,' he ordered, as the latter sprawled at his feet. '*Aeroporto. Pronto.*'

The man grinned ingratiatingly. He had a gold tooth and several black ones.

'*Si, signor.*'

They flew out of sunny Genova and set down in chilly, cloudy, gusty Geneva less than an hour later. Their passports, genuine and forged, earned no more than the most perfunctory of inspections. They were reunited with their luggage at the carousel, passed through the green Customs lane unchallenged. It was as Lux had expected yet in an important respect he was treading virgin ground: after a job he invariably travelled solo. Much as he loved the woman by his side the professional that was ever alive in him resented the increased responsibility with its attendant increased dangers.

From Geneva they travelled by Swiss Railways to Lausanne. Not long into the journey Ghislaine suggested a joint visit to the toilet and not for the purpose of bladder or bowel relief.

'I can't wait,' she had pouted, when he rebuffed her suggestion.

'We're almost there,' he grumbled. He was not in the mood.

Not to be denied, she embarked on a campaign to change his mood.

When the train trudged into Lausanne's grey but excruciatingly clean station, it was – unusually for Swiss Railways – twenty minutes late. Two of its passengers at least hadn't even noticed.

'Sheryl had composed a scorcher of a speech. It was designed to scare the shits out of every head of state with a nuclear or biological programme.'

Gary Rosenbrand to Thierry Garbe, freelance journalist, 19.03.1999

*   *   *

It was a little after six when Sheryl Glister woke up in the luxury apartment in the west of London. It was daylight and the street below was already winding up to the rush hour. A compulsive early riser, she went to the kitchen and brewed coffee while she worked on the speech she planned to offer BBC News later today, as soon as the story broke.

When a pyjama-clad Gary Rosenbrand wandered in, yawning and scratching under his armpit, she was already on her third draft.

'Hi,' he said, wondering what his wife would say if she knew he and Sheryl were sharing an apartment. She would automatically assume they were shacked up together. Back in 1992, when first he signed on for Greenpeace, Sheryl had indeed essayed a fairly blatant come-on but when he made it clear how things stood with him and Jenny, she had retreated in good grace. She had been man-hungry in those days all right, still was a bit, though her technique had mellowed, was less aggressive.

She waved a sheet of paper at him. 'Grab yourself some coffee, Gary, and tune in to this.'

'Sure.'

He poured it black, added a hefty dollop of sugar and sat opposite her at the round table.

'On Sunday 2nd June 1997,' she read from her notes, 'Jacques Chirac, President of France, was executed by an organisation committed to saving our planet for future generations. According to the laws of man we committed murder in the first degree and will therefore be liable to pay for our crime.

'Under those same man-made laws Jacques Chirac and the leaders of other like-minded nations are permitted to murder our planet and need fear no retribution. They may poison and pollute, blight and despoil this wonderful, extraordinary, unique planet of ours and be allowed to sleep easy in their beds, untroubled by laws or conscience. They may ultimately destroy the home of the human race, which destruction will result in the murder of six billion human beings, and no hand will be raised against them. Only nature will punish them – the tiny, tiny minority of guilty – as it punishes us, the multitude of innocents. Unlike man, Nature does not discriminate and she does not forgive. There is no appeal against Nature's judgement.

'By this act of retribution against all criminals such as Chirac, we, the members of an international society dedicated to protecting planet Earth against the depredations of the human race, give notice to all heads of state and government who design, build, test, stockpile and deploy weapons of mass destruction of any kind, be they nuclear, chemical, or biological, that unless they desist from such activity and proceed to destroy all such weapons under their control, they too will die.

'They will not – regrettably – die a lingering death from radiation burns or sickness, or an agonising one from the effects of a chemical or biological attack, deserving though such deaths may be. Nevertheless, *they – will – die*.' Eyes shining, Sheryl looked across at Rosenbrand. 'What do you think?'

Rosenbrand mock-applauded. 'Bloody fantastic. Don't change a word. Only one problem …'

'What's that?'

'They haven't announced Chirac's death yet.'

Sheryl frowned. 'Hey, that's right. They should've by now. I was so wrapped up in my speech I forgot we're still waiting for confirmation. Switch the radio on, G.'

* * *

Radio 4's eight-thirty news was mostly devoted to continuing recriminations over BSE, and pleas for John Major to get on his bike. Nothing remotely as earth-shattering as the assassination of the French President.

'They're suppressing it, the bastards!' Sheryl said through her teeth.

'Yeah, maybe,' Rosenbrand said, ripples of worry extending across his forehead. 'Or maybe it didn't happen.'

'Lux phoned with the code word – JC crucified. Do you think I'm going deaf or something?'

Rosenbrand lifted the last slice of toast from the rack and scraped the burnt patches from it. Wished he was home with Jen who made perfect toast.

'Maybe he was lying.'

Sheryl rounded on him, her expression savage. 'Don't be such a fucking defeatist! What would be the point? The deal is he gets paid on confirmation by newspaper, radio or TV. No confirmation, no pay. It's not as though he could get away with it. What would be the *point?*' she repeated.

Rosenbrand outwardly agreed with her. In private his doubts were mounting. It was inconceivable that, a whole day having elapsed since the supposed assassination, news of it had not been released.

'No,' Sheryl said, clutching the neck of her silk robe together as if to prevent Rosenbrand from peeking down her cleavage. 'They're keeping it quiet to avoid internal unrest. Don't forget there are rumblings of rebellion in the wings. Ever since Chirac laid his rotten eggs at Mururoa dissent has been simmering below the surface. Somebody – Juppé or the Interior Minister, Debre – is keeping the lid on it.'

Rosenbrand bit into the cold toast; a blob of marmalade stuck to his top lip.

'You're probably right. The next news is at nine-thirty. Keep your fingers crossed.'

No file existed on Dennis Lux, either in conventional written form, or on the computer files. The subject of a previous record was never raised so Barail, who answered all questions but volunteered nothing, omitted to mention that, true to his accord with Lux, he had removed all physical reference to the American assassin and obliterated all traces from the central computer. Not that it would have helped Acting Commissaire de Police Philippe Mazé, now leading the hunt. Lux had disappeared and so had Agent 411. It was fairly safe to assume that the double disappearance was not a coincidence. The report of the DCPJ officers assigned to watch Lux's house pointed to her having gone of her own free will. It was perplexing. It was inexplicable. At some juncture in their manufactured romance had she ceased playing a part and really fallen for him? Yet she had been giving feedback on his movements right up until the day before the assassination attempt.

If nothing else they had photographs of Lux, taken by the surveillance team when he stayed in Menton. They had blown up well and as Mazé eyed the head-and-shoulders snapshot selected for circulation to the press he could understand why a woman with normal appetites might fall for a man with the American's looks, killer or not. Even a policewoman; which she wasn't strictly anyway, more an administrator.

To add to Mazé's woes the Minister was blaming Le Renard for Lux's getaway, and Le Renard in turn was blaming Mazé. Nothing new there, except that it used to be Barail who passed the bucks from above. Now even that cushion was gone. Mazé released a great sigh into the smoke-clouded air of his office. Sometimes it was hard being a cop.

Lausanne, Switzerland, 3 June 1996 (afternoon)

'We had barely arrived in Lausanne when he confronted me with what he had learned from Commissaire Barail, that I was not a reporter, not married. He took it well. That and the rest.'

Ghislaine Fougère to Enrique Dubois, Lieutenant de Police, DCPJ, during interrogation, 28.06.1996.

* * *

The view from the balcony of the sixth-floor penthouse apartment was of a plain of water so flat and still as to appear iced over. The French shoreline on the far side of Lac Leman was duplicated as a mirror image and indistinguishable from the real thing.

A small motorboat arrowed out from the Swiss side, pushing an inverted V before it, and the mirror illusion was lost, the image shimmering then dispersing.

Lux flipped a cigarette butt far out beyond the balcony and turned to the woman he loved: she was in an outdoor lounge chair, watching him, her chin resting on her knuckled hand. Her eyes were big and fathomless.

'Anything wrong?' he said.

A tiny shake of her head, a smile that flickered like a candle flame caught in a draught. She was dressed in jeans and a skimpy white top that made it hard for him to focus on anything but her breasts.

'I was just looking at you. I like to look at you.'

'You might have to go on looking at me for a long time,' he said and went to sit in the empty chair next to her. They held hands, a natural union of the flesh, a shared desire for tactile contact.

'Do you own this place?' she asked.

'Not me. It's Eddie's.'

'Eddie?'

'Keating. The guy with the boat.'

'I see.' Ghislaine mulled this over but saw no reason to pursue it. 'Are you going to tell me what happened yesterday? Why we had to leave in such haste, in such mystery?'

Lux was in no hurry to come clean. He had heartsearched at length how much truth she could take and still not be repelled. To his astonishment and rising unease the media had not yet reported Chirac's death. Upside, this made it easier to hold off telling. The longer they were together, consolidating their relationship, the higher his chances of keeping her.

'For now you'll just have to trust me,' he said. But the entreaty sounded stale, past its sell-by date. He had used it before, maybe this was once too often.

'I trust you to love me and not to hurt me,' she affirmed, her phrasing carefully chosen. 'But we must share everything, even our darkest secrets, otherwise the trust is one-sided, *n'est-ce pas?*'

'At least I haven't lied.'

The statement carried an undertone that she immediately pounced upon.

'Are you suggesting I have?

'I know you have. For one thing, you're not married, you're divorced. For another, you're not a journalist, you're some sort of functionary. Why didn't you share those secrets with me?'

Her faced paled but she was not cowed. She kept her chin up, lacing her fingers with his.

'How do you know this?'

He had half-hoped she would deny it. 'It's true then.'

'Yes. It is true.'

He let go her hand, looked away. The boat was distant now, its buzzing motor no more obtrusive than the bombination of a fly in the clutches of a cobweb.

'If you will allow me, I will explain and then perhaps *you* will explain because you too have lied, in spite of what you say.'

Lux wondered how much she knew and how much would be guesswork. He masked his consternation behind the lighting of a cigarette and was satisfied to note the lack of tremor in the famously steady hand.

'Before I tell you,' she went on, 'there is one thing above all that you must hold in your mind – I love you. So long as I love you and you love me, here, now, without reservation, all else that came before is of less consequence than the fall of a leaf from a tree.'

Lux expelled smoke to sully the seemingly pure Swiss air.

'I do love you,' he said, though the avowal didn't trip from his tongue with quite the usual spontaneity. 'Now – tell.'

'Very well. I work ... worked, past tense ... for the RG.'

Not being a Frenchman, Lux's perception of the structure of the justice department was meagre.

'So what? Who cares who you worked for? History is history.'

He tossed a wandering lock of hair from his forehead and leaned towards her to kiss her. For once her response was lacklustre.

'I don't think you're listening.' Her voice hardened. 'I worked for the RG. The *Renseignements Généraux*. The Government.' And when Lux still looked blank, 'Oh, for God's sake, Dennis, it's a *police* department!'

He sat forward, digesting, disseminating.

'Why tell me now? You say "worked", past tense. So you used to be some sort of cop, now you're not. Now you're with me, knowing I'm a criminal of some sort. It doesn't change anything. It's still history, if you say it is.'

Now she too was leaning forward. Her face was troubled.

'You still don't understand completely. I worked for the RG until two days ago. I was working for them when I met you. Our meeting was engineered.' She pounded the chair arm with her clenched fist. 'I was planted on you!'

Even spelled out, the implications were slow to seep into his brain.

'If you were planted on me,' he said, speaking slowly and a shade unsteadily, 'you must know why I was there, at the Crillon place. And if you know why I was there you must also know or can guess what I did yesterday. So how come you're here with me? To arrest me?'

She shook her head violently, causing her hair to swirl across her face, veiling it completely.

'I love you, my darling. Unconditionally. I love you so much I don't care about anything but being with you. I quit the RG to be with you. I have turned a blind eye to your crime which, in any case, must have failed. Not only that but I have become your accomplice. If it is in my power to help you escape justice I will do it. Whatever is necessary, I will do.'

'When did you make this decision?' he said with a hint of harshness. Her fine professions of love and loyalty were not enough to ameliorate the hurt and the sense of treachery.

'I did not *decide* to love you, *crétin*.' She reached for him tentatively but he shied away like a naughty child fearing a blow. 'When we met at the Crillon estate, of course I was there to entrap you. You can thank Barail's loose tongue for that; it was due to him we were able to predict where you would be. At any rate, for some weeks after that our affair was for me no more than a job. I kept track of you when I could, though it was out of my hands when you were away. It did not make my job very easy.' A shaky laugh. 'Not that you should care. Well, anyway, I began to like you a little bit, then quite a lot … I was a little mixed up. It was around the time you stayed with me in my apartment … was it only last week?

It was then when my feelings for you became stronger than liking. From there it was but a short step to loving you.' She laughed again, only now it had a bitter timbre. 'Ironic, is it not, that the role I acted out has now become real life? You could say it serves me right.'

She fell to her knees at his feet, her features crumpling, her eyes glistening with the tears that somehow he was certain would never be shed.

'Do you want me to beg forgiveness? It was not a noble thing I did, though it was for the right cause. And if I was ignoble, so were you, in what you did ... tried to do. So we cancel out each other's ignobility. What matters is that I love you and you love me.'

To Lux it was akin to the final denouement in a banal Hollywood melodrama. He could almost believe he was watching this up on the big screen instead of participating.

In the street directly below tyres squealed as someone braked too late, an unusual occurrence in stolid Switzerland. No crunch of metal ensued. It served though to jolt Lux from his trancelike state, to liberate his vocal chords.

'No, sweetheart. You don't have to beg anything. I wish we had met some other way but it's nobody's fault.'

'That's not all,' she said.

'Christ.' His tone was soft but the sentiment behind it was full of feeling. 'What else?'

She swallowed. 'All that we said and did was recorded.'

'Oh, for Christ's sake! Are you telling me you were wired?'

It was standard police procedure in entrapment cases, so he should not have been surprised. Inside though, he squirmed a little to think that it was all on record to be sniggered over in the corridors of law and order: every endearment, every rutting grunt, every twang of overstressed bedsprings.

'Hold me, darling,' Ghislaine said, opening her arms to him. 'Tell me none of it matters because yesterday is not today and truth is better than lies, however much it may hurt.'

So he held her, rocking her as he spoke, and in the warm closeness of her he discovered that she was right. It did not matter in the least how they had come together. Looked at from another angle, it she had not been a policewoman and he not a hired killer, they would never have met at all and this woman – this intelligent, beautiful, courageous, exciting woman – would not be here in his arms. Far from feeling injured he should be grateful.

Yet it was a lot to digest, especially for a man who was seldom prey to his emotions.

'I need a drink,' he said.

'Let me get it,' she said, jumping up, in her relief some of her customary *joie de vivre* restored. 'I think I will join you.'

'Make mine a stiff one.'

Paris St Germain, 3 June 1996 (afternoon)

Finding Lux and Agent 411, not to mention Simonelli, will be a major challenge. I assume they are together. We seem to have let the whole bunch slip through our fingers other than Barail, who effectively gave himself up. Through a contact of C-G's at Scotland Yard we also checked out the London number Barail had provided.

Extract of report dictated by Philippe Mazé, Commissaire de Police, CRS, 04.06.1996. Filed 05.06.96.

*   *   *

Le Renard had given him the task of co-ordinating the round-up of Lux and Simonelli. It was not CRS work or even CRS business, but by sticking his neck out he had qualified for a place on the team, vice-captain to Le Renard's captain.

Where to start? Lux's Menton home had already been searched to the point of demolition without yielding up a single incriminating speck of evidence. As for Simonelli, he might never have been. The only trace at the *comte's* chateau in Venoy was an empty pack of Disque Bleue in a waste bin in the room he had occupied. It provided a first class set of fingerprints that they didn't need.

No, there remained but a single tenuous link, the most gossamer of threads – Agent 411. Except that she was incommunicado. Only once, out of a score or more of attempts, had he got through on her cellphone and even then she cut him off without speaking. Thereafter it had remained stubbornly switched off. Whether a willing or reluctant confederate, she was with Lux, of that he had no doubt. Hence, she had it within her means to deliver up the American.

His head ached from pummelling it for solutions. Hundreds, thousands, of policemen were out there asking questions and getting nowhere. More than likely the couple had left France within hours of the assassination attempt. By now they could be in … in … Mazé tried to think which country was farthest away on the globe. But of course, dolt – New Zealand! Among the Greens, that was where they would seek refuge.

He would have smacked his forehead with the heel of his hand had that not been a tendency of Barail's. His former boss was now a pariah in the service and any imitation of his mannerisms, subconscious or not, was best avoided.

He reached for the telephone to set in motion another string of enquiries on the other side of the world.

*   *   *

In his austere office on the floor above, Le Renard was about to tap into the international old pals' network.

The telephone number Barail had been tricked into providing began with the area code 0171. Inner London. Easy enough to match a UK number to an address if you had connections in Scotland Yard's Special Branch, as Le Renard did.

In less than a minute he was making his request in mangled but fluent English to John Gough, Detective Chief Superintendent and an ardent Francophile. Sussing out an address, even for an ex-directory number, was routine for policemen on both sides of the Channel. Gough promised to transmit it via Le Renard's direct fax line by no later than five o'clock local time.

For favours such as this there is always a *quid pro quo*. Before the week was out a case of valuable 1978 Châteauneuf du Pape would be delivered to the Gough residence just outside Surrey's stockbroker belt.

Hampstead, London, 4 June 1996 (morning)

'You know, you really do have to hand it to the French. When it comes to self-interest, they have no respect for international frontiers or international law. They are quite literally laws unto themselves. They are definitely not wimps.'

Sheryl Glister to Thierry Garbe, freelance journalist, 25.03.1999

⋆   ⋆   ⋆

Summer had come to London literally overnight. Temperatures were up in the mid-eighties by noon when Sheryl Glister and Gary Rosenbrand sallied forth from their penthouse eyrie for what should have been a five-minute walk to the Benihana Japanese Restaurant. It was not destined to last even a minute. They crossed Finchley Road, dodging the endless flux of metal. As they reached the kerb on the other side a Ford Scorpio drew up beside them. Sheryl was preoccupied with detaching her shorts from the crease of her bottom and paid it no heed; even Rosenbrand, who was not in dispute with his shorts and was nearer the kerbside, barely glanced at it. A beat too late he realised what was about to happen.

'Sheryl …!' He intended to add the injunction 'Run!' but the blackjack that connected with the back of his skull removed the power of speech not to mention motion, and he sagged into the arms of his assailant.

A black man in a kaftan who was coming along the street, fingers clicking to the music from the Walkman headphones clamped to his skull, shouted 'Hey!' All four men from the Scorpio froze and simultaneously looked towards him, as synchronised as a stage act. Seeing that he was outnumbered four to one, the black man had second thoughts, did an about-face, and retraced his steps at the double.

While this was in progress Sheryl was indeed running – without any encouragement from her colleague. She bumped into a startled postman, scattering letters left and right, before plunging into the open doorway of a florist shop. A woman behind the counter squealed as Sheryl blundered through, two jean-clad men in pursuit just short of grabbing range. Without slowing to ask directions Sheryl continued at a lick through another open door at the back of the shop. It led to a corridor just wide enough

311

for two people to pass. At the far end the oblong of another doorway and beyond it some sort of loading zone by the look of it. As she passed into the corridor she flung the door shut behind her, the thud of wood connecting with flesh and bone a small triumph.

It bought her a slim respite. Just long enough to scrabble the Mace spray from her pocket and adopt a defensive stance. The door was hurled open and the first of her pursuers came hurtling into the corridor.

A single squirt from the spray was enough. A green-hued vapour jetted viciously from the nozzle, dousing the man's face.

'*Mes yeux!*' he shrieked, covering his eyes after the damage was done. The CRS gas had blinded him and he would stay that way the best part of an hour. For good measure, as he crashed against the wall, Sheryl brought up her knee and crushed his balls flat. A second shriek, even louder than the first, and he was down, thrashing and squirming at her feet. His companion, pulling up beyond the range of the spray, whipped out a compact automatic and snarled at her in French.

Sheryl snarled back in ripe Anglo-Saxon and took off for the exit, gambling that he wouldn't dare gun her down in public. Sure enough, no shot followed her, not even as a warning.

Bursting from the doorway into the loading zone, she almost tripped over an empty carton. She staggered but stayed on her feet. Opposite her, a row of garages with up-and-over doors. No haven there. To the left was a brick wall too high to scale. She turned right and, thankful to be wearing sneakers, sprinted towards a steeply-inclined street at right angles to the loading zone. A scruffy fat man unloading a large carton from a white van gawked at Sheryl as she flew past. He was still gawking when the gun-brandishing Frenchman popped out of the same doorway, yelling 'Stop or I shoot!' in what the fat man later described to the police as 'a funny accent'.

A rickety removal van grinding up the incline in low gear proved to be Sheryl's salvation. She ran right up to it then alongside, pacing it while grabbing the handle of the passenger door. A young black man in a ragged once-white T-shirt gave her a startled look as she wrenched the door open.

' 'Ere, 'ang on a minute,' he spluttered.

'Help me,' she panted, hauling herself up into the cab without invitation. 'A French bloke is chasing me.'

Nothing is calculated to arouse an Englishman's Galahadian instincts more than a distressed damsel – especially one wearing tight shorts and no bra – fleeing from a *French*man.

Now it was the driver's turn to protest as his companion slid along the bench seat to make room for their guest. Sheryl slammed the door and depressed the locking plunger while frantically winding up the window. There came a bang on the side of the van. Then the Frenchman's face bobbed up beside her, hammering on the glass with his fist. He shouted at her in his mother tongue. Sheryl poked her tongue at him and reinforced it with a stiff middle finger. At least he wasn't waving the gun any more.

'Piss off, Froggy!' her young saviour bawled; and to the driver, 'Give 'er some stick, Don.' And Don, middle aged with glasses, obligingly coaxed another mph out of the protesting pantechnicon.

'Thanks both of you,' Sheryl said, flashing the young guy a breathless smile of gratitude.

'Don't mensh.' He stuck out a hand. 'I'm Duane.'

'I'm Sheryl,' she said and laughed wildly at the craziness of it all.

In the door mirror she saw the Frenchman drop back, throwing up his hands in admission of defeat. As the removal van came to an intersection and slowed, he jogged away off the edge of the mirror, presumably to report his failure.

Or partial failure. They still had Gary, Sheryl reminded herself.

'Nah then, what was all that about,' Duane said as she flopped back in the seat, blowing strands of hair from her sweaty forehead.

He was wearing cut-off jeans and she became aware that his thigh was pressing up against hers, flesh to flesh. Admittedly space was at a premium, but she guessed it was good old-fashioned male lust at work, notwithstanding the minimum ten year age discrepancy. Well, a thigh-to-thigh snuggle was the very least he deserved.

'What's it about?' she said back to him. 'If I told you, you'd never believe it.'

Don, the driver, nodded understandingly, as they crested the incline. 'Fuckin' French. Can't fuckin' trust 'em.'

'Where do you want us to drop you?' Duane asked as they swayed and bounced downhill with little semblance of control.

Not back at the apartment, that was for sure. Not yet. She had her wallet containing credit cards and some cash, so had the wherewithal to get off the streets. She needed to figure out what to do about Gary (if he wasn't beyond anyone's reach), to contact Barail, to get out of England, or London at any rate …

'I don't rightly know,' she said at last and threw in an arch smile. 'Any suggestions?'

The Citroën XM was parked on the corner, where the Impasse de l'Ecole joined the Rue de l'Agent Bailly. From there it commanded an unrestricted view of the entrance to the school. Inside the car were Lieutenant de Police Enrique Dubois and Brigadier Leveque, his regular sidekick. It was half-past three and the first egress of children was spilling from the open double doors into the playground and the sanctuary of their waiting parents, mostly mothers. A childish chatter arose, amplified by the narrow street.

Marc Fougère came with a friend, a girl of about the same age. They ran up to a youngish woman wearing a stylish black and white dress. She hugged the girl and dealt Marc a kiss on each cheek. As she walked them through the wrought-iron gates, one per hand, Dubois and Leveque closed in.

'DCPJ,' Dubois intoned, allowing her a long scrutiny of his ID.

She was a woman of some sophistication, not readily intimidated by authority. She looked him up and down. '*Vous désirez?*'

'This boy must come with us,' Dubois informed her in his most officious voice.

'Are you mad? As you can see he is a child and in my care. He is not mine to hand over to you.'

'*Qu'est qu'il y a,* Juliette?' Marc asked, looking up at the woman, his handsome little face screwed up in puzzlement.

'We are policemen,' Dubois explained to him pompously. 'How would you like to visit a police station?'

He had no children of his own and none of the appropriate skills. He had been given this job only because the top brass were trying to confine the officers involved to those who were already 'in the know'.

The woman called Juliette was not prepared to back down so easily, but her protests were as pebbles hurled at a tank. Dubois was implacable. Yet she drew the line at letting Marc leave with the DCPJ officers unaccompanied.

'For all I know you could be *pédés*,' she snapped. 'You have the look.'

Dubois allowed the insult as the price of getting the woman to co-operate.

She and her daughter rode in the Citroën with Marc, Dubois and Leveque to the Bois de Boulogne, there to meet Acting Commissaire de Police Philippe Mazé.

In a soundproof basement room below that where Commissaire Barail had talked his heart out, Mazé faced Gary Rosenbrand across a metal table whose legs were screwed to the bare concrete floor. Whereas Rosenbrand was alone, Mazé was flanked by Lieutenant Gruyon, a CRS colleague, and Capitaine Krynicki, of the DCPJ.

Above them a powerful strip light glared. It emphasised the room's absence of colour and made the four men look anaemic. Krynicki's pale blue suit was faded to a nondescript grey, and even Mazé's scarlet tie appeared as a pallid pink.

It was also as cold as the interior of an igloo, chilled by air conditioning to an uncomfortable 12°C. Rosenbrand, still clad in the shorts and short-sleeved shirt he had been wearing in balmy London, hugged himself to keep warm. Somewhat to his own surprise, he found he was not afraid of these stony-visaged policemen and to hell with the reputation of the French security forces for brutality in their treatment of enemies of the State.

'*Allons-y,*' Mazé said.

Gruyon switched on the recorder and muttered briefly into the microphone. He and Mazé then lit cigarettes and puffed away for a while in total silence; Krynicki waved smoke from his air space, looking none too pleased.

Understanding that this was all part of the preliminary softening up process, Rosenbrand kept his gaze fixed on a point midway across the table where a zigzag scratch was apparent (years ago an interrogee had somehow smuggled in a knife which he duly plunged into the hand of the interrogator, passing through flesh and bone to scar the painted surface of the table itself).

Mazé spoke little English, hence his questions and Rosenbrand's answers, if any, would be passed via Gruyon [Author's note: for the purpose of this narrative the dialogue will be presented as if it were all in English, spoken directly between Rosenbrand and Mazé.]

At last Mazé stubbed out his cigarette. '*Alors, petit bonhomme …*'

'Now then, little man …' Gruyon translated faithfully.

Mazé glared at him. 'You do not have to interpret every single utterance, Lieutenant.' He turned back to Rosenbrand. 'We know who you are and who you work for. We know you plotted to kill

President Chirac, using a professional assassin. We know that through him you caused the presidential helicopter to be destroyed yesterday on 2nd June resulting in the deaths of all on board. All that is now required is for you to confess and provide the names of all persons involved in the financing, the planning, the organisation and the execution. Not a lot to ask, *hein*? Your co-operation will make the difference between twenty-five years in a top security prison with no privileges and ten in an open prison.'

'You're bluffing,' Rosenbrand said, not very convincingly. 'You've got nothing on me.'

When Gruyon relayed this, Mazé remained poker-faced while inwardly seething. The New Zealander was correct in his assessment: the only link between him and the crime was his association with the Glister piece. For all the hard evidence they had on him, he might be no more than her boyfriend.

'Let us dispense with the verbal jousting,' he said with a glibness that belied his frustration. 'You are cold and I am tired and would like to go home. It has been a long day and my temper is a little frayed, you understand.'

'Stuff your temper,' Rosenbrand grated. 'You can't hold me. You've already broken the law by kidnapping me in London. I'm a foreign national, mate. Do you think Sheryl Glister is going to just forget me? If I know her, she'll be talking to the press by this time tomorrow. How do you think the story will look on the front page of every newspaper?'

Rosenbrand had exposed the flaw in Mazé's tactics and privately he did not dispute it. Those morons from the *Sécurité Extérieure* had let the woman slip through their hands. She had gone underground and nobody had a clue where she was now. On the other hand, Mazé reasoned, Rosenbrand could not be entirely certain of this.

'I am sorry to disappoint you, my friend, but Mademoiselle Glister is in an identical room to this one, answering more or less identical questions.'

'Come off it,' Rosenbrand sneered, chafing his bare arms to keep the circulation going. 'If you ask me, your goons – the ones who chased her – came back empty-handed. Go on, admit it. She got away, didn't she?'

'We had other goons, as you call them, out looking for her. Take my word for it, she is right here in this building.'

'Fuck you, mate. I don't believe it.' Rosenbrand pushed his face close to Mazé's. 'Best thing you can do is open that door and give me the plane fare back to London, or better still Auckland. If you're really nice and make it first class, I'll even sign a statement promising not to tell.'

Krynicki, thus far a non-participant, jabbed a finger at Rosenbrand.

'We have uzzer ways of keeping people like you from opening zair mouths,' he said and his tone was vicious.

'Shut it!' Mazé commanded. His brief from Le Renard had been unequivocal. Stay within the written rules. No violence, no threats of violence. An effective emasculation of standard police interrogation techniques, but there it was.

He lit a cigarette, took a couple of deep pulls, appreciating the soothing balm of nicotine.

'Very well,' he said, letting the cigarette droop from his lip the way he had seen it done by Hollywood-style cops. 'Let us approach the problem from a different angle ...'

Three hours and thirty-seven minutes later the interview was terminated with six pages of prize-winning fiction and a pyramid of cigarette stubs to show for it. A dog-tired Gary Rosenbrand was escorted to a stark but clean holding cell one floor down. He was given a cooked meal, a glass of red wine, and for entertainment a French magazine of which he understood barely one word in a hundred.

Prisoner B was issued with an airline ticket and exiled from France indefinitely.

Extract from SECRET memo from CG/CRS to Minister of the Interior, 06.06.1996. Filed 13.06.1996.

*   *   *

They came for Barail after dark. Six of them, not speaking, not meeting his eyes. They handcuffed him and escorted him from his cell, oblivious of his protests and demands to know where he was being taken. Down a passageway lit as bright as day, its walls painted a brilliant gloss so white that it hurt his eyes. Out through a steel door with electronic bolts, activated by a key card. A second door, then a third, opening onto a street devoid of traffic. Tree-lined pavements, eighteenth-century architecture. The air was muggy after the air-conditioned cell block.

A black car was waiting, driver at the wheel, engine running. They bundled him in the back and hemmed him in on either side. Another slid in beside the driver. As the car took off he asked again, '*Dites – où allons-nous?*'

Predictably no one enlightened him as to their destination.

On through the streets of Paris. To begin with, Parisian though he was, he was utterly lost. Not until they crossed the Seine with the floodlit Notre Dame on their left was he able to get a fix on their whereabouts. Instead of entering the Latin Quarter they turned left immediately on reaching the *rive gauche* to follow the river. Once, they were stopped by a red traffic light opposite a bistro; people were sitting at tables on the pavement. The car's window on the front passenger side was open a fraction and through it trickled the murmur of conversation, the rattle of plates, and even – or was he imagining it – the smell of food cooked to perfection and garlic. Two girls, sitting opposite each other a few metres from the road, glanced incuriously at the car. He fancied one of them smiled at him. Such was his yearning for contact with the world from which he was now exiled that he found himself smiling back.

Then the lights went to green. The car shot forward and the impression was gone if not forgotten.

At Ivry they switched to the Boulevard Périphérique, still

bustling with traffic long after the rush hour. They crossed over the marshalling yards. Again, he asked, plaintively now, where they were bound. Again the response was nil.

On their right the Olympic Stadium at Porte d'Ivry slid by, dark and silent. Here he was blindfolded. The man beside the driver opened the dashboard locker and extracted a slender plastic box about the size of a toothbrush container. He snapped it open and passed a hypodermic needle to the man directly behind him. Barail's head turned towards the source of the sounds, as he tried to identify them and their purport. At that moment the car left the Périphérique via the unnamed exit before the Porte d'Italie. At the end of the ramp they made several changes of direction in succession before entering a private driveway bordered by flowers and beyond them lawns where sprinklers were at work. A discreet sign loomed in the headlights: CREMATORIUM in tasteful fancy gold lettering on a black background.

The man with the syringe ejected a miniature geyser into the air.

'Now, Commissaire Barail, we are about to send you on a long holiday. Somewhere hot. Do you like it hot, *Commissaire*?'

Lausanne, 5 June 1996 (morning)

'It never seemed quite real, being with him finally. Like a dream. And dreams don't last, do they? Commissaire Mazé woke me up.'

Ghislaine Fougère to Enrique Dubois, Lieutenant de Police, DCPJ, during interrogation, 13.06.1996.

* * *

The sun was hardly up when the call came on Ghislaine's cellphone. She came awake, groaned groggily.

'Somebody's gotten a sense of humour,' Lux mumbled into his pillow.

Ghislaine dragged the phone off the bedside cabinet to note with a tingle of concern the identity of the caller.

'It's my mother,' she said, and into the handset, '*Maman? Qu'est qu'il y a?*'

Lux, half-awake, half listened. The sudden gasp, the exclamation, the terse monosyllabic responses, the final, '*D'accord. Au revoir, Maman.*'

'The *bastard*!' she said in a choking voice and the bed undulated as she bounced off it. 'If he hurts Marc I'll kill him!'

All drowsiness fled from Lux. He sat upright. A naked Ghislaine was rummaging through a drawerful of underclothes, alternately cursing and sobbing.

'What is it?' Lux asked, slithering across the bed towards her.

She stepped into a pair of black panties and spun round. With her hair still mussed and no make-up, she looked like a waif.

'That swine Mazé has taken Marc,' she sniffled, heeling tears from her cheeks. 'I have to go to Paris – right away.'

Lux was beside her at once, cradling her in his arms, her shuddering body melding with his.

'We go together,' he said.

'Don't be a fool,' she said, her mouth against his collar-bone. 'You can't enter France. It would be a pointless sacrifice.'

'Not if you want Mazé killed, it wouldn't.' Lux was joking, but she took him in earnest.

'No. That is not the answer.'

She delayed another precious moment to kiss him full and hard on the lips, a reaffirmation of her love for him. It disturbed him. There was something final about it. More final than could be

320

attributed to just a few hundred miles travel and a day's absence. But if she shared his presentiment, she was not letting it show. She was back sifting among her undergarments.

'I must hurry. You will drive me to the airport?'

'Don't you think we should check flight times first?'

'Ah, I am so stupid.' She hooked up her brassiere, pushing out her chest as she did so, a pose that Lux found intensely erotic. 'Will you make enquiries for me, darling?'

He nodded and went in search of a telephone directory.

*   *   *

The drizzle that started around ten depressed Simonelli, creature of the sun that he was. This was only his second visit to Switzerland and it had rained the other time too. Why would anyone choose here as a bolthole? he wondered, when sun, sand, and warm seas were so near in the opposite direction.

The best part of two days spent casing the apartment block on Avenue du Lac and waiting for Lux or his woman to appear had finally borne fruit that morning when Lux drove into the parking lot alone.

From a bench by the lake, Simonelli, his face shaded by a newly-purchased umbrella, had watched the American lock his car and make for the entrance to the building. He made no move to intercept him. This was not some flabby businessman he was taking on. Like all hits it would require painstaking planning. Before all else, he needed to get inside the building, check the layout, and identify two alternative escape routes. Out of practice he might be, tired of living he was not.

Here she was, millions of dollars at her disposal, fretting in a sleazy bed-sit in the East End of London. On the run, in a manner of speaking. In England, yet a fugitive from the French Government. Not only that but she felt bad about Gary, about not having stuck around to lend a hand. No matter that if she had she would most likely have joined him on a ride across the Channel to face the thumbscrews and hot irons of a French torture chamber.

She felt bad physically too. She had woken with a migraine and with Duane on top of her, bonking away. He was insatiable. His sex drive licked Rafael's into oblivion. The pounding in her head hadn't been helped by the pounding in her snatch, though she didn't say him nay.

After the quickest shag in her living memory he was off to work, a slice of Vegemite-smeared toast in hand, a cheery 'So long, girl,' on his lips. Leaving her to while away the day as best she could in this dump of a bed-sit. Bed-*shit* would be more appropriate.

She stood before the cracked window and stared down without appreciation at the tiny yard, cluttered with used tyres, engine parts, and sundry junk. Even in the sunlight it was a pretty crappy set-up; on a grey day it must have been dispiriting beyond measure. How did people live in such squalor and still stay upbeat?

Just as worrying as her predicament, not to mention Gary's, was the absence of news about Chirac's death. Three days gone by and still the media were mute on the subject. No mention even of an attempt. Chirac was still alive, that much she now had to accept. It looked as if Lux had either fouled up or cried off. Either way or some other way it amounted to the same thing. Pity. She had read him as a man of his word. The financial loss was not to be airily dismissed either, though the prospects of recovering it were slim to zero. God, what a shambles. Her first major project and she had made a balls of it. If Eddie had still been around he would have booted her out, no mistake.

Her head hurt. She rummaged in her bag and split a pack of Paracetamol and swallowed four tablets without water. It was time to move on. She had restocked on clothes, make-up, tampons, and the other necessities of female life. Plus some auburn hair colouring which she was about to put to use. Then, hopefully before Duane came home and pinned her to the bed, she would be off to Ramsgate by hire car, from there to Zeebrugge by ferry, from Zeebrugge by train to Brussels, and from Brussels by air to any-bloody-where-at-all outside Europe.

At Ghislaine's insistence the venue was her mother's apartment, off the Square de Montholon. She wanted friendly witnesses, just in case. Mazé was already there when she arrived, sitting on a hard chair at the great oval dining table that had been in the family for three generations. By his elbow an empty cup, coffee stains around the rim. Her parents sat at the table too, as far from Mazé as it was possible to be, as if they feared contamination. When Ghislaine whirled in, her face drawn, her clothes crumpled from the flight, they rushed to greet her. Tears were shed by all three. Mazé looked on. If he was impressed by the display of emotion it was not reflected in his expression.

'What is this all about, my dear?' her mother quavered, dabbing her eyes.

'Have you done something wrong?' Her father, a near-cripple with arthritis but a bit of a martinet, was always ready to suspect his only daughter of misbehaviour, despite having no cause to do so.

'Later,' Ghislaine said, a shade brusquely. 'First I must deal with this … gentleman.'

Suffering from travel fatigue and her early rise, she flopped into the nearest armchair. This spacious yet cosy apartment with its unfashionable address had been her home from her early teens until her marriage. All at once the familiar surroundings – the gloomy furniture built to last forever, the brass fittings, the rococo ornaments, the perpetually faded wallpaper – were hostile, sullied by Mazé's presence, the outlook over the square no longer pleasant to behold. Even as the thought struck her she revised it: it was not the policeman's presence that was so repellent, more her own culpability. He was here because she had placed herself outside the law.

'Where is my son?' she demanded of him.

'Hello, Ghislaine,' he returned, not insensible of her feelings, yet not remotely swayed by them.

'Where *is* he?' she repeated, tearful, close to breakdown.

'Safe and well and not far from here.'

Ghislaine did not doubt it. They had no reason to harm the boy. Not yet.

'So what do you want from me, you … you …' An adequate pejorative failed her.

'Can't you guess?'

Ghislaine was permitted fifteen minutes alone with her son in a cheerless, sparsely furnished room with a bare light bulb and barred windows. The boy was hardly perturbed by his abduction and removal to Roissy, close enough to Charles de Gaulle Airport for the whistle of jets taking off and landing to form a constant accompaniment.

'*Ne t'inquietes pas, Maman,*' he said stoutly as she cuddled him, weeping despite her resolve not to. 'It's not bad here, and I've met lots of new uncles.'

Some uncles, she thought bitterly. Any one of them would kill him to order.

The fifteen minutes passed like seconds and no extension was granted. A last cuddle, another cascade of tears that Marc wiped from her cheeks with sensitive fingers, before she was bundled away by two beefy CRS men.

She demanded to speak to Mazé. Neither man even bothered to answer. She refused to move so they lifted her off the floor by her arms and conveyed her to the waiting car, and from there to the airport for the 13.50 Air Inter flight to Lausanne. And made damn sure it didn't leave without her.

Lausanne, Switzerland, 6 June 1996 (afternoon)

'You won, you bastards.'

Ghislaine Fougère to Enrique Dubois, Lieutenant de Police, DCPJ, during interrogation, 13.06.1996.

* * *

A warm rain was falling when Ghislaine's flight touched down at Lausanne Airport. Good as his word, Lux was there to meet her as she emerged from Customs with her overnight bag.

Their coming together was subdued. A touch of lips, a token hug.

'How are you?' he enquired, relieving her of the bag. His tone was compassionate but the eyes that probed her face were more speculative than concerned. For, in the hours alone, he had dwelt upon the tactics behind the police seizure of Ghislaine's son. His conclusions did not bode favourably for their relationship.

'A little tired,' she confessed, softening the negativity with her dazzling smile of old. 'And you? Did you miss me at all?'

'Like I'd miss my head if I lost it.'

She tucked her arm through his and they walked to the exit. To the passing observer, just another couple, albeit more attractive than the average.

In the Range Rover Lux had hired locally they drove to the apartment, conversing only in stilted monosyllables. The backcloth of grey skies added to the gloomy atmosphere in the car. Under it the orderly streets of Lausanne, oddly deserted for a weekday, appeared drab and inhospitable.

Back at the penthouse, while Lux percolated coffee an exhausted Ghislaine collapsed into an armchair to stare listlessly out across the lake, blurred behind a veil of drizzle.

'Are you going to tell me what happened?' Lux said, leaning on the breakfast bar as the percolator dribbled.

'Of course. But later. First I must rest. And think.'

'Alrighty. No rush. Not from this chicken anyhow.'

She wouldn't meet his gaze, behaving almost as if she couldn't bear to look at him.

He lit two Gitanes and took one to her with the coffee, though she didn't much care for the brand. When she drew on it, it made her cough.

'Sorry,' she said and gulped a mouthful of black unsweetened coffee. 'How can you smoke them without filters?'

'It takes practice and leather-lined lungs,' he quipped.

As she replaced his cigarette with one of her own bland Stuyvesants, he lit it for her.

'Thank you, darling.'

Until this morning she had always made the endearment sound like a caress. Now it just sounded mechanical, much as it had been with his wife after a couple of years of wedlock. A habit, a knee-jerk.

'Are you going to lie down?' he asked.

'Yes. I did not sleep well last night. This evening we will talk.'

She reached for his hand, squeezed it. It was an empty comfort. She was trying to behave normally towards him but he could tell it was an act. During her short absence her face had grown lines that had no business there. She was as beautiful as ever, only now it was a subtly flawed beauty, a glimpse of the future Ghislaine that he would have preferred be postponed for some years.

Lausanne, Switzerland, 6 June 1996 (evening)

*The report of the Swiss Police is enclosed with Simonelli's statement,
such as it is. Much of the former appears to be speculation, and of the
latter to be fiction.*

*Extract from SECRET memo from CG/CRS to Minister of the Interior
17.07.1996. Filed 21.07.1996*

*   *   *

Evening came early and brought more rain with it. Lux sat before
the TV, absorbing little of its clacking effluent, as the darkness
enfolded him. Around nine Ghislaine wandered in, wearing a
towelling robe, smelling of bath salts and yawning. She switched
on the lights and joined him on the couch.

'We must talk,' she said, perching sideways to face him, her
arm along the back of the couch, brushing his shoulders.

Lux used the remote control to kill the TV.

'I know.'

His tone was resigned. He could have told her what she was
about to say.

'I love you,' she said, and shuffled closer, making body-to-
body contact.

'I know that too.'

'Then you will understand that what I must do is not because
my love for you is less than it was.'

Lux took a drag on his cigarette, the only solace immediately
available to him.

'But Marc is your son. To save him you have to sacrifice me.'
Her mew of distress moved him to look at her. 'It's okay,
sweetheart. I don't blame you. You have no choice.'

She laid her head on his shoulder, stroked his thigh with her
left hand.

'Thank you for understanding. Thank you for not hating me.'

Despite his melancholy he was becoming aroused by her
caresses. He restrained her.

'You want me to stop?' she queried, incredulous. His sexual
appetite normally recognised no bounds.

'This isn't the moment.'

'You are right. To make love might make me weaken.'

'I wouldn't let you, because my conscience wouldn't let me.'

Moved, on the verge of tears, she said, 'And to think your wife said you had no humanity. Kiss me, darling.'

In a way he would have preferred to part without the ritual of a farewell kiss. Even so, he held her to him and applied his lips to hers almost savagely. When at last they broke off she was flushed and her breath was coming in little explosions.

'You do it so well,' she said unsteadily.

'Yeah. Lifelong practice.'

Ghislaine opened up space between them and let him see the compact automatic she was pointing at him. Her hand was not quite steady but that made the weapon no less dangerous.

He was more amused than afraid.

'You're a cool one. Were you holding that all along?'

'I'm sorry,' she said. 'You know I have to turn you in.'

'You have to try,' he amended.

'If I don't, they'll kill Marc. Mazé told me.'

Lux believed her, if not Mazé's threat. Yet she wouldn't dare gamble Marc's life on the possibility that her boss was bluffing. Her maternal instincts were strong.

'You'll have to kill me,' he told her as she rose and backed away, beyond his reach.

'No, I won't. To disable you will be enough. Your knee ...' She altered the angle of the gun barrel accordingly. 'Or your foot.' Another alteration.

The warning was enough to make him revise his tactics. Enough to make him take her seriously. Enough to convert him from lover to killer – and as a killer he had no equal.

The lunging kick when he delivered it was unexpected. He was as supple as a ballet dancer. His foot slammed into her gut and instantly bent her double. The explosion of pain caused her grip on the automatic to contract and a tiny round left the muzzle in a dart of flame to graze Lux's side, just north of the hip. So light was the bullet that it lodged in the arm of the couch and went no further.

Ghislaine was on her knees, hugging her stomach, still miraculously clutching the gun yet incapable of firing it. Lux prised it from her and she offered no resistance. Instinctively he noted the type and calibre – a Manhurin PPK, modelled on the Walther and chambered for .22. He pocketed it.

'Sorry, sweetheart,' he said, truly contrite, as he stooped over her.

Her mouth opened but only to emit a groan. He helped her to the couch, left her there rocking back and forth.

Done with sentiment he hurried to the bedroom, raided his wardrobe for two neckties and returned with them to the living room. He bound her wrists together in front of her and half carried her to the pine dining table to strap her to one of the legs. By then she had ceased squirming though her face was white and sweaty.

Satisfied that she was immobilised, he returned to the bedroom to tend his wound. Detaching his shirt from it made his eyes water. It was weeping blood, but not to excess. He cleaned it up painfully as best he could and smeared it with some antiseptic cream that he found in the bathroom. It stung, making him hiss through his teeth. Finally he swathed his midriff in a whole roll of bandage, also from the cabinet's first aid stores.

Next, he gathered his belongings and dumped them carelessly in his valise. When he was done he left the valise by the entrance and went to check out his captive. She had recovered enough to call him an unpleasant name.

'Now don't be mean, honey,' he said. He felt a louse, but he wasn't remotely tempted to untie her. 'You did your best. They can't punish you for failing.'

'You don't know them.'

'If I thought they would hurt your boy if I didn't give myself up, I'd do it and take my chances.'

'Words are cheap,' she scoffed. 'Go on then, Jackal – run. Save yourself.'

'Jackal?' He gave her a quizzical look. 'Is that what your people call me?'

'Yes. It is apt.'

But no verbal blow could bruise him now. The transformation to professional was absolute.

'Goodbye, sweetheart. God bless.'

She made no answer, simply turned her head away as a final gesture of rejection. He shrugged and left her. At the door he collected his valise and towed it into the corridor. He shut the door and made for the lift. As he touched the button he heard the motor whine into action.

*   *   *

The apartment building was clearly upmarket and incorporated all the usual security devices. The entrance door could only be unlocked by inputting a code on the digital lock. Visitors were required to buzz their hosts to access the communal lobby. In addition CCTV cameras were trained on the lobby. They could easily be taken out of commission but Simonelli judged it unnecessary. As a rule the TV receivers were located in the entrance halls of apartments and only viewed when a visitor arrived. To beat the system took little ingenuity, only patience. Simonelli positioned himself in a dark corner of the porch to wait. He would slip through the door next time it was used, posing as a bona fide visitor. If someone objected that would be their hard luck.

His passport was not long in coming; a car swung into the parking lot. He ducked back into the shadows as its headlights swept the entrance. Moments later the engine died. Doors slammed, followed by the tap of at least two pairs of high heels on asphalt.

A pillar, a good foot square, occupied the centre of the porch. Simonelli darted behind it, placing it between himself and the approaching women.

'*Enfin. Je suis bien fatigué,*' one of them complained.

'*Moi, non,*' the other responded. 'I'm just hungry.'

Simonelli edged around the pillar, keeping it between him and the women as they crossed the porch. As one of them selected the access code she obligingly announced the digits out loud: '*Huit quatre quarante-huit.*' A tongue click. 'I ought to change that. Using my date of birth always reminds me how old I am.'

The other woman cackled.

Simonelli memorised the figures: eight-four-forty-eight. So she had been born on 8th April 1948. He wordlessly praised the woman's stupidity.

He gave them time to ride to their floor. It began to drizzle, softening the glare of the street lights. Music started up in a ground floor apartment, thud-thud-thud. As a teenager Simonelli had been a rock aficionado like all his contemporaries, but this techno stuff was just monotonous. No melody. Or was this just a sign of ageing?

Five minutes had passed. He advanced on the door. His thin fingers picked out the numbers on the lock – 8-4-4-8. A metallic click as the bolt was released. He pushed at the door and it swung back. A last glance behind him. The building opposite was an office block, darkened except for a yellow light over the entrance. No passers-by.

Half a dozen strides saw him to the lift. The indicator above the doors told him it was stopped at the fourth floor. He pressed the call button and fretted at its unhurried response. It eventually sighed to rest at ground level and the doors parted. Inside it was mirrored on three walls and plushly carpeted. The control panel showed seven floors, from RC through 1 to 5 topped by P for penthouse.

Simonelli thumbed the P. The doors hummed shut. The lift began its weary ascent.

His image was replicated to the left and right into infinity, zillions of ever-diminishing clones. It was disconcerting. He loosened the automatic in its shoulder holster. It wasn't much of a gun. 6.35mm calibre. A handbag gun. A moll's gun. Any serious adversary would laugh if he threatened him with it. The thought made him quail. Lux was as serious an adversary as they come.

He tugged the gun free, operated the slide, then lowered the cocked hammer. One round in the chamber, six in reserve. Small calibre slugs will kill surely enough if planted where it counts. But even a magazine-load might not be enough to stop Lux dead and prevent him from shooting back.

The lift was creeping past the third floor. Sooner or later, probably later, it would reach penthouse level. He wasn't yet at the point of no return, he reassured himself. Not yet committed to following through. He could always descend without getting out. And why not? Why risk his life for a paltry five million francs when he had just made four times that amount for acting as a go-between? It was not as if he was short of money in the first place. The more he questioned the rationale, the less sense it made to go through with it.

A hard contract was not to be defaulted on lightly. You put yourself at risk of retribution. Yet would Barail spend more of his illicit earnings on punishing Simonelli? He didn't think so.

The lift slowed. A chime sounded for those passengers who needed a wake-up call. Simonelli looked down at the gun in his hand. Maybe he was too old to be making a comeback as an assassin. Maybe it was time to go home and drift into a well-heeled retirement in some far-off place beyond the reach of the law.

The lift had come to a stop. The doors chugged open. A man in a dark blue blouson and chinos stood there, valise on the floor beside him, a bag slung from his shoulder. He was clutching his side as if it were paining him.

'Lux!' Simonelli momentarily froze.

'What the fuck …?' Lux's eyes dropped from the Corsican's face to the gun he was clutching and his reactions were a blur.

Marginally more prepared, Simonelli had only to lift the automatic and fire. It was advantage enough. He pumped out five of the little bullets (never leave yourself with an empty magazine) as fast as his finger could trigger them. *Crack-crack-crack-crack-crack*, no louder than a snapped stick. They may have sounded puny but all five struck home where he intended.

Five hits in the chest put Lux down on his backside, his own gun – an automatic even smaller than Simonelli's – slipping from his grasp to bounce once and lie still, at the Corsican's feet. He sat there on the carpet, supported by the wall, a surprised expression on his face and five red roses blooming on his shirt front

Simonelli hesitated, torn between stepping from the lift and, like the commanding officer of a firing squad, administering the *coup de grâce* and getting the hell out before Lux produced a hidden gun as he had once before. No man could live with five holes in his chest, he decided, and hit the lift button. Lux still sat there, now canted over slightly to the left. Eyes unseeing, the red splashes merging to become a single stain over his heart which, against all probability, continued to pump. Then mercifully the doors closed like stage curtains on the final death scene in a play.

The lift descended. Simonelli sagged to the floor, dabbed perspiration from his forehead. His nerves were shot. The hand that held the gun shook like that of a lottery winner receiving a record-breaking cheque.

When the lift sighed to a halt on the ground floor he reeled out into the lobby on boneless legs. But for a man passing on a moped, who took him for a drunk, no one saw him lurch from the building and, guided by self-preservation rather than judgement, make his stumbling way to his car.

Among his acquaintances of longstanding Le Renard counted one Jacques Legoff, a political columnist for *France Soir.* Legoff was in his late fifties, in the news business since before de Gaulle came to power, and nobody's fool.

Two days previously an *Ordonnance* from the Ministry of the Interior had been circulated to all newspaper and periodical publishers. It made reference to rumours of an assassination attempt on President Chirac and issued a total clampdown on all reporting, be it of fact or fantasy. However, the latest buzz circulating the media world was that the powers-that-be had had wind of the contract in advance and let it go ahead so as to snare the whole cabal. What was more, the assassin had actually penetrated the security screen, made a successful hit, and got clean away. Fortunately or unfortunately for France, depending on your politics, he only blasted to bits a helicopter pilot and two dummies, done up as Chirac and his wife.

Determined that these rumours should be substantiated or laid to rest, Legoff invited Le Renard to lunch at La Terrasse Fleuri in the Inter-Continental Hotel. So exclusive and expensive was this most *bleu* of *cordon* establishments that, owing to the adverse impact on his expense account, the columnist only ever dared use it when the stakes were high and the informant exalted.

Though it was again a day of warm sunshine they dined inside amidst the plethora of flowering shrubs to which the restaurant owes its name, in a discreet corner where they could not be overheard. Legoff, shortish with close-cropped grey hair that stood up like bristles, was an untidy eater: he wore his napkin tucked in his collar to save his tie from the inevitable shower of debris.

During the starter course he seemed content to discourse on everything but the President's wellbeing. Only when the main course came – *filets de rouges profilés* for Le Renard, *ris de veau* for Legoff, the second cheapest item on the menu – did he unleash his bloodhound skills. With the departure of the waiter came the abrupt switch from gentle sparring to the equivalent of a punch below the belt.

'Did you catch the assassin yet?' he asked, in a 'by the way' manner, affecting absorption in the contents of his plate.

Not even Le Renard, for all his encounters with the press and consequent suspicion of its motives and methods, was quite prepared for such bluntness. Fortunately his gaze was also on his plate and stayed there while he composed an answer.

'You've had your ear to one too many keyholes,' he said, shovelling rice into his mouth.

'Don't prevaricate, my friend.'

Now Le Renard lifted his eyes to the newsman. 'Did you not receive the *Ordonnance*?'

Legoff dismissed the ministerial decree with a wave of his fork. 'You and I are old friends. What is an ordinance to twenty years of lunching together?'

'A good question, Hervé. One day I will ask myself.' Le Renard sipped his wine. It was a Petit Chablis and just acid enough to titillate his critical palate. 'For the present you must do as you are told.'

Legoff grunted. 'Don't I always? Don't we – the whole news industry – do as we are told? We are positively supine. To step so much as a millimetre out of line would be more than my job is worth.'

'Not to mention your life.'

A morsel of veal shot off Legoff's plate and across the white table cloth, leaving a spoor of mushroom sauce.

'Do not make jokes about such things,' he said, retrieving it.

'It was barely a joke. Though I should not need to say it, do not trifle with ordinances in general and this one in particular.'

'I never have. But can you tell me nothing, even off the record?'

A waiter hovered, enquired if all was to the gentlemen's liking. He was sent away entirely reassured, just as he expected to be.

'Off the record?' Le Renard trusted Legoff as much as any other journalist – not at all. In the ordinary way he might have let drop a hint or two, nodded a rumour through, corrected an item of gossip. On this story though, he was gagged. His boss, Jean-Louis Debre, had left no margin for discretion. Denial was the official line. Not even a simple 'no comment' was enough.

'The ordinance referred to rumours, did it not? It rejected these rumours as mischief-mongering. It forbade any reporting even of a speculative nature. That is all I have to say on the subject.'

Legoff stared, his resentment plain to see. 'And that's it? That's all you're going to feed me?'

'Correct.'

'Nothing about an organisation called Greenwar?' Legoff was angry now and not trying to hide it. 'Nothing about an act of revenge for the nuclear testing we did in the Pacific?'

'If you wish to report on the subject of this Greenwar movement or on the tests, you are free to do so. Simply do not link either or both to any tittle-tattle about contracts on the President.'

Legoff ripped his napkin from his collar and pushed back his chair. It squealed on the block flooring and caused several heads to turn reprovingly in his direction.

'You insult me, my friend: me, my integrity, my profession, and … and our friendship.'

'Some things are bigger than friendship,' Le Renard rejoined.

As the columnist whirled away out of the restaurant, an outwardly unmoved Le Renard resumed his meal. It was far too good to waste out of pique. In any case, it now looked as if he would be stuck with the bill.

It was to be the final meeting of the key figures in the Jackal affair; the concluding chapter. Better still, the epilogue.

Le Renard reported to the assemblage that the threat to the President's life had been removed, leaving the 'for now' qualification unsaid. He formally ruled out any further attempts by the clandestine green organisation, claiming, without evidence or justification, that they had been reduced to a demoralised rabble. Ending on this upbeat note, Le Renard delegated to Mazé the CRS response to Interior Minister Jean Louis Debre's request for a breakdown of results.

'Not a chronological account,' the Minister elaborated. 'Just a status report on the protagonists.'

Le Renard affected not to notice Mazé's resentful glance at being handed this poisoned chalice. By rights, the head of the department should take the rap for the bad as well as credit for the good.

When Mazé spoke though there was no suggestion of rancour in his voice.

'Commissaire Barail, who acted as contact and informant and joint-co-ordinator for want of a better title, has been dealt with. Rafael Simonelli, who was the original recruiter of Barail and shared the co-ordination with him was arrested in Switzerland the day before yesterday on suspicion of murder. A formal application for extradition is being prepared. He was also close to the Glister woman, whom I shall come to shortly.'

'So far so good,' the Minister murmured.

Mazé shuffled his papers around. '*Alors,* the Jackal, whose name we now know to be Dennis Randolph Lux, was shot to death in Lausanne, seemingly by Simonelli, on 5th June.'

'Very obliging of him,' Le Bihan, the Foreign Minister's Chef de Cabinet observed.

'As we are all aware Agent 411 became emotionally involved with Lux,' Mazé continued. 'As a result she absconded with him and in so doing became an accessory after the fact. She is under arrest and will be interrogated by the DCPJ very shortly. Charges will almost certainly be preferred against her.'

'We must be sure she keeps her mouth shut.' This from Roger Billaud-Varennes, right-hand man to Debre at the Ministry of the Interior.

'*Evidemment,*' Le Renard said.

'Other than that only one other French national was involved – Monsieur Le Comte d'Arbois, who is also to be charged as an accessory, though he claims to have been unaware of the plot and of Simonelli's fugitive status. It may be difficult to prove otherwise.'

'He is unimportant, surely,' Le Page said. 'There is no suggestion that he was a party to the assassination attempt, merely that he was doing Barail a favour.'

'In any case,' Debre said, 'that leaves only the Greenwar people unaccounted for, in particular the Glister woman.'

Mazé moistened his lips. They were about to enter territory where the results were less likely to earn him plaudits.

'As has been reported, the man, Gary Rosenbrand, was … er, arrested on 4th June in London. This man was a companion of the Glister woman, though it seems to have been a purely professional relationship. His precise role is unknown. In any event, despite subjecting him to a total of … ' Mazé's index finger roamed over his notes, came to rest near the foot of a page, 'eighteen hours interrogation, we were unable to obtain either an admission of complicity or any inculpatory evidence to use against the Glister woman.'

Debre was ill at ease with the term 'interrogation'. Interviewing officers often got carried away by their enthusiasm and their natural wish to obtain a result.

'Nothing unauthorised occurred during questioning, I trust,' he said, to cover himself.

Le Renard, equally anxious to keep his reputation clean, said, 'Instructions were given verbally to Commissaire Mazé prior to interrogation of the suspect and subsequently confirmed in writing. Any violence and intimidation was firmly forbidden.'

'*Non, Monsieur le Ministre,*' Mazé said in answer to the Minister's query.

'Where is this man now?' Le Bihan enquired.

'He is held incommunicado, at Hubert Monmarché, pending instructions.'

Le Renard began to speak but was out-decibelled by the Interior Minister. 'Release him at once.'

'*Oui, Monsieur le Ministre.*'

'With an apology,' the Minister added, 'and luxury travel facilities to any destination of his choice outside Metropolitan France. And make sure he knows that the President is alive and in perfect health.'

'*Oui, Monsieur le Ministre.*'

Debre rested his hands on the blotter before him, arranged to expose the optimum two centimetres of white shirt cuff.

'Good. This leaves the infamous Mademoiselle Glister, does it not?'

Mazé's sigh did not travel far enough to reach the Minister's ears. 'The same squad from the *Service Extérieure* that arrested Rosenbrand attempted to arrest Glister as a simultaneous operation. Regrettably, she escaped and has gone to ground.'

'So you have lost her,' the Minister said.

'We have not given up,' Le Renard asserted. 'The DSE is still scouring England.'

'Call them off. The operation is cancelled herewith.'

Le Renard didn't dispute the ruling, and Mazé was merely relieved, glad to be shot of the whole imbroglio.

'Gentlemen,' the Minister said, his gaze skipping from one face to the next. 'The operation is to be considered terminated. Renard, I would like your concluding report on my desk one week from today, with all 't's crossed and all 'i's dotted.'

Le Renard acknowledged. That would keep Mazé out of mischief for a few days.

'That will be all, thank you,' the Minister concluded.

Mazé and Le Page were the last to vacate the room.

'That's a turn up for the book,' the DCPJ *Commissaire* said. 'I never expected to see the day when France let a gang of assassins off the hook.'

'This is different. One of them is American, and the other a New Zealander, which is worse. After that *Rainbow Warrior* cock-up and all the fuss about the nuclear tests no president is going to risk upsetting those bolshie buggers again. If we did, I wouldn't put it past them to declare war on us!'

A statement from Mme FOUGERE was required for completion of the report. Commissaire de Police MAZE secured her co-operation.

Extract from memo from CG/CSP to Minister of the Interior, 10.06.1996. Filed 12.06.1996.

*   *   *

Mazé scarcely recognised the woman who was led from her cell. She wore a prison dress – a grey, drab, utterly shapeless garment. Her hair was scraped back and held in a plastic clip. Her face was bare of make-up and her mouth had acquired a downturned set that soured her whole expression. Most of all the vivacity, the glow that complemented her looks was absent.

'Are they treating you well?' he asked as they walked together to the interview room.

'I am fed, my bed is comfortable. They don't use violence towards me. Not the physical kind anyway. What more could a prisoner ask?'

As they settled on their respective sides of the table, Mazé offered her a cigarette. Gitanes, the brand favoured by Lux. They made her cough but she was in no position to be choosy.

'The purpose of this interview is simply to find out if you will co-operate. By which I mean tell us all about your involvement with Lux and all you learned of the Jackal affair beyond the twenty-odd cassette recordings you supplied us before you decided to cross over the line. The sessions will not be conducted by DJCP officers, nor by me, although I may drop in from time to time. Expect them to last several days.'

'As you say, you already have all the cassette recordings I sent you,' Ghislaine pointed out, funnelling twin streamers of smoke from her nostrils. 'What more is there?'

'Cassette recordings provide much that is invaluable. They are not evidence, and we received nothing after 30th May.'

'If you intend to use what I tell you against me in court I don't have to say anything.'

Mazé wafted away the film of smoke suspended in the air between them.

'Understand this, Ghislaine. This case is not going to court. All we wish to do is tidy up loose ends for a report to the Minister. Tell the truth, co-operate, and you may yet escape with a few years in prison. If your change of heart and allegiance did not come about until after the assassination attempt you will not be considered an accessory before the fact. If this is the case, convince us. If it isn't, admit it. Clear?'

Ghislaine nodded.

'Good. Now, if you are ready, I will send for the interviewing officers. The senior of the two is called Enrique Dubois ...'

It was ten o'clock in the morning and the Commissariat de Police in Rue Thorel was as busy as a bus terminal. Like a small boat bobbing on a stormy sea the petite woman with the iron-grey hair done up in a bun forged through the bustle. At the information counter she found herself alongside a fat Arab woman who was haranguing a ginger-haired policeman in mangled French. Something to do with a gang of hooligans daubing racist slogans on her kitchen window.

A policeman who looked young enough to be the grey-haired woman's grandson came over from his desk. He was tall, very erect and impeccably-groomed.

'*Madame*,' he said, seeming as eager to please as a puppy.

'I wish to speak to an officer,' she said, meaning someone of exalted rank.

'*Très bien.* I am an officer,' he said, assuming she was using the term in its generic sense. 'How can I help you?'

The woman was about the size of a twelve-year-old. To make her feel less intimidated he reduced his height by resting his elbows on the counter.

He had a sympathetic face, she decided, and let drop her intention of demanding to see someone more senior.

'*Je m'appele* Madame Duplessis,' she said, fiddling with her handbag which she held before her on the counter as if to create a protective barrier. 'I live near here, just off the Square de Montholon. It is about my daughter.'

'Yes?' The policeman did not yet draw the pad of report forms towards him. Time-wasters outnumbered serious complainants by 2–1 and like all policemen he abhorred form-filling, even when it was justified.

'She is missing. She has not been home for over a week.' She gave the counter a diffident thump with her bag. 'A whole *week*, young man!'

The gendarme inwardly assessed the age of the woman, putting it at around fifty-five, which in fact flattered her by a couple of years.

'How old is your daughter, *madame*?'

'She will be thirty in November.'

'Well, now,' the policeman said, selecting his words with great circumspection. 'Do you not think she is old enough to come and go as she pleases? Does she live with you?'

'Not normally,' Madame Duplessis said, raising her voice to compete with the continuing verbal torrent from the Arab woman. 'However, that is not all: she has a son, aged seven. He too is missing.'

A missing child was a more serious matter. The policeman finally conceded that a report could not be avoided. He picked up a pen with a chewed end and regarded it with distaste for the chewing was not his doing.

'The child has also been missing for a week?'

'A little longer in fact. Ever since the police took him away.'

The policeman had been about to start writing. Now he stared at her.

'The police took him away? Was he in trouble?'

The woman shook her head. 'No, no, it was nothing like that. My daughter works for the police, or at any rate the RG.'

'The *RG*?' The policeman's eyes widened. This was getting too deep for a trainee *Gardien de la Paix*. It had the smell of something more than a routine missing person. 'Wait here a moment, please.'

He started towards a door to the side, then stopped after a few paces and turned.

'What is your daughter's name?'

'Fougère. Ghislaine Fougère.'

He repeated it to himself and resumed his forward progress. Madame Duplessis waited, occasionally drumming her fingers and listening abstractedly to the Arab woman scattering abuse over the ginger-haired policeman, whose powers of osmosis seemed limitless.

It was some time before the young policeman reappeared. He was accompanied by a pot-bellied man in a rumpled suit.

'*Bonjour, madame*,' the latter smiled. 'My name is Parizon, Lieutenant de Police. We have made enquiries with the RG and they maintain that your daughter transferred to the CRS in March of this year.'

Madame Duplessis blinked at him. 'I was not aware of it. But what has it to do with her disappearance?'

'Nothing perhaps,' Parizon conceded. 'But I thought you should be aware of it. In any case, we checked with CRS headquarters and they told me ...' He shook his head. 'It is very strange that your daughter has said nothing.'

'What did they tell you, these CRS?' Madame Duplessis said impatiently, supposing that this plodding policeman would get to the point sooner or later.

'Simply that she and her son have been sent on a long holiday.'

AFTERWORD

DID ANY OF IT REALLY HAPPEN?

Fact blurred by fiction? Fiction built on a foundation of fact?

In September 1996 a French freelance news correspondent called Thierry Garbe allegedly received an anonymous telephone call at his Paris Montmartre apartment. The caller claimed to have in his possession a secret Government dossier concerning an assassination attempt on President Jacques Chirac, arising out of his decision in 1995 to resume nuclear tests in the Pacific.

Though sceptical, Garbe agreed to meet his anonymous caller at an isolated spot near the south coast of the Brittany peninsula. The informant took precautions to ensure that he was not being lured into a trap, including sporting a false beard, false nose, and dark glasses. Other than wiring himself to record their conversation, however, Garbe played it straight. His desire for the exclusive rights to the story far surpassed any notion of public duty.

The informant handed over extracts from the dossier, including a lengthy report dated March 1996 from the Director General of the CRS (*Compagnies Républicaines de Sécurité* – the security body that includes the presidential bodyguard) to the Minister of the Interior. The report set out how a clandestine militant organisation of New Zealand origin had hired a professional killer to assassinate the President of France in retribution for the nuclear tests at the Muroroa Atoll.

The report further attested that a government minister and a senior officer in the CRS were implicated, together with a notorious Corsican terrorist. Other key participants were a New Zealand multi-millionaire, and two green activists, one American, the other a New Zealander. The assassin was an American, resident in France at the time, ex-husband of a French socialite and member of the aristocracy.

The assassination was foiled when the CRS infiltrated the cabal. However, they failed to bring the instigators of the plot to justice. These individuals remain at large to this day.

The informant would not disclose how he came by the dossier. His price was one million French francs *en liquide*. He and Garbe parted, having arranged to speak again on the telephone forty-eight hours later.

During these forty-eight hours, Garbe negotiated with a major French magazine (rumoured to be *L'Express,* though they steadfastly deny it, maintaining that they 'don't spend that sort of money'.) to pay the asking price. A rendezvous was arranged between Garbe and the informant for delivery of the dossier, but the man didn't show up and nothing more was heard from him.

Garbe was not about to let the story go. Funded in part by the unnamed publication, in part by his modest savings, he spent the next sixteen months tracking down the informant and eventually came up with an identity – a middle-ranking civil servant at the Ministry of the Interior, by the name of Vincent de Poilu, one of whose minor duties was to supervise the shredding of confidential material. Via further backdoor enquiries among de Poilu's fellow officials, Garbe learned that the man had quit the department the day after his second telephone conversation with him, when the arrangements were made for the handover. The rather seedy apartment in Gennevilliers where de Poilu had lived with his wife proved now to be occupied by an Algerian family, who were no wiser than the civil servant's colleagues as to the couple's whereabouts.

The magazine's flagging commitment was revived by this development, and Garbe was authorised to hire a private detective. On 21st August 1998, nearly two years since de Poilu first made contact, the detective reported that he had traced the de Poilu couple to an apartment in the Belgian town of Louvain, living under the name of Wargniez.

Hot-footing it to Louvain, Garbe cornered 'Wargniez' at the small electrical goods store of which he was manager. By a combination of bribery and intimidation, he persuaded the former civil servant to co-operate. Despite his terror of discovery, Wargniez/de Poilu admitted that he had held onto the six-hundred-page file on the assassination attempt. It was lodged in a safe deposit box at the Cera Bank, in Parijsstraat.

A new deal was clinched for the same price as before, and this time the exchange went ahead (though Wargniez/de Poilu and his wife have since gone missing again).

Burning midnight oil, Garbe read the report from end to end and realised that he had on his hands a scalding hot property. Too hot, in fact. No French publishing house would dare publish it, as it would be all too obvious that secret government papers were the source, though his employers would be free to sell the foreign rights with impunity. However, something about the account still troubled Garbe: it was incomplete. The principals behind the assassination attempt referred to throughout as 'G' and 'R' were still at large and their whereabouts uncertain.

The magazine concurred in Garbe's view that the account could only be sold abroad, but before passing it on to their foreign rights agent they commissioned Garbe to try to trace the people who issued the contract on the life of President Chirac.

Money was no longer an object. Garbe flew to Auckland, New Zealand, and easily obtained the name of the man whom it was suspected had financed the operation, if only indirectly – one Edward Nixon. Nixon apparently left New Zealand for good at the end of 1995 and died in the USA in April 1996, of cancer of the liver, shortly before the attempt on Chirac's life.

Garbe appeared to have reached an impasse. The only remaining avenue of enquiry was Greenpeace. At their headquarters in Auckland's Parnell district, he met a leading woman activist, who insisted on remaining anonymous. This woman, accordingly anonymous in Garbe's notes, was unable to throw further light on Nixon's involvement, but a passing remark about two leading militants, who coincidentally quit Greenpeace in the autumn of 1995, stirred up the reporter's curiosity. The two renegades were named as Sheryl Glister, an American woman, and Gary Rosenbrand, a Kiwi ('G' and 'R'?); the former was living 'somewhere overseas', but Rosenbrand had a house in the Auckland North Shore suburb of Takapuna. He was believed to be no longer active in any environmental movement.

To persuade Rosenbrand to see him, Garbe made a nuisance of himself. Only when he threatened to expose the New Zealander as a leading participant in the plot did his resistance collapse. At his one and only interview, Rosenbrand co-operated in adding much 'between the lines' material. More importantly, he told Garbe where he could get in touch with Sheryl Glister, putative leader of the breakaway faction.

Garbe flew to Hawaii and paid an unannounced call on Ms Glister at her Honolulu apartment. She was not at home, but by literally camping on her doorstep until the small hours, he was able to confront her on her return. Unlike Rosenbrand, she readily agreed to an interview, and Garbe was able to strike up a rapport with her in the hour that followed. The intelligence she supplied during the session was off the record, though Garbe secretly recorded it, and could not, she insisted, be publicised 'until my death'. She did relent enough to allow him to quote the last few lines of their conversation, recorded as follows:

Garbe: 'What's your next move, Sheryl? Will you quit?'

Glister: 'Not me. Heck, my work is no more over now than it was in 1995. Out there are still nuclear weapons, still governments playing with them, still megalomaniacs threatening to use them. India and Pakistan, for instance. What a pair of beauties!

[Laughter]. Their leaders need their heads cracking together. A simultaneous execution would be kind of apt, don't you think, Thierry?' [Prolonged laughter].

In the end, nobody would publish the report and the magazine that had recruited Garbe was obliged to write off its investment. But Garbe himself was far from done with it. He had kept a copy of the whole dossier. He returned to Honolulu in March 1999 and over a period of two weeks persuaded, bullied, and cajoled Sheryl Glister into filling in the gaps in the chronicle, and ultimately agreeing to his commissioning a book on the subject.

The author, then living near Grenoble in France, was roped in to 'novelise' the mish-mash of documents and notes. Garbe summarized the report and his recordings of the interviews with Rosenbrand and Glister, while the author introduced dialogue, dramatization, and most notably fleshed out a relevant love affair that the official report voyeuristically dwelt on at some length.

This narrative is, therefore, based roughly one-third on the report produced by the Ministry of the Interior, which incorporates reports from other government departments and personnel, one third on the interviews with Glister and Rosenbrand, and one third on the author's storytelling skills. It is for the reader to judge how much of it really happened.

AUTHOR'S NOTE

In 1971, a book entitled *The Day of the Jackal,* written by freelance news reporter Frederick Forsyth, was published. It was an account of an assassination attempt on the life of Charles de Gaulle that purported to have taken place in Paris on Liberation Day, 25th August 1963. A deserved worldwide bestseller, it has twice been made into a movie, though the second one had little in common with the book.

At the time of publication there was speculation as to how much of Forsyth's tale was fact and how much was fiction. Nobody really knows for sure to this day. Probably it was a bit of both. De Gaulle certainly survived a number of assassination attempts, that much is a matter of record. The 'Jackal' affair was to be the last recorded attempt on the life of a French president for over thirty years.

The only similarity between Forsyth's narrative and mine is the target – the President of France, in this case Jacques Chirac, the incumbent at the time in which the events are set. Thierry Garbe, the French journalist who brought the evidence to me swears the story is true. Not all of the facts stack up, though many do. Anyhow, I took Garbe's material at face value, added some colour to the black-and-white of the evidence by fleshing out the principal players, introducing some personal strife, and creating quite a lot of wholly imaginary dialogue. Having said this, sections of the dialogue not invented by me are based on hearsay from a key player, and the rest is verbatim, for reasons that will become apparent as the narrative draws to a close.

Only one of the key players remains unidentified to this day – the French government minister who, if not actually a conspirator, was privy to the plot. The motives behind his complicity are not clear and seem unlikely ever to become known.

Finally, the names of some people and places have been changed, and some haven't. Those of the protagonists still living will know which. The rest will have to speculate.

L L, September 2012

Printed in Poland
by Amazon Fulfillment
Poland Sp. z o.o., Wrocław